FROM THE MATCH

SCARS OF ICHOR

BOOK ONE

ADRIAN TKACZYK

BOOK ONE OF THE SCARS OF ICHOR TRILOGY

FROM THE MATCH

ADRIAN
TKACZYK

Cover Illustration and Character Illustrations by Denny S.
You can find more of their art on:
Instagram (@deetrinity)
Tumblr (@detrinity)
Twitter (@detrinityart)

Cover Design by Adrian Tkaczyk
Interior Book Layout by Adrian Tkaczyk

Published by Quinton Li Editorial

@thneskos
www.thneskos.com

First Paperback Edition 2023
Printed in the United States of America

ISBN 9780645681543

To my sister, Tara, who was my light even on the darkest of nights.

TRIGGER WARNINGS

The following topics are essential to the plot of the *Scars of Ichor* series and intrinsic to its narrative.

- Alcoholism, Alcohol Abuse, Relapses Involving Alcohol
- Depictions of Depression, Suicide, and Self-Harm
- Opioid Addiction, Opioid Use, Opioid Overdoses
- Past Emotional, Physical, Sexual Abuse
- Past Torture, Victim Blaming, Domestic Violence, Murder, Past Grooming
- Psychiatric Hospital Stays (Voluntary and Involuntary)
- Parental Abuse, Parental Neglect, Parental Abandonment

Readers sensitive to these topics should proceed with caution or forgo reading this novel and the rest of its corresponding series all together.

THE PROLOGUE

DANTE ALONSO HIDALGO

GOALIE #12

OCTOBER 25, 1996

ZODIAC SIGN
SCORPIO

FAVORITE FOOD
SINIGANG

MAJOR
UNDECIDED

PROLOGUE

CELENA

TODAY WAS THE BEGINNING of my newfound status among the like of an eternal mythos. Because with the stroke of a pen, I had become the first woman scouted onto a once all-male NCAA team in all of the institution's history.

The covenant made by self and my forthcoming coach, Clayton Alonso, was a perfect arrangement. Sure, it had first ruminated among the basis of talent, but now play among the college sphere an equal to the men meant one thing: squashing my brother and father where they stood among their corresponding positions of rookie and head coach now gracing the Wesley Cardinals. Of course, in Clayton's vaulting me through a glass ceiling, he also wanted to irk the deplorable man I called a father. Anyone who knew anything about hockey was well aware of my father and Coach Clayton's famed and equally bloody feud documented across shared NHL careers in which my father would retire a hero but Coach Clayton had not.

I knew better than to ask which party had instigated their mutual dislike of each other, but I knew my father despite my wishes to see myself absolved of the indignant fate of calling him family. After all, he would not allow a man he deemed undeserving—like Coach Clayton—steal his spot as the first-round pick among the 1993 NHL Draft when he believed the right to lay claim such was his first. Truth be told, all signs pointed to my father, Andrei, being the party to first irk Coach Clayton and later spurn their agreement to see themselves hate each other. Although, even if Coach Clayton was not the kind of man to instigate violence like that of my father, I did not think that the matter of finishing it was a fate entirely beneath him either.

The coming press conference was my first showcasing to the world as the answer to whether or not women should play separate or with the boys. Coach Clayton had been at a total loss on how to present me in terms of appearance. I knew adhering to something strictly feminine would see me reduced to the butt of some kind of joke. If I swung to the other end of the spectrum, it would see myself a pariah based on stranger's assumptions that had no use other than to give me kindling on a fire now burning to prove them wrong. I settled for something in the middle. My favored bold, smokey eye and red lip. Touched up, bleach blonde roots kept atop shoulders of a tailored suit coat and an unbuttoned collar. Heels were out of the question considering I had no use for them other than to see myself made a fool in trying to walk in them. Coach Clayton had agreed, and so I had donned shiny, leather oxfords with yellow stitching instead.

A one-sided compromise had been made in terms of who would be delivering the remarks to the gathered press, being that Coach Clayton would handle their stupidity and I would say nothing. I didn't find a need to argue with him on such when he had continued to live under their spotlight since first gracing the New York Rangers in his debut season and I did not. After all, I trusted Clayton Alonso with my legacy. And I figured my coming showcasing was something that had to be included in our newfound partnership if we wanted it to work knowing neither of us could begin to afford failure.

I examined myself in the mirror before placing my hair in its usual, high ponytail at the top of my head. I saw movement in the glass and turned to the crash that followed. I gazed upon a boy I had been informed of in the wake of my scouting, being Coach Clayton's nephew, Dante Hidalgo.

He was easily twice my size despite our noticeable age difference. His head was shaved in a buzzcut. Sharp, defined, cheekbones gave immediate access to the deep, rumbling brown covering the pair that was accessorized with a thick, raised scar dragging down from his left side. Patchy facial hair was sprinkled atop a smirk kept behind the lip of a bottle of vodka, and I watched Dante take a swig before rising from the pile of hockey equipment he had fallen into. He then noticed me staring at him, and raised his bottle in an exaggerated, drunken toast to then say, "Congrats, Celena. First woman scouted onto a men's team in all of NCAA history. Only took us 2,103 years to get this far, no?"

"You look a little young to be drinking that."

"You of all people should know Schaffer is my sober jail, no?"

"And yet here you are. At Schaffer. And very much not sober."

"Touché."

Dante took another swig from his bottle as he seemingly lurched forward in my general direction. In the past I would have flinched at such. However, I had been raised in a house dependent on violence and knew I could come out of its brunt withstanding despite the obvious difference in stature between the two of us. I pushed him backwards a good inch, and Dante recoiled beneath the weight of my palm in an obvious drunken stupor. He turned to me. Dante was smiling as if I were the most interesting person he had ever met, let alone heard of in the wake of his uncle agreeing to let me join his roster despite the college sports world now wanting me dead, squashed, and gone. After all, playing for the women's team meant I could not cut my brother and father down at their knees. Truth be told, if there was anything anyone could come to count on in terms of my coming college career was that it was entirely fueled by spite. Some might say such a mindset is not entirely healthy. However, if it was the reason for me still being able to call my life my own, I didn't think it was nearly as degrading as others would come to suggest.

I looked Dante up and down. "And is Coach aware you're drunk right now when I need him now more than you do?"

"Now, is that any way to talk to the first line to Tito Clayton's pet project?"

"A man without a future will not dampen mine."

"Ouch," Dante said, smiling beneath the lid of his bottle.

Wooden heels against a solid floor came towards us in a uniform, staccato rhythm. Clayton Alonso was now in our range of sight, gazing between me and his drunk nephew. He was wearing a transparent, white barong tagalog paired with black pants and dress shoes of the same shade. His expression was stern, unflinching, and equally foreboding. It washed a sense of fatherly comfort over me I had not felt in the longest time since the passing of my mother. The lines etched into his aged face looked between Dante and me. Then, he settled his gaze upon his nephew and the bottle of vodka tucked into his chest in a feeble attempt to hide it.

Coach Clayton gave a long, drawn-out sigh before taking the bottle of vodka from his nephew's grip. Dante laughed before Coach Clayton hoisted him off the ground and slung him over his shoulder as if Dante were weightless. It was an impressive effort considering the drastic difference in terms of their corresponding sizes. Coach Clayton then looked at me, frowning to then say, "I need you to wait out for me here until I handle this. No talking to the press without me, got me?"

I smirked a bit knowing he had seen right through my ruse. "I'll be fine, Coach. You take care of this and come join me once it's settled."

"The second coming," Dante called with drunken cheer.

"You, be quiet," Coach Clayton called. He then turned back to me to say, "Thank you, Celena. I will be back as soon as I can be. Until then, sit tight."

Coach Clayton walked out of the women's locker room as Dante gave me a toothy grin and a thumbs up. Even if he was being nothing short of a pain in my ass, I found his drunken candor somewhat charming. I knew better than to think the circumstance that saw him inebriated was anything righteous. Considering the matter of his age and the history I had been told in even first agreeing to play for Clayton Alonso, I knew it could never be such. It had been agreed upon that Dante would join us during our daily Schaffer practices, and I would do my best to pay him no mind. Coach Clayton did not trust his nephew alone because of the well documented history of self-destructive tendencies Dante would see through should he be left unsupervised. I found no reason to argue with these perquisites required of me in signing a four-year contract for the Schaffer Lions. Just because I had no family left did not mean I would resent Coach Clayton for having his own. I of people knew it was pointless to feel scorn over something that was long past grieving anyway.

A shape peered from the crack of a now ajar door at the front of the locker room. An unknown man had come to join me inside of my same height of six feet even. Contrasting myself was the brown smeared across his face—a few shades deeper than Coach Clayton's—but still infinitely richer than the porcelain beholding to my own. Freckles dotted the bridge of his nose and seeped into his cheeks. A mop of curly, black hair sat atop of his head, and I could see he was easily very handsome. He was holding a bouquet of flowers, which he stuck out for me to take. Hesitant, I accepted the olive branch shown by the man before me.

I watched him then say, "I'm staring on the Schaffer Lions too. Name's Conner Villanueva. I'm looking forward to working with you, Celena. If any of the guys give you problems, you let me know, and I'll handle it."

"Last I checked I don't need a savior, let alone a man to do that for me," I answered, examining the flowers to find they were my favorite, being water lilies.

"You're right, you don't, but you should know a woman attempting to join what was once a boy's club is going to be a lot more difficult than you might think." Conner glanced back at me to say, "I just want you to know you have me on the Lions as an ally. That's all."

"Well, it's appreciated, Conner."

"Where's Coach Clayton?"

"Handling his drunk nephew. I was just about to go out and tame the press in his absence."

"Like hell you are. Wait here until he comes back. Do you really trust the all-male reporters to have anything of substance to say, Celena?"

"Point taken," I answered.

Conner smiled. We turned to the noise of press cameras flashing and an indistinct male voice playing on the television in the lounge area of the locker room we were standing in. The man before the camera held an uncanny resemblance to Coach Clayton in nearly every facet of his appearance from his eyes to his skin to his short, black hair. He smirked at the camera as if he had long ago declared victory in a war only he had been fighting. It was a cause that had once been righteous, but with time had warped beneath the weight of his own ego for an unfounded arrogance to now take its place. I knew men like him well. Men who took until all had been taken. Men who hurt the women they claimed to love because of their past now clouding their present. I knew nothing of value would come from between the pair of his pink lips, and that much would be confirmed when he was asked by a nearby reporter, "What are your thoughts on Celena Božović joining the Lions, Xavier? After all, it is your uncle's hockey team."

Despite the familial linking him to Coach Clayton, I knew there was no value this man held other than to get a rise out of me from a press that already wanted me dead. I thought they had run out of credible people to interview if they were asking everyone along Coach Clayton's family tree their unneeded opinion about my gracing of the Schaffer Lions. Conner glanced at me, and I met his gaze. We watched each other before turning back to the television to wait for Xavier's answer.

"I think she's clearly too dumb for her own good if she thinks she can handle being on a men's team. What happens if she falls victim to men's locker room talk? Essentially, she is a *distraction*. And when you're playing a sport, the last thing a man needs is such. It's like giving a dog a Wagyu steak and telling him not to eat it. We all know what's gonna happen. He's gonna eat it."

My eyebrow twitched. Conner then muted the television. Coach Clayton came back into view. He moved to look between the two of us when I straightened my posture and he then said, "Dante is handled, for now. What's this, Conner?"

"I figured someone should welcome her," Conner replied, staring at me with a tense expression. "After all, it's going to be a difficult enough fucking season playing for a college team let alone one where you are unwanted."

I did not meet his gaze. "I'm not the kind of woman to back down from a challenge."

Conner looked hesitant to then say, "No, but as long as hockey is a team sport, you will need your team to help you get where you need to be. And I of people know how much you cannot afford failure, Celena Božović."

"Point taken, Conner Villanueva."

Conner smirked a bit, as if he was expecting my coming violence. I met his gaze, settling on a smirk of my own before turning back to Coach Clayton. He took the flowers Conner had gifted to give them back to him and then say, "Hold these while we go out there and declare war, will you, Conner?"

"Let's hope the coming damage is detrimental," Conner answered.

"For Andrei, Elliot, and Xavier," I added.

Coach Clayton looked at me perplexed as to what his other nephew had anything to do with my coming humbling. Conner then—seemingly on instinct—turned off the television as if not to give illusion to the coming fire laced in my rebuke. Coach Clayton then deemed it a mere coincidence. He began to talk towards the designated press room and turned around when he saw I was not following behind him to say, "C'mon, Celena. The sooner we do this the sooner we get this over with."

I gave a nod, glancing back at Conner who met the gesture with one of his own. Coach Clayton led me out of the locker room only for the two of us to be greeted by the incessant flashing of press cameras upon our entry. Coach Clayton slyly linked his arm in mine, guiding me to my place amid the jarring white surrounding my peripheral vision. He placed me into my chair before moving to his own and then adjusting the microphone only at his end. The cameras did not cease once he said, "Welcome, everyone. Thanks for coming. We're here to discuss Celena Božović and the hopes we have for the season. I will be the delegating party, so all questions will be asked to me."

The shouting that followed could have shaken every conceivable corner of the Earth, most potently—and cruelly— this room. The combination of the continued flashing and the insatiable, overbearing rumble that was an attempt to get Coach Clayton's attention was least to say, disorienting. I turned to find him unfazed by the overbearing, external stimuli that could have easily sent anyone else into full vertigo. He used his careful, steely gaze to then assess the situation with a clear, rational head atop his shoulders. How he could begin to do such in spite of our current shared circumstance was beyond me. I thought maybe he was right and that letting him handle my current showcasing to the world was not a move that would see us shot in the foot before we had even run out of the gate.

"You," Coach Clayton said, pointing at a male reporter. "Your question was?"

"What makes you think this woman will not lay victim to male locker room talk? After all, your nephew said the same thing earlier."

It was as if something had been awakened inside me, once lying dormant my entire life but now itching to be let out. I rose from the seat to stare down the male reporter. All eyes in the room then turned to me, but I did not break beneath the collective force of their judgment. I watched him cower beneath the weight of my pointed finger, and I smirked knowing I had him exactly where I wanted him. I then made sure that my voice rose above the noise surrounding me to shout, "Next time you ask a stupid fucking question like that, ask me. I can assure you; I am not some meek, hopeless woman who needs saving. Now, all of you will *sit the fuck down and be fucking quiet.*"

Everyone heeded my orders. I did not look at Coach Clayton but moved to take the microphone from his range of motion to then answer Xavier's accusations in saying, "Your own fantasy of what you think I am is not reality. I am here to play. I am here to win. I am here to see the name Celena Božović is among the like of an eternal mythos like the famed and equally great Achilles. I am here to see that Clayton Alonso's is reborn with a newfound partnership between he and I that will redefine his legacy. If I was here to entertain your skewed and equally unwanted hope of me being subservient and forever dependent on the men around me to be something of value, I would not be here, and we all know that. So, does anyone have something of fucking value to say, or can we call it a day and I'll come back when you do?"

The men looked among each other, at loss as to what their next move should be. I scanned the room before settling on the only female reporter in the room before pointing to her and saying, "You may ask me the rest of the questions from here on out since I know you will not ask anything fucking stupid. What's your name?"

She rose from her seat holding her pen and notepad in hand to say, "I'm Dylan Rivera. I'm the new hire among the local Boston ESPN network. My question is actually for Clayton."

I placed the microphone back in Clayton's range of motion. I then sat back down before the two of us stared at each other. The faintest trace of respect was smeared across his face despite me refusing to follow his lead. We then turned back to face Dylan when Coach Clayton then leaned into the microphone to say, "Go ahead, Dylan."

"Why did you pick Celena to break this glass ceiling? We all know this moment has been a long time coming in the collegiate sports world, so my ask is why now? What makes Celena different than any of the other women who had once hoped to do the same?"

Clayton did need time to think about it when he answered, "Celena is the kind of talent you only see once in a lifetime, Dylan. And when you're a coach, naturally you want the best to play for you. And the best is what I got when Celena agreed to join me here at Schaffer. Nothing more, nothing less."

I noticed he did not acknowledge our shared hope to scorn Andrei, but I knew better than to think it would be in our shared interest to admit to such. Instead, I turned back to the quiet that had washed over the makeshift press room. I promised myself then I was going to do everything in my power to prove the men gathered—and Andrei, Elliot, and Xavier—wrong no matter how much blood they would shed in the process.

ACT ONE

ROBYN HERA ZARAGOZA

RIGHT WING #24

AUGUST 23, 1994

ZODIAC SIGN
VIRGO

FAVORITE FOOD
FLAN

MAJOR
FASHION DESIGN

1

DANTE

WATCHING THE STADIUM CLOCK strike twelve, my most haunting of nightmares had finally been realized.

Because with the dawn of the new hour, I was now twenty.

And very much not dead.

Death and I were the oldest and fondest of friends. Truth be told, our relationship was every bit toxic, codependent, and— some could argue—abusive as the stereotype of the Grim Reaper our society had led us to believe it to be. Most people viewed the quintessential end intertwined with our mortality as this almost entitled and equally sordid man who took without a care for what the taken would come to leave behind. I could see why people feared it, or even why they did everything in their power to stave it off with phony products or illusive fountains of youth. But I never really saw it the same way. Truth be told, I found comfort in death. You could even say I welcomed death.

I loved him in a way few people ever could; with this fierce and limitless indignation that even in my most desperate and equally undeserving hour, he could finally make all my suffering cease. That even someone as pitiful and infinitely hopeless as I had finally done something right by cutting out the root of the sadness at its very source, being life itself. And I had promised myself this day would never come, but here I was.

Now twenty.

And still very much not dead.

My uncle had confiscated all my favored vices I would need to cope with this infinitely sickening milestone. He had refused to shave knowing I would repurpose the blades for a perfect baptism made across my arms to wash away my original sin blood. Tito Clayton had also refused to keep any alcohol in the house we shared knowing I would gorge on the habit should I find myself unsupervised. The pitiful dwelling he called a home was akin to a jail knowing I was not trusted outside the confines of its popcorn ceiling without someone else present.

Any pills had been stored somewhere I was ignorant to, and I thought Tito Clayton was smart for such. After all, my yearly tradition during the dawn of my birthday always coincided with an emergency room visit whether thanks to something externally illicit or something internally heinous. Whether I had vodka, blood, pills, or tears—sometimes all four—to show for the intake, it did not change that this wretched and equally morbid day did nothing to remind me I had failed. It was a promise I had made myself since the age of twelve after I was dropped off on my uncle's doorstep like second-hand, unwanted garbage. The transfer of powers in regard to my guardianship was seen through by the very people who were supposed to love me without fault. But I think we don't need to divulge into the entirety of my vast and infinitely pitiful sob story. Mostly because we all know the coming ending to it anyway.

I took out my package of cigarettes from the pocket of my ripped, black jeans. Tito Clayton always went on about how buying pants with rips in them was a waste of money, but I could care less what a man who only wore Schaffer tracksuits had to say about my fashion choices. I then pressed around my pockets for my chrome lighter that was the only remnant left of the family I had been forced to leave behind eight years ago. I examined the polished silver. The inscription of my father's name and birthdate glinted in the overhead lights as I thumbed my fingers over the carved-in edges.

The letters were displayed in a pleasing font whose name I could care less about. I read the words 'Quentin Rivera Hidalgo' for an endless minute in hopes it would conjure up a face I had long forgotten in our agreed upon silence. I could not find a matching image to go with the man who had hand in raising me, nor could I find the face belonging to the woman who, too, had helped. They were long forgotten strangers. They were no longer family. They were a caricature of what family should be. And maybe knowing such meant any hope for recovery had long been dead. Shot at point blank range with its corpse long forgotten beneath the brush of a forest who would keep its secret until there was nothing left to show for the crime but bone.

I took a cigarette out from the flimsy, cardboard packaging. Images of the horrors that would befall me if I refused to quit were superimposed on the back, and I gave a laugh. After all, who needed to worry about cancer when in the first few minutes of this sickening holiday you had just promised yourself you would now never live past twenty-one?

I placed the cylinder to my lips. I flicked the fork of my lighter until it rendered a flame. I placed the ember to my cigarette before releasing the fork which snuffed out the remnant I no longer needed. Once I was sure my cigarette was burning, I took a long and equally needed drag. I exhaled the remaining smoke from my nostrils as an unfounded calm began to wash over my body. I loosened my shoulders. I relaxed my back. The nicotine was now doing its job to see me remain sane enough to come out of this hour alive, and maybe, that would be enough for now. After all, another visit to the emergency room would only screw over my tito more so than it would me. We only had one other goalie, being my best friend Chase. He was decent, sure, but when a former first round NHL draft pick trains you in the sport before you can even walk, you're bound to be good. And in the realm of talent, it wasn't braggadocious to say I had it. It was simply a fact.

Footsteps came toward me in a uniform manner. I could tell by the steps the person was wearing sneakers, and I knew it had to be one of two people considering the hour and the place. I did not turn to face the intruder, instead saying, "Tito. I told you I needed to be alone."

No answer came. I thought Tito Clayton was trying to play coy with me, so I turned around. And to my surprise, it was not my uncle who greeted me, but the captain of his Schaffer Lions, Celena Božović.

Celena's rugged features greeted me behind a firm expression. Her nose was warped ever so slightly to the right, a sign to show for repeated breakings. The sport we played was neither forgiving nor kind, but Celena, too, knew this truth well. After all, being the first woman scouted onto a once all-male NCAA team was not for the faint of heart or weak of mind.

Celena had carved out her position at the top of the Lions's hierarchy through obscene determination, calculating strategy, and sheer, indisputable talent. Every man who held power or influence in the college sphere wanted her squashed, dead, and gone. But Celena took their vitriol without so much of a complaint and her head held high. Truth be told, I thought her effortless grace and equally formidable strength to withstand such abuse unflinching was infinitely admirable. I would always admire her for staying true to what she believed in no matter who or what it cost her. And I knew with her standing before me considering the date and the hour meant that much was about to be put to the test.

"You're not allowed to do that here," Celena said.

It was not so much a scolding as it was an empty threat. Tito Clayton did not like the stench of tobacco knowing he had been clean of the vice since my thirteenth birthday. How he quit without any kind of aid was beyond me. However, I knew better than to think I could do the same when the other means to cope with this beyond pointless existence had been stripped of me in even agreeing to play for him in the first place. Maybe in the afterlife I'd come to scorn him for such. But for now, it was this rose-colored lens of recovery he had been looking at me through that was the only thing keeping me alive anyway.

"I shouldn't be alive, Celena. I have every reason to cope."

Celena tilted her head upright ever so slightly. She crossed her arms and then parted her thin, pink lips to say, "Then, is a happy birthday beneath you?"

I smirked a bit, blocking the expression with my hand to take another drag of my vice. "Every bit as calling Elliot or Andrei your family."

Celena laughed at that. I did find some comfort knowing I was one of the few, carefully chosen people who could even think of making a joke at her expense. I did not know what I had done to earn such a right, but Celena always thought there was more to me than this street that could only ever lead to the same dead end. Ever since I had met in her freshman year here at

Schaffer, she had weaved tall tales of how we would come to take the NHL by storm; a famed and equally hallowed duo of offense and defense that would see us achieve glory, riches, and infinite respect. Celena could very well have been selling me this pipe dream since childhood in hopes it would give me something to live for. And I hoped she found some comfort in knowing I liked the product she was selling. However, thinking I was worthy of such or even being able to afford it were two very different things.

I was a man on borrowed time. I had been staving off my inevitable end for some unbeknownst and equally unconscionable reason. I didn't want to say I was still here because I wanted to be. Truth be told, killing yourself is a hell of a lot harder when people actually want you here despite all you've done to push them away. Maybe knowing I would see through my own demise despite such made me infinitely more heinous than the people I had promised I would never become. But such crimes did not need to be answered for now. Right now, all I needed to focus on was Celena Božović and the acrid taste of nicotine that felt like a pair of hands wrapped around the width of my neck. Closing the space between the bruises as I lost all resolve to fight back knowing the fate I would soon meet was one I could never, truly be above.

"I suppose you're right," Celena said. She swept her gaze up and down the length of my body. "But I suppose I should rip off the Band-Aid."

I motioned for her to continue before taking another drag from my cigarette.

"Robyn Zaragoza wants to transfer here."

Time had seemingly come to a complete and total stop. Despite my tether to sanity and rational thinking being frayed knowing the date, I was still in a clear enough state of mind to realize what Celena had just said. Despite what little I chose to know about my older brother, I was more than aware that Robyn Zaragoza was the woman he called a best friend. Mostly because her and the same older brothers Celena and I did not constitute as family all kept each other company as some kind of deranged and equally detestable friend group. So knowing this, it only begged the question, what the fuck was Robyn Zaragoza doing on my front doorstep in a place we all knew she was unwelcome?

I already knew the answer to that question as soon as I had asked it. I glanced at Celena to watch her head move back to face mine, and I knew the firmness in her expression meant she knew this too. Robyn Zaragoza had betrayed Xavier Hidalgo in a scorning so barbaric it meant her life was now in the balance. It's not that I didn't think Xavier was capable of solving his own problems, but despite my wishes, we were brothers. And that meant I knew the fucker whether I wanted to or not. It was no secret a relationship with Xavier was not so much on equal footing as it was who he could have some kind of influence or power over. This was so when they did something he did not like, he could punish them as he saw fit. By no means a healthy way of dealing with your own problems, yes. But considering I did the same thing except at my own expense, I was in no place to judge.

I took another drag of my cigarette, then dislodging a clump of ash with my pointer finger. The remnant fell onto the concrete beneath my feet, and I ground it out with the ball of my platform, combat boot. The cinder left an insidious, black mark as if to warn me of the fate that would befall me should I let Robyn Zaragoza into my refuge unvetted. But I knew the truth of the matter was something both infinitely more complicated than Celena could begin to suggest, and that it was something I had yet to earn the right to know.

Despite all the work I had done to see myself absolved of morality, it did not change I still had its truth entrenched in every part of my being. Trying to justify your self-destructive behaviors despite what damage it caused to those around you was a kind of mental gymnastics I would probably have earned gold in a very long time ago. But doing such did not mean I knew deep down that it would always be wrong. It could even be evil. It could very well send me to hell like the same Catholic doctrine that had saved my tito from the brink of death would come to suggest.

And while this sense of degradation at the expense of self was something I was more than fine with seeing through, extending this same skewed sense of conscience to others would always be wrong. I was the only maker of my own destiny. While

I could have some influence over others, it did not change that I could never be the final say. And tell me, what righteousness would be found in casting Robyn Zaragoza out headfirst because of my dislike of her knowing this was probably the only shot she had left? I'll answer that for you. It would always be wrong. And it would always make me among the like of the same people I had promised through equal portions of tears, blood, pills, and liquor that I would never become.

"You say the word and I will send her back to the nothing she came from." Celena inched closer. Considering the height difference of her bleacher and mine, in this rare instance she was taller than me. "If she will prevent you from being something great, I could give a fuck who she is and what the fuck she wants."

I took another drag of my cigarette. I didn't think Celena would like the coming answer, but I was the last person to lie. "She can stay."

Celena raised an eyebrow. "You want her to stay?"

"Why else would she be here if Xavier didn't fuck her over?"

"She could be a mole. I don't trust her as far as I can fucking throw her, Dante. And you would be smart to do the same."

"You know it'll never be that simple. This is Xavier we're talking about." I pointed to the thick, raised skin starting at the bottom of my left eye that dragged down the edge of my jaw.

"Since when is the man who gave me this a man of moral standing, Celena?"

Celena pursed her lips. She looked as if she were going to spew venom from the length of her tongue when she then said, "You're right. But don't lie and say she didn't have something to do with their sins too."

I knew she was right, but I knew better than to correct her outright. I crossed my arms and raised the pair of fingers holding my cigarette upright to then say, "You wanted my permission. And I say it's granted. Or, is your own judgment clouding your rational thinking?"

Celena did not answer, only to reply, "I'll tell Coach, then. But don't think her being here means I will stop my effort into making you something great."

A chill ran down the length of my spine. I don't know what was infinitely more sickening, that the greatest hockey player to ever live saw this inherent worth in me I would never be worthy of. Or, my allowance of Robyn Zaragoza to find refuge among the same people she had once helped to scorn. I put my cigarette back between my lips, using my fingers to keep it in place. I then took a long and much needed drag. This entire conversation was making an already terrible birthday morbidly worse than what I could have ever expected it to be. Truth be told, all I wanted to do was sleep and forget this day had ever happened. I knew Tito Clayton was more hesitant to see myself admitted to another ward, and what good did they even do anyway?

Plus, the added factor of my newfound dependence on alcohol complicated such plans to see myself escape my depressing reality. I was not stupid. I knew getting admitted to the psychiatric ward was a temporary solution to a lifelong problem. It only paused your issues since when you got out, the same problems would be waiting for you when you got back. I knew the only way to really, truly see myself free of the confines of this mental illness was to even admit there was a problem to begin with. But truth be told, I was comfortable in this state of constant degradation. I liked the home I had made here. And I found no need to uproot its foundation just because other people had been stupid enough to care about a man who was only destined to kill himself before his coming college graduation.

Does this mindset make me a bad person?

Yes.

I'm well aware it does.

But change and I are two things that never saw eye to eye. And when you've been hellbent on self-destruction for the past eight years, changing is a hell of a lot scarier than staying this way ever could be.

I knew Celena was going to expect me to shut down the very notion that my life had this inherent value only a fool could attribute to someone like me. But in the past four years I had known her, I knew Celena was not a liar. I knew that when she said something, it came from equal parts of her soul and mind.

It had her entire backing and sense of honor behind it whether it was something someone wanted to hear or not. Celena was a good, just, and equally honorable woman. She had a strong sense of morality. Unlike mine that had been twisted by eight years of a still unmanaged mental illnesses, which could very well have shrouded my own sense of judgment. I wanted nothing more than to call her a liar and tell her to stop telling me things I knew could never begin to be true. But seeing this perfect, all-encompassing glint encircling the blue surrounding her pupil, I knew she was right. That, and I knew deep down that arguing with her would make me a liar. And if there was anything I would never want to willingly become, it was a fucking liar.

"You're greater," I answered in hopes the deflection would get her to change the topic. "What am I compared to the future great endless generations of young girls will look up to as a titan of the sport?"

Celena smirked a bit.

I knew this meant she had seen right through my ruse.

"My greatness, Dante, does not diminish yours."

I was quiet.

"And truth be told, I am not the kind of woman to lie especially when my own character and judgment comes into question. So, you can pull that shit with anyone else on the Lions, but not me. You should know me better than that, Dante. After all, you are the only person here who holds any real skill that is at all comparable to mine."

"Thanks, I suppose," I replied, nauseous. "But what are we going to do about Robyn's newfound presence? Do you really think she could be a double agent, Celena?"

"Only time will tell," Celena said, tilting her head to the right. "We need to keep an eye on her. Her girlfriend is transferring with her. I think you know her."

"Who is she?"

"Lisanna Wilson."

I knew the name and face the moment the words came from between Celena's lips. Whenever there was a family get together orchestrated by either halves of my family, Lisanna's aunt was always there with her niece in tow. Truth be told, most of the other children gathered there did not like me much due to Xavier's influence, but Lisanna—for some reason—was the exception. We would hole up in my room, talking for hours free from the unwanted ears of the adults around us. Never about the past but only the future she had once tried to convince me was worth seeing through until the end.

Knowing she was Robyn's girlfriend, I could now bestow enough of my trust into Robyn Zaragoza. That is, until she had proved her loyalty to the Lions rather than to the man who had dared to scorn her. Some could argue such was not fair, but when your brother has been actively trying to end your life for the past eight years, even this allowance to have Robyn come here was beyond generous. I didn't like to think of myself as a good or just person. After all the damage I had wrought upon others at my own expense, I didn't think that much was even true. But even if I could never say I was a man of moral standing, I was fair. And refusing Robyn refuge here at Schaffer because of her past would never be fair.

"Ah," I replied after a bit. "I'm going to say something that you're not going to like."

"You trust Robyn?"

"Not exactly," I answered. "But I trust Lisanna. And that gives me enough backing to extend a tentative truce to Robyn. Until we can be sure she's not working for Xavier, like you said."

Celena watched me before saying, "And I trust you. So, I'll extend the same to Lisanna and Robyn. Maybe not all of my backing, but enough of it that they can stay. I'll tell Coach."

Celena took something out of her hoodie pocket. It was a small, gift-wrapped item adorned with a gaudy, red bow. The wrapping paper had the words 'Happy Birthday' superimposed in an equally annoying font, and I moved my gaze back up to Celena's cobalt blue eyes to see she was—of all things—smiling.

"Happy birthday, Dante."

"I don't want anything."

"Well, that's too fucking bad."

I couldn't help but laugh. I took the object from her thin hands smeared in an even shade of porcelain. Celena moved them back to her side, and I placed my cigarette back between the part of my lips to tear the packaging off. Beneath it was a tiny, black box. I glanced up at Celena to watch her say in an obvious excitement, "Chase, Breanna, Davi, and I pooled our money to get you something. It's not much, but I think you'll like it."

I moved my gaze back to the box to lift off the lid. Beneath was a matte, black lighter engraved with my full name, Dante Alonso Hidalgo. I never liked gifts to begin with, and I never found a point in asking for them when celebrating something as morbid as my failure to see my own life cease. But moving to inspect the lighter in the cool, tinted stadium light, I realized, this year wouldn't be so bad. That is, if the coming transfer of Robyn Zaragoza wouldn't soon lead to the downfall of us all.

2

ROBYN

I **WAS WELL AWARE** I had come to Schaffer University a
traitor.

The reality of my transfer was not lost on me. I knew I was
every bit unwelcome and unwanted as anyone who once called
Xavier Hidalgo her best friend would expect to be among the
court of his scorned. Truth be told, coming to Schaffer
University was a last-ditch effort to see myself reclaim a life that
had—up until a month ago—been dependent on Xavier
Hidalgo. Our once intertwined truths included the share of our
faults, quirks, and traits I had tried so hard to absolve myself of
since getting out of rehab and being forced to rebuild my sense
of self without him. As of now, I was unsure if I could ever bring
myself to forgive him. Maybe I never could. Maybe with time the
wound he had smeared across the walls of my heart would
become less monstrous if I dared to address its truth. But such
did not matter now. Mostly because I knew surviving my

assassination attempt meant addressing the truth of the crimes I had committed. And it meant facing the inevitable consequence of actions I had chosen to see through despite knowing the damage they would wrought to the few people I could really, truly say I loved.

I walked inside Tito Clayton's house to find the decor was nonexistent. I could tell by the furniture and the way the pieces were arranged that the only people who dwelled between its painted over, white walls were men. A clear feminine touch was all but nonexistent, and it only deepened the pang of fear taking root in the pit of my stomach. That it was too late to dare and start over and become the person I had promised Lisanna I always would be. I had not seen my girlfriend since my initial intake after waking up from my overdose, and truth be told, facing her after what I had done was a confrontation I was all but dreading.

It's not that I feared Lisanna and what she would come to say. It's not that I didn't want to take responsibility for the hurt I had wrought upon her. I knew my newfound status was the same like of a man who had been so heinous to hurt her before. It was a truth I could not begin to live with myself knowing what I, too, had done to her. I ached for Lisanna to find it in her heart to forgive me. But hoping for such did not change the matter of worthiness. And knowing what I had done, I would never be entitled to the same kindness she had given blood to give to me despite all she had been forced to endure.

I walked into the kitchen. The tiled floor did not aid my step considering the matter of my six-inch stiletto heels. I had been barred from makeup, dresses, and heels while in rehab, and it was all but miserable not being allowed to dress up to my usual overdressed attire. After all, I needed everyone who gazed upon me to know that I was something every bit unobtainable as they hoped I could never be. I needed the general populace to know that no matter what they gave to hold a candle to my pristine, infinitely flawless image, it would be an effort in which they would never be successful. I remember Xavier making a comment saying I never went anywhere without looking red carpet ready. Even if I knew now he was every bit abhorrent as he was reprehensible, it did not change that in that rare instance, he was right. Although, I could no longer say such with the same confidence knowing I was now one of three names atop his hitlist who could only ever pay for what he deemed a betrayal in blood.

The door to a bedroom opened to reveal two people I knew well. Being my twin brother Conner Villanueva and Xavier's ex-girlfriend, Davi Salvatella.

I didn't think either of them had much reason to keep each other in their company. Conner had no history with Xavier like Davi and I did, so I found no reason to think there was anything suspicious with their agreed upon congregation. Truth be told, this was the first instance I had seen Conner face to face. Mostly because of the more than incompetent and equally bureaucratic foster care system that did little to keep families like our together rather than apart.

We had the same everything, which would have made sense considering the fact that he and I were twins. Truth be told, looking at Conner was akin to looking in the mirror. Our skin was the same hue of brown, dotted with freckles that poked out from the respective cloth covering the shade. Dark, honey brown eyes watched me between an expression that looked equally unsure what to make of me as I was of him. It's not that his hesitation offended me. Because truth be told, I felt the same way. After all, what the hell were you supposed to make of a man who had your same face you never knew existed until a month ago? Who was now standing before you every bit a stranger as you could safely assume your same parents never wanted you to be?

I knew better than to dwell on such a truth. I didn't think I would be able to stomach it sober anyway. Instead, I moved to gaze upon the safer half of the pair before me, being Davi. She looked nearly identical as she did back when we traveled in the same circles, with the exception of her hair now dyed in a short, bleach blonde bob. Hooded, black eyes free of bruises greeted me with an unblemished and equally untainted expression that gave no illusion to what she was thinking or feeling. Seeing her standing before me without any kind of blood, gashes, or bruises dotting her body was a strange sight in and of itself. And knowing such meant I should have known better than to think she was the safer option to gaze upon as I once thought. Mostly because we both knew she was the only other woman on Xavier's hitlist. And this meant she was another one of the Lions I had excused Xavier's abuse toward incorrectly assuming he would never extend the same brunt to me.

A palatable silence thick enough to be torn apart with a pair of fingers lingered between the three of us. I glanced between Conner and Davi a last time before attempting to be the bigger person and say, "Conner. Davi. How lovely to see you both."

Conner and Davi looked at each other. Davi brushed her arm against Conner's. It was a motion I knew meant there was more to the nature of their relationship than either party was going to tell me outright. I filed away the evidence to be asked about later. For now, my focus was coming out of this conversation with enough of my dignity intact that it would not see me relapse. Rehab may have taught me ways of how to cope with this inherent dislike of the person I was that saw me abuse opioids to begin with. But the thing about this is that rehab is a temporary solution to a lifelong problem. After being discharged, I knew the problems that had been put on hold would be brought back to the forefront knowing I had to face their inevitable consequences. I knew what to do that would see me remain clean. I had been taught the skills needed to see through such. But that would not matter because the problem that even saw me resort to getting high to begin with remained knowing my parents were never going to get back together. And while I knew I was not seeing through my attempt at sobriety alone, it did not change that it sure as hell didn't feel that way.

"You're certainly taller in person," Conner said after a bit.

I pointed at my shoes. "A girl can like her heels, no?"

"I suppose so," Conner replied, almost quiet. "I have to ask, Robyn. What do you make of the two of us standing before each other? Despite all the powers at play, who did everything in their power to see this day never came?"

I thought that was a beyond loaded question to ask someone when you were meeting them for the first time. The truth of my relationship with Conner was not lost on me knowing I had escaped the foster care system before holding any real memory of it, and he had not. I knew this metric was not so much a privilege as it was sheer luck. I think Conner would hold a right to be resentful towards me because of such, even if the horrors of his past was a truth still unknown to me as of now.

Maybe I would never be worthy to know, and maybe he would never tell me. But standing here before him, I knew I wanted nothing more than to be the family he could never really say he had. After all, this truth was the only reason as to why I had wanted to transfer to Schaffer before the matter of Xavier's betrayal upended such plans. And I didn't know if Conner was in the right state of mind or even the right place to welcome me knowing I was every bit a stranger to him as he was to me. But that did not mean I was not going to give everything I had to show him what wonders a cohesive, family unit could do. Even if the one in which I had based this notion on was every bit broken as I once thought it never could be.

"You can save the psychoanalysis for once you two get to know each other," Davi called.

Conner looked at her, frowning.

"What?" Davi asked, the least bit sympathetic. "You're asking her to dish out a truth God only knows you're worthy of in your first meeting. In the meantime, we have bigger fish to fry in terms of Robyn's new reality."

I swallowed down the lump in my throat.

"Like the matter of Xavier."

I knew such was coming, but the pang in my gut remained despite my best efforts to see it repressed. I glanced at Davi to see her expression was equal parts stern and unflinching.

She crossed toned arms to then say, "You know every bit as I do that we're equals, do you not?"

"I know that much," I answered, somewhat sheepish. "And I'm sorry, Davi. I'm so fucking sorry I did not do anything to stop what he had done to you."

Davi bore the weight of my apology evenly atop her broad shoulders. She contemplated my attempt to extend the olive branch with careful thought. Conner gazed upon her; their height difference infinitely drastic considering Davi's more than unassuming height of five feet even. Davi did not face Conner. Instead, she gazed upon me. She pointed her finger painted over in a deep, sultry red to say, "Tell me, Robyn. What makes you think you got out unscathed?"

I didn't follow. "What the hell are you talking about, Davi?"

"We all know Xavier's capacity to manipulate. We all know his relationships are not so much on equal footing as they are founded in imbalances of power. Xavier is evil. Xavier is wicked. And tell me, what makes you think you, too, are not a victim of his signature trait of violence?"

Conner was already watching me. He probably had no idea what the hell Davi and I were talking about, but I didn't move to meet his gaze. Instead, I swallowed down the lump in my throat a second time before croaking, "Yeah, but he respected me as a person. You and Dante can never say the same. I was his best friend, Davi. I have a hell of a lot to atone for knowing such."

"I'm not ignorant to that, Robyn. But just because you think Xavier respected your autonomy does not change the obvious matter of the truth. Just because he fed you the fantasy your friendship was on equal footing does not mean he actually believed such. Sure, you're complicit in not standing up to him. But you're sure as hell not entirely responsible for actions *he* chose to see through. Save the pity party for someone who wants to hear it. But I will never be the one."

Before I could rebuke the very insinuation of what Davi had said, the front door to Tito Clayton's house clicked open, and two men walked inside. One I recognized as the only tether keeping me alive. And the other third of the trio who Xavier wanted equally dead as Davi and I.

Dante Hidalgo was a towering height. His stature was so formidable that he easily commanded all attention when he walked into the room. He wore mismatched shades of black, with his jeans having rips at the knees. A turtleneck covered most of his neck and arms. His skin was the same range of a deep brown as the one belonging to Davi, myself, and the brother before me, contrasting his uncle whose own was a few shades lighter. Dante's face was framed on either side by long, shoulder-length hair that was accessorized with a goatee and a pair of dark, rumbling eyes. And, of course, dragging down from the bottom of his left to end at his jutting jawline, was the scar Xavier had carved into Dante's face during a long and equally distant family holiday eight years ago.

Another silence loomed over the five of us. Tito Clayton was the first to move, and he commandeered my bags I had left near the door. He did not leave the four of us alone, but I moved to look at Dante who was already staring at me. He gave the filthiest, shit-eating grin I didn't think anyone but him could possibly begin to manage. I expected something wicked to come from between his pair of thin, brown lips, and that much would be confirmed when he said, "Robyn Zaragoza. How lovely to finally meet you, dearest."

The sarcasm was not lost on me. Instead of stooping to his level, I said, "I did not come here to start shit with you, Dante.

You are the last of any concern on my already crowded list of things I need handled. And you can hate me all you want. You can even want me dead. But the one thing you will not do is disrespect me. Are we clear?"

Dante looked incensed, but before he could reduce me to cinders with the fire laced in his rebuke, Tito Clayton moved his hand instinctively to his nephew's shoulder. Dante then bit his tongue, eventually settling to say, "Whatever. You're not welcome here. I need you to know that. And should you be some kind of double agent in disguise, I will be the least bit kind with your eventual punishment."

Dante shook his uncle off him, then exiting from the front door. Conner and Tito Clayton looked at Davi who sighed and then said, "I'll handle it." Davi turned to look at me. "And we'll finish this conversation another time. And truth be told, I wouldn't take Dante's animosity to heart. He's vindictive even if I don't think he has much reason to be."

Davi followed Dante outside, closing the door behind her. I turned to look between Tito Clayton and my brother, then saying, "I have to ask, Tito. How the hell did you even find me to begin with?"

"Conner did one of those DNA tests last month. Seeing as I am his step-in guardian, he came to me first. Then, I called you, and now we're here."

I glanced at Conner.

Conner then said, "I want you to know that even if it's a big adjustment for you to come here, Robyn, I don't take your sacrifice lightly. I know how hard it can be to start over. And I want you to know that you're not alone. I'm here for you should you need me to be."

While Conner had no reason to lie, that did not mean believing him was as simple as he would expect it to be. I gave a smile and then said, "Of course, Conner. Let's hope the coming year will be kind on us both, no?"

Conner met my smile with one of his own.

Tito Clayton then turned to Conner to say, "I'd like to talk to Robyn alone, Conner. Is that alright with you?"

"Of course," Conner said, nodding. He glanced at me a last time before exiting to say, "It was nice to meet you, Robyn. I really do hope we can be the family our parents always wanted for us to be."

Conner smiled before exiting from the same door as Dante and Davi prior. I turned to Tito Clayton who was still holding my bags to find a prominent five o'clock shadow dusted across his face. His expression had many lines to show for his age and the hardships I knew he had been so unjustly forced to endure. I may not have known the entire story of Tito Clayton's life from start to finish, but I knew enough of it. It was a fucking miracle he was standing before me and offering me refuge from the man who would not rest until I was six feet under. I glanced down Tito's Clayton's arms that were obscured by even lengths of cloth. I brought my gaze back up to his own to see he was already staring at me. His expression washed this sense of fatherly comfort over me knowing the emotion he was conveying was one that told me that as long as I was one his Lions, I would always be safe.

"Have you talked with Lisanna?" Tito Clayton asked in a tone I knew meant I could no longer ignore the issue of my betrayal now that I was out of rehab. "She's moved into her dorm. She told me she wanted to talk to you."

"I haven't, no," I answered, every bit meek as I was afraid. "I can't face her after knowing what I have done, Tito."

"You can and you will," Tito Clayton answered. "I did the same in my own recovery after pushing away everyone I held dear. Truth be told, if Ciara had not picked me up from the hospital after my last overdose, both our stories would have very different endings. And we both know I hurt her too. And I think where your issue lies, Robyn, is that you don't think you have the capacity to be forgiven."

"Why would I?" I croaked. "I know what I've done. I know what I'm responsible for, Tito."

"You are right that you are responsible for what you've done, Robyn." Tito Clayton moved to stand before me, and I glanced down at him. His expression told me he was not going to budge on the point he was trying to make. "But I think holding yourself to this unobtainable degree of perfection is unrealistic. It does nothing but make you hate yourself. You're going to make mistakes, and you are going to fuck up in your life. But it's what you do in the aftermath after your fuck up that defines you. You have a choice to make. Either be a coward and lose the one thing you still hold dear or acknowledge the pain you've caused Lisanna and refuse to do it again. The choice is yours. But even I know you don't want to lose her. I don't think you'll survive it."

We watched each other.

"Because, Robyn, I barely did."

Tito Clayton glanced at me a last time before turning around with my bags in tow to point at the door Conner and Davi had entered from before to say, "That's your room. I'll move your bags there. And Davi is right, don't take Dante's animosity personally. The man does not have a single nice thing to say about anyone. I think he gets that much from me."

Tito Clayton walked into my room when I grabbed my phone from the chasms of my purse. I unlocked the glass slate to open my messages and text Lisanna.

im ready 2 talk when u r just lmk when and where

Later today at the Nora Wilson Hockey Center. Tell Tito Clayton you'll be with me and he'll allow you to go.

Tito Clayton walked back into the living room as he then said, "Get some rest, Robyn. It's been a hard and long transfer. You need all the beauty sleep you can get."

I didn't answer, only giving a nod. I retired to my makeshift prison cell. I then prayed to a god I could never bring myself to believe in that the coming confrontation with the only woman I could ever love would not see me reduced to a pitiful pile of ash.

3

DANTE

TODAY WAS THE DATE of Tito Clayton's yearly tradition to usher in the season where he and his Lions—old, new, and staff—would be invited to his house for a typical Filipino soirée. It had been something I was forced to attend since he had agreed to be head coach of the Schaffer Lions when I was thirteen. This was my first year present as a member underneath his ranks; rather than the same archetype of the son who could not be trusted outside his guardian's immediate supervision.

Considering my history of a myriad of self-destructive behaviors when left to my own devices, I understood the logic behind my presence despite then not having aged into the proper rite to see me have any standing among the people gathered like they did amongst each other. It's not that I disliked being deemed a kind of mascot by Tito Clayton's Lions. To be entirely transparent, it saw me acquire a new tether to a steady supply of alcohol I would not have otherwise. That is, until Celena's tenure began, and she banned the—once all male—Lions to supply me with such vices.

I had gotten to know most of Tito Clayton's past Lions well before aging into the rite of becoming one myself, which was how Celena and I had first become familiar. I suppose graduating from the role of captive to a man of some kind of standing was something to be proud of on the surface, but the reality that I was still every bit a prisoner was not lost on me. After all, what else was there to call my own tenure here at Schaffer when I was sentenced to house arrest unless I had some kind of chaperone present? I knew the only way to see myself be given some kind of leeway in terms of my own freedom was to admit there was a cause seeing me restricted to begin with. But knowing the change that would come with such meant admitting there was a problem in terms of self, and this truth did not change that change and I would always be two things that would never see eye to eye.

Even if it meant freedom.

And even if it meant life itself.

I had spent the rest of my birthday helping my uncle cook a vast array of cultural dishes that were now resting atop metal frames and covered in aluminum foil atop our linoleum countertops. Their smell had blended evenly inside my nose to illicit memories of the home I had been forced to leave behind at age twelve without a say in my coming banishment. I knew better than to be bitter about what was now said and done, but it did not change that there was some resentment I harbored for the silence that followed. I could understand why Xavier did not talk to me considering he hated everything it was that I stood for, even if I didn't know what I had done to deserve such. My parents on the other hand, I knew better than to award such comforts. After all, they were every bit the wielders of power and influence in our relationship, and it may have taken me a long eight years to realize such, but wrong could I have done to earn their scorn as a child?

I knew better than to dwell on the matters of my past when the means to cope with it was banned in the confines of my uncle's campus home. Chase skipped over to sit next to me, his mullet now dyed a bright, cotton candy shade of pink that, least to say, bewildered me considering the gaudiness of it. Black eyes curved at the fold squinted as he greeted me with a smile, and I glanced at the birthmark resting at his chin, then moving my gaze back up to his own.

Chase then said, smiling wide, "Like it, Dante?"

"It's certainly *something*, I'll give you that."

"Girls like men in touch with their feminine side. Right, Davi?"

I turned to look at Davi who was leaning atop the back of the leather couch with her head resting in her hand. She glanced at me before turning to Chase to answer, "Truth be told, more masculine guys are more my type. I like them strong and dependable." Davi glanced at me again before turning back to

Chase to say, "What makes you think Celena will even notice, Chase? She's already got so much on an already loaded plate anyway."

"She'll notice," Chase cooed, every bit confident as I didn't think he had much right to be. "Progress may be slow, but it's still progress."

"A man fond of the long game," Davi said. "I can't say I feel the same."

Chase looked at Davi with raised eyebrows and accusatory eyes that I knew were accusing her of lying. Ignorant to what was the truth or not, I glanced at Davi who smirked a bit at the unsaid comeback. Neither party bothered to explain to me what they meant by their exchange, but I could care less about the truth of it when the gossip of others was something I would never be interested in discussing with anyone, even my two best friends. I fiddled with my lighter before moving to pocket the item, the front door to Tito Clayton's house then opening to reveal the new people making up the Lions staff, being Takeshi Oba and Ciara Wilson.

The only one of the three to whom I held a personal connection was Ciara. She had been involved in my life since I had been dropped on Tito Clayton's doorstep a long eight years ago, and I knew there was more to their relationship than either making up the pair would ever begin to divulge me in. Not to say I minded living in a state of ignorance in regard to the nature of their relationship. I just didn't think I had done much to earn the truth. Even if I was above any and all kinds of gossip, I would want Tito Clayton to tell me himself, on his terms and when he was ready to do so in a way that did not back him into some kind of corner. But regardless of such comforts, it was easy to piece two and two together. After all, Ciara wore the same platinum band at the dip of a gold chain that Clayton wore on the middle finger of his left hand. It could very well have no meaning other than to make a kind of shared, agreed upon fashion statement, but I knew my uncle. And the way he looked at Ciara Wilson could not be anything but love in its most virtuous form.

Tito Clayton was never the affectionate type. There was this obvious hesitancy in expressing more intimate emotions that I could not really judge him for when I was guilty of the same exact behavior and doing so would just make me a hypocrite. But issues of intimacy aside, I knew Tito Clayton loved me. After all, why would he continue to hold hope I would agree to a stability he was forcing upon me when I had proved an endless amount of times before I was incapable of such? What else is there to call our relationship when he was the man to find me after nearly each of my suicide attempts, holding me in this unyielding, iron cocoon made up of cloth covered arms until I whisked away to the hospital where he would then refuse to leave my bedside?

You could very well say that Tito Clayton's love was something I was entitled to considering he was my father in every sense but blood, but I would disagree. Mostly because after my parents gave me to him like some kind of unwanted and equally repurposed yankee swap gift, he did not refuse them outright. He did not argue with his life now upended and his new game of house where he would be expected to play the role of step-in father to a child who was every bit a problem as his parents—and even his brother—knew he was. Tito Clayton chose to love me. And truth be told, he didn't fucking have to. And if he hadn't, I knew the long and sordid tale of self would have a very, very different ending.

Ciara gave me a smile, and I responded with a nod. She cradled an aluminum baking dish in her hands, and the three of us then turned to Takeshi Oba to see he had two children in tow. Both men met my gaze, with my attention focused on one of the pair.

He was handsome. Even if I never liked to stoop so low to find others attractive since doing so when I was simply going to kill myself come my college graduation, it did not change that this stranger's overall bone structure was more than appealing. Every angle was jutting; carved by a careful and loving hand akin to a bust of a long dead Roman emperor's long forgotten lover. Eyes of an alluring, endless black seemed to examine me with the same interest I held for him. High cheekbones were accentuated by his long hair being tied back in a short ponytail at the center of his head. His lips were thin, pink, and the perfect accessory to adorn rich, brown skin the same color as the sands making up the dunes of the seemingly endless Sahara Desert. In a sense, his own presence was akin to the same wonder that came with a place as inhospitable as such. Mostly because I knew if I were ever to be stupid enough to see through this attraction I harbored, it would mean I would have failed in my mission to see myself dead, and arguably worse, I would be forced to share this misery I selfishly kept to myself with someone else.

And truth be told, I do not think anyone would come to like its constant state of corrosion like only I ever could.

The other man was uninteresting. He was handsome, sure, but nothing really to marvel at. I could tell by the way he both dressed and carried himself that harboring any kind of affection for him would only prove to be pointless in the end. He and the other man I, too, did not know seemed close, sticking by Takeshi as he greeted Tito Clayton with a hug.

When Tito Clayton had first taken the position of head coach of the Schaffer Lions, he only agreed to his post with the caveats of tenure and his ability to pick his staff. Every member making up his supporting network that was from the last administration prior to my induction had been either fired outright or dismissed and filled with those my uncle had kept close over the years. I didn't think it had much to do with the sake of the game, and truth be told, Tito Clayton did not really care of such when it came to coaching like his self-proclaimed arch nemesis—and Celena's father—Andrei Božović might. Tito Clayton had a long history of NCAA titles to back up his talent for guiding wayward youth, but it was an open and equally undiscussed secret that the current players making up his roster were not so much about skill as they were here in an attempt to keep my deranged older brother at bay. After all, I knew firsthand how Xavier would do anything—even forgo morality—to get his point across. And maybe we were alike in that sense but differed in whose blood would come to pay its price. But I knew better than to dwell on such sober. I didn't think I would come to survive it anyway.

I rose from the couch to tilt my head over a try bedroom door. It was no secret that during Filipino parties like this, the adults talked shit about their kids and coworkers in their shared dialect with voices so loud their chorused laughter was enough to shake the entire building. I didn't think anyone here spoke the same native language as Tito Clayton, but I knew, nonetheless, that the topic at hand would be gossip, and I still refused to see myself involved. Tito Clayton caught the three of us attempting to make our grand escape to then say, "Anak, you need to eat before you hole up in your room."

Davi and Chase glanced at me.

I then answered for the three of us, "Then, the rice is done, I take it?"

"It has been since you got here," Tito Clayton answered. "Besides, you have to say hi to our guests anyway."

I motioned with my hand for Davi and Chase to go to my room without me. They did not follow my instructions, instead, standing behind me as I walked over to greet the Lions staff gathered. Ciara gave a smile, moving to place both hands on my arms and giving them a faint squeeze, before saying, "Dante. How lovely to see you."

"It's good to see you too, Tita," I answered.

Tito Clayton glanced at me. I nodded, moving to press the back of her hand to my temple. Ciara smiled again, then saying, "You know, Clay, he doesn't need to bless me. We're all family here."

"I'm aware, but tradition is still tradition," Tito Clayton answered gently. He moved to glance at Takeshi to then say, "And Takeshi too."

Both of the children gathered behind him glanced at me. I did not meet their gaze but blessed Takeshi as I had blessed Ciara before. Takeshi smiled and brought his hand back to his side to say, "My, Dante, what have you been eating? You're huge now! You totally don't get the height from Clay, that's for sure."

"Maybe he's not mine," Tito Clayton replied.

I laughed at that. "I don't think I am, Tito."

Tito Clayton smiled slightly and placed a paper plate and plastic silverware in my hands. He then motioned to the food gathered before us, then looking past me to the other children gathered to say, "You guys need to eat too. We have a long season ahead of us, and if we're going to knock the Wesley Cardinals down a peg, we need to be strong enough to do so."

Davi, Chase, and the two men I did not know gave a nod. I was the first to put portions on my plate, starting off with even parts pancit and white rice, then adding two empanadas, bistek, and a serving of the beef stew Ciara had brought onto my plate. I waited for Davi and Chase to do the same, and once our plates were colored in a vast array of food, we began to make the trek over to my room when one of the two men I did not know said, "Hey, wait up for me and my brother, will you?"

Chase and Davi looked at me, mostly because they knew I was not fond of strangers. While this much was true, I would make an exception considering the circumstance and setting.

I then gave a nod before looking between the two strangers to say, "I'll need to know your names before I let you into my room."

"Alexei," Alexei answered, pointing at himself.

The other man came up to his right.

"That's my brother, Rue. We're Takeshi's kids. And we're both starting here as the new Lions, so I hope you'll come to welcome us with just enough grace."

Chase moved to stand between our two factions, picking up where I would never bother to leave off. "Chase Zhu. I'm the other goalie, with our star and future great, Dante over there." Chase pointed at me, then moving his finger over to Davi. "And Davi Salvatella, left defenseman."

"Left defenseman? I'm one of those too," Alexei said, moving his gaze up and down the length of Davi's body with pleased lips.

Davi smirked herself, doing the same to then say, "Then, I suppose we really are meant to be, aren't we, Alexei?"

Alexei laughed, moving to cover his face with his hand almost instinctively. It was rather obvious they were flirting with one another, and while I would normally not care for such, Davi's history with my older brother changed such prejudices. I then said, "Well, are you lot coming to my room or not?"

"We are," Rue answered, his voice an ever-hypnotic drawl like unruly ocean waves before a coming hurricane. "You can lead us, Dante."

I looked him up and down. I felt Chase's gaze upon me, but I did not meet it. I walked over to my bedroom door, opening the wood as the other Lions gathered followed me inside. I retired to the nook of my window that was deep enough to be sat in, cramming my more than gargantuan stature into the carved in drywall. I opened the window before digging into my portions, and I watched Rue and Alexei claim their seats atop my bed. Davi sat in a chair at my desk with Chase leaning next to her. We all began to eat in silence. Once finished, I fumbled around for my cigarettes. This was the only section of Tito Clayton's house where I was allowed to smoke considering the giant window which brought in a more than annoying draft in the now present wintertime season.

I placed a cigarette between my lips, grabbing my new lighter and flicking the fork until I had rendered a flame. I then placed the cinder to my cigarette, making sure it was burning before snuffing out the fire before pocketing my lighter once again. I blew the smoke out from my nostrils and made sure the stench did not fill the room as I blew the trail out into the nearby earth of the Schaffer campus. Chase and Davi did not bat an eye at the ritual, but I caught Alexei and Rue staring at me with interest.

"You look like you've never seen someone smoke in their entire life," I said dryly.

"I just don't think you have much of a place to be doing that considering the sport we play," Rue said.

Alexei looked at his brother with an expression as if to say he was treading on thin ice. That much was correct, but for some reason, the remark did not annoy me as much as I thought it would coming from Rue's mouth.

Instead of cutting him down at his knees, I said, "Well, I still get the job done on the ice, don't I?"

"You do. You're very talented. It's one of the reasons as to why I wanted to come to Schaffer to begin with."

I blocked my expression with my cigarette. I then said, "Charming. You kiss up to everyone's ass like that, Rue?"

"No, not particularly," Rue answered. "It's not really kissing up if it's the truth, no?"

"Fair point, but I'm beneath any form of flattery."

A silence lingered.

Chase must have known I was not going to play nice with strangers who had yet to prove their own worth, so he said, "So, tell us, Alexei, Rue, what brings you to Schaffer?"

"To play hockey, obviously," Alexei answered for the two of them. "Truth be told, Schaffer was the only place that offered. And like hell was I going to blow such a golden ticket."

Rue glanced at me. I had no idea why, but I met his gaze as I flicked the ash from my cigarette onto a nearby ashtray. He looked me up and down before moving back to look at Chase, and I did the same to see Davi was now the one speaking.

"But you know of Celena's presence, no?" she asked, batting her eyelashes. "After all, we went from twenty-four players down to twelve after she was named captain because all her male counterparts refused to take orders from her."

"She has every right to be arrogant," Alexei said. "If I was half as good, I would be too."

I glanced at Alexei to then say, "Good to know you know your place. Word of advice, Celena's respect is not given. It is earned. And the more you take my advice to heart, the easier the coming season will be on all of us."

Alexei gave a nod, then finishing his food. He looked around my bedroom to find everyone else had done the same in the time passed, and he rose from my bed to say, "I'll collect the trash. Anyone else want to get more or join me?"

"I will," Davi cooed. "Did your dad bring the empanadas? They're amazing, by the way."

"It's my mom's recipe," Alexei said, obviously buying Davi's flattery. "He doesn't make them as good as her, but they're still pretty good." Alexei turned to me. "You need anything while I'm out there, Dante?"

"No," I answered.

I then stuck out my trash for Alexei to take. He collected my paper plate and plastic silverware, then doing the same among the people gathered.

Eventually, Chase and Davi rose to their feet to join him, with Chase saying, "I gotta get that recipe from your dad. Seriously, I think he put something in them to make them so addicting."

Alexei laughed, joyous and equally content. "We'll hound him when we throw this away. Let's get a move on before the adults are finished talking shit about all of us."

Davi and Chase laughed at that, exiting my room after closing the door behind them. I glanced at Rue who remained, and he stood upright. Rue walked over to stand before me, his height and mine eye to eye considering the matter of my relaxed posture. I stared at him, with his endless eyes of volcanic glass staring back when he stuck out his hand.

"What is that for?" I asked.

"Give me a cigarette."

"I thought athletes don't smoke."

"I can make an exception this one time."

I laughed at that. I took out my cardboard box filled with my current favored vice and fished out a cigarette to place it into Rue's waiting hand. His skin and mine scraped against each other for what seemed like a fraction of an insignificant second, but we both turned to stare at each other as our shared touch lingered. His gaze was equal parts this unspoken yearning and this unflinching affection I knew better than to think I could ever begin to understand. The way Rue looked at me was as if I held this inherent value I knew I would never be worthy of no matter how much blood I gave to see such atoned for. The way Rue looked at me was as if I was the answer to a prayer he had asked time and time again that God had once refused to answer; until the two of us were standing before the other with his hand against mine and our bodies conjoined in some kind of sacrilegious ritual that I could never begin to comprehend whether it be drunk off my ass or—as I was now—sober.

And it only made me ask myself, what the fuck had I ever done to deserve someone looking at me like that? What made him even think of me—this unworthy and equally repulsive sinner—in such a light knowing I could never really say I had done anything to deserve such a fucking thing? I knew better than to think of such a haunting truth. Instead, I retracted my hand knowing such dangerous thoughts were just another facet of life that would soon drive me to madness and see me take a life I had deemed long ago could never be worth living.

"You need a light?" I asked, holding my cigarette between my fingers. I used my other hand to fish around for my lighter when Rue shook his head.

"No," Rue called, leaning closer.

I stood frozen as Rue leaned into my space. He placed his cigarette against mine, then flicking his gaze up to my own. We watched each other, his end and mine pressed together in the same unholy and equally blasphemous act as when our hands first came together what seemed like an endless eternity ago. Seconds felt like years. Minutes felt like eons. Light, heated puffs of his breath danced across the bridge of my nose, sending this sickly shudder down the length of my spine. When Rue withdrew, the breath I was holding escaped from the confines of my ribcage. He blew the smoke from beneath his filter out from his mouth, and I turned away. I tried to ignore the pang in the pit of my stomach that told me should I ever stoop so low to see this attraction through, it could only ever fucking kill us both.

4

ROBYN

I WALKED INSIDE THE Schaffer hockey center named after Lisanna's murdered mother with a fantastical hope that she could still love me despite what I had done to her.

I knew I would never be entitled to such again knowing I had hidden the truth of my addiction from her for three months. I knew what I had done, and I knew the weight my mortal sin came with. But not being able to face her would only make me among the same as her coward father, even if I knew in saying such he and I were already among equals. The gravity of the coming situation was not lost on me, but I knew I had to focus on the ability to see myself withstanding knowing accountability was something Lisanna had every right to wrought. Because if I really was going to become the woman I had always promised her I would be, it meant acknowledging the wrong I had chosen to do and making an effort to learn and heal from it together. But the caveat of the latter was that I was no longer entitled to such. It was entirely up to the only woman I could ever begin to love if I was worthy of forgiveness or not. And to be entirely transparent, that was a *terrifying fucking feeling*.

I walked into the stadium housed within the confines of the Nora Wilson Hockey Center. Alternating blue and white banners atop the rafters greeted me upon entry, and I moved to examine the long history of Schaffer championships. I then noticed the four years in which Tito Clayton had his stint here as a student before being scouted as a first-round draft pick in the '93 NHL season. Truth be told, his odds were already abysmal to make something of himself in this sport considering the matter of stature, nationality, and just the reality of hoping to go pro. After all, everyone who ever plays a sport one day dreams of playing professionally with little credence to see such culminate. But despite the odds, Tito Clayton had made a name for himself, only to lose it all in the wake of his first and only Stanley Cup win.

I knew Tito Clayton was a perfect, shining example I could use to show myself that I was capable of a sobriety I could never quite believe I was entirely deserving of. Yes, it's true I knew my worth, and yes, it was true I was not shy about reminding others of such when they mishandled me. But the matter of what others thought of me and what I thought of myself were two, very different things. It's not that I hated myself and needed myself dead by any means necessary like Dante fucking Hidalgo. It's just that my mistakes were so heinous—so unforgivable—that it only made me ask myself, what could I ever do to possibly be deserving of atonement? What had I done in this lifetime or the infinite ones before this to say I was worthy of the love I had been given when I dared to hurt these same people like they didn't mean fucking anything to me?

I nearly fucking died keeping the secret of my addiction from my parents and Lisanna. What could I ever do to make something like that right? I knew none of those same people would deserve to lose me at the hands of self because for some inconceivable reason, they loved me as I did them. But knowing this did not change that I deserved to die for hurting them in this way. That I was no longer worthy of my life as it was because I had treated it as if my say so was the only one that mattered. And maybe no one would ever come to understand such as intimately as I did word for word and beat for beat. And truth be told, I hoped nobody could so that when I did see through my self-destruction, it would make the coming murder easier for everyone around me to digest.

I spotted Lisanna sitting at the home bench. She was wearing her favorite pink sweater, making her skin the same shade of peach glowing in the bright, overhead stadium light. She turned to face me, offering a smile kept between thin, pink lips and electric, blue eyes. The same freckles I would always get lost in counting dotted the bridge of her nose and seeped into pink cheeks. Her expression told me she was willing to hear out my side of the story, even if I knew better than to think I would ever be entitled to such knowing what I had done.

I took a cautious step forward. And another. And then made brisk pace until I was before the only woman I ever wanted to love; the two of us the only remnants of a past we both had tried so hard to absolve ourselves of. It was a truth I knew meant neither of us could ever attempt to show another, and maybe it was not unfounded to say I had confidence in my ability to somehow make Lisanna see my side. She tapped the seat next to her with her thin, dainty hand, and I did as she asked, sitting next to her. I crossed my legs and let the silence that had taken root between us fester long enough until I got so sick of it to dare and speak.

"I know I fucked up," I said, quiet.

Lisanna turned to look at me.

"But I don't want to lose you, Liz."

Lisanna still watched me as if she were holding her breath.

"Because Tito Clayton was right. I don't think I'd come to survive it."

Lisanna gave a nod, placing her elbows atop her knees and interlocking her fingers. She seemed to be thinking over her response carefully, and while the circumstance did not warrant such comforts, I still found some ease in her ability to think of me as someone still entitled to such.

"You know, you could have told me what it was you were doing. I would have gotten you help. I don't think it's the matter of your addiction that bothers me, Robyn. It's the fact you hid it from me. It's the fact you didn't think I loved you enough to care until it all reached a crescendo, and I had to stay by your bedside from the ambulance ride to when you got admitted to rehab."

Lisanna fiddled with her fingers.

"We both know there is no one else who can begin to understand the other like the two of us can. You're the only remnant from my past I still choose to hold onto. And it's like you completely disregarded that truth for the sake of, what, *fucking Xavier Hidalgo*?"

"I know this," I replied, quiet again. "I know what I did hurt you, Liz. And I am going to try so fucking hard no matter what it costs me to never fucking do this again. You don't have to believe me. But it doesn't change that I am going to try. I am going to try so fucking hard; I promise. I promise on the grave of my dead fucking parents. I can't promise I won't fuck up ever again. But I am going to try. Really, I will. On everything I am and everything I have."

Lisanna gave a smile, moving to lean back and turn to face the ice before us. "That's all I could ever ask of you, Robyn." Lisanna glanced at me, her eyes the same fire in them I had not seen since before my overdose a long month ago. "And know, you will never have to do it alone. Because I'm always going to be here. I promised you forever. And I am not the kind of woman to break such a covenant because things get hard."

Lisanna was quiet again before saying, "But if you are struggling, you need to let me know. You need to be honest. I can't promise I won't be upset, but I will work on it with you.

Together. Do you really think I would not have reached out to Tito Clayton and have him offer you refuge if I didn't think you were capable of change?"

I bit the inside of my cheek so hard I could taste blood. Between the splatter, I croaked, "But I became just like your—"

Lisanna moved her hand to cover my mouth. Her expression was cool, jaded, and equally mysterious. I could not tell what emotion I had dared to elicit in daring to compare myself to the coward she called a father, but the truth lingered in the air like the smell of a pungent and equally repulsive perfume. Lisanna tilted her head down to gaze into my brown eyes, the blue beholding to her own telling me speaking ill of a man better off dead while warranted, was a truth that was better left unaddressed and equally unsaid.

"Don't say his name. Don't say his title either."

I obeyed, giving a nod beneath the skin of Lisanna's cold, calloused palm.

"You are right that you both have hurt me. You are right that you have both betrayed me. This fact is not lost on either of us. I know this truth has been weighing on you since you've had time to process it. But what makes you and *that fucker* different is that you are capable of change. And what of my father can say the same when he paid the price of his inability to atone for his mortal sins in blood?"

Lisanna retracted her hand from my lip, moving to hold both my hands in her own as she turned to face me. I, too, faced her. We stared at each other with this unspoken emotion I knew meant she still loved me as I always would love her. The person I once was did not matter. All that mattered was the act of atonement I had dared to see through knowing the woman overseeing my penance had the capacity to forgive.

And even if I would never deserve Lisanna Wilson's unconditional love, it did not change that she had dared to show it to me to begin with. That despite all the pain and all the trauma she had been forced to endure by the man who was supposed to love her without condition and without fault, she had dared to reclaim such affection and show it to me. I was not stupid. I knew that Lisanna was right and there was no one else on this same planet who we could attempt to teach how to love the other when such had been contorted due to our circumstance.

But standing before her, every bit in love with her as I had always been since that long and equally distant middle school classroom all those years ago, I knew I really didn't fucking want to love anyone else. I could only ever love one person this way, and truth be told, she was the only woman I really wanted to share this kind of intimacy with. And that would always be Lisanna Wilson. The love of my life. The woman who had dared to teach me how love should feel. Even in the wake of my parents's bitter and equally bloody divorce that saw the definition of such warp beneath the weight of each halves of my family's inability to admit to the crimes they had both committed.

Lisanna smiled, moving to cradle my right cheek with her hand. I met the skin with my own, glancing between her pink lips and back up to her blue eyes. Lisanna then said, smiling, "It will be hard going forward. But, truth be told, Robyn, I don't think I would even want to live this life without you. I don't think I'd come to survive it either."

"Then until death do us part, my love?"

Lisanna laughed, interlocking her pinky with my own. "Until the world stops fucking spinning, my love."

I smiled, moving to place my lips against Lisanna's. She kissed me with the same passion I had once assumed she could never feel again for me in this lifetime. But it was with her cherry lips gloss smeared evenly across my tongue that I thought, maybe, the effort to see through sobriety would not be as scary as I had once thought it to be.

5

DANTE

CHASE, DAVI, AND I claimed a table dotting the outside of a café housed on the Schaffer campus. It was known between the three of us that I would probably be smoking, despite the campus mandated banning of such among those who congregated among its greens. A stupid rule I found no need in upholding, yes, but if I were to willingly go against a mandate, I would do it in a way that did not see it be at the expense of strangers, as long as they did not bother me as I was actively trying not to bother them.

I did appreciate the gesture on both the part of Chase and Davi that they would go so far to make me comfortable, and I knew this was a testament to the friendship we shared in spite of all I had done to drive them away. Well, maybe it was not so much the matter of actively driving them away as it was that I did not feel like I had really done anything to earn their companionship. After all, I was going to be dead after my four years here at Schaffer were up, and despite this, I had let Chase stay and even befriended Davi during her tenure here after she was dropped off on my uncle's doorstep bruised, bloody, and broken by a stranger—who had by all means saved her life—in the wake of Xavier's violence. Perhaps that was why dying itself was so scary. Maybe that was why I had never managed to fulfill my promise of seeing through my own execution, and even when I had come close, had been saved from the brink of death by a miracle of the same vein that had happened so many times it could no longer be a coincidence.

Instead of letting the very notion of my life and what it was worth fester like a grotesque, open sore, I took a sip of my black cold brew to wash down the taste of tobacco saturated evenly across the length of my tongue. I did not really care much for smoking or the mess it came with. The only reason I did it was because it was a socially acceptable way of harming myself that my tito allowed, and what did I have to worry about cancer and the like when I was simply going to be dead come four years from now anyway?

The matter of the people I would come to leave behind did not leave my mind despite the coming caffeine buzz. I then wondered what would become of their lives in the wake of my suicide. I knew they would never begin to forgive me for such a thing, nor did I think the matter of moving on would be as black and white as I hoped for it to be. Being here and daring to care for other people meant I owed them the same existence I had come to scorn for the misery entrenched in living it. Sharing yourself with people meant they were entitled to the most basic of respect and human decency, and what respect was there to be found in killing yourself the day after you graduated college knowing the damage that would come to lay in its eventual wake?

Such a mortal sin would never ever leave you deserving of any kind of penance. It did not matter if it was seen through by an equally unforgivable clergy or by self, barefoot atop a carpeted bedroom floor washing away your mortal sin in a steady stream of red mixed into even portions of an equally blasphemous salt. I suppose that's why people who come to take their lives when living would pay its price in the afterlife thereafter. After all knowing the guilt that came with the murder was something that would absolve self, but would only come to pass it on to the people you would leave behind. Such a truth was not lost on me; no matter how much blood I had already given to see myself absolved of it. To be honest, I knew better than to dwell on such without the crutch of a tapering bottle of alcohol, washing away my same mortal sin down my throat to then gnaw on the skin residing in the bottommost pit of my stomach.

"Ugh, I'm not looking forward to practice," Davi said, taking a sip of her coffee. "How many dollars we putting on Celena punching a cocky rookie?"

Chase and I knew better than to bet on such slim odds. Chase, however, rose to the defense of the woman he wanted to make a wife to say, "Fifty saying she does not punch anyone."

"Done," Davi replied. "Say, what do we make of Alexei and Rue Oba?"

Chase answered, "Alexei seems to like you. I have to ask, what are your thoughts on that, Davi?"

"Well, I'm all for sexual escapades but something tells me I have enough in terms of that," Davi answered.

I didn't think Davi would come to welcome this question, but nonetheless, I asked, "Have you ever thought about dating since my brother?"

Davi bore the weight of my asking evenly atop both her shoulders to then reply, "No. Should I be, Dante?"

"I mean, after all he did to you, I don't think you need to, but I suppose morbid curiosity got the best of me." I felt like I was going to puke when I then replied, "Are you still hooking up with Conner?"

"It's kind of inconsistent," Davi admitted casually, like the entire reason as to why I hated Conner was not because he was hooking up with Davi despite liking our other teammate, Breanna Kim. "But it's still very much a thing."

Chase answered for me to say, "But we all know he and Breanna are into each other, right? I mean, he can only outrun his feelings for her for so long. And he's kind of using you as some kind of outlet."

"I'm not ignorant to the nature of our relationship," Davi replied, unfazed as she checked over her short, red nails. She seemed somewhat annoyed that neither Chase nor I understood what Conner and her did in terms of their relationship. "And Breanna is equally guilty in that regard, need I remind you. She was hooking up with the head of Kappa Sigma for God knows how long. Until I hear the words come from Conner's mouth that he likes Breanna and is only using me for a means to an end, I see no need to buy into hearsay."

"That much is true, yes," I answered, almost quiet. "But you deserve a man who treats you better than fucking Conner Villanueva."

Davi's expression softened, dimples imprinting between both her cheeks. She smiled, then answering, "Thank you, Dante. That means a lot. I hope you know you do too. If you even believe in love still."

"In glimpses," I admitted, honest. "Very small ones, but in glimpses, nonetheless."

Chase spoke between our accusations to say, "You seem to believe such in terms of Rue Oba."

I felt like my stomach had begun to gnaw in on itself. "Now, what the fuck are *you* talking about, Chase?"

"Don't play coy," Chase said, smirking a bit.

It was a tell I knew meant there was no point in arguing with the point he was making. While that much was warranted most of the time, I knew better than to let Chase talk of such fantasy unchallenged considering the subject was something as grave as commitment.

I then said, "And what makes you think I'm in love with Rue Oba?"

"Now, I never said that," Chase said, taking a sip of his coffee. "But you seem *interested*. And how many times can we say you were actually interested in someone, Dante?"

Now I knew the tell had done its job. Mostly because there was really no point in arguing with Chase when he was, of all things, right. Least to say, having a best friend was a double-edged sword. I loved Chase as I would a brother. He purposely failed his freshman year of high school with me so we would still be in the same grade for each of our corresponding graduations. He saved my life a long and equally distant year ago when the weight of the future I had always promised myself I would never have had become too heavy of a cause to bear. And this was all well and good, but the matter of worthiness did not change I would never deserve such graces. What good had I ever done to be worthy of mourning? What righteousness had I ever seen through to be deserving of love? I knew the answer, and I knew better than to speak it when it was every bit cruel as this same life had proven to be despite all I had given for change. And I could never begin to forgive myself knowing the same damage I inflicted upon self would come to befall the man I called a best friend, who would never begin to be deserving of the pain that came with it.

I glanced at Davi. Her curved, brown eyes looked me up and down before moving to block her expression with her hot coffee cup. I was unsure why she looked so annoyed at the very mention of Rue since I didn't think she had much reason to be. After all, I listened to her recount her sexual escapades that came with fucking Conner Villanueva, so what made my own any different?

I crossed my arms, answering, "Yeah, but nothing is ever gonna come of it. You of all people should know that, Chase."

"But do you want something to come of it, Dante?"

"Why are you asking me that?"

"Because I don't think you've asked *yourself* that."

I thought over the question. Chase was right that I had not asked myself what I wanted of Rue Oba, and quite frankly, I didn't really want to look inward and be so selfish to answer it in its truth. I was content with this impasse the two of us seemed to have been caught between. Because daring to venture past it was equally immoral as any cardinal sin considering the fate soon awaiting me. All of us here at Schaffer knew I had forbidden myself from having a future come my looming college graduation. And would there ever be justice for this affection I harbored if I saw it through—and arguably even more heinous, have it dared to be reciprocated—only to be the man who would take it away knowing the damage that would lay in its wake?

It's not that I didn't want to let myself feel these emotions, and it's not that I didn't want to explore them if Rue were to ever stoop so low to feel the same. It's just that it would never be right to dare and love someone else when I did not even like myself. It would never be fair to love someone else knowing the end foretold to me since my brother branded me a long eight years ago: death, self-destruction, and seeing myself as collateral damage in who would have to answer for the crime Xavier Hidalgo had willingly committed.

I knew better than to dwell on such in a clear state of mind. I took out a cigarette and my lighter, bringing the flame I conjured to the cylinder stuck between my lips. I put my lighter back where I had found it. I then took a drag, moving my hand to block the exhale of smoke from getting in either Davi or Chase's face. The nicotine washed enough of a calm over my body that I would come out of this conversation withstanding, and I answered Chase to say, "It's death either way."

But still, I knew that wasn't much of an answer at all.

Chase replied, without missing a beat, "I don't think liking Rue will end in ruin. I don't think liking anyone else will. Truth be told, Dante, you're still here for a reason. Each and every time you have sought to end your life, it's never worked. You only get so many coincidences before it becomes fate." Chase took a sip of his coffee, his expression almost sage. "And you would be an idiot to think you can outrun something as sordid as fate."

I knew Chase was right but answering to such would do nothing but leave a bitter taste in my mouth. Instead, I took a sip of my cold brew after placing my cigarette between my stocky fingers. The silence that followed was haunting, but I knew daring to admit to the gravitas of feelings better left unsaid would be infinitely more sickening than daring to speak them ever could be.

6

ROBYN

THERE WAS A KNOCK on the door to my bedroom, and I moved my book to rest atop my made bed before answering it to find it was Tito Clayton. His expression conveyed no worry, and he parted thin lips kept between his prominent five o'clock shadow to say, "Alexei is here to see you."

"Do I look like I know an Alexei?"

"Nice try. Alexei is Conner's foster brother. You would be smart to give him an allowance if you really want to become the family Conner never had."

I bit the inside of my cheek. "Do you really think that's possible?"

"Anything is possible with hard work, Robyn."

"That really doesn't do much, if any, to answer my question."

"All I'm saying is that if you want to offer Conner that, you have to be content with the rejection that comes with it. I know

Conner, but not well enough to say what he wants from you. After all, you're the one who came here. He never asked you to do that. So, you're really playing in his court in an already uphill battle in terms of everything else that's going on with you."

I didn't think I would come to survive this answer, but, nonetheless, I asked, "Then, do you think I can actually be sober?"

"What kind of answer would you like, firsthand experience or that of step-in father?"

"I think the firsthand experience answer will drive home the point more than sugarcoating it will."

Tito Clayton watched me, then saying, "Well, from my personal experience is that sobriety is a group effort. Truth be told, shipping you off to rehab was window dressing for the NCAA and NESCAC to allow your transfer onto my team. Rehab can only do so much if you don't have the proper support network or the want to even want to get better."

Tito Clayton and I watched each other.

"Which stems into my next question, do you want to get better, Robyn?"

I thought over the question. On the surface, the answer was obvious, and that was that I needed to see through sobriety to still have enough standing to lay claim to everything I loved. It was not lost on me what being clean would then entail. While not only quite literally solving all my problems, would see me spend the rest of my life with the woman I loved. It would finally see me as an equal worthy enough to be at her side after being able to look my addiction in the eye and slay its monstrous, gargantuan head without two more emerging from the stump. I knew that in order to become the good, just person everyone had believed me to be, it meant giving up the pills that were not only rotting me from the inside out, but also rotting the bridge I had made the choice to build in daring to share my life with someone else. Even if I knew this truth as intimately as Lisanna did, it did not change how I felt like I did not deserve it. And it would never change that I would never deserve my own happy ending which went hand in hand with the equally nauseating truth that I would never be deserving of sobriety.

I knew this logic probably made no sense to anyone else but self. Maybe even daring to speak it to Tito Clayton would see me reduced to a pitiful pile of ash with the fire laced in his coming scolding. But what had I ever done to deserve the happiness that would come with being clean knowing the damage I had already wrought? It was not lost on me that I had already dared to hurt Lisanna. I knew what wrong I had made the conscious choice to see through in choosing those tiny, white pills over her and our relationship. I knew there was no redeeming myself in the eyes of both the only woman I loved and the eyes of the same god my parents believed in that I could never bring myself to in his choosing to create me broken. And as soon as I had thought such, I knew there was only one other person alive who could begin to understand my apprehension in terms of sobriety and the dependent clause of being undeserving that went hand in hand with it.

And that man was Dante Alonso Hidalgo.

I knew Tito Clayton would understand this truth too. But in daring to confide in him my deepest and most intimate parts of self, it did not change that it would come across to me as the same kind of failing as the one I had seen through at the expense of my parents. Tito Clayton may not be my father in any sense other than figurative, but I could not bring myself to tell him the truth when doing so meant seeing through the same effort in terms of sobriety I could never be deserving of. I had made the choice to hurt everyone I loved. I had made the choice to become the same monster undeserving of love I had promised Lisanna I would never become. And tell me, how could I ever begin to admit such to Tito Clayton when the same niceties I had grown tired of would be his response? He would then tell me I would always be deserving of the same things I could never possibly be, like I had never made the active choice to harm the people I claimed to love as if they never meant anything to me to fucking begin with.

I smiled. "Alexei is waiting for me."

I knew Tito Clayton saw through my deflection. But instead of speaking on it, he looked me up and down before moving out of my way to say, "I'll be in my room if you need me."

Tito Clayton retreated back into his room, his gaze lingering on me for a few seconds before the door closed behind him. I then walked out into the living room of his house to find Alexei Oba waiting for me, a tense smile strewn across his face that made up the rest of his more than rigid posture.

Alexei's skin was light, almost a kind of gold smeared across his body. The shade was accessorized with folded, black eyes on either side of a straight nose that was flat at the tip. His face was almost square-shaped, contrasting his adoptive brother. Where Rue was sharp and defined at every angle, Alexei was soft and round. He ran a hand through his short hair. Alexei gave a smile that made me feel a bit better at the circumstance shared between the two of us, even if I was equally unsure what to make of Alexei Oba as he was to make of me.

"Robyn," he called, a hint of gentleness tucked between the words spoken. "I wanted to talk."

"About Conner, I presume."

"Truth be told, we have little in common for anything else."

The honesty made me laugh a bit. In hopes to ease the obvious tension taking root between the two of us, I then said, "Then, how much money you putting toward your brother making a move on Dante Hidalgo?"

"I'm not betting against such abysmal odds," Alexei called with a laugh. "Although, I think your money would be better put to use if Dante will ever come to realize my brother is into him."

"Fair point. Dante would be the last person to ever pick up on your brother's interest." I crossed my arms, sweeping my gaze up and down the length of Alexei's body. "So, Conner. What is it that you feel the need to tell me, Alexei?"

"I grew up with Conner in the foster care system," Alexei answered, almost quiet, like the ghost of the past had come back to haunt him in recounting things better left unaddressed and equally unsaid. "I was adopted by Takeshi when I was twelve. I've kept in contact with Conner since then, and I want you to know that what you want of him and what he is willing to give you may be at odds."

"Are you saying being the family he's never had isn't something he's interested in?"

"All I'm saying is that when you've grown up in a place devoid of any kind of family, it's hard to reclaim what such means when you have no metric to base it off of." Alexei leaned back on Tito Clayton's peeling, leather couch to then say, "It may not be fair, but I know Conner may be resentful towards you for escaping a system he did not have such privilege to. Jealously is one hell of a drug, and if you look at your offer on a bare bones level, it would come across to him as almost this entitlement because you've had everything he's ever dreamed of and want to offer him something he has a kind of fucked up view regarding."

The ignorance to my own circumstance amused me. Not that Conner was entitled to give me such graces, but I thought giving me the benefit of the doubt was not as hard as Alexei was suggesting it to be, even if such may not even be entirely fair. "He seemed fine with my presence when I first landed at Schaffer."

"I mean, he had no idea what the fuck to make of you. Could you really blame him, though? He had no idea you existed until a month ago, beholding to everything he realized long ago he could never have. And then you come here to his makeshift home to offer him the one thing he has held a scorn for since he was a child, while having it nearly all your life. I know Conner may not be actively vindictive and want you to pay for such a thing like Dante might, but you have to understand he may be apprehensive. Maybe even jealous if it's not right for him to be."

I wanted nothing more than to reduce the obtuse and equally entitled Alexei Oba to cinders. He was right in the sense that he was the only in I had in terms of my brother knowing I was still very much the traitor among the people who lived among the place he called home. A humbling would come, yes, but I needed to first deduce if Alexei was willfully ignorant to my own circumstance or just plain stupid. "So, are you on my side or are you actively against it, Alexei?"

"I'm on your side," Alexei offered without hesitation. "I just don't want either of you to fuck up this chance up. That's why I'm offering you help, or a kind of in regarding my brother."

Despite the stupidity Alexei had once spoken, I felt my stomach twist in a knot when I then said, "Then, I suppose I should ask you, Alexei. Would he want for us to become family?"

"I know he wants to, Robyn. But I know he doesn't know what a family is or what family means. The closest thing he's ever come to it is me and Tito Clayton. I mean, Tito Clayton is technically and legally his guardian anyway. But we'll get into that later. In the meantime, I offer you a truce."

Alexei rose from his seat, clutching his practice duffel bag in one hand and offering me the other. I glanced at the shape before moving to place my hand in his, shaking on the truth that we would both make an effort to teach Conner Villanueva what a family was and the weight that such a covenant came with.

7

DANTE

I **WALKED INTO THE** living room of Tito Clayton's house to find Robyn Zaragoza sitting on his couch. Her long, black nails were typing across the glass of her phone screen, and she was seemingly ignorant to my presence.

It was no secret I did not like Robyn. Truth be told, I did not think we would ever reach a common understanding once her time here at Schaffer was over in a year, so I found no reason to see myself among her good graces when she was by all means, a terrible fucking person. After all, what else was there to call her knowing she made a conscious choice to keep Elliot Božović and Xavier Hidalgo among a sickly court of her so-called best friends? I may not be some kind of rocket scientist, but on the basis of morality, it was obvious Robyn's virtue was skewed considering whom she kept close, and what she had dared to excuse. And I was not blind to such a fact no matter how much she liked to pretend that simply transferring to Schaffer had seemingly absolved her of its truth and the weight it came with. She may have Tito Clayton and Lisanna fooled that she was this good, just, and equally honorable woman, but I would never be as naïve. You could argue such a bias may not be fair, but as long as Robyn had called the brother who wanted me dead her best friend, I saw no reason to see myself uphold the expectation to be unbiased when she was equally as complicit as I was in that regard.

"Staring," Robyn said, not looking up from her phone.

"It's just the fact you look so obscenely ordinary I can't help but gawk," I answered.

"I have better things to do than get into a spat with you of all people, Dante," Robyn said, her typing seemingly growing faster with each passing second. She then looked up from her phone with a scowl to address me in saying, "A man can only have so many issues, Dante. Do us both a favor and pick one, and get it fucking fixed instead of bothering me, will you?"

"Same goes for you," I barked. "The woman who claimed to be Elliot and Xavier's best friend is now among the court of their scorned. Endings don't get sweeter than that, huh?"

"You praying for my downfall only goes so far when you're on the brink of total calamity. Don't think I'm above the fate of pushing you off."

"I'd drag you down with me, Robyn. Last I heard, hell is beautiful this time of year. I hope you bring sunscreen, so I don't get burned on our way down."

Robyn rolled her eyes. The door to Tito Clayton's room then opened to reveal my uncle carrying his practice mandated clipboard. He donned his same Schaffer tracksuit he always did during practice days, and I watched him look between us to then say, "Well, we're still alive, so that's a better start to the day than what I thought it would be."

"Not for long, though. How do we know Robyn here won't kill me in my sleep like some kind of sleeper agent?"

"First, that's not even what a sleeper agent is. Second, you think I would get my hands bloody to kill you of all people? You're going to do the job for me. That's just unneeded work on my already beyond busy schedule."

Tito Clayton pressed his lips together to contain his laugh. Annoyed, I turned to Robyn to then say, "And what exactly is on your busy schedule? Ruining my life? Fucking over my entire college career with your unwanted presence?"

"I never set out to do that, but I'll take my wins where I can get them," Robyn replied, unfazed. "I came here as a last-ditch effort to see my life still have value. Ruining yours along the way is just an added bonus, asshole."

Before I could spat back at Robyn, the door to the bathroom opened and Davi joined us in the living room. She then commandeered her bag that was kept behind the leather couch Robyn was sprawled across. Davi looked between the three of us to then say, "Am I missing something?"

"Nothing of importance," Tito Clayton answered before either Robyn or I could. He then looked between his Lions to then say, "And we will be doing everyone's physicals before practice, so that means meeting the new team doctor, Bruna Allenbach. We also have a new assistant coach, Takeshi Oba. You three are going to not create any problems, understood?"

"Yes, Coach," we chorused, even if I was unsure such was even possible with Robyn present.

"Great. Now, the walk isn't bad to the Nora Wilson Hockey Center, so we'll be walking. Dante, you're in front. Davi and Robyn, you two are in back of him. I will be keeping the end of the line. Should any blood be shed between any of you, I will make sure you regret it. Got me?"

"Got you, Coach," we all said again.

"Good, now, rank and file, Lions. We already have plenty of work cut out for us in terms of the new season."

Tito Clayton ushered us out of his house with a waving of his clipboard making up our practice itinerary. Then, he led us out onto the patio linking his house and the Schaffer campus before locking the door behind him. I did not know much of how Tito Clayton had come into possession of what I now called a jail cell, but I assumed it used to be student housing before my uncle had moved into the three-bedroom flat and called it a home. After all, it was about only a block from the Nora Wilson Hockey Center, which Tito Clayton had erected among the buildings of the Schaffer campus after receiving his first NHL paycheck. Who the building was named after, I was unsure. Truth be told, I had never heard my uncle discuss a Nora let alone mention her, but in doing the mental math, I knew she was related in some kind of way to Lisanna since the women in her family seemed to share the same last name.

Tito Clayton unlocked the front door of the Nora Wilson Hockey Center, but when we walked inside, the lights were already on. I knew this meant our captain, Celena Božović, was already present. I had not seen her since the end of the Schaffer hockey season last year when she was eliminated from the playoffs. Not because she lost the game, mind you. She very much had conquered against my brother in their famed and equally hallowed rivalry. Both sides had been at each other's necks since they both started in the college hockey world three years ago. It was no secret both wanted to lay claim to the NESCAC hockey crown that neither of them had yet been deemed worthy enough to inherit in their shared college tenure.

To be fair, Celena had technically accomplished that much despite her own teammates wanting her equally dead as the officials making up the college sports world did for her breaking of a glass ceiling. The forthcoming NESCAC Championship was hers in everything but title since she had eliminated the Lions from the championship game after breaking my brother's collarbone good enough it would need surgery in the semifinals. There were rumors that the move had been intentional, but either way, Xavier fucking deserve it after dragging her name through the mud before every and any press camera he could find. I held no pity for a man who simply got what was fucking coming to him. But that did not mean the Lions who remained felt the same way. Truth be told, most of them had come to resent Celena for the move. When Tito Clayton deemed her captain, it was the straw that broke the camel's back and saw them all transfer to different teams since they refused to take orders from a woman, let alone one they deemed undeserving like Celena Božović.

The three of us walked past the trophy case documenting Tito Clayton's many NESCAC Championships. Painted over, white brick held up the walls surrounding us on all sides. Its virtuous hue was accessorized with horizontal stripes of our corresponding royal blue making up our team colors. The overhead, fluorescent lights combined with the squeaky, linoleum floors gave this illusion of the walls closing in the further you wandered down the hallway that led us to the locker rooms. The same bench dividing the now gendered spaces in two remained as the last time I had seen it.

Tito Clayton then looked at me, tilting his head over to the men's locker room to say, "You're up first, Dante."

"Why not Robyn? She's new here after all," I answered in hopes my deflection would work.

Tito Clayton's annoyed expression told me he was not at all buying it. "Nice try. But those who are unkind to their fellow teammates will face their fears of doctors and go first."

Robyn stood behind Tito Clayton to then flip me off. I rolled my eyes before heeding his warning and walking into the men's locker room. It was the same as I had left it as an honorary mascot among the Lions during Tito Clayton's current stint as head coach. It was a status I did not mind since most of the men among their ranks were equally complicit in my alcohol dependency since they would supply me with a means to abuse it. But Celena had made it clear when she started here that the black-market trade of supplying me with the same vice I was bound to was something she would no longer tolerate while they called her a teammate.

Back when I was still this wide-eyed teenager, I thought the men who would purchase vodka for me were the coolest. Effortlessly charming, and the kind of adult I hoped one day I could be too. Someone who simply gave me what I wanted when I asked for it, despite what was needed for me and my own best interest. When you're more impressionable and equally naïve, adults of weaning morality seem so much more tolerable than those who uphold virtue.

Probably because unbeknownst to the child I once was, these adults were equally complicit in my own undoing. They were giving me the means to see myself dead before I turned eighteen like I had promised myself at a distant birthday celebration a very long, eight years ago. But when you're young, dumb, and hellbent on self-destruction, this was one part of the perfect equation to see yourself go down in flames. That no matter what would then catch fire once you turned into a pitiful pile of ash, the damage was said, done, and equally irreversible as you always hoped for it to be.

I walked into the locker room and scrounged the rooms to find a woman I did not recognize but assumed was Bruna Allenbach. She was tall and the first thing I noticed about her was her straight, auburn hair and piercing, green eyes. She looked me up and down, freckles dotting the bridge of her nose to then say in a thick, palatable German accent. "Dante, yes?"

"That's me," I replied.

"Come in, let us get the physical over with."

I gave a nod, my stomach gnawing on itself considering my fear of doctors in any possible variety. Bruna adjusted her stethoscope hanging around her neck accessorized with solid gold bands to then motion to the examination table covered in a thin, flimsy paper before her. I looked around the room to see it was the spitting image of the doctor's office as seen in my childhood but without the childlike decorations that would put someone of that age at ease. Bruna then began to scrounge the cabinets. I sat atop the table, fiddling with my thumbs. I watched her don purple, plastic gloves before listening to my heartbeat.

"Breathe in," she said.

I did as she asked.

"Breathe out," she added.

I, again, did as she asked.

"Good, good." Bruna then moved to the painted over, white brick wall that had some kind of instrument taped to it. She took off the cap on the device before placing a new one on and using it to examine my ears. Then, after giving a satisfied nod, she again removed the tip of the device. Then she sunk her fingers into my jaw to then say, "Open."

I opened my mouth.

"Stick your tongue out. I know you've done this before, and I don't have time for your fear to get in the way of my job."

I figured she had a point. Something about the combination of her accent and the scolding that came with it compelled me to listen. I stuck out my tongue as she then examined the inside of my mouth before moving the light to my eyes without warning. I blinked, once, twice.

Bruna then said, "Move your eyes with the light."

She moved the tool to my left as I followed it with my gaze. Then, I did the same as she maneuvered the light to my right. Bruna then gave a nod before moving to place the object back where she had found it. Then, she grabbed a little hammer before knocking it on my kneecaps which jerked out in response. She then said, "Good reflexes. Needed of a goalie."

"I must get it from Tito Clayton."

Bruna laughed at that. "I suppose we should slay the beast of the elephant in the room. Your alcoholism."

"It's not—"

"No, no, there is no arguing with my professional opinion. After all, Tito Clayton gave me access to your medical records. You went to rehab for it before you started here. Have you had anything to drink since?"

"No," I answered in a rare bout of honesty. "I promised Tito Clayton I would quit in becoming one of his Lions."

"Good, and you will continue to be sober or else I will have to do something about it," Bruna said.

"What could you possibly do to help me, lady?"

"Let me put it this way, Dante. You either stay sober, or I will tell the NCAA of your problem, and they will sort out your punishment. Tito Clayton will give you as many chances as you need. But me, seeing the damage it has caused him, will not be as forthcoming with such graces. As I've said, I've seen their consequences firsthand. And as long as you feel no remorse for the wrong you have committed, I will not feel bad for giving you a much needed tough love approach. Now, get out. Our time is finished, and I see no need to coddle you any longer."

I swallowed the lump in my throat. Then, I exited the locker room with Bruna's words weighing down my chest until their collective force left bruises against the brown skin smeared atop my rib cage.

8

ROBYN

DANTE CAME BACK TO join us in the hallway before the men's and women's locker rooms. Tito Clayton then turned to me and said, "It's your turn, Robyn."

"Can't Davi go?" I asked knowing this would be the first time I was facing my mother since getting out of rehab. "I don't need a physical."

"Nice try, but if Dante faces his fears, you have to too even if you didn't instigate any animosity."

Dante's lips curled into a satisfied smile when he then said, "See, Robyn? All is fair in love and war."

"Like you even have the mental fortitude to know what that means," I replied, moving past him to enter the men's locker room.

The door closed behind me before I could hear Dante's reply. I moved past the lounge area housing royal blue recliners scattered around a flatscreen television kept atop the wall on my left. Then, I walked into the area of the locker room where the hockey gear was stored for each player in their corresponding, wooden cubbies. Dividing each half was a wooden bench, and past it a few feet were showers, sinks, and bathroom stalls kept atop alternating, white tile. The mirrors ahead of me kept atop the vanities housed in the bathroom area caught a glimpse of my reflection, and I stared at the woman before me, unable to recognize who she had become before ducking my head away to gaze at the ground beneath my feet.

I glanced at the cubby to my left to find it belonged to Dante. His number twelve was staring back, haunting me like the coming vision of my mother. I knew she would come to berate me for disregarding everything I had built for myself and my future for reveling in the shared disease of addiction with Xavier Hidalgo. My mother was a very simple woman. She was brunt, honest, and equally uncouth when it came to telling me how she felt about decisions I had made with my life. I knew she loved me, and she knew I loved her. And how could I dare and face in the wake of my failure knowing the damage it had wrought upon her and my father in the process? Every sinner may be entitled to redemption like the same Catholic doctrine my father upheld and had once tried to instill in me too. But if that were true, what did it make of a sinner of my same like; who made the choice to choose sin over virtue, despite knowing what damage would befall in the process?

I'll answer that for you.

It meant I was created with an overhead, looming density of failure with my equal among the like of Judas Iscariot.

And that much would always be true no matter what act of penance I made a feeble attempt to oversee in the eyes of the same God who had dared to create me broken.

Ignoring the pang in my stomach, I shook my head and strode forward, meekly opening the door housing my mother's name atop a plaque. I found my mother, Bruna, and my father, Max, waiting for me behind the wood.

Least to say, seeing them inhabit the same space since their divorce was an odd sight in and of itself. It was no secret my mother still held resentment toward my father for leaving her that my father did not harbor for her since he was the party to first instigate the coming abandonment. Max and Bruna had raised me in a marriage of convenience, and no love was shared between either of them in an attempt to make the union work.

And knowing this, I did hold some scorn for them both. They still chose to raise me in spite of their shared incapability and thinly veiled, loveless annoyance with the predicament they had caught themselves in. Although, I was unsure if that made me ungrateful knowing my alternative was the same truth Conner had lived all his life. A man without home. A brother who I could only hope to show it to despite its metric being equally dead as I almost had been after my overdose and washing up to Schaffer's shores a traitor.

"Mom," I called. "Dad."

They looked at each other.

"It's weird seeing you two together."

"We decided it's time we talk about your addiction as a family," Max said, gentle. It was a roundabout way of considering my feelings in a coming scolding that my mother did not think had much founding. "We're always here for you, Robyn. As your mother and father, we always will be."

I bit the inside of my cheek.

Bruna then said, "And I have agreed to help Clay here at Schaffer among his staff to keep an eye on you and your sobriety."

I knew I would never be entitled to trust again knowing what I had done, but I did not think the matter of babysitting me was all that fair either.

"We're in this struggle together, Robyn. And I need you to know that going forward."

"How can we be in it together when you and mom can't even tell me why you two separated? When we are every bit no longer a family as you both know we aren't?"

"Just because your father and I are not together does not mean we love you any less," Bruna answered.

I realized even in the wake of my overdose they would still refuse my expectation of honesty. I don't know why, but I felt compelled to show it to them instead.

"Then, show me that. For the love of God, *fucking show me that.*"

Bruna and Max looked at each other, but I did not stick around to hear their coming answer. Instead, I exited the locker room to find Tito Clayton and Dante waiting for me. Dante was sitting atop the bench separating the two gendered spaces, looking at me with perked up eyebrows and his lips a tight, thin line.

I turned to Tito Clayton to then say, jabbing my finger at him, "You did not have to see that my parents babysat me in the one place I was devoid of them in moving out."

"That was not my intention in hiring them," Tito Clayton responded, cool and firm. "I needed supporting staff who would help me lie to the NCAA and NESCAC. Seeing that having you and Dante on my team was a liability, I needed complete and total loyalty from the people surrounding me knowing that while you both need me, I cannot jeopardize Celena's last shot at finally cutting her father and brother down at the knees. I will help you all that I can, yes. But I will not see that my other players are neglected in that process."

I glanced at Dante, who met my gaze. I stared at him. I wondered if there was more than what I currently knew poking out from the surface in terms of him being a liability in the same way I had become one among Tito Clayton and his Lions. I knew Xavier wanted us equally dead, even if Dante did not want to believe this same truth because his prejudice clouded his better judgment. But staring at him, I could see his expression was conveyed in a way that was hesitant. Almost this mixture of fear

I would come to out him as a liar, or worse, someone of my same truth.

An addict.

A liar.

A person who chose a vice over the same people they loved knowing such could never see them entitled to redemption no matter what remorse they would hold to it thereafter.

A sense of calmness washed over my body knowing we were brothers and sisters in arms, only for it to be replaced with this newfound ache taking hold of my chest. Because I knew what had spurned us both into the corresponding vices we were bound to, being the man I had once called a best friend who Dante also called a brother.

Tito Clayton then spoke, jarring me back to the present as I turned to watch him say, "I'm asking you to trust me, Robyn. I would not have had your mother among my staff if I did not trust her."

"And how do I even know this grand scheme of you protecting me against Xavier will even work, hm?" I asked.

I saw Dante look at Tito Clayton through the corner of my eye, but I did not turn to confirm such. Instead, I stood my ground and stared at Clayton Alonso, waiting for his coming answer.

He looked annoyed to then say, "Because would Lisanna really have reached out to me in the wake of your circumstance and asked for me to offer you refuge if she did not think I would keep my word?"

I was quiet.

Tito Clayton then said, "I am not asking for us to be best friends. I am not asking you to even like me. All I'm asking for is your trust, and I will treat your life like it is my own. Otherwise, this will be a very long year for all of us. Can we work together, Robyn?"

"We can," I answered. "I suppose I should get ready for practice."

"We can discuss this without the present company," Tito Clayton replied, giving a nod. "Dante, you are to wait here until the locker room is empty for you to change and you are to go nowhere else, are we clear?"

"Crystal, Tito," Dante said. He looked at me but did not give a dig. He slunk down the wall he was sitting against and left his limbs displayed gangly atop the bench he was sitting on.

"Robyn, will you come with me?"

"Sure. It's not like I have anything better to do."

Tito Clayton did not address the annoyance in my tone, but he walked into the men's locker room to find it was empty except for the two of us. There was no remaining sign left of my parents, and I did not find that the air of animosity to show for their mutual dislike for each other had lingered. Tito Clayton led me over to his office. There was a corresponding plaque reading his full name, Clayton Rivera Alonso, and title 'Schaffer Head

Coach' carved into the royal blue plastic, with the indented edges painted over in white.

He opened the door and held it for me when I walked inside his office to see the entire space was barely large enough to accommodate either of us. Kept behind a desk accessorized with a clunky, dated computer monitor, and buried in paperwork and files were team pictures of each season he had coached since my father had been his reference in getting him the job at the start of the 2009 season. I wondered how deep their friendship ran knowing my father was not the kind of man to go out on a limb for someone who had not already proven their worth in terms of their relationship. Max always talked fondly of Tito Clayton, but there was always a twinge of bitterness tucked between each word I could not begin to understand.

There was only one chair for me to sit in, kept across from a large filing cabinet. Tito Clayton sat in his office chair, motioning for me to take the only seat cross from him. I narrowed my eyes before doing as he asked, sitting atop the scratchy and equally stiff cross between a chair and a recliner for Tito Clayton to then say, "I do not think you are being very fair to me, Robyn."

"Well, I don't think having my parents here to babysit me is very fair either."

"You just got out of rehab. How will I know you will not relapse? You're acting like I did not tell you I understood your struggle when you woke up from your overdose, and I was there at your hospital bed. You're acting like I am some unwanted onlooker in your saga rather than an active participant. And you tell me again, Robyn, how is that fair?"

I was quiet.

Tito Clayton then leaned forward in his chair to add, "You don't have to like me. But I am the only thing keeping you from death. And I think on that metric, we should at least learn to tolerate each other, no?"

"Then, how is it that you can offer me protection from Xavier?"

"Because I have leverage over him that sees him cater to keeping him at bay." Tito Clayton watched me to then say, "I'm sure you know how much he loves his mother. It's knowledge that will see her disown him. And he knows if he crosses my threshold, I will reveal it. But I don't need to explain to you the inner workings of my other nephew since you knew him a hell of a lot better than I ever could."

I studied Tito Clayton's face to see his even shade of tan taut across his wide, flat nose. I thought the deeply set lines etched across his forehead and scattered throughout the rest of his expression were the most obvious sign to show for the hardships he had so unjustly been forced to endure. I knew in coming to Schaffer University that Tito Clayton and I were two people of the same truth. The difference between my world and his was that he had dared to look the effort of sobriety in the eye and slay the belly of its beast.

It was an effort I had yet to think I was even deserving of let alone comprehend, but it did not change Tito Clayton was this seeming gleaming success story on what sobriety could do for you. But Tito Clayton's victory aside, it did not change that his current peak was preceded by my current darkness. It was a truth I knew my father knew more intimately than I ever could. I knew both his best friend and then soon after his daughter would be caught in the thralls of their own dependency. The pain that went hand in hand with loving a woman like me was not lost on me. And knowing what I was responsible for, how could I begin to think I was deserving of such a thing when all I could ever do to something as pure and equally virtuous as love was bring upon its ruin?

Tito Clayton seemingly read right through my expression. His next reply was as if he could read the most intimate parts of self I had made a conscious effort to stay hidden.

"Things will get better, Robyn."

"Can you promise me that?"

"Only if you're willing to let them be."

It was more than obvious to me now that things as they were now were not working. I had my mother now babysitting me at a self-imposed sober jail. The man I once called a best friend wanting me equally dead as his younger brother and his ex-girlfriend. And hurting the woman I wanted to one day grow old with like she had never meant anything to me to begin with. I knew choosing the pills over the life I had been given could only end in death. After all, everyone had instilled such in me at rehab until my ears had become so tired from the words and their corresponding syllables that I tuned out their warnings entirely.

But I could not bring myself to see myself free of this weight that was beholding to my own addiction. Not when it meant facing the reality of the person I was beneath its truth; a woman I had made an active choice to see buried under the same weight of that sickly, orange and white bottle. I did not think I would come to even like her. And even if I did, how could I begin to live with myself knowing all I had done to desecrate her memory in seeing myself bound to a man who no longer loved me as I still loved him?

I smiled, warm, sweet, and equally shallow. "Of course, Tito Clayton."

He had seen right through my ruse. Instead of pressing the matter further, he moved his stocky fingers to rub his temple. Then, he leaned over in his chair, pressing his elbows atop his knees and said, "I'm not going to tell you something you don't want to hear, or that you'll make an active choice not to listen to. But know, when the time comes, you'll realize I'm right. And for both your and my sake, Robyn, I hope it's before it's too late."

I smiled again. "Are we done here, Tito Clayton?"

"We are," he replied, tired. "Now, get changed for practice, will you?"

I did not reply. Instead, I rose from my seat and exited the locker room office; the cardinal sin of my refusal to see through sobriety weighted evenly atop both shoulders.

9

DANTE

AFTER A FEW MINUTES, the men's locker room door opened and a familiar face joined me outside in the hallway.

Rue Oba was just as handsome as I had remembered. His rugged and equally masculine features caught the fluorescent lights at just the right angle. It made his brown skin glow in this almost kind of ethereal quality I don't think I could ever begin to attribute to anyone else. Rue looked equally surprised to see me as I was of him. I thought such was strange on both ends. We knew the other would be present since this was the first practice to start the Schaffer hockey season, meaning all the Lions—old and new—would be gathered. Neither of us commented on such, but I noticed Rue smiled at me as if he had never made the gesture willingly before, his teeth and lips beyond crooked but infinitely charming.

I looked him up and down, eventually settling on the brown staring at me to say, "Rue. Nice to see you."

"Yeah, you too, Dante," Rue said, his voice dark and equally poignant like unruly ocean waves hitting against a jagged and equally immovable coastline. "Did you help Coach make all that food we had at his party?"

"I did, yes," I answered, glancing between his lips and eyes. "Those empanadas were brought by your dad, right?"

Rue nodded.

"They were pretty good too."

"When he makes more, I'll be sure to give you some."

A silence lingered. I didn't find it awkward, and there was this hunch in my stomach telling me Rue didn't either.

"Cool. I'll see you at practice, then."

"Yeah, guess so."

We watched each other.

"It was good to see you," I said.

"You too, Dante."

I glanced up and down the length of his body a last time before moving past him to enter the locker room. The door closed behind me, and I tossed my duffel bag onto the floor next to my designated cubby to find all my gear resting neatly inside. I sat inside the raised edge, moving to undress myself to exchange my all-black attire with a hockey required base layer. I then began to pile on my more than cumbersome and equally excessive goalie armor. Maybe saying it was excessive was not entirely true knowing the entire point of my position as goalie was to get solid concrete launched at me at more than concerning speeds. Nonetheless, the process to see myself not break all the bones in my body or lose more of my teeth was still least to say, fucking annoying. When I went to fish out my practice jersey from the bottom of my duffel bag, I spotted my repurposed water bottle that housed my stashed vodka I had only allowed myself to use in the case of a more than dire emergency.

I had forgotten it had been housed in the confines of my duffel bag, mostly because Tito Clayton routinely searched every part of my room with this small and seemingly insignificant exception. I suppose that only added to the truth I had a problem when I would go out of my way to hide it. Maybe there was merit to what Tito Clayton and all those stuffy, arrogant, and equally incompetent therapists and psychiatrists had agreed upon. That I was this hopeless, innocent victim of the horrors of life and that I needed *their* help to fix what they deemed a problem.

Sure, the spurning of my mental illness may not have entirely been my fault. Maybe it was, but only the same God and I could never bring myself to believe in and his perfect foil of my older brother would know the answer to such. But I don't think that meant I was totally innocent of the fallout that transpired after I saw this illness hold me beneath the clenches of piercing, yellow teeth. After all, who made the choice to cope with it by destroying himself? Who was the man who sought to end his own life, despite knowing what pain it would cause the people he had dared to love? And he, too, could never promise them a future because he would simply never allow himself to have one?

There only ever could be one answer.

And the judge, jury, and executioner of the Dante Alonso Hidalgo tale would always be the same man who had never wished to live it.

Once my hockey gear was on, I grabbed my goalie stick and began the trek to the ice after hiding my repurposed water bottle beneath my discarded black clothes. I saw all my teammates gathered at the home bench, and I moved to skate in the middle of the line they had formed. Both people on either side of me scooted over to accommodate my presence.

I watched Tito Clayton ignore my tardiness to then say, "Welcome, Lions. Old and new. We're going around and doing the same icebreakers you've all had to do in your class. Name. Position. One interesting fact about yourself, major, or what you hope to get out of the season. Let's start with Dante. My nephew."

All eyes turned to me. I knew this was a dig at my stalling, but I didn't take offense to Tito Clayton's retribution when it was warranted. I then parted my lips kept beneath the cage making up my goalie helmet to say, "Dante Hidalgo. I'm the other goalie. And fun fact about myself? Well, I'm banned from the Kappa Sigma house for destruction of property."

"What the hell did you break?"

I turned to look at the man behind the question. I could see he was easily more than pleasing to look at, with sharp features jutted in pleasing angles, and the perfect amount of birthmarks dotting the even shade of tan kept beneath them. Electric, blue eyes kept between an expression of pure shock looked at me as if I had just said the most fascinating accusation ever spoken. A thick, Irish accent soaked up every one of his words, and it added an overall pleasantness to his first impression I realized gave me no reason to dislike him. And truth be told, for me to even say such about someone had to mean the apocalypse was nigh, hell had frozen over, or Xavier had grown the capacity to be a decent fucking person in our time spent apart. And I had little hope to think the last would ever culminate knowing how a man like Xavier Alonso Hidalgo was every bit beyond saving as myself; the man who had to bear the brunt of his scorn.

I smirked a bit, then saying, "You know that weird, little atrium they have?"

He glanced around as if to seek permission to his underage drinking.

Tito Clayton then answered, "What you do off my time is none of my concern unless it is at harm to yourself or another, Damien."

Damien nodded, turning back to me to say, "Yeah. I'm familiar."

"There used to be a chandelier there."

Damien didn't follow.

"I broke it."

Damien covered his mouth with his hand, but not before a glimpse of a laugh seeped from the part. He looked at me, flabbergasted to say, "*How the fuck*, do you break a chandelier, Dante?"

"Simple. Be drunk, nearly three hundred pounds, and hang off it, Damien."

That seemed to have broken the ice among the new Lions who erupted into laughter. I laughed too. Until I moved my gaze upon Tito Clayton, whose face was taut in an obvious tenseness. After all, the entire escapade of getting drunk and subsequently banned from the only fraternity on campus with decent pickings was because of the same alcohol habit I had deemed myself above. I ducked my head away, moving to glance down at my pair of skates.

Tito Clayton then said, "Now, we'll be going from my left to my right."

"Right," Celena said. "Celena Božović. Captain of the Lions and center. Interesting fact about me is that I'm originally from Romania. Hence the accent."

"Did Coach scout you all the way from there?" Rue asked, and I turned to stare at him. I had not realized we were next to each other, but we watched each other before Rue peered past me to wait for Celena's answer.

"No, I have lived here since I was sixteen," Celena answered. "But before that I lived in Romania."

Alexei seemed to be asking for death when he then said, "You're related to the head coach of Wesley, right? And you're probably Elliot's sister then too, right?"

Celena smiled, full of malice and equal parts ice. "Are you stupid, or do you want to lose both your legs before the start of the season, rookie?"

"Why didn't you just play for them, then?" Alexei asked again.

I glanced at Chase. He smiled as if Celena chewing out a man asking stupid questions was the reason he had fallen in love with her to begin with. I turned back to Celena to watch her shed her gloves and stick to know then Alexei was as good as dead.

Celena seemingly teleported to stand before Alexei, who was standing at the other end of the makeshift line the Lions had formed. She moved to grip Alexei's jersey with her left hand to pull him closer before settling to say, "Word of advice if you don't want to lose your fucking fingers, rookie. You do not mention the family I have left behind. Unless, you want to lose that and some of your fucking teeth. Get me?"

"Woah, woah, chill, I didn't know it was such a sensitive topic. I didn't mean any harm by it."

"You see, Alexei, I have to deal with men of your same like every waking moment since I made the choice to play here at Schaffer. I have cut men like you down at their knees, and I will not hesitate to do it again if you think I am a woman who will take your idiocy sitting down. This is my court, where I rule unchallenged. And should you want to stay here, *you will learn to play by my rules.* Get me?"

Alexei swallowed the lump in his throat to then say, "Got you."

Celena did not stick around to wait for Alexei's answer instead collecting her discarded gloves and stick to retreat back to her post.

Breanna, who was next to her, then spoke, "I am Breanna Kim. I'm a right defenseman, and a fun fact about me? Well, I grew up in France before moving here for college."

"What's France like?" Damien asked.

When I turned to look at him, I noticed all the women making up the Lions followed my stead. It was not a secret Damien was exceptionally attractive, even if I could just tell by looking at him that the brunt of his pleasing bone structure would never come my way. My issues with intimacy aside, it was never a crime to admire an attractive man who was just that. After all, how else was I going to entertain myself during the downtime at practice if I didn't have a nice hunk of flesh to sink imagined teeth into?

I knew Damien was going to cause drama among the women on the Lions. After all knowing just by looking at him what way he swung in the pendulum of human sexuality, I wondered who would lose some teeth laying stake into him first.

Truth be told, before starting at Schaffer there really was no kind of who-was-sleeping-with-who drama considering our entire line up for the past few years was all men, and the only woman gracing our roster was Celena. It's not that Celena didn't have the capacity for sexual escapades, it's just I didn't think anyone—except Chase—was really worthy of her time.

After all, our roster went from twenty-four players down to twelve after Tito Clayton selected Celena to be the captain of his personal pet project. Because the men who were now ranked under her had refused to take orders from a woman who knew her worth and was not afraid to remind others of it when they were stupid enough to forget it. I may not think of myself even within the same vicinity of someone like Celena in terms of talent, but it was her unflinching dedication *to be something great* that never failed to leave me with this sense of celebrity whenever I was in her presence. She was the kind of woman you knew would redefine the role and expectation of what one could be for the women who would follow her thereafter. And how could I not help but feel this ache in my chest knowing that she wanted me at her side through it all when I had never done anything to really, truly deserve such?

I knew better than to think on that truth sober. I had been weaned off of vodka in rehab, and I had been banned from any other of my toxic coping mechanisms in the wake of agreeing to play for my uncle. I shook my head. Then, I moved to watch the next Lion who could come to introduce himself to see it was the very man I loathed with every part of my being just like his fucking sister, Conner Villanueva.

"Conner Villanueva. I'm the other right wing. And fun fact about myself? Well, I suppose I can go with I'm planning to get my doctorate in psychology and become a therapist."

"Do you even have the brain capacity for that?" I asked.

Conner looked irritated to then say, "Oh, I have plenty, fuckhead. Because I know a fucking alcoholic when I fucking see one."

I don't remember the violence I instigated, but I remember coming to and being atop of Conner Villanueva; my gloves and stick long shed with blood dripping down his nose. It was as if I had come to bear witness to the crime committed. Conner used my realization of morality to gain the upper hand and shove me until he was now atop of me. He, too, had long shed his gloves and landed his clenched fist into my left eye where my branding had been etched into the skin a long, eight years ago. Under normal circumstances, this would have spurned a total and complete mental breakdown, but I did not respect Conner enough to have his violence get under my skin. Truth be told, since I had started here at Schaffer, it was simply an expectation rather than an exception. Not that I disliked throwing blows with a man who was incapable of being a good person. I guess the predisposition to be an asshole must have been genetic as both Conner and his sister were the waking embodiment of such traits. Oh, well. I didn't have much time to think about that now.

Right now, I wanted to lay craters into Conner's freckled face knowing any man who was stupid enough to start shit with me would come to learn I would *fucking finish it*.

Conner and I tousled around for what felt like an hour, and everyone's attempts to separate our opposing factions proved to be futile, mostly because our dislike for each other was far beneath verbal warnings that we both knew neither side would listen to. With my head against the ice, I jerked my left fist into his nose, the crunch of his cartilage warping beneath the weight of my knuckles. Conner cried out in an obvious pain, moving to cover the length with his hands as I then attempted to use this opening to see myself do more damage. Such hopes would be thwarted when I was yanked up to my feet by two pairs of hands, with Chase and Davi moving to stand between the two of us. Breanna, Lisanna, and Robyn helped Conner to his feet, and I turned to face the people behind me to find Rue and Celena.

Celena had an expression conveyed on her face as if to say she was growing tired of my fondness for violence. Rue looked at me as if he understood my viewpoint but disapproved at my indignation to get my point across at the expense of self. Celena's annoyance I could stomach. Her disapproval and her anger toward the violence wrought was borne evenly atop both my shoulders. But Rue looking at me as if the fate of an instigator on a one-way course to his own self destruction was one I had always been above?

I could never begin to stomach that.

I would never begin to be worthy of that.

And I wanted nothing more than to wipe the very notion of such an expression off his equally annoying, handsome face. But for some reason, I chose not to see it through. And I wondered if I would ever tell him that he was now the only person I had willingly chosen to spare the fate of my scorn knowing I had failed everyone else. It was a truth I ached with my entire being for the people I loved to say the same as Rue Oba standing before me, perfect and equally unobtainable as only he could be.

I turned away from Rue knowing I would not be able to stomach the messages conveyed by endless pools of black and an equally sharp and straight nose. I picked back up my gloves, helmet, and stick, turning to gaze upon the pair for a last time before skating off the ice, moving back to sit on the bench kept between the women's and men's locker room.

Footsteps came toward me, and I did not look up to meet them until hockey skates were in my immediate vision. Chase was standing before me, effortlessly cool and infinitely comforting as I watched him toss me something. I looked down at my lap to find a carton of cigarettes and the lighter I gifted him during our first meeting in middle school. Back when we were forced to become friends after being actively ostracized by our peers for reasons I could give a fuck about since their truth didn't change what had already been wrought.

The lighter wasn't anything special, made up of a cheap plastic. I had written my name on it in Sharpie that was fading from the oil smeared across foreign fingers. It was an annoying, bright, and equally gaudy orange, mostly because when I had stolen it, it was not so much about style or practicality. It was more about making a statement of morality during teenage years I had no idea how I had even survived. Maybe there was some guilt knowing I was capable of living this long because I had never planned to. Or, maybe it was guilt for failing myself and being unable to fulfill a promise I had made every birthday since I was twelve. After all, what good was this so-called life when all I had to show for it was its misery and the scars that went hand in hand with its truth knowing that I was a man every bit beneath the finite freedom of death as I ached not to be?

I ignored the weight such a question came with. I opened the package of cigarettes to claim one from the cardboard, placing it between my lips. I hunched over, placing my elbows to my knees as I struck the fork of Chase's lighter to render myself a flame. I covered the ember from outside wind with my other hand before bringing it to my cigarette. I lit the length before moving to lean against the wall and taking a long, much needed drag. The buzz saw my more violent tendencies wither beneath the taste of the nicotine, sending an unfounded shudder down my spine to look at Chase, who was already watching me.

"You have something to say," I replied, blowing the smoke out from my mouth.

"Do you want me to be nice or do you want me to be real?"

"All I've ever wanted of you, Chase, was to be real."

"Then, let us help you."

Chase was quiet.

I was quiet too.

"Losing you is something I would never be able to live with myself after the fact. I don't mean this in a way to guilt you, obviously, but it's just the truth. After I found you on that bathroom floor with those pills and all that blood scattered all around, the threat of your death has haunted me ever since. And, Dante, even if no one else may want you here, *I do*. And I hope and pray that's good enough if not for forever, then for now."

"It is," I answered before I could really think on it. "It will always be good enough, I promise, Chase. But I will never think I'm worthy of it. It's just not possible, and for that, I'm sorry."

"Do you really think I would show you this friendship if I didn't think you were worthy of it?" Chase asked. "Truth be told, I have made the choice to stay. I have made the choice to carry some of the weight of your demons because I know even you are entitled to redemption. It's never too late to change, Dante. You still have an entire life ahead of you. And I don't think the lot of us Lions would come to forgive you if you were to take it from us."

I didn't answer, moving to take another drag from his whittling cigarette. Chase smiled as if he expected this much, sitting next to me before taking out one of his own from the package. I was still holding his lighter and struck the fork to give him a flame. He never liked my smoking to begin with, but I knew this exception was a gesture of kinship that meant he would stay by my side even when I had done everything in my power to drive him away. I knew better than to think I could ever be worthy of such, but with his arm pressed against mine and the smell of burning tobacco shared between us, it didn't mean I didn't want to try.

1 0

ROBYN

BREANNA, CONNER, LISANNA, AND I sat in the men's locker room as my mother began the process of cleaning my brother up.

I wondered if Bruna would ever come to welcome Conner into our already broken family even if I didn't think there would be much use of him there. My parents still actively disliked the other knowing the marriage I had once believed was idyllic would be exposed to be built upon equal deceit from both parties who chose to see it through. While they never extended the same venom to me as they did each other, it still stung knowing the perfect life I once had fell apart in an instant. Although, I knew better than to grieve it when both of my parents were infinitely happier apart then I would come to learn they ever were together. I suppose that is the hardest lesson to learn growing up. That your parents are every bit human as you know you are, and they are incapable of perfection no matter how much you ache for them to be.

"I'm going to snap your nose back into place," my mother said, the same thick, German accent soaking up most of her words. In the time she had moved to America, it had mellowed out into the same American drawl as mine. However, there were glimpses where her Germanic ancestry poked through despite her best efforts. "It's going to hurt."

"I can handle it," Conner said, seemingly annoyed that Bruna would warn him of such. I knew my mother would not take such sitting down, and that much would be confirmed when she snapped the cartilage back into place without any kind of warning.

"Fuck! You could have warned me," Conner cried out.

"Niceties are for nice people," Bruna replied, unsympathetic. "And until you act like one, you are not entitled to my good side."

Bruna began to wipe the blood from Conner's even shade of brown, eventually discarding her gloves and bloodied gauze once finished. She glanced at me when I tilted my head to the door. My mother nodded, moving to exit and leaving me alone with Breanna, Lisanna, and Conner with a silence thick enough to be torn apart with an even pair of fingers.

"Do you want me to like you or not?" Lisanna asked, her tone nowhere close to easing the tension taking root between the four of us.

"Why would you not like me?" Conner asked, obviously unsure what he had done to earn my girlfriend's ire.

"Disrespecting Dante like that," Lisanna replied, crossing her arms. She tilted her head upwards slightly, moving to look down at my twin brother who was sitting atop the bench separating each half of the cubbies where our gear was stored. "I get you don't like each other, but does calling him an alcoholic in front of the entire team make any fucking sense in your mind or are you just stupid?"

Conner was quiet, now clutching an ice pack warped around his nose. "Dante is every bit beyond saving as we both know he is, Lisanna."

"And what do you have to say about your presence here, then?"

"I don't follow."

"You were given a second chance. Foster kids are shot in the foot before they even have a chance to learn how to walk. Tito Clayton gave you that. He gave Robyn that. The sister you just told you could give a fuck about by not extending grace or any ounce of sympathy for a man of her same struggle." Lisanna looked Conner up and down. "Truth be told, if you're going to say shit like that, you have no place to be a therapist. It's the kind like you that made the entire process of healing even more fucked than it could ever have been doing it on my own."

Conner looked at Breanna. When she did not offer him aid in her expression, he then turned to me. I agreed with the point

Lisanna was making, yes, but I did not want to butcher my relationship with my brother right out of the gate knowing all I lost to even be in his presence. I looked Conner up and down to find him frown, turning to face the concrete beneath our feet.

I glanced at Breanna, who met my gaze before turning back to Conner to say gently, "Conner, I think what Lisanna is trying to say is that you need to be more sympathetic to the struggle Dante and Robyn share. Imagine if someone had said something like that about your own. I don't think you'd come to forgive them either, no?"

Conner was quiet, eventually turning to face me to then say, "Sorry, Robyn. I meant no disrespect in my dig on Dante. Truth be told, he just pisses me off so fucking much I can't really think through my anger when I see him."

"It's ok," I said, smiling a bit.

Conner returned the gesture.

"But, for the sake of our relationship, I would think more carefully about what you say about addicts considering I am every bit one like Dante. Even if all of us here would rather me not be."

A silence lingered.

Lisanna then said, "What made you hate Dante so much to say something like that, anyway?"

"It's all stupid," Conner replied dismissively. "I don't think it'd make much sense to any of you lot anyway."

Lisanna lurched forward when I caught her, moving to lean into her ear to say, "We're still strangers here, Liz. Getting them to trust us will take time, so be patient."

Lisanna glanced at me before moving back to her original posture when the locker room door opened to reveal an irate Clayton Alonso. While so much was not shown in his calm, cool, and collected expression, his presence conveyed otherwise as I watched Conner wither beneath its weight.

Tito Clayton then said, "I would like a word with Conner."

None of us moved.

"Alone."

That was the only cue we needed. Lisanna filed out of the locker room first, with Breanna looming in front of me and me taking post at the end of our makeshift line. I hesitated, unsure if Breanna would answer any question I wanted to ask her, but ignoring all logic and reason, I said, "Breanna. A word, if you don't mind?"

Lisanna glanced at me, and I waved her off. She gave a nod before moving to exit, leaving Breanna and me alone in the hallway before both locker rooms. A tenseness lingered. I was unsure if it was entirely based in my imagination, or if it had founding in the woman standing before me with a smile pressed between thin lips and framed on either side by pink hair. After all, it was no secret what I had dared to excuse being friends with the man who had abused Breanna without doing anything in my power to stop it. Even if I had not been friends with Elliot during the time where the violence took place, it did not change how the guilt for choosing to ignore its truth was a fate I had been grappling with since arriving on Tito Clayton's front doorstep a traitor.

I wanted nothing more than to admit what I had dared to excuse. I wanted nothing more than to admit I was born with this inherent, original sin of trying to fix a man who had long ago deemed himself above fixing. While this person was not Elliot Božović, it did not change how his and Elliot's fate were now intertwined knowing Elliot was the man who had replaced me in the wake of what Xavier deemed a betrayal. I had given blood to see through the redemption of Xavier Hidalgo. And maybe that wouldn't hurt as much knowing the man I saw greatness in had never seen the same in me.

"You seem close with Conner," I replied, watching her carefully. "I don't think just anyone would be there for him in the wake of Dante's violence."

Breanna gave a tight-lipped smile. "We are, yes. I hope you can learn to be too."

I gave a smile of my own, more than aware of her deflection. "Even if I may never be entitled to such, Breanna. I wanted to say I was sorry."

Breanna feigned an innocence I knew better than to believe when she said, "For what exactly, Robyn?"

The words coming from between my lips tasted every bit sour as they did sweet. "For being friends with Elliot despite what he did to you."

Breanna was noticeably taken aback, giving a flinch at the use of her ex-boyfriend's name before. Eventually, she adjusted to bear the weight that came with it evenly atop both her shoulders. She crossed her arms, moving to look me up and down before saying in a quiet, "You weren't friends with him when we were together. Why the hell are you apologizing, Robyn?"

I hesitated before settling with, "I knew what he did. And yet, I made the choice to be friends with him regardless. Are you telling me you don't find that as heinous as I do?"

Breanna smiled. "I don't think the answer to the question of guilt is as black and white as you are saying it is. If it's safe to assume Elliot is a terrible man, why do you think you would not come out of your friendship with him unscathed?"

"What do you mean exactly?"

"Elliot and Xavier are two in the same, yes? They are terrible men, with Xavier going so far to date Davi when she was a junior in high school while he was in college because it allowed him control. And tell me, Robyn, what makes you think you were above their signature, mutual trait of manipulation?"

I was quiet knowing she was ignorant to the truth.

Breanna continued, moving to stand before me. I was still taller than her by a head. Even with the absence of my heels, I felt as if her presence was grander than I once thought it to be. She smiled again, eventually settling to say, "You may have things you need to answer for and atone for. You could very well be a bad person, and you could very well be among the same like as the men you once called your best friends at Wesley. But, Robyn, you can do something neither Elliot nor Xavier will ever be capable of."

"Being?"

"Change."

I couldn't help but think Lisanna had said something to Breanna even though I knew better than to think that much was true. And I knew both of them were right in saying that I was capable of healing, and the men I had tried to see through the same during my time at Wesley were not. I had given nearly everything in an attempt to spurn such change onto both Elliot and Xavier only to have the pair attempt to assassinate me the moment I sought out the same for self. I knew there was an inch of credence to what both Lisanna and Breanna had said, and I knew they were every bit right as I could never bring myself to accept they were. After all, what had I ever done to deserve someone—let alone Elliot's virtuous ex-girlfriend—to look at me in such a light?

I could very well be beating a dead horse with this warped sense of self that told me I would never be deserving of such a thing. And even if I knew better than to think years of internalizing my parents's mutual hatred of the other was a reflection of myself, it did not change how *it still felt that way*. There was nothing a long-needed apology for their dislike for each other that could begin to fix such a branding when it had already been imprinted against the brown of my flesh. The deed was done. The curse was set. And there was nothing anyone— including myself—could ever begin to fix it. After all, I had given years in an attempt to dare and say such, and what else did I have to show for it but the pain I had already made the choice to wrought upon the same woman I claimed to love like she never meant anything to me to begin with?

Breanna smiled a bit as if she could see the most intimate parts of self I had long ago made the choice to keep hidden. She crossed her arms before propping up her left with her elbow to say, "You don't believe me, do you?"

I knew better than to answer.

But I think my expression did such for me when Breanna then replied, "You don't have to. But it does not change what is and isn't the truth. I used to spend years asking myself what I had ever done to deserve Elliot's mistreatment of me. And the answer to that question will always be *nothing.*"

Breanna stepped closer, then continuing, "Their mistreatment of you is not some kind of divine punishment, Robyn. It was never a reflection of yourself, or a price you had to pay. It will only ever be the reflection of them and their inability to accept and acknowledge the wrong they chose to do. And truth be told, I think you should realize such sooner rather than later, or else, we'll have nothing to show for Elliot and Xavier's shared sins but your corpse."

I swallowed hard. Breanna gave a tight smile before moving to tap my shoulder to exit, and her words haunted me her entire way out.

1 1

DANTE

I WALKED BACK ONTO the ice of the Nora Wilson Hockey Center to find my teammates gathered around the home bench as I had left them. Chase followed behind me, the two of us skating over when Tito Clayton dismissed the other Lions present with a wave and a nod.

Celena then said, "C'mon. Shooting drill. I'll show you all how it's done with Chase in goal."

Chase, Rue, and Celena glanced at me before filing out and allowing me and my uncle some privacy for his coming scolding. I watched him give a tired, drawn-out sigh before moving to rub his temples with his right hand. Then, he moved the shape to join the other making up his crossed arms with his signature clipboard with our practice itinerary tucked underneath his armpit. I moved my gaze back to his own. His stubble was growing ever more prominent thanks to the razors that had been banned from his house knowing the use I would see them repurposed for. I swallowed the lump in my throat, banishing my inability to be the man Tito Clayton always saw me as into its pit—and like the cautious optimism once held for things to really, truly get better—was now forever lost and never to be found again.

"You know I say this each and every time you instigate violence, and I know each and every time I know you will not listen," Tito Clayton said after a bit.

I bore the accusation evenly atop my shoulders since we both knew it was true. Denying it would simply make me a liar, and if there was anything I would not stomach myself becoming, it was that. I then replied, "Just give up and let me waste away, Tito. It'll save us both all the grief that comes with loving a man like me. Just let me go. *Please.*"

Tito Clayton had an annoyance creased into every line of his aged face to then say, "And what kind of man would that make me should I give up on you? How would I later live with myself knowing your death could have been prevented, and I chose not to stop it?"

I was quiet.

Tito Clayton continued, "You can paint me out to be anything you want, anak, but you cannot paint me out to be the villain in this life we've come to share. I am not saying what you are going through is not hard, but the truth of the matter is, you are not letting anyone help you."

"If we're going to have this argument again, I don't want to start the season off this way, Tito."

"It's only an argument if you make it one," Tito Clayton replied quickly. "You act like I don't know exactly what you're going through. You're treating me like a stranger rather than the man who raised you. Tell me, Dante, is that any bit fair?"

The use of my first name made me shudder. I tried to defend the bare bones thread my honor was hanging by to say, "I am not opening up to another psychiatrist or therapist just for them to tell me lies on how I am fixable. Or, to tell me I am doing this entirely for attention and that medication is the only way to save me when I quite frankly *don't even want to be saved.*"

Tito Clayton was quiet, creasing his thin lips into a straight line. He moved to glance at me, as if to say this cause to have me see through this life he was forcing me to live was not one he was going to relent on so easily. And, yes, it meant a lot to me that he would care, but it also annoyed me that he could not give an inch to see the point I was trying to make.

"I'm not saying getting professional help will magically fix you, anak." Tito Clayton watched me carefully as if he was trying to drive home the point he, too, was trying to make. "All I'm saying is that you need to let me help you. We don't have to see therapists or psychiatrists if you don't want to. You simply have to first admit there is something about you worth saving. Do you really think I would die on this hill if I didn't think it to be true, hm?"

I was quiet again.

Tito Clayton continued, "You can call me every name in the book. You can hate me. You can say I'll never be your father, so I should stop acting like one. You have every right to hate me because of your circumstance, but you cannot hate me for refusing to give up on you. You cannot tell me your life holds no value when I have been tasked with making you see such when you were dropped on my doorstep eight years ago." Tito Clayton adjusted his shoulders to say, "I won't give you this same lecture since we both know you have yet to listen. But, Dante, if you keep walking down this path, you won't figure out there's something worth saving until it's too late."

I watched my uncle, still as the dawn before Christmas morning.

"After all, we both know each time we've sought to end our lives, we have failed. And you and I both know why, even if only one of us is capable of accepting this as the truth. And truth be told, Dante, you will never know what you have until it's gone. I don't think you'll come to survive it. Because quite frankly, *I barely did.*"

I knew better than to speak and address the truth. I knew it would make me equally heinous as the outside forces that wanted me to see through the hopeless cause of my own destruction. I knew my uncle was every bit right as I ached for him not to be. But, like the coward I always would be, I did not address such then and did not think I would have the courage to anytime soon. Instead, I ducked my head down and skated over to the goal, where Chase was waiting for me, and the drill had been halted to accommodate my presence.

"You want a stab at it?" Chase asked, smiling.

I glanced at the line. I saw Conner and Alexei were up next. I then turned back to Chase to say, "A little humbling can go a long way."

"That it can," Chase called sagely.

He moved to glance at Celena to ask permission for the changing of the guard. She gave a nod, and Chase skated over to hover at the home bench where I had just been lectured. I then took his place beneath the goalie crease, getting into a readying position that would see me reclaim my dignity in the wake of my more than characteristic violence at the expense of Conner Villanueva. I slapped my stick atop the ice to indicate to my challengers that I was ready for their coming humbling, and when I watched Alexei skate towards me first, I already knew what to expect.

It's not that Alexei was any bit talented. Sure, he was good enough to play here at Schaffer, but his skill set was nothing to really marvel at compared to that of Celena—or some could even argue—my brother. I think the arrogance that came with his scouting showed in his demeanor that everyone here was just as good as he, so therefore, this gave him enough of an inkling to build a kind of entitlement on. I think the best way I could begin to describe it was that his head was so big in terms of what he thought of himself. He obviously did not extend the same gravitas to others, even when they were marginally better than him.

I don't think this is a bad thing to perpetrate inherently. Truth be told, it was only asking for a coming humbling because the reality in any sport you play is that there will be people far better than you could ever hope to be. Celena was leagues ahead of my own talent. Even Tito Clayton in his prime was a force I don't think I would come out alive in facing. And since Alexei was Rue's brother, I would give him the benefit of the doubt that he was just ignorant to the truth rather than actively choosing not to listen to it.

Alexei skated forward, moving his puck to his left side before attempting to fake me out and shoot at my right-hand side. I knew Alexei knew I was left-handed based on the punches I had just thrown, so he was obviously trying to exploit the weakness of shooting on me on the side I was not dominant on. Truth be told, the move was elementary, and I could see it coming a mile away. For the sake of stirring the pot, I faked an attempt to guard the right half of the goal. I didn't move my entire body to deflect the would-be direction of the puck. I knew considering my stature, investing in a movement like that would cost me, since where I lacked in speed, I made up for in strength. The bait I had so blatantly put on the fishhook was easily swallowed whole by Alexei Oba, and I watched him quickly move the puck to his right side and fire. I moved back to the right-hand goal, catching the puck within the net of my goalie glove for the sake of dramatics. Alexei looked stupefied, and I'll admit, seeing his flabbergasted expression at one of the easiest saves in my entire hockey career since I could hold a stick *almost* made this whole living thing worth it.

"And we've come to learn the world does not revolve around you, Alexei," I called, unsympathetic. "We all have to learn that much eventually, no?"

"Don't start shit with me, Dante," Alexei replied. "Because I'll finish it."

"Will you now?" I replied, moving to stand upright. I skated over to face Alexei to find I had a good six inches on him in terms of height. Maybe the goalie armor was not as cumbersome as I once thought it to be. After all, it did help the effort in making my more than gargantuan stature all the more dramatic. I moved to shove the puck into Alexei's chest, sending him back an inch to give a malice-ridden smile to then say, "You have a place here. And it sure as hell among my same like."

"If you keep talking about me and my brother like that, I'll make sure you regret it."

I knew he was talking about Conner but knew better than to ask the invasive question as to why they called each other such. I then leaned in and said, "You're challenging a man with nothing to lose, Alexei. And truth be told, you won't come out alive when I have every bit of a reason not to either."

I skated back over to the goal, waiting for Conner to then shoot against me. He glanced at Alexei, who mimed a salute before getting behind the last person in his own line. Conner charged forward, not bothering to try as he shot in the left-hand corner, which we both knew was my stronger half of the goalie net considering the dominance of the right side of my brain. As he skated away after flipping me off, I knew it was going to be a long fucking season, and the ego among the other Lions was going to make it all the more unbearable. That is, without the undiscussed factor of seeing my older brother again for the first time in a long, eight years come our looming season opener.

12

ROBYN

I **WALKED OVER TO** the women's locker room to find Celena Božović waiting for me.

It was no secret neither of us were not any bit allies as I was now a traitor among Xavier's court. After all, I used to keep the company of the same man who wanted me dead, and his only equal who wanted Celena dead in equal measure. I knew better than to think such a sin could be forgiven without making an effort to either amend it or even dare to acknowledge its truth. But looking at the malice tucked between the blue surrounding Celena's pupil, I knew better than to dare and try when it now became obvious that we would only come out of this conversation with burnt bridges and equally cindered truths.

Celena moved her gaze up and down the length of my body before settling on my brown staring back to say, "You know you're not welcome here, right?"

"If you want to ruse me up, I will not fall for cheap parlor tricks," I replied. "The Lions can only handle so much ego, Celena. And you would be wise to not bear the brunt of such scorn because it will only come back to bite you in the ass if you want to finally beat Xavier and Elliot before your college career is over."

Celena smiled; the same iciness tucked between the part as if it were coming from Xavier's lips. A shudder ran down the length of my spine, but I knew better than to convey such to other side on the battle of ego taking place between her and I. I was not ignorant to fact I had enough that it could provide for two, and knowing such, meant I would not submit to Celena's degradation without a fight. I may not like the person I was now, but that did not mean I would let others exploit such a trait when it was obvious they only meant to do so to gain an upper hand they would never have otherwise.

I moved to rest my hockey stick atop the concrete beneath our feet. We watched each other, daring the woman before us to speak first even if the tension shared did enough of the talking for us. Since I had dug into Celena's pride, I figured she was entitled to an insult of her own. Even if I knew we would never come to like each other considering the matter of what I had done and what I had excused, that did not mean I would continue to treat her unfairly. After all, my time as her brother's best friend was now entirely beneath me knowing what he and his better half had done to me.

"And you would be smart to learn your place and learn it fast," Celena replied. She moved to stand before me, and because of the lack of high heels, we were the same height of six feet. "Or, the coming teaching will not be so kind to you, Zaragoza."

Before I could bark back some kind of insult conjured from the depths of my stomach, the door to the locker room opened almost on some kind of cue as I watched Lisanna join the two of us in the hallway. She stood at me right, crossing her arms when Celena looked her up and down in a less than accusatory manner than she had me. Celena then retracted back to her starting post to say, "You both are guests here. And the sooner you learn that the easier this transfer will be on the two of you. You're only here because of Dante's grace, and I need you both to know that. Mostly because if it had been left up to me, I would have reduced you back to the very nothing you once came from."

"Do you really think Tito Clayton would allow us both entry to his pet project if either of us were some kind of double agent in disguise, Celena?" Lisanna asked. "You are a smart woman. But it seems your dislike for Xavier and Elliot is clouding your better judgment. You like to forget Robyn is just as much of a victim of their shared trait of violence as you and Dante are. I'm not saying you have to love her like I might, but I'm asking you both to be fair. And tell me, what is fair about attributing Robyn to be among the same like of men we all know are incapable of change?"

Celena did not answer Lisanna's accusation, instead, saying, "You two so much as think of blowing my one shot left at knocking those men down a peg, and you will regret it. And while you're here on my ice, you play by my rules. And if you give nothing but your absolute best, then you can play elsewhere."

Celena walked past the two of us and into the women's locker room. I didn't really want to stick around and be graced with more than annoying presence, so I turned to Lisanna to see she had read my mind when she then said, "We can find some place to cool off until she's out."

"I honestly would love nothing more," I replied, smiling.

Lisanna met my smile with one of her own. The two of us began to explore the Nora Wilson Hockey Center in a comfortable, homey silence when we heard footsteps coming towards us. Davi came into view, her expression tense and equally tight as she did not address either of us to move past us and enter the women's locker room. I watched her until she was out of eyesight, turning to look at Lisanna. She then said, "Do you want to check in on her?"

"I don't think I have much reason to," I replied.

"You were the one who dropped her off on Tito Clayton's front doorstep, Robyn, that gives you plenty of reason to be the one to comfort her."

"Point taken," I replied. "I'll see what's wrong. I think I can face Celena despite it."

"If she ever does something stupid, you tell me." Lisanna's expression was firm and equally unyielding. "And I will handle it, ok?"

"I love you, Liz, but I have never needed someone else to fight my battles for me," I replied, smiling. "But we can discuss this later. In the meantime, wait for me here once I'm finished."

Lisanna gave a nod. I walked back down the hallway and into the women's locker room to find Davi sitting on the bench dividing the locker room in two. We stared at each other as I closed the door behind me with a click. She glanced at my left before bringing her gaze back to my own. We watched each other, a tense silence taking root between us when I then said, "You look upset."

"You would be right," Davi replied after a bit. "Robyn, do you really think we can become people free of the clenches of Xavier's teeth?"

I really had no idea what this had to do with her current emotional state, mostly because I had assumed Davi already knew the answer to such. I didn't think the burden of reminding her of the answer we had once agreed upon was an annoying one, but I couldn't help but think she would find little credence to such a truth since her expression conveyed such. She seemed to be in this unfounded state of hopelessness I could not begin to understand. Mostly because what did she have to be hopeless about when the fact she was standing before me was every bit proof of her ability to live despite what Xavier now wanted for us both?

The fact Davi and I had even survived the time spent with Xavier—where we would become the only two people who would see him scars, flesh, and all—was proof that there was hope for either of us to live free of the confines of his will. I knew this, and I knew Davi knew this too. But seeing the pain entrenched in her expression told me that like the matter of my own worthiness, she just could never bring herself to believe such. And how could I begin to tell her lies on the matter of worthiness when I, too, was incapable of believing it? After all, seeing it through would only make me some kind of liar akin to the like of the man we had given nearly everything to dare and escape. And if there was one level I would always refuse to sink beneath, it was exactly that.

I knew better than to give a long winded and equally unwanted rant on inherent worthiness neither of us would want to hear. Instead, I said, "Do you remember that night I dropped you off here at Schaffer last year?"

"How could I forget?" Davi asked. "After all, I nearly lost my fucking leg the way Xavier broke it. It was a miracle I could even walk again. I remember how the bone was literally poking through the flesh."

"Why do you think I saved you that night?"

Davi watched me, her brown eyes glinting in an endless circle. "Truth be told, I don't know, Robyn. You were never my friend, and I was never yours. We knew of the other, but did not know each other. I was every bit a stranger to you as you were to me. So, tell me, why did you save me the night Xavier tried to murder me?"

I swallowed the lump in my throat to say, "Because I always believed you could make something of yourself if you were freed from the chains that bound you."

Davi was quiet.

"I knew that if I did not save you, you would have died in his dorm room. I knew there would be some fake story about how you tried to kill yourself because Andrei would have been convinced by Elliot to cover it up, and knowing all the championships under his belt, Wesley would have listened."

I stepped forward, moving to crouch down until Davi and I were eye level. She moved her gaze to meet my own, and I shed my hockey stick and gloves to the locker room floor to then hold her hands, thumbs circling around the brown skin making up the back of her palm. She watched the motion for an endless minute before moving to meet my gaze, her expression softening when I then said, "I'm not saying rebuilding our lives without the man we would both come to love is going to be easy. Truth be told, my identity is every bit dependent on the man I called a best friend as yours is calling him a lover. But we have one thing he never could."

"Being?"

"Each other."

Davi was quiet, a smile now pressed between thick, red lips.

I then spoke, "We don't have to face the unknown alone anymore. Because we have someone who really gets what it's like to be loved by someone like Xavier only for him to take that much away from you when he deems it convenient. The only mistake we made was doing what we needed for self rather than himself. You and I did nothing wrong, Davi. And I will really, truly believe that until the day I die or the world stops spinning. Whichever comes first."

"I'm glad then," Davi said after a bit, still quiet. "Do you think Xavier ever really loved me?"

I moved my thumb to trace a circle over Davi's skin to then say, "No. I don't think he ever did. Truth be told, Davi, I don't think a man like him is even capable of such. Not when he refuses to acknowledge all the wrong he has done, and blames it solely on the pain he, too, was forced to endure."

Davi then said, "Do you think he'll ever become the man we always hoped for him to be?"

"Maybe," I said, honest. "But we should stop killing ourselves praying for such to happen at the expense of self when he has, for now, given us both the answer."

My phone rang in the net of my duffel bag, and I gave a smile before moving to stand upright and walking over to my left to find the ghost of a vice I had left behind.

Because sitting next to my ringing phone and tucked inside the pocket was a bottle of Oxycontin.

I did not know how it got there. I did not know who had put it there. But all that mattered was that it was standing before me, staring at me with haunting, glossed over eyes. The spheres of an insidious, indignant red told me I needed to see through self-destruction to ever be worthy of the love shown to me by the people who would never deserve the loss that would soon befall them. But I could not show such now. Instead, I took my phone from the pocket where my own executioner laid next, answering the call without bothering to check who was calling. "Hello?"

"I've been made aware Xavier has shown his face on the Schaffer campus. You are to either come to my house, or find someone and stick by them until I give you the call that it's clear to leave where you are. Get me?"

"Got you, Tito."

"Who's with you right now?"

I glanced at Davi who met my gaze. "Davi."

"And where are you?"

"The women's locker room."

"Share your location with me while I go and find Dante. Lord knows where he is considering he does not have a phone." Tito Clayton paused for a moment to then say, "I know Lisanna is nearby. I've already altered her of the threat. Stay put until she finds you. Mostly because she's one of the few people I know who can knock that fucker who is my other nephew down a peg."

"Of course, Tito."

I glanced back down at the orange and white bottle of pills waiting for me in my duffel bag.

"I know better than to think I could ever do the same."

"Good. Now, I have to get going, but like I said, share your location with me. We'll regroup once I, too, knock Xavier down a peg."

I hung up the phone, moving to place it back in the net pocket of my bag after sharing my location with Tito Clayton as he had asked. I then examined the bottle of pills with my hand, trying to be as discreet as possible when I caught Davi's gaze on the back of my neck. We watched each other, daring the other woman before us to speak first when I broke all resolve and shoved the pills into the depth of my duffel bag, covering the cylinder with my clothes before turning back to Davi. She looked at me as if she, too, would keep my newfound secret. And I prayed to a god I could never bring myself to believe in. That I would somehow find a strength I knew I didn't have to remain sober, so I would not see me lose the one person I could not afford to lose.

1 3

DANTE

I **EXAMINED MY REFLECTION** in the mirror as the scar carved into my face shrouded me in an ever welcome whisper of self-degradation.

I moved my finger to the skin, the length hovering above the keloid for an endless minute before I sucked my breath in and placed it atop the flesh. A sickly shudder ran up and down the length of my spine, raising bumps against my thick, toned arms that scratched up against the fabric of my turtleneck. The sensation made my head spin in this seemingly endless circle. It gave me the same sense of vertigo as if I had downed enough liquor to be sentenced to retch up my mistake above the rim of an unknown toilet seat for the rest of the night.

Truth be told, it would require an ungodly means to get me that drunk to begin with considering my stature and knowing my secret stash would never warrant such inebriation, I suppose I was—for now—safe from the fate of being a drunkard. That is, until I found a new means to acquire the vice that had been banned from me in every other conceivable context. After all, Kappa Sigma was the only place worth stealing from since their wares were so numerous no one would notice a couple bottles going missing. And tell me, how was I ever going to begin to cope with this sadness entrenched in the very founding of my being without something at the expense of self?

I didn't ask anyone to understand my mindset or even dare to agree with me. But I wanted everyone in my life to respect the fact I could not live with the person I was now. There was nothing to like about this man who could only ever hurt the people he cared about knowing a future was something he could never promise any of them. Not even to the uncle and best friend who had both dared to save him from the brink of death. Everyone could very well be entitled to redemption, but I knew I was the only exception to such a metric. Because what had I ever done to deserve such? We all knew the answer, and I don't think I could ever be so heinous to speak it aloud. But refusing to acknowledge such a truth as it came from between a pair of lips did not make it any less poignant. I knew the dawn of my end was drawing ever nearer with each second, minute, and hour that passed of my already pitiful existence. But despite the only end I would be deserving to meet, it did not change that my tito was right.

Because each time I sought to end my own life, I had failed.

After the first time it could very well have been luck. After the second, a mere coincidence. But when the total was drawing closer to the halfway mark of a dozen, luck was not a scale I thought would be fair to measure my survival on since I did not think such would even be true. Tito Clayton would have argued divine timing and intervention. Others could very well have argued fate. But knowing what my tito had said, I knew the real reason as to why I had failed in seeing through my own execution.

And it was because *I really did not want to die.*

Maybe this could have been a sort of coming to God moment that would save a man already beneath such graces. However, I already knew that despite this revelation, there was nothing I would begin to do to change my life as I knew it now. Mostly because who was I as a person without this sadness? Where did the man known as Dante Alonso Hidalgo start, and where did he end free from the confines of this depression that had long ago swallowed him whole? I knew better than to think I could ever answer such unless I saw through a recovery that was needed to understand such an inconceivable truth.

But the fact of the matter is, I did not know anything about this man I had been seemingly cursed to live as other than his misery. There was nothing else to define the matter of self but destruction. Whether seen through beneath razorblades, sloshed evenly in my stomach with equal portions of straight liquor, or in a haze of tiny, red pills that would be thrown up the rest of the night in an empty room where no one spoke of the crime committed, except hospital mandated counselors who would never really, truly *get it*. I had spent nearly half of my life teetering on the edge of total calamity. I had long ago butchered the boy I once was only for the man I am now to rise from a dead child's corpse. And tell me, how could a man so heinous to dare and see through such a crime ever be entitled to salvation?

I moved my hand to the mirror, placing my palm against the cool glass as if to remind myself the man staring back was every bit real as I hoped he never could be. That this person watching me behind the gaze of haunting, black eyes—every bit a monster as only he would ever begin to know himself as—was the man I had chosen to become. Knowing such, I wanted to puke up the last remnant of each and every one of my original sins in the nearest toilet and flush them away in the hope it would become a kind of makeshift baptism.

But I knew such could never begin to be warranted when they had already seeped into the people I had dared to love in return knowing they would never forgive me for the final, third act of the Dante Alonso Hidalgo story. And maybe the same Catholicism I could never bring myself to stomach would see me cast out the same eternal salvation once promised to man if they simply believed in it. But I was above such cheap parlor tricks in terms of entitlement. Mostly because it did not change the matter intertwined with its truth, being worthiness. And there was nothing I could begin to do to begin to be deserving of such a thing.

I walked back out into the locker room, pulling my wet hair back into a tentative ponytail. I saw the glint of something poke out from the chasms of my duffel bag, and I fished around from beneath my clothes to find an old friend, being two unopened bottles of a favored, liquid vice.

I really had no idea how it had gotten there. Truth be told, I could give a fuck how it materialized in my possession, mostly because seeing it before me meant it was just that. I smirked a bit, taking each bottle out from the chasms of my bag to twist them open. I sniffed the rim of each to find the smell was too pungent to be anything else but alcohol, and I gave cautious look around before moving to cover my newfound stash with the clothes they had once been caked under. I closed my bag, moving to adjust it over my shoulder as I walked out into the hallway of the Nora Wilson Hockey Center to find Ciara Wilson waiting for me, smiling neatly and dressed in her usual unassuming and equally humble attire.

I never really had much of an opinion on Ciara Wilson. Mostly because while I knew she and my tito were close, she was never a kind of step-in mother like one would expect her to be considering the nature of her and my uncle's relationship. I never saw a need to ask invasive questions on the shared platinum band they wore, or why whenever family was gathered Ciara would be present despite not being tied to the Alonso tree by blood. I also knew the woman whom our hockey arena was named after was related to her but not much else. Mostly because I had so many things to worry about in terms of self that bothering to fill in the gaps between mental breakdowns with gossip I think would have made me even crazier. All of it was stupid anyway. I never got the point of Chase divulging me in our teammates's sex lives since it was quite literally none of my fucking business anyway.

Ciara was around the same age as Tito Clayton, but she did not look anywhere near as old as he did. Truth be told, I didn't think Tito Clayton cared much about his appearance. Mostly because when you're living to survive, things as unimportant as looks are on the last of your long list of things that you need handled. Like I had said, Tito Clayton never told me everything he had been through from start to finish. But the thing about my uncle is that he was very much a public figure for a good portion of his life. And being one meant his life was well documented on the Internet. I mean, Tito Clayton had a fucking Wikipedia page, so what was going to stop me from doing some digging when it was all public knowledge? By no means a fair use of my time, yes, but I needed to know if the man who was hellbent on my recovery had any credence to such a claim. And truth be told, maybe it made me infinitely more heinous than Xavier could ever be knowing the answer.

"Dante," Ciara cooed as if I were her unruly child. "Got a minute?"

My duffel bag felt like stones weighing down my corpse after it had been thrown out to sea. But I had done this song and dance of lying an infinite amount of times before, so I knew its four for four beat like the in and out motion of my own breathing. "Of course, Tita Ciara."

She smiled. "What do you want for your future, Dante?"

I thought it was a stupid question to ask. "You know the answer to that, don't you? After all, I don't think Tito Clayton didn't tell you."

"Yes, that much is true. But I want to hear you say it out loud."

I didn't like the corner she had backed me into. "If you have something important to say, please, get to it."

Ciara stood before me, and I gazed down at her. She fiddled with the same platinum ring she always wore that my uncle had the other matching half of. I noticed a gold charm of a cross strung next to the band, and it made me wonder if Ciara was the force that saw Tito Clayton a believer.

"You know, your uncle and I have been lovers for some time now." Ciara smiled as if talking about my uncle could ever come from an emotion of fondness. "We never told you or Lisanna when you were younger since we didn't think it was the time. But it plays into the grander point I'm trying to make, so bear with me, Dante."

"And your point is?"

"I know you know the journey to sobriety Clay is currently seeing through. After all, how could you not when he's every bit a celebrity as he never really wanted to be."

Ciara smiled, warm, gentle, and equally maternal.

Truth be told, the gesture made my stomach begin to gnaw on itself.

"But what you do not know is that Tito Clayton fell out of touch with all his friends now among the Lions staff." Ciara tilted her head. "He pushed us all away because of his addiction. Truth be told, when he called me in the hospital after his last overdose, we hadn't talked since he got terminated from the Rangers. He never told me he would be clean. He knew better than to promise me such. But, he had no one else left. And I was there for him because he needed someone. Because he was the only man alive who could understand my grief."

I didn't want to ask such invasive questions, but I knew this tied into the woman whom our stadium was named after. Ciara must have picked up on my curiosity, since she then said, "You know Clay understands you. You know he has seen through the same arduous changes you will need to uphold should you want to—maybe not be happy—but to be ok. And you have something Clay never did."

I knew the answer, but I was still arrogant to ask, "What is it?"

"People who will support you should you see it through."

A silence lingered. I felt my rib cage begin to concave into the flesh beneath, poking all my organs once confined until my blood seeped from the gaps. Before I could dare and admit that Ciara was right, Robyn and Davi came into view. Their expressions were equally tight as the one beholding to self despite little reason to warrant such since they would never care about the point Ciara was making like Chase or Tito Clayton might.

Another herd of uniform footsteps came towards us, and I turned to watch my tito and Lisanna join the four of us. Tito Clayton's expressions softened by the slightest of margins when he gazed upon the three Lions Xavier needed dead at any conceivable cost despite none of us doing anything to warrant our heads on a pike. I glanced behind me, back at Davi and Robyn to see they both met my gaze, studying my face until I lost all resolve to answer for the accusation tucked between their eyes. I turned back to gaze upon Tito Clayton to watch him begin to inspect me, turning my face with his calloused hands. I did not gaze back at my bag to warrant the search and seizure of my only tether to stability, and I knew such tricks had worked when I watched Tito Clayton move to do the same to Robyn and Davi.

I didn't think anything we had done at practice would begin to warrant such behavior—not counting my breaking of Conner Villanueva's nose—when I remembered the commonality linking the three of us, being the brunt of Xavier Hidalgo's scorn.

And I knew then that this meant Xavier had been to the Schaffer campus, the only conceivable place I had once thought to be safe from me. And I knew better than to dwell on such a truth that would warrant both a complete and total mental breakdown and a relapse of all my favored vices, so I focused instead on the factor of my newfound dependence now given to me by an imagined icy smile and malice-ridden glare.

I didn't think Xavier knew much about me in the eight years we had been actively kept apart. Truth be told, I was more than comfortable with the silence shared knowing any hope for a constructive conversation was long past the two of us. After all, what was there left to be said between us knowing he needed me dead to come to terms with something I could only assume he had yet to accept or even address in terms of self? I didn't think it was fair that I had to pay for whatever damage was wrought upon the brother I had made an active choice to forget. But as soon as I had asked myself such, I knew I was just as complicit of such in terms of my own myriad of unmanaged problems even if the motive behind our shared sin was infinitely different. Xavier intended to see me hurt. And I could never begin to say I was not guilty of the same considering all I had done to wash the same original of my very creation away.

And I realized the newfound weight of my gifted bottles of vodka meant Xavier wanted to spurn my own inevitable self-destruction faster than the pace it was already steamrolling towards. I realized then that him giving me the scar on my face was not so much about justice in terms of his own righteousness as it was a hope to elicit a reaction that would cost me my life as I knew it. That Xavier was not some clumsy and equally arrogant man who carelessly harmed others without care of its consequence. The truth of the matter was that Xavier was vindictive, calculating, and smarter than I had once assumed he was. Xavier knew the damage he was causing. Xavier knew he was hurting people by seeing that they pay for what he deemed a betrayal in blood.

And I think the most heinous of all, was that he did not care.

Xavier wanted to hurt me.

Xavier wanted me to suffer.

And I knew then I could no longer group myself among the same like of a monster who knew the damage he had wrought but did not care about the people who would come to pay its price.

14

ROBYN

"**WE'RE ALL SAFE AS** I can now see," Tito Clayton said, cutting through the silence taking root between me, Lisanna, Davi, Ciara, and Dante. Tito Clayton then moved to accuse Dante and I of something, looking between us to say, "Have we been safe this entire time?"

I glanced at Dante before answering. He adjusted his duffel bag resting atop his left shoulder, moving to meet my gaze. I knew the tense stare, timid eyes, and lips pressed together in matching, thin slits making up the whole of his face well. After all, it was the same expression I displayed when lying to the people who I owed honesty to in regard to my own addiction. I think it was safe to assume Dante had a new supply to taper in regard to one of his banned vices; a truth Xavier had made a conscious effort to learn in hopes it would see Dante answer the question on who would have the last laugh in regard to the ever-depressing Dante Alonso Hidalgo tale. Xavier could care less who wrote the ending, as long as it ended for a reason I did not think any other person would come to know but me. And maybe standing before Dante knowing this truth would not hurt as much if I was not the only person alive who Xavier had dared to confess it to.

I knew Davi and Breanna were right when saying I did not have a hand in the hurt Xavier had wrought upon the Lions. However, I did not agree with the truth they were trying to spin that Xavier had manipulated me in seeing his side. Mostly because at one point in time, Xavier had loved me as I had once loved him. Whether the platonic affection we shared was housed between the shelves of the Wesley library we had met under the guise of studying that would never be accomplished. Or, when he babied me after I had caught a particularly unforgiving strain of the flu that saw me bedridden, and my body fighting against me every inch in attempting to heal from it. Or, even most intimate of all, helping court Lisanna when I realized she was the same first love that I had fallen out of contact with ten years ago, who had moved away after her mother was murdered. Even if he did not still love me still, I knew better than to think I could be so calloused to sever our relationship as cleanly as he had in the wake of what he deemed a betrayal.

And maybe this even mix of anger and melancholy would not have swallowed me whole if the betrayal that saw me cast out of Eden really was not even much of one at all.

I moved to address Tito Clayton, bearing the lie Dante and I now shared evenly atop my shoulders. I smiled, warm, inviting, and equally two-faced to answer, "We are all unharmed, Tito. We have been. Xavier did not show his face to either of us."

I watched Dante exhale in the loosening of his body language. Tito Clayton had not been watching him, mostly accusing me of being the deceitful party. I thought that much was warranted considering what I had just done. After all, while Dante and I shared the common axis beholding to the realm of addiction, I was more susceptible to its teeth mostly because my struggle with sobriety was new. While Dante's was all but nonexistent, Dante either did not have immediate access to it thanks to his uncle's intervention, or he was simply very good at hiding it. And knowing the truth of addiction as intimately as the three of us did, we all knew better than to think the latter was anything other than the truth.

And Tito Clayton did not know the tells that would out me. After all, lying and addiction went hand in hand, and I had gone out of my way to make a conscious effort to see them repressed. I liked to believe doing so would lessen my inevitable betrayal knowing that as long as I kept the truth hidden, life would remain the same. But what I knew now was that the thing about every lie, is that the other side of its face will always come to light no matter how much bedrock you cake it under. After all, such was true in terms of my life knowing I had hidden my opioid habit from Lisanna for a good three months. And maybe seeing my façade dependent on the man who had first thought the stranger atop the staircase of a Sigma Chi party was the same Lisanna Wilson who had left me behind ten years ago was what saw me outed.

But I knew better now than to think there was anything I could do to avoid the truth. And having Xavier tell it in the most grandiose way—only he could begin to conceive—did not come from a place of betterment. Truth be told, Xavier wanted me to meet the same fate he had once tried to see through as Davi and Dante before me. Outing my addiction to Lisanna was just an added twist of malice now resting in the pit of my stomach; with the blood of Xavier's betrayal seeping into the consistent shade of my brown skin hidden beneath even lengths of cloth that contrasted the peach beholding to his own.

"Well, not all hope is lost then," Tito Clayton answered. He glanced at Davi, who I had not noticed was wearing sweatpants and a hoodie in a matching shade of yellow. "Thanks for warning me, Davi. Where did you hear that he was coming here?"

"Elliot still talks to me," Davi answered, the words rolling ever so perfectly off her tongue. "Truth be told, I think he feels bad about his part in me and Xavier's relationship. Doesn't mean I can't use his conscience against him when he never did anything when Xavier beat me until I was black and blue."

I winced. I glanced at Davi to watch her meet my gaze, looking me up and down before settling to say, "What forgiveness is owed to him when he refuses to cut out the source that saw me abused, anyway?"

"I suggest you make up your mind on where I stand on your own," I replied, curt and between a scowl. "I know what I have done, Davi. The truth is not lost on me. And you can deem me under the context of any kind of status you want, but you will not lie to me when it comes to matters of my own redemption."

Davi was quiet. She turned to face Dante, glancing down at his bag before settling her gaze against mine again to say, "Dante, let's get out of here."

I was annoyed at the two-faced nature of Davi's remark. I knew trust would not be warranted when I had done nothing to earn it, but I did not think her intention to mislead me in regard to my atonement was very fair. Granted, I would never be entitled to such a thing, but something did not feel right in the pit of my stomach in regard to what was said. I knew better than to think on such now when the prejudice Xavier had conditioned me to believe was going to take an effort to unlearn. And maybe that meant starting with being honest in regard to my inevitable relapse, but I could not bring myself to bear the weight of entitled responsibility like Dante before me. Maybe that made me equally a coward. But I would not need to answer for such now when I had a new array of tiny, white pills to do the atonement for me.

Tito Clayton then looked at Ciara to ask, "What did you talk to Dante about, Ciara?"

"Nothing important," Ciara answered. "It's not anything that hasn't been said already anyway."

Tito Clayton met such with a nod. I finally brought my gaze to look at Lisanna. She was already staring at me, seeming to dissect my body language and expression with careful thought. I knew better than to think she would ever know I was now lying to her again. After all, I had gotten away with it for three months while she lay ignorant to the problem that would come to kill her the same way it would kill me. The thing is, though, she would survive it. And I never would. Not when I was making a conscious effort to no longer be righteous like the man on the Lions of my same truth.

ACT TWO

CELENA BOŽOVIĆ

CENTER #27

AUGUST 25, 1994

ZODIAC SIGN
VIRGO

FAVORITE FOOD
BLINCHIKI

MAJOR
SPORTS SCIENCE

1 5

DANTE

I **WALKED INTO MY** new English class to see a man who looked as if he hailed from the same island nation as Tito Clayton and me. However, his skin was much deeper than the shade beholding to my uncle. His nose was the same wide and equally flat shape of my own, and he gave me a smile as if the two of us were the oldest and fondest of friends that I did not return. Instead, I retreated to claim a seat in the back of his classroom as he then began to instruct us on a lesson about grammar I did not need to pay attention to since I already knew what it was he was talking about.

Instead, my mind wandered to the newfound vice in my immediate disposal, being the bottles of vodka now hidden in the depths of my duffel bag; the only conceivable place in the confines of my prison cell where I knew Tito Clayton would not search. I knew going so far to hide my new access to the poison was not being very forthright nor honest in terms of self. I knew doing so very well made me a bad person. And maybe Robyn Zaragoza was not as bad as I once thought when she would make a conscious effort to help me hide my newfound truth. But I knew better than to think the sense of camaraderie between Robyn and I had come from some kind of righteousness. After all, what was there to call us knowing we would keep the open secret of our addiction no matter what harm it caused to the people around us? I thought the only term fitting was cowardice. We were not brothers and sisters in arms, united in a shared struggle. We were cowards bending beneath a shared weight, who would help the other lie even if telling the truth was the only way to quite literally solve all our fucking problems.

I glanced at the clock above the board my professor had been lecturing with. There was about thirty minutes left of the class, and I was counting down the seconds until it was over. I had been required to find a new one. My old college composition professor had taken a dislike for my so-called 'outburst' when I told him the reason why no one passed our most recent test was because he simply could not teach.

I'd come to learn in my academic career that most teachers and professors do not care so much about the subject as they do about power and control. Maybe this new class would prove to be different, but I held little hope for such when the power dynamic between student and professor was one—in my experience—not so much one of mutual respect as it was about making the party beholding all of the power feel better than the one that held none. I mean, respect is not something everyone is entitled. It is something that is earned. And knowing such, why should I give it out to academics who obviously cannot teach and leave the work to the students who are there to learn?

"Alright, we've gone through everything we've needed today, so I'll let you guys out early. Remember the homework is the quiz in Canvas, ok?"

The shuffling of backpacks took the place of a thank you. I slung mine over my left shoulder, walking past the professor's desk when he then said, "Dante Hidalgo if I'm not mistaken?"

I turned to him. "The only. I take it introductions would make sense considering I am the new student in your class."

"That they would. I'm Max Zaragoza. You probably know my ex-wife, Bruna Allenbach."

"That I do. Was it you who set up my tito with the job here at Schaffer?"

"Correct, I was the party that told Clay he should apply. Your uncle and I have been old friends since we first met here and played hockey together. Of course, I was never as good as him to hope to go pro, but I was decent enough to help him get to those NESCAC Championships."

"That's all he could hope for, I think," I answered.

Standing before Max Zaragoza, I knew that he was the party Tito Clayton had scorned in regard to his own sobriety. That is, before he had pushed everyone away to revel in his own favored vice until his last overdose. It would be then when he realized he now had no one left, calling Ciara in an attempt to reclaim the life he had made a conscious effort to sacrifice in exchange for a high that would never give him anything back. And there were so many questions I wanted to ask Max in regard to how he had come to forgive Tito Clayton, or even if he ever had. But the expression looking at me with careful and watchful study told me such an ask would not be warranted until I had agreed I, too, had a problem. And to be honest, I did not think I was ready to admit to such. At least, not while I was sober enough to bear the weight of its truth atop my shoulders anyway.

"You don't have to think there's any merit to what I'm saying, Dante," Max said after some thought. "But I'd like you to listen."

I swallowed the lump in my throat to then say, "Of course, Professor Zaragoza."

"I have been on the other end of addiction in terms of my daughter and in terms of my best friend. And before you rebuke me, I just want you to know, should you need it, I will be an unbiased viewpoint in terms of it should you need it."

"Of course, Professor Zaragoza."

He smiled. "My office room number is on the syllabus. It's open to you should you need it, Dante."

I gave a nod, feeling my stomach begin to swallow itself whole as I exited the classroom to find Chase and Davi waiting for me.

"You good, Dante? You look like you've seen a ghost."

I shook my head, swallowing the lump in my throat to then say, "No, yeah, I'm fine. Let's go to the dining hall, shall we?"

Davi and Chase looked at each other. Neither party probed further. Instead, we walked to the dining hall in silence with Chase and Davi's hands on my back as they guided me out.

16

ROBYN

"**HOW IS PRE-MED** treating you, Liz?" I asked, taking a sip of my coffee.

Lisanna peered above her homework. "I'm teetering on the edge of a complete mental breakdown, but the thing about me, is that I'm good at balance."

I laughed at that.

Lisanna smiled too.

"Have you talked with Aspen at all?"

Lisanna frowned. I did find some comfort knowing I was the only person who could begin to talk about her past considering I was the only remnant of it she had made a conscious choice to hold onto. And I knew better than to dwell on such when the matter of my addiction complicated such things, but we didn't need to think about such now when there was no circumstance that would warrant an immediate relapse. I knew with Xavier now having a bounty over my head the latter would reach an inevitable crescendo, but right now, it was a distant and equally unaddressed memory that held no point other than to dwell on the matter of my own misery.

"I have not."

"I know he still writes you. What harm is there in writing back?"

Lisanna looked as if she were going to spew venom from her tongue when she then said, "I can't bring myself to face him knowing I'm the only reason he's locked in there, rotting away when the powers at play have thrown away his key."

"The failures of the American justice system are not your fault and neither is Aspen being trapped in it either. You were a child, Liz. Who in their right mind would blame a child for something like that?"

"You know who," Lisanna replied, now annoyed.

"Well, he can't answer for such now can he? When he's very much dead like he fucking deserves to be?"

Lisanna was quiet, then glancing down at her scientific equations to then say, "I know your heart is in the right place, Robyn. I know you want nothing but my best interest at heart. But I cannot bring myself to answer Aspen when it sure as fuck feels like I'm the only reason he is there."

"He made his choice to take the blame knowing what it would cost him," I answered in a hushed tone to not give illusion to the others gathered around us that were discussing something as heinous as murder. "And, my love, I cannot let you continue to blame yourself for that when he held all the power, and you held none."

Lisanna opened her mouth to answer when we turned to the presence looming at our table to find it was a woman I had seen before, but as to where, I was unsure. She was easily beautiful, with a long, curved nose that was a perfect centerpiece to sharp and equally defined face. The shape was smeared in an even shade of taupe, with a birthmark resting at the ride side of her chin framed on either side of long, straight hair dyed in a fading gradient of blonde to brown.

She smiled, looking between us to then say, "Lisanna and Robyn, right? The other girls on the Schaffer Lions?"

"We are," I answered for Lisanna and me. "You are?"

"Leila Johnson, I'm on the Lions too." She smiled. "I didn't get to introduce myself at practice considering what went down. But I'd thought I'd say hi since we're teammates and all."

"Why don't you sit with us?" Lisanna asked. "Truth be told, I can't stand most of the people on the Lions, and I would like to chat with someone who doesn't seem as unbearable as the rest of them."

"Oh, yeah, of course!"

Leila pulled up a chair. She placed her books atop the table, smearing them across the surface as I studied the texts belonging to her. I noticed they were all beholden to freshman required classes, and I wondered if my father would be among the ranks of her professors considering he taught one class for freshmen at Schaffer, being college composition. After all, without his position of tenured, academic standing among the Schaffer staff, Tito Clayton would not have had the means to acquire his own as head coach of the Lions when the matter of his sobriety was still new and equally unvetted. I suppose there was some comfort knowing that even despite the damage both had wrought upon their relationship, there was still enough of a foundation to dare and look the pain in the eye and attempt to mend it. I glanced at Lisanna, wondering if we could ever begin to do the same even if I already knew the answer. It was a truth I could never begin to speak aloud knowing its shared weight was something I had yet to be worthy of whether it be sober or having taken enough pills to finally believe I was.

"What's your major?" Lisanna asked, moving to rest her chin atop her raised hand. "I'm pre-med."

"Pre-med?! How the fuck are you even alive, Lisanna?"

Lisanna smirked a bit, glancing at me as if to say she had taken a liking to Leila. She then turned back to address her accusation to say, "That's the thing about being a first-generation college student, no? Doing the work no one else could begin to do for us?"

"Yes, yes, I suppose you're right," Leila answered. She looked at me. "And you, Robyn?"

"Fashion design," I answered. "Truth be told, I have a final I'm expected to design an evening gown for, and I'm totally lost at what to think of." I held up my sketchbook, flipping through the blank pages. "See? Nothing."

"Maybe you need a muse," Leila answered. "Lisanna could do that for you, no?"

We laughed.

I then answered to say, "Art needs to come from emotion to dare and attempt to move people. And tell me, what emotion other than fatigue can I feel knowing I'm stuck here at Schaffer as a prisoner?"

Lisanna looked at me, but I did not meet her gaze. Instead, I tapped my long, acrylic nails atop the table the three of us were gathered.

Leila then said, "Your life doesn't have to be defined by your mistakes, Robyn. I don't think that much is even fair in regard to yourself. Anyone is capable of change. Even you. Even Xavier."

I knew better than to let Leila's ignorance to the truth of her last remark get to me when I knew such could never be true. It's not that Xavier was not capable of change. Truth be told, Leila was right in the sense everyone was no matter how undeserving they might seem to be. Hell, even Dante was capable of such a feat even if I knew both he and Xavier would refuse to see it through. Xavier and Dante were two sides of the same coin. One lay damage to others in payment for what was done to him, and the other destroyed himself to atone for the same mortal sins.

The latter was a truth Xavier, too, knew well. He had given Dante the scar on his face knowing the genetic predisposition for collateral damage at the expense of self as seen in their shared mother's side. Xavier may be cold, calloused, and equally cruel, but he was never stupid. After all, what else was there to call him knowing he had only ever introduced me to my favored vice of tiny, white pills in hopes to get me hooked, so he would have complete and total control over me when—what he called—a betrayal demanded such?

And truth be told, the only comfort I found in his cruelty was that he, too, was dependent on the vice we had abused under the guise of healing, even if I knew better now than to think such had ever been true.

Lisanna then answered for me, as if she could read my mind to say, "Everyone is capable of change, yes. But to lump Xavier in such an equation is idiotic knowing he refuses to see it through."

Leila got quiet, frowning to say, "I didn't mean—"

"I know what you meant, but next time I would steer clear from a topic you don't know much about and speak on it as if you do."

Leila frowned, but eventually nodded as a palatable silence now had taken root between the three of us. I then answered in hopes to lessen it by saying, "I don't take it personally. Truth be told, if I did, I think I would have gone insane considering how charming Xavier is when he wants to be." I then crossed my arms to lean over to the table to say, "So, while we're all here, what should we take bets on in the coming season?"

"You gamble?" Leila asked, trying to play off her obvious interest.

"Only when it's at others's expense," I replied, smirking. "There are three things I think are worth putting money on. You want to hear them, Leila?"

Lisanna laughed. Mostly because she already knew of my fondness for all pursuits involving gossip as long as it was not at my immediate expense.

Leila then said, "You already mentioned them to Lisanna. I take it."

"That I did. Considering there is no one else on the Lions who could begin to understand my fondness of such, I thought you might like to know."

"I'm in your care, Robyn."

I smiled, flipping my hair to one side before saying, "Well, I know Chase is into Celena. I also know Damien is going to cause drama because of the matter of looks. And lastly, it's rather obvious to me Dante is into Rue and Rue is into Dante."

"Dante is gay?" Leila asked innocently.

"A man does not look like that and be anything else but gay. Don't tell me you actually thought Dante was hot," I replied.

"Dante is handsome," Lisanna answered. "You were friends with Xavier, who is his older brother. You're so shallow

I don't think you have the capacity to be friends with anyone you don't deem nice to look at."

I laughed. "What, is it so wrong to want my immediate company to look as good as me? I can't have ugly people bringing down the group average."

"You say that like you didn't fuck Pia before we started dating."

"And? You did too."

Lisanna smirked a bit. "I can see we have the same type, do we not?"

I returned the gesture. "It would make sense. Truth be told, looking at anyone else but you since we started dating is enough to make me break into hives."

"Good to know you still have a brain in there."

"And it's good to know you're still capable of having a decent conversation about something other than school."

Leila looked between us, lost. Lisanna and I burst out into a shared chorus of laughter, when Leila then said, "Yeah, let's get back to stuff I know about too, huh?"

"Right, right," I answered. I looked at her. "So, we can bet on any of those things, or we can bet on something else. Since you're new to our ritual, I'll let you pick."

"These are all good options. Except, truth be told, betting against Rue and Dante is simply a losing cause knowing no one has ever looked at me like that."

"Smart woman. Don't worry, I'll sucker someone else into it to get a fat wad of cash."

"Then, what about Davi and Damien becoming a thing?"

Least to say, the proposition had exceeded my interest knowing I knew Davi's history with men more intimately than Leila could ever hope to. I knew it was an easy means to win a few hundred dollars, so I offered my hand and said, "You have a deal, Leila Johnson. Hundred bucks going to the camp that Davi and my brother become a thing first, ok?"

Leila smiled, bright and equally radiant as we shook hands to cement our covenant made in blood. I turned to Lisanna to see she was smiling, small and equally fierce to then say, "And I'll add fifty bucks to Leila's cause too."

"Betting against your own girlfriend? How in bad taste of you, Liz."

"I live for the drama of it all, Robyn. It's fun."

"No wonder we're meant to be, no?"

Lisanna laughed at that. And I felt my heart begin to beat against the confines of its cage as I tried to bury the looming threat of failure knowing I could never give her what she needed of me.

17

DANTE

DAVI, CHASE, AND I claimed a table near the exit of the dining hall.

Its name was I had yet to memorize since I had only been on campus for a month, and most of that time was training for the looming start of the hockey season. Truth be told, my life held little value outside the expectation my uncle had placed upon me in terms of a talent he and Celena had deemed me worthy of. I would never begin to know what I had done in my life to be worthy of such a thing, and maybe I was better off never knowing since I didn't think I would be able to digest the answer anyway.

Truth be told, I knew I would be able to stomach such coming from my uncle since it could be argued he owed me such courtesies. But the same truth coming from Celena would do nothing but leave a sour taste in my mouth after its weight had spurned a complete and total mental breakdown between equal portions of pills, razorblades, and vodka. And knowing such an end was something I could never possibly be above, I wondered if the coming death of what she claimed would soon become the other half of the future of the NHL would be mourned, despite knowing that in the end, none of it would come to matter.

I pushed my Schaffer food across my plate, staring at the foreign shapes making up my salad. My sweet tooth had been all but butchered in the wake of coming to Schaffer since my uncle forbade me from anything sugary or processed knowing it would curb my performance as his starting goalie. I knew better than to argue with such since it was his position as head coach that even saw me obtain an all-expenses paid, full ride at his alma mater since any children of Schaffer staff were entitled to such.

It made me wonder why Robyn had decided to go to Wesley instead of Schaffer since she, too, would be entitled to this financial gain knowing her father had worked here prior. While I would have no prior knowledge to be beholding of such information, I had seen Robyn around the Schaffer campus during my own babysitting sessions under the careful watch of my uncle, before either of us had aged into the rite to attend. Maybe her parents were rich. Or, maybe such handouts were beneath her. Either way, I was unsure really what to make of Robyn Zaragoza, mostly because I knew now that she was a woman of my same truth.

While no one was telling me the truth of Robyn's transfer outright, I knew she had covered for me in the wake of my newfound fix pertaining to one of my favored vices. And this could only ever mean she knew the truth of my addiction like she did the matter of her own. Maybe knowing this meant she could not be as bad as I had once thought, but I knew better than to think such when our shared trait of a newfound camaraderie was not at the expense of self. In any other context, her standing by my side could very well have been admirable, and it may have even changed her already deplorable standing in my mental hierarchy. But we both knew what her solidarity meant in terms of being clean, and even if I don't think it was entirely warranted, I knew better than to take such as an extending of the olive branch as it was a matter of self-preservation. Because I had yet to know where Robyn's loyalties lied. Even if this lingering aftertaste smeared across the length of my tongue told me I should know better than to attribute her selfishness to anything other than the commonality of our shared truth as brother and sister bound to our corresponding vice.

"Dante," Davi called.

I turned to look at her.

"You haven't said anything the entire time we've been here," Davi answered.

I glanced at the now empty seat once beholding to Chase. I then turned back to Davi to see her expression looked as if she had read right through my silence.

"Sobriety?"

"Something like that."

Davi frowned, moving to cross both her arms. "Then, I suppose I should ask, have you had any suicidal thoughts recently?"

"Thoughts, yes. But a plan is all but impossible when you're in an improvised sober jail thanks to your straightedge uncle."

Davi frowned, moving to rest her hand above my own. The same shade of brown shared between us blended into a continuous, even lacquer. She then smiled, moving her thumb to stroke the back of my hand as I brought my gaze back to her.

She then said, "I want you here, Dante. I know it's hard to believe, but it's true. Would I really lie to you in regard to something as important as your life?"

I knew Davi was right, but I didn't think believing her was as easy as she was suggesting. The truth of our shared trait of depression meant she understood the bout of my own more than someone else might. However, that did not mean she could understand it word for word and beat for beat when the circumstance that spurned it had been removed from her but was still present in my own life. I glanced down at her hand again, watching the painted over lengths of red circling my skin as if the motion would free me of this inherent, original sin that was my very creation. Instead of daring to answer such, I moved my other hand to prop up my head.

I turned back to Davi to then say, "Your mom. Has she tried to contact you? Has Xavier?"

Davi shook her head. "No. It seems neither party is interested in me any longer when I have long ago burnt that bridge. I suppose the same thing could be said about your own."

I sighed, moving to play with the food on my plate. "If Xavier or my mother tried to contact me, I don't think I would be having this conversation with you."

"You know you are going to be miserable the rest of your life if you don't make an effort to change. Right?"

"I'd rather be miserable than change when I don't think I would even come to like the person I would become, Davi."

Davi opened her mouth to speak when a uniform herd of footsteps came up to her left. We turned to the noise to find Rue Oba staring intently at the two of us. Davi looked him up and down before retracting her hand, deeming him a cause beyond saving. Rue smirked a bit, the gesture confident and equally crooked as he moved to sit next to me. Chase opened his mouth to indicate Rue had stolen his place, but Rue waved his hand to dismiss the accusation. Chase looked between us before I, too, indicated it was fine. He then adjusted the weight of his new position evenly across his shoulders to sit next to Davi.

Chase then said, "I found Rue in line when I was checking out for my food. Hope you don't mind I brought him along."

"I don't care," I answered.

Chase looked at me as if he didn't believe me.

I knew better than to argue with him.

"So, Rue, how do you like the Lions so far?" Chase asked.

It was no secret he was more socially inclined than Davi and I might be since neither of us could say we were fond of strangers. Truth be told, I didn't think Rue was that much considering we had shared a cigarette under a thick chill of the fall season wafting into my room from an open window. I wondered if he could still smell the mixture of the crisp, winter air, earthy tobacco, and the feeling of his breath dancing across the bridge of my nose like I did.

"It seems fine," Rue answered casually. "I didn't really want to play hockey in college, but Celena came to my school and told me I should play for her. And here I am."

"Celena did that?" I asked.

Everyone turned to me, but I only had eyes for Rue. He met my gaze, eyes dragging down the length of my face to settle on my lips to say, "She did, yes. Alexei was only offered a position on the Lions because I told Celena I would not go without him."

"And they say chivalry is dead," I answered, laughing a bit. I moved my food across my plate again before pointing my fork at Rue to say, "Truth be told, it would have saved me more of a headache if you didn't let Alexei onto the Lions."

"You're just vindictive," Rue answered.

I perked my eyebrows up in surprise as Davi and Chase exchanged glances at each other. My lips curled into a satisfied smile, and I eventually turned to face Rue. I placed both my crossed arms atop the table, crooking my head to face his own as he glanced at my eyes before moving back to gaze upon my lips.

"Not everyone is out to get you. You're on a team, and you might as well be a team player, no? Alexei is just standing up for his brother who, need I remind you, you broke the nose of. You can play coy with anyone else on the Lions, except me. I'll see right through it each and every time, Dante."

I laughed, propping up my head with my hand to say, "And who made you an expert on all things Dante Alonso Hidalgo related?"

"I know you," Rue replied. "And besides, even if I didn't, you're the easiest man in the world to read. All you want to say is across your face anyway."

Chase moved to speak, but I did so first, settling to say behind my smirk, "Aren't you just the most interesting man I have ever met, Rue Oba."

Rue smirked a bit.

Chase then said, "Well, you two seem to get along. Truth be told, I have never known someone who can challenge Dante and get out with any of their teeth."

"When Rue does it it's not stupid," I replied as if that should answer the question even if I knew better than to think it did. But even knowing such did not change that the answer was every bit the truth as I was unsure if I wanted it to be.

"I see," Chase said, equally unconvinced. "But, I guess I should ask the basics, what's your major, and what do you plan on doing after school?"

"I'm a fine arts major," Rue answered, moving to chew some of his campus mandated burrito bowl. "I want to be an artist when I graduate. You know, making money for my paintings and have them displayed in some stuffy gallery."

"Because you hope to be among the same stuffy like?" I asked.

"No," Rue answered. "Just to prove someone like me can break into their stuffiness despite all the barriers at play that I know don't want me there."

"Fascinating," I called. "You are strange."

"Is strange good?"

"Very," I answered, still smirking a bit. "At least, I can't think of it being anything other than good in this context."

Chase then interrupted to say, "You single, Rue?"

Chase glanced at me. I knew he was asking for my sake, but the last thing I was going to do was see through this attraction when all it would do was kill us fucking both.

"I'm open minded even if my interest is already skewed a certain way to a certain person," Rue answered.

I didn't think that was much of an answer at all.

Davi then said, "So, you like someone. Is what I'm getting at."

"I do. I think you know him well. Since it seems we tend to swing in the same direction."

Davi scoffed. Rue smiled, slow, cold, and equally coy. I didn't think it really had any kind of malice behind it as it was a playful declaration of war. Considering the matter of attractiveness, I suppose it was naive to think Rue would not already be spoken for. After all, he embodied every facet and trait of what I thought a man should look like and what a man should be. There was a twinge of jealousy when I gazed upon him which I could not differentiate between wanting to be him or wanting to be liked by him. The emotions had blurred into this cohesive, unfamiliar gnawing. I knew better than to think I could decipher it whether it be in my current state of mind sober, or so drunk off my ass it would inebriate all motor functioning knowing a blackout was imminent.

Maybe that's why I found comfort in vodka to begin with. Mostly because it allowed me to feel and process the emotions I would never allow myself to address sober, and I would never have to remember the weight and degradation that came with their truth the following morning knowing the liquor had purged them from every conceivable orifice of both mind and body. The erasure would reach a point where I could be normal—and even stable again—without doing the mature, emotional labor of facing my problems and daring to address their truth. Maybe that made me a coward. Maybe I would never be anything but. But I did not need to think on such now. I still had four more years of going through the motions until the question of my life and what it was worth would beg for an answer. After my tenure at Schaffer was over, I would no longer be under the watchful, protective eye of my uncle, who only needed me here to prove something to himself in regard to his own recovery.

"I hope you know I'm not the kind of woman to give up easily," Davi called, bringing me back to reality.

"And I'm not the kind of man to be intimidated," Rue replied, smiling. He seemed equally sure on where he stood in this person's mental hierarchy and that Davi ranked beneath him.

"Alright, you guys can hate each other, but not while I'm here and my job is to make all the Lions like each other."

We all turned to Chase.

Chase then said, "So, you mentioned Conner is Alexei's brother. Why didn't you say he was your brother too?"

"Alexei was adopted from the foster care system when we were twelve years old," Rue answered, no emotion poking through the words. "They were in the same foster home and grew up together."

"Imagine, being brothers with Conner Villanueva," I replied.

"He really is not any bit as bad as you make him out to be," Rue replied. "He's always treated me fairly. I don't think we can say the same thing about you in regard to other people."

Chase and Davi moved to speak, but I raised my hand to answer, "Are you always so sharp with your rebukes? What the fuck makes you entitled to claim to know me as intimately as you do?"

"The fact I know you are content with being this miserable because you know nothing else about yourself besides it. And that you refuse to fix yourself because you've found a home in this constant state of self-degradation to the point you can't imagine yourself without it."

I smirked again, then saying, "My, my, my. Rue Oba. Aren't you going to make a beyond pointless hockey season here at Schaffer *all the more interesting*."

18

ROBYN

I **WAS STILL ON** the rotation of needing to be supervised wherever I went on the Schaffer campus. Considering Lisanna was preparing for the looming date to take her exams to get into medical school, I knew better than to take up her already precious time with something as pointless as being my designated chaperone. I was not the kind of woman to ask anyone of such a thing, but Breanna had volunteered her time for some unbeknownst reason.

I'll be honest, I didn't think we had much in common or any kind of inkling of a foundation to build any sense of camaraderie atop of. But I knew better than to comment on such since I was already detested by everyone else on the Lions, and the last thing I needed was another reason for the lot of them to hate me. I would never be entitled to Breanna's kindness, but if she was willing to dare and show it to me knowing the damage I had wrought, I knew better than to be arrogant enough to say no to such a thing.

I walked over to the treadmill, setting the speed to something low since I was on the cool down period of my workout routine. I saw movement out of the corner of my eye to find Breanna take up the machine next to me, seeming to be at the same step of her own workout as me. She offered a smile, settling to say, "Robyn, I was hoping we'd be able to chat."

"About what, exactly?" I asked, hoping it did not come off as rude as I knew it sounded.

"Well, you are the sister of Conner, who neither of us knew you existed until a month ago. I think that gives us plenty to talk about."

"You seem close with my brother," I replied. "Do you like him?"

Breanna smiled, low and equally sweet. I knew better than to prod, so I moved my gaze back to my feet.

She then answered to say, "We're close, you could say. But nothing official. I mean, I'm thinking of hooking up with Damien, truth be told."

I cursed under my breath knowing the money I had set aside would not be won by any party who lay privy to it. I did not let such show on my expression as I then said, "You and Damien? What makes you think of just fucking him?"

"He's handsome, and I'm on the prowl," Breanna replied.

"You're a bad liar."

Breanna smiled. "Well, your brother and Davi have been shacking up for a good few months, and I'm the last woman to get in between something like that. I mean, if Conner likes her, he likes her, you know?"

The drama between my teammates suddenly clicked in a perfect instance. "And you like Conner. But he won't commit. Or, you won't commit. Or, maybe even an equal mixture of both."

"Conner wasn't kidding, you really are smart," Breanna said with a laugh. "No wonder you got a full ride to Wesley. I heard you were valedictorian of your graduating class. Is that true?"

"It is, yes," I answered, meeting her smile with one of my own.

It felt strange getting along with someone I had been conditioned to hate, but I thought I didn't dislike Breanna as I used to. Truth be told, the narrative Elliot had spun of her as the cruel, vindictive woman who instigated violence against him, and he could only hope to defend himself, was one I realized then that could never be true. After all, Breanna never held any of the power in their relationship. I mean, how could she when Elliot towered above six feet and she was a measly five?

"School has always been easy for me. I've never struggled with any subject. I suppose being a jack of all trades really is better than being a master of one."

"School is by all means a scam, but it seems you're an excellent con-woman."

I stared at Breanna.

"In regard to school, of course."

"Right, right."

A silence lingered.

Breanna then said, changing the subject, "But, as I was saying, Davi and Conner have been sleeping together for some time. No one knows on the team except me since it's an open secret Davi likes Dante, but we all know there's no hope for such in regard to his... Well, everything. And I think Dante doesn't like Conner because he's sleeping with Davi, so who knows, he may actually like her back. Truth be told, the Lions are an interfucking mess, and I think you're smart for being above such noise."

"Interfucking is beneath me when I already love a woman and will love her until the day I die," I replied, laughing a bit. "But, why have you and my brother not gotten together, if you don't mind me asking?"

Breanna frowned. "You won't tell anyone?"

"Unless it's at the expense of your sanity and safety, my lips are as good as sealed."

"Well, it's going to be touchy, but I don't want you to blame yourself, ok?"

I knew the subject would now shift back to Elliot. Despite what little hope I held for myself to follow through with such, I said, "Of course, Breanna."

"Well, we know Elliot was not very kind to me. I've gotten over it, but Conner has something that's happened to him in regard to his own past that we can't meet me in the middle with. It's kind of frustrating, to be honest."

I was quiet before saying, "I don't think you're being fair."

"To whom, Conner?"

"Both my brother and yourself."

Breanna looked at me as if I had grown another head. "Why the hell would I not have been fair to myself, Robyn?"

"You aren't calling what Elliot did to you what it is."

"And what was it?"

"Abuse."

Breanna stared at me, expression and lips tight.

"There's nothing else to call it but abuse. Giving him the benefit of the doubt is giving him the higher ground he's robbed you of the entire time you were together. You owe him nothing anymore, Breanna. You owe yourself the truth. You owe yourself honesty."

Breanna's mask cracked by a fraction of an inch. For a brief moment, I could see the scared, timid victim Elliot had forced her to become in the wake of his violence until an empty, people pleasing smile once again found its home on her round, unblemished face. I wanted to tell her she could confess what she had been forced to endure and I would never be so heinous to tell a soul. I wanted so desperately for her to find it in her heart to forgive me even if I knew I could never be worthy of such. And I wanted with every part of my being to be the good, just person I could never bring myself to be while under the influence of Xavier Hidalgo; where he fed the most delicious and unforgiving of poisons knowing doing so would leave me dependent on him for the rest of my life.

I was not ignorant that the truth of our relationship now was not so much on equal footing as it was on differing statuses beholding to addict and supplier. Even if Xavier's own addiction brought me some comfort knowing he, too, had not come out of his taking unscathed, it did not change how rebuilding my life without him was all but impossible. And there was only one other person alive who could begin to understand such, even if she now hated me and had every reason to.

A crowd had begun to gather around one of the gym televisions, which was a strange sight in and of itself knowing no one who would regularly come to one would care about such. I had now noticed a wash of quiet dust over the room when I glanced at Breanna. She met my gaze, and we turned back to the television to find Celena's father and head coach of the Wesley Cardinals, Andrei Božović, before a camera, arrogant and haughty as ever.

I glanced at Breanna who met my gaze a last time before moving to join the crowd gathered. I followed behind her but kept my distance. Someone raised the volume, and I turned back to the television to watch the interview unfold. It was no secret the Wesley and Schaffer hockey teams wanted each other dead since the rivalry Tito Clayton and Andrei harbored in the NHL had carried over into their careers after their time with the league had ended. I may have only known a scant amount of information as to how deep the animosity ran between both schools knowing I was not beholding to the same expectation playing before for Wesley's female team. But based on the interested parties surrounding me on all sides, I knew either school would only ever be satisfied until an even coat of blood from the other had been smeared across the curves and protruding shapes making up their knuckles.

"Andrei, welcome. You rarely do interviews, so I'm glad I've been given this opportunity to talk to you."

"The pleasure is all mine," Andrei called.

The same thick, Eastern European accent soaked up his words as seen in his only and eldest daughter. Now that I thought about it, Elliot's was not as prominent as the others in his same familial lineage.

"Now, championships. Clayton Alonso used to have a sort of monopoly in regard to NESCAC titles under his belt during his tenure as head coach of the Schaffer Lions. We all know of your famed rivalry as documented in your shared NHL careers. I suppose the question I'm trying to ask is, what's the secret that has seen you achieve great success?"

"Simple, do not have women play on your team."

Whispers began to shroud the people gathered. The camera panned to the interviewer to find she was of the same gender

Andrei had made a conscious effort in insulting. She bore the weight of his sexism evenly atop her shoulders, crossing her legs and adjusting her posture accordingly to then say, "I take it you think the partnership between your daughter and Clayton Alonso has not been as fruitful as we can all assume Clayton expected it to be. Why is that?"

"Celena has too much ego to lead a team," Andrei said.

I glanced at Breanna to see all her attention was fixated on the almost hallucinatory vision of her ex-boyfriend's father before her.

"Truth be told, Clayton only scouted her in hopes to get a dig in on me. And it worked out for both of them since they both wanted to scorn me and prove me wrong that women have no place in a sport where the men rule unchallenged. But as you've said, ever since Celena has graced the Lions's roster, there has been not a single championship won by the famed and equally great Clayton Alonso. And there is only one factor in such. And it is my firebrand daughter who is trying to play a man's role in a place a woman cannot meet it."

The interviewer cleared her throat, glancing at her notes. She moved her gaze back to Andrei Božović with a glare so venomous I was convinced she was going to unhinge her jaw and swallow him whole.

"Speaking on that, Celena, arguably, has the best statistics in the entire NCAA. The only player who comes close to her in terms of talent is Xavier Alonso, but he has never been quite the same after she broke his collarbone last year in the midst of their playoff game."

I winced knowing that break was the catalyst that saw the both of us supplied with our prescription of Oxycontin. The image of those same tiny, white pills clouded my vision. I bit the inside of my cheek. I hoped the copper finish of blood would give me something else to think about other than the almost muscle memory of getting high with a man who no longer loved me as I still did him.

"What I'm getting at is that your daughter is probably going to become the first woman to grace an NHL team. She is destined to be something great in a way few others can say the same. Celena has always had the potential to be something greater, and she always will. I just think your blatant sexism is clouding the obvious matter of her skill."

Andrei laughed. He adjusted his suit coat to then say, "Then, why don't you have her come on here and answer my accusations for me? After all, if she is any good like you say, she will stop the petty, immature silence she had decided to take since her first scouting knowing she is scared of the truth." Andrei then smiled again, settling to say, "After all, playing such stupid games for a man who likes to shoot up heroin rather than do his fucking job will warrant such stupid prizes, no?"

I got so sick of hearing Andrei speak I pushed through the crowd to stand at Breanna's right. She did not turn to face me, instead, saying, "Well, you heard him didn't you, Robyn?"

I nodded.

Breanna didn't meet my gaze, then saying with venomous lips curled into a coy smile, "Looks like the coming hockey season? *Well, it's fucking war.*"

19

DANTE

IN THE WAKE OF Andrei's interview trashing his daughter and my uncle at each and every mention, Tito Clayton had summoned all his Lions at the Nora Wilson Hockey Center to deal with the aftermath.

Truth be told, I had only seen Celena angry less than a handful of times, and even I knew better than to purposely get in her way in the aftermath. Celena was not so much violent with her anger as she was unpredictable, and anyone being stupid enough to push one of her buttons would ultimately pay the price for it. I knew keeping her and Alexei separate would be crucial in seeing no bloodshed between her and her Lions. Considering my size, I knew the role of mediator in the wake of any kind of violence was not so much an ask of my tito as it was a requirement. I didn't mind such, though. After all, that was the entire point of seeing me gain all this muscle anyway. I might as well put it to good use since I would never be strong enough to face the man I hoped to wrought it upon anyway.

I knocked on the door of the women's locker room. No answer came, but I knew despite such I would be welcome inside knowing the gravity of the situation and the people gathered. I motioned for Chase and Rue to follow, and Davi gave a nod as she kept company of the other Lions gathered outside knowing an irate Celena was something better dealt with by people who knew what the hell they were doing. Not that I thought Rue had much experience in that regard, but he had Celena's respect knowing she went out of her way to scout him to begin with. And to be honest, that would have to be good enough for now since I wanted to have more cards in my deck should they be needed than having Celena call my bluff.

Walking inside, I could feel Celena's anger take hold around the width of my neck. She did not look up to meet our presence, and I glanced at Tito Clayton to see him give a nod. Breanna was sitting next to Celena on the bench, comforting her with a hand tracing circles around her back. Tito Clayton gave me an expression that told me while she had yet to lay waste to the locker room, that did not mean such was not imminent. I didn't think Celena would be in the wrong for such anyway. I may have nothing to show from my parents but a lighter and an agreed upon silence, but I don't think I would be able to stomach pure, unadulterated vitriol taking its place like Celena had been subject to since starting on the Lions three years ago. And truth be told, even if my parents weren't any better in such regard knowing their silence could be a front to disguise hate, I don't think I envied Celena withstanding it and probably never would.

I sat in the cubby before her. Celena moved piercing, blue eyes up to my gaze as we watched each other. I leaned back, crossing my arms to say, "Do you want comfort, or do you want me to keep it real?"

"It's not going to be what I want to hear regardless," Celena answered.

"Then, I say you go on that show and bite back. Maybe even hit your father a bit for the sake of their ratings."

Celena glanced at Tito Clayton.

He answered, "Going on Dylan's show will simply give Andrei what he's looking for, Dante. It's playing into his hand in terms of what he wants of both me and Celena."

"You can speak for yourself, Coach, but you cannot speak for me," Celena replied, turning to look at my uncle.

Tito Clayton did not flinch at the venom tucked between each of her words.

"Listening to you is how I fucking got here to begin with," Celena spat. "Painted out as this hopeless woman who can't even speak to what the men around her say about her. You've babied me long enough. I say let me show my fucking teeth. Or else, all they're going to think of me is some fucking pushover who runs in the face of vitriol."

Tito Clayton crossed his cloth covered arms to then say, "You're right."

Celena was quiet, as if she had realized the animosity laced between her rebuke was unfair.

"I have been protecting you not letting you do press interviews when your father and your brother—and even my other nephew—did everything to tear you down to any camera they could find. After all, we know how everyone reacted to your first, and I wanted to prevent that kind of unfair fallout again.

Tito Clayton watched Celena with careful thought. "I knew what would come with my scouting of you. Andrei was right in the fact our partnership helps us both scorn him, and that was a factor in our agreement for you to play with me to begin with. But what you have to realize is that Andrei is a man who instigates. He is a man who wants you act on emotion rather than reason, so you embarrass yourself and play into this image as an emotional, vindictive woman he so desperately wants you to be. I've protected you from this while you are under my care because you are my Lion. And as long as you play for me, my job is to keep you safe."

A silence lingered. Celena tucked her head back to gaze at her feet, kicking one forward. She rested her chin atop her propped up palm, her expression quizzical in regard to her next move. I glanced back at Chase and Rue who met my gaze.

Celena then said, "You were right in protecting me, Tito."

Celena met Tito Clayton's gaze, her eyes glinting in an endless circle.

Tito Clayton kept his expression a firm and unyielding neutral.

Celena then said, "And I owe you for that. You could have very well fed me to the wolves when I first started here, but you didn't. And I am forever indebted to your sacrifice, but you cannot baby me forever. If I really do hope to be the first woman gracing the NHL like you've always told me I will be, that means fighting my own battles. Maybe not alone, but with me at the helm. And if there's anything I know how to do, Coach, it's make a fucking fool of the men in my family."

Tito Clayton didn't miss a beat when he said, "Then, I suppose I should give Dylan Rivera a call. We're all good here?"

"Yes," the five of us chorused.

"Good. I'll be in my office. Knock if you need me."

Tito Clayton swept his gaze across his Lions that were gathered, eventually retreating back to his office with his door clicking behind him.

A silence lingered.

Chase then said, "It's not fair how they treat you, Celena."

"I came into this post knowing what would come," Celena answered. "Feeling bad for me is pointless in every regard."

"Doesn't make it any bit right as we all know it isn't," Chase said, quiet after a bit. His voice was soft spoken and gentle, an obvious affection tucked between each word. "You never deserved to be treated this way. And I'll always believe such no matter who says otherwise."

"Thank you, Chase," Celena said, somewhat rigid. "It's good to know the Lions are on my side, I suppose."

Breanna glanced at me. I met the suggestion laced between her folded, brown eyes to then say, "You would be an idiot to think we'd let you do this alone, by the way."

"I thought so," Celena said. "Which is why you're doing the interview with me."

Least to say, it was the most outlandish thing I could have expected to come from between her lips. Quizzically, I replied, "And what makes me qualified to do so, Celena?"

"You have accusations to answer to in regard to your brother, too," Celena replied. "And this is where I intend to announce our partnership to the world. This is where I intend to give you a future, for the world to see. You have a choice to make, Dante. Either let Xavier win and kill yourself, or spit in the face of the man who marked you by letting me make you something great."

Celena didn't stick around to hear my answer, standing upright. She glanced at Breanna before saying, "The choice is yours. But you would be smart to make up your mind before we go on Dylan Rivera's show, and I do not look like an idiot for believing in a man who could never believe in himself."

Celena flipped her hair, exiting the locker room. Breanna followed her out, her gaze lingering on me for a few seconds before the locker room door closed behind her.

I did not like the corner Celena had backed me into; the choice of either failing her or failing self. After all, I knew the weight my promise that I would kill myself at twenty-one came with, but the weight of letting Celena down would mean extending such cruelty to a woman who would never begin to deserve it. I suppose that's the reason why one of the signs of suicidal ideation is isolation. Mostly because tying a noose around your neck sure is easier when every connection to this earthly tether had long been severed before your spinal cord could begin to say the same. There was this unconscionable comfort in loneliness. Because I knew that should I take my own life, there was nothing I would come to leave behind. That even if there was no one left to care, you had been given what you ultimately wanted, being the mortal fate of an end. I wondered what I had ever done to deserve for the people who loved me to stay at my side unflinchingly despite all I had done to drive them away. But I knew better than to think of the matter of inherent worthiness sober. Mostly because I don't think I'd come to survive it anyway.

I turned to Rue, who was already staring at me, face tight and equally unreadable. He tilted his head down to my level, then saying, "What did Celena mean in saying the man who marked you?"

"Ah." I pointed at the scar dragging down the length of my face. "My brother, Xavier. Team captain of the Wesley Cardinals. He gave me this when I was twelve years old."

Something told me to look at Chase. I turned to watch him look between us, his expression conveying one confusion knowing I was not the kind of man to give out secrets for free. I knew something was different about Rue, but what attribute was not like the other people in my life, I was unsure. Maybe it was jealousy that had taken hold of my mortal frame and refused to let me go, but this pang in the bottommost depths of my stomach told me such could never be the case. Maybe it was not so much jealousy of his sense of self as it was jealousy over his purpose; how there was something grander at play in his future, and I could never begin to say the same. And as soon as I had asked myself that, I realized such had just been disproven in Celena's declaration to make me into something great on a national stage. And the unknown between us lingered knowing I would never begin to piece it together, whether it be sober, or so inebriated that an answer would be sloshed in the bottom of my stomach with a generous portion of hard liquor.

I watched Rue speak to say, "I'm going to make him pay for what he did to you, Dante. I promise."

I smiled with no meaning behind it to then say, "You sure can try." I rose from the cubby to then say, "You would not be the first. And you certainly will be the last."

"You deserve to be avenged," Rue answered, almost quiet.

"Don't you think I already know that?" I asked, trying to mask the emotion laced in my voice. "I have tried so desperately to see through such myself. If you want to see through a lost cause, by all means, go ahead. But don't say I didn't warn you it was every bit pointless as I know it is, Rue Oba."

I didn't stick around for an answer. Instead, I exited the women's locker room to change into my practice gear unbothered.

2 0

ROBYN

I **WALKED INTO THE** stadium housed in our hockey rink. Davi was sitting at the top bleacher gazing down at me, crossing her arms. Her expression was equally unreadable as her body language. I then watched them settle and deem me a cause worth hearing out. I thought while I may not be entitled to such, it made things between us even considering her less than favorable treatment of me prior. But thinking on such, I didn't think that much was even true. After all, we still knew what it was I had excused in regard to the past we had once shared, but we were now each trying so desperately to forget.

I stood a bleacher below Davi, who was dressed in a sweatpants and hoodie, fur lined boots resting atop the seat before me as I dusted off my dress. We stared at each other, neither party having the heart to break the silence when I got so sick of the noise I said, "Thank you for hearing me out, Davi."

"I was unkind to you in the wake of Xavier's presence," Davi replied, turning to look me up and down. She smiled slightly, a gesture I felt comfort in even if I knew better than to think such was warranted. "I'm sorry I snapped at you. But him coming here brings out the worst in me. I hope you understand."

"I do," I said, almost quiet. "I want you to know, I don't regret dropping you off here on Tito Clayton's doorstep. Quite frankly, I don't think we would be before the other had I not."

Davi was quiet, tilting her gaze back to the concrete holding up our feet. She then said, "Do you even remember what made him so angry, Robyn? All I remember is the fallout. Nothing before, nor nothing after."

"I don't know either," I replied. "To be honest, all I can remember is what you looked like. Your leg warped in the wrong direction and your blood. So much of your blood."

Davi nodded slightly. "They told me it was a miracle it could even still work. He didn't break the bone, fucker fractured it into pieces. The recovery was a bitch, but I suppose being able to still say I'm here is a miracle, no?"

"I am one of two people, including you, who know that truth as intimately as you, Davi."

Davi was quiet again, retreating her legs to hug them into her chest. The blonde rested her cleft chin atop her knees, then moving to place her cheek above the bone. I gazed at Davi's face—free from taint and blemish as seen through by a man who found comfort in hurting her—before looking out onto the ice of the Nora Wilson Hockey Center. To be honest, I wondered what Nora would come to think of Tito Clayton erecting this stadium in her honor knowing what having the money and status to do so cost him in the process. I had only met the woman responsible for bringing my girlfriend into this world a handful of times, but the one thing I had learned about her in the wake of her murder was that Tito Clayton loved Nora the same way a Renaissance man loved his ever-reluctant muse.

After all, what else was there to call such when Tito Clayton had forever immortalized the woman he loved in a medium— while not as awe inspiring as oil paints smeared across a canvas— still equally as intimate knowing she had been erased in every sense while alive, but now had something dedicated to her that even the evil she called a husband could not, too, strip from her? And I found some comfort knowing the fucker responsible for her butchery was long gone, and that his final resting place was one absent of the family he had been the force to break to begin with.

Thinking of Nora made me think of Davi. Mostly because Nora's truth was one Davi, too, would have met should I not have saved her in the wake of Xavier's signature trait of violence. Even if I could not remember the circumstance that warranted the beating, it did not change that the aftermath of his calloused and equally barbaric wrath saw her teeter between the line of life and death. The Fates stretching the string tying her to this earthly tether until I made the conscious decision to beg them not snap it. It was then, carrying Davi and her bruised, battered, and equally broken body in my arms that I drove three hours in total silence to Schaffer University and left her on Tito Clayton's doorstep in hopes he would do what I never could, being stand up to the nephew I had once called a best friend. And I suppose there was some comfort knowing my effort had worked, but there was this pang in my stomach that began to gnaw on the flesh knowing I had done nothing to stop Xavier's violence, only helping Davi with the clean-up that came after.

Davi glanced at me as if she could read my mind. I knew she was the only other person alive who could begin to understand what it meant to have your sense of self dependent on a man who would come to betray you. While Davi had argued that Xavier had never respected me as a person, I knew such could never be true knowing Xavier—at one point in his life— had loved me like he would a sister. That for a brief moment of time we spent together, our relationship was on equal footing and affection knowing we each had once called the other our best friend.

Davi could never begin to say that same.

After all, what equal footing was found in a relationship where one party had yet to be an adult and the other already had established a sense of self that could not be easily manipulated as Davi's knowing she was a child? I know such could never begin to be forgiven, and that there was no excuse knowing I had done nothing to stand up for her except when the beating was so heinous its truth could no longer dare to be ignored. And I wondered how I could begin to show her I was sorry. Of how the two of us could begin to rebuild our lives in the absence of the man we had built nearly our entire sense of self around knowing he was now every bit gone as we once thought he never could be.

I spoke, my voice barely a whisper I was unsure if would be heard or not, "Davi, how do you rebuild your life without Xavier in it? You grew up as his girlfriend, and I was dependent on him in terms of my own sense of worth. How did you do it?"

Davi smiled like I was too naive to understand her truth as intimately as I knew my own. She turned back to the ice of the Nora Wilson Hockey Center to say, "You're acting like I have an answer for you when even I'm unsure how to answer your question."

"Then, do you regret coming to Schaffer?"

"I don't regret you saving me, if that's what you're asking. I could have refused your offer. I could have told you to let me die there. But I didn't."

"Why didn't you, then?"

"Even someone like me holds onto hope whether founded or unfounded." Davi thought for a moment. She looked at me, and I met her gaze to see her smile with the slightest writhe of pain attached to it. "I liked to think I was capable of rebuilding my life free of Xavier's influence. But what I like to think and what is actually true are two, very different things."

"I wouldn't have saved you from him if I didn't know you were."

"I know that, Robyn. But what I think and what I feel do not always see eye to eye."

I was quiet, then settling to say, "Then, what if we dare to do so together?"

"What, find our sense of self when it has been stripped of us in every sense by a man who betrayed us both?"

"Exactly, Davi."

Davi was quiet, as if she could not bring herself to believe me. I smiled slightly, then adding, "We don't have to be enemies. I know I may never be entitled to forgiveness, but I'm making the effort to atone for my past now, and I think it's better late than never. And I'll help you reclaim your life free of his influence, if you would be so kind to extend the same to me."

Davi moved her head to face me, eventually sticking out a pinky from her outstretched right hand. "Then, promise me that we'll rebuild our lives without him."

I stepped forward to lock my pinky with her own to say, "I promise, Davi. From now until death do us part."

Davi laughed, retreating her arm to hug her knees as we watched our teammates file onto the ice of the Nora Wilson Hockey Center in a comfortable silence.

2 1

DANTE

I **SKATED ONTO THE** ice of the Nora Wilson Hockey Center. Celena was dividing our team into corresponding halves for a makeshift scrimmage, and she turned to me to then say, "Dante will be on my team."

"That's not fair whatsoever," Conner called. "I'm going to get destroyed if you're both on the same team, Celena."

"Then, it should be good that you're on my team," Celena answered, smiling a bit.

Conner met the gesture with one of his own. "You I can tolerate. Dante? Not so much."

"Feeling's mutual, love," I said, blowing a kiss. "Now, how many shots are you going to miss with Chase in goal? I'm thinking your odds are zero for twenty. Let's hope I'm wrong for both mine and your ego, no?"

Conner flipped me off. I did the same before standing at Celena's right for her to then add, "Off my time, you two. I already have enough on my plate and do not need you two to add killing each other to it, we clear?"

"For now," I answered.

"Ignore him. I understand, Celena."

"Great, now that that's settled, I will have Davi, Leila, Conner, Dante, Breanna, and Dante on my team. The other will be Chase, Rue, Lisanna, Robyn, Alexei, and Damien."

Robyn crossed her arms and raised her eyebrow in a sharp arch. "I agree with Conner, why do you and Dante get to be on the same team? It's like you're asking us to lose."

"This is not a democracy," Celena replied, unsympathetic.

Lisanna said without missing a beat, "No, but it is a team sport. Or, is your head so big for your body any hope to remember anything has long past us?"

Celena jerked forward in Lisanna's range of motion when Conner stood between the pair. I glanced at Breanna who met my gaze, but did not address the accusation laced between my gaze to settle back to look at Conner.

He then said, "Easy, Celena. You know Lisanna is right. Even if we don't like how she said it."

Celena looked him up and down before recouping her losses and then saying, "My point still stands. Don't like it? I heard Wesley has rolling admissions. Let Elliot know I miss him oh, so, dearly, will you, Wilson?"

I tried to suppress my laugh as a cough. Lisanna noticed regardless and rolled her eyes before skating over to the opposite side of the ice where Celena and her team were congregating. Conner looked me up and down before miming his hope for my coming decapitation with his stick. I then tripped him in a response, which earned a curse. I didn't stick around to hear it, moving over to stand behind the goalie crease before me could hope to retaliate.

Davi then skated over to say, "You know there is a new fraternity on campus, right?"

Least to say, I had no idea what this had to do with me. "And why would that be in my best interest, Davi?"

"Because they hate Kappa Sigma, so I think your ban would not transfer over."

I felt this out of body panic begin to wash over my body. A sense of doom and misfortune soon to come now ruminating in the pit of my stomach. If I were to stoop so low to see me acquire a new fix in terms of my favored vice, it would mean relinquishing my promise made to Tito Clayton in even agreeing to play for him in the first place, being sobriety. I had been through the extensive and equally grueling detox once before; with the ward's black, caged windows and empty, white walls housing no décor. Other than artwork made by other patients who knew they were not going to remain clean once their time here ended as I knew it too. Since that admittance last year, I had kept my promise. But even I did not know how long such graces would last. Especially when the threat of facing my brother again loomed before me in terms of our season opener. I had not seen him in a long, eight years. And truth be told, I did not think the answer of how to face him and see myself withstanding was as righteous as I hoped for it to be.

I did not understand why Davi seemed to be enabling my signature trait of deceit. After all, we all knew the damage that would soon befall us Lions if I were to see it through in this instance. Another detox. Another failing of the people who did not deserve such of me no matter how much I had tried to convince them this sickness was what *I* wanted. After all, being so heinous to share this life with others, despite not wanting it yourself, meant you owed them the same truth of staying here. I knew if I died, it would simply pass my grief onto them; the people I would come to leave behind. And I had tried so desperately to absolve myself of this through a makeshift baptism beneath the same vice I had gone a year without. But now, a consistent means to abuse was in my tangible reach, washing away the memories I had been trying so long to outrun.

The other woman on our team, who I assumed was Leila, skated over to the two of us. Davi and I glanced at her, for her to then say, "What are you two talking about?"

"The Sigma Chi party tonight," Davi answered.

Leila raised her eyebrow in a sharp arch. She then looked as if she were going to challenge Davi on her prompted invitation, when Davi then said, "You don't have to come if you don't want to, Dante, but Conner invited me. Like I already told you, they hate Kappa Sigma, so odds are you can go without any kind of issue."

"Truth be told, Davi, is that really a good idea considering his—"

"It'll be fine, Leila. Promise."

Leila gazed upon Davi to then say, "I don't think it will be fine. We know Dante's circumstance, and I am unsure why you seem to be—"

"It's fine, Leila," I answered. "So, what are their pickings like, Davi?"

"Not sure," Davi answered, sly. "Looks like you'll have to come and find out."

Before either Leila or I could reply, the whistle blew from the circle at center ice. Tito Clayton then said, "So, we playing or chit chatting? Off my time, please."

I waved him off, but Leila and Davi looked at each other before Davi skated away. Leila then glanced at me before saying, "If Davi is your friend, why is she enabling your behavior?"

"I wouldn't be alive if she did," I answered.

"You're a terrible liar. And between you and me, Dante, you need to learn to keep better company, or else the coming fall will bruise your ass on the way down."

"I could say the same about you being her friend."

"She's not my friend. And if she were, I wouldn't let her enable my addiction for God knows what, Dante. You're a smart man. Don't let your loyalty cloud that, or our rival team won't be the only thing soon dead."

Leila looked me up and down before skating over to her corresponding post, and I stared at her before Tito Clayton blew his whistle and the state of play had begun.

Relegating myself back to the task at hand, I watched Celena win the face-off, but Rue was a looming threat behind her. Alexei and Damien began to close in on Celena, who pushed the puck before her. Considering how there was no one there, an obvious confusion was shared between Alexei and Damien. They glanced at each other while Celena skated between the gap now formed between them. She shoved Alexei for good measure before moving back to collect the puck, but Rue had skirted around the pair of defensemen who were closing in on Celena to lay claim to the puck instead. Celena, however, was not going to let her play be in vain. I watched as Davi checked Rue hard enough to leave him tumbling across the ice; a pretty impressive feat considering her height of five feet and his height of six feet.

Davi then passed the puck back to Celena who was waiting to receive it, long past the defensemen who were still trying to catch up to her and prevent her from scoring. Rue had brought himself back to his feet, but by the time he had managed to regain his balance, Celena had shot on the goal. Chase had saved it, but nonetheless, the seemingly instant humbling coming right out from the gate was nothing short of humiliating.

Tito Clayton blew his whistle, stopping play. Celena collected the puck from Chase, and they exchanged words before she moved over to the face-off circle. Tito Clayton then oversaw the changing of guard. Rue and Celena were on the face-off, and I watched Tito Clayton blow his whistle for Celena to win again. Truth be told, I was curious how the other team was going to put a stop to the sheer, grandiose force that was Celena Božović, and I readied myself in the case of a miracle.

Their strategy was to have every player except Chase make an attempt to curtail Celena and her exploits rather than giving any focus elsewhere. Lisanna and Robyn loomed in front of Celena, while Alexei and Damien loomed in back. Rue then was the one to take her on, checking her into the boards before managing to steal the puck from her by the skin of his teeth. Now that Celena had been knocked to the floor hard enough that it would give them a few extra seconds, each player was now in their corresponding positions in my defending zone. But seeing as the focus had entirely been on Celena for the past few minutes of play, that meant Conner, Leila, Davi, Breanna had been left unguarded.

Rue passed the puck to his brother. Breanna then intercepted it, skating up the ice as Leila and Davi guarded her on either side in case the other team would be stupid enough to dare and try to get between them and their coming goal. Conner charged forward, past everyone else on the ice and deep into the attacking zone. Celena was waiting for them in the neutral zone, and Breanna passed the puck to her. Celena then did not hesitate to slap the puck towards Conner. Conner flicked it off the ice, landing it in the left-hand corner of the net, which was Chase's blind spot considering the matter of his left-brain dominance. Chase cursed loud enough for me to hear him, when Conner raised his fists triumphantly before being engulfed in a congratulatory hug by his makeshift teammates.

"C'mon," Alexei called, fierce and equally indignant. "One more go around. I've got what it takes to take you on, Celena."

Celena smiled, breaking apart from her hug with her other teammates to then say, "Alright. One last go around, and if you score against me, you will be deemed worthy of the very air you breathe, rookie."

Rue skated forward, but Alexei stopped him mid stride. "No, Rue. I need to handle this on my own."

Rue looked hesitant to comply with his brother's wishes but ultimately relented. The rest of our teammates relegated to the home bench. We knew this coming humbling was something that would be needed to either bolster up Celena's status as untouchable, or see Alexei's rise above his expectation of failure. Celena then glanced at me, signaling with her stick Alexei's coming decapitation. I smirked before getting in a readying stance, with Rue overseeing the face-off. Tito Clayton blew his whistle. Rue dropped the puck. And the coming battle for the future of the Schaffer Lions had begun.

Celena let Alexei win the face-off, but in a way that made it seem like her past gravitas had been entirely based on the metric of luck. Alexei took this bait so blatantly placed on the fishhook as he commandeered the puck with ease to then charge towards me at full speed. Celena loomed closely behind him, waiting for him to develop an unfounded sense of confidence before sinking her teeth into the flesh of his neck and rendering him immobile. Alexei glanced back at Celena before turning back to face me, deeming her a cause every bit hopeless as his own.

Celena gracefully skated up to his right. Alexei, so obscenely confident in his hopeless cause to best Celena, did not notice her until she had maneuvered her stick between himself and the puck, taking her spoils for herself. Alexei now realized Celena was next to him, and I watched her lips curl into a smile before she cornered him into the boards and checked him with a deafening thud. Alexei remained on the ground as Celena moved over to shoot against me in goal. She aimed at my favored left-hand corner without much effort behind it, and her shot was easy to save. She loomed before the goal crease as we gazed upon Alexei, who was still sprawled across the ice like a lifeless rag doll.

I didn't think I should pity someone as stupid as Alexei Oba, but nonetheless, my morality peaked through its shallow dusting of dirt I had caked it under when I then said, "You didn't have to be *that* mean."

"A stupid man needs to learn his place eventually, Dante. And who says I am beneath the humble fate of being a teacher?"

I laughed. "You're so full of shit. You just get off on cruelty."

"What can I say, I like my men pathetic."

We both laughed at that. I gazed upon Alexei to see he was still writhing in an obvious pain, and no one among the Lions had dared to help him to not earn Celena's ire. Knowing I was immune to such a fate, I figured I would be the party seeing through his redemption. I glanced at Celena to then say, "Now, if you will excuse me, Celena, I will be cleaning up your mess."

"Broken bones don't stain white. For future reference."

Celena skated away, back over to the home bench. I moved to stand before a now immobile Alexei Oba to offer my hand. He looked at me as if I were some kind of out of body hallucination, when I then said, "Get up, Alexei, if you want any shred of dignity to remain."

"And if I don't want to?"

"Celena is entitled to an I told you so."

"Point taken."

Alexei accepted my offered hand, rising to his feet as we stared at each other. He didn't say anything, instead, retreating back over to the home bench where Tito Clayton and the rest of our teammates were waiting for us. Tito Clayton gazed upon his notes scrawled onto his clipboard in an illegible chicken scratch to then look among his Lions and say, "Good or bad news first?"

"Bad," Damien said. "That way the good news can cheer us up."

"Well, bad news is that we have our work cut out for us. We are nowhere ready to take on the Wesley Cardinals come our season opener. Good news? Well, we have plenty of time to work on the bad to make it not so bad in time for the NESCAC Championships. But I'm going to need you to help me here. We need no more ego clouding our sport, which, need I remind everyone, is a team sport. Got me?"

Tito Clayton did not accuse any party outright, instead, sweeping his gaze among his Lions to distribute blame evenly. Not that any of us meant it, but we nonetheless chorused a collective *Yes, Coach* to appease him. Seeing right through our feeble attempt at misleading him, Tito Clayton then said, "You're all terrible liars. Don't forget, we have conditioning tomorrow morning. You guys are late? Ten extra sets of suicides for you when we go back on the ice the day after."

We all groaned collectively.

"I don't want to hear it. Now get out of my hair while I go plead a strong enough case to Mother Mary that we don't make total asses of ourselves against Andrei and his Cardinals."

Tito Clayton waved us off. I took this cue to lead us to our corresponding locker rooms, moving to sit atop the bench between the pair to wait for my male teammates to finish changing. Davi then loomed before me, waiting for our teammates to file into their respective changing areas to then say when we were the only two before the other, "You coming to that Sigma Chi party?"

"I'll be there," I answered despite the gnawing in my stomach after what Leila had said. "I'll meet you there, ok?"

"It's next to Reed Hall, you'll recognize it from the banner making up the Greek letters. Conner won't be there since he has plans."

"That's good, I suppose."

"Yeah."

"Well, I'll see you there."

"Yeah."

Davi smiled before moving to exit into the locker room. I tried to ignore the pang of fear that had taken root in the belly of my stomach; its bitter twinge now making an effort to climb up the chasm of my throat. I shook my head, giving a feeble attempt to relegate my train of thought to something morally virtuous when the men's locker room door opened. My teammates filed out, only sparing a glance for me. I glanced at Rue, who met my gaze as the two of us stared at each other for an endless minute before I lost all resolve and looked away. I felt Rue's gaze linger upon my own for a few seconds longer, but I did not meet it knowing my coming circumstance.

I rose from the bench to then enter the men's locker room to find it was empty as I had hoped for it to be. Instead of being so heinous to answer the question of my sobriety outright, I showered and donned my change of clothes. I put my items of loaned gear in their corresponding places before packing my duffel bag and slinging it over my shoulder. I then walked out of the locker room and into the hallway to find Leila waiting for me, which least to say, was odd. It was a shared, understood truth that we had nothing in common let alone enough of a basis of a relationship to call each other friends. So, it only made me ask myself, what was she doing before me playing the role of one when I had never given her a reason to?

"I realized we've never introduced ourselves," Leila said. "Leila Johnson."

"Dante Alonso Hidalgo," I replied, smirking a bit. "I have to ask, what the hell is this?

"This is an intervention," Leila said, pointing between us. "And if you know what's good for you, Dante Alonso Hidalgo, you will come with me."

Her insistence was charming. Even if under normal circumstance I would never have listened to anyone without any kind of standing in my mental hierarchy, I found her case poignant enough to be compelling. "Alright, I'll go with you. If you tell me where it is you're going."

"The stands," Leila answered. "I'm too lazy to walk back to my dorm, so me and my friends will be hanging out there. That cool with you?"

"Is it cool with Tito Clayton?"

"Now, your uncle doesn't need to know everything that goes on behind the scenes. But I think he'll find some comfort knowing everyone in our company will be a Lion."

"Then, that gives us all the more reason for me not to snitch," I answered. "Lead the way, Leila."

Leila mimed a salute, leading us back to the ice of the Nora Wilson Hockey Center to find two people waiting for us, being Damien and Breanna. I really had never made an effort to interact with either of them prior but found it odd they would be among the company of what Leila called an intervention. Truth be told, I did not think I had the social gravitas to come out of this coming conversation withstanding since my tether to such graces—Chase—was not present. But nonetheless, we ascended to the bleachers until Leila claimed the top, leaning against the back wall. I sat next to her, leaving a seat of space before taking out my package of cigarettes and gifted lighter. I took one from the box, placing it back in my duffel bag. I kept the sliver between my lips before striking the fork of my lighter to render myself a flame. I inhaled. Then, exhaled. I blew the smoke away from the people gathered, when I caught Breanna staring at me with interest, "I see you like your gift."

"I do," I answered, awkward.

I was unsure what to think of Breanna Kim when it was no secret she liked Conner Zaragoza. What she saw in him, I was unsure, but I would never be so arrogant enough to ask. I took another drag from my cigarette after leaning forward. I placed my elbows atop my knees and kept the vice between my pointer and ring finger of my left hand.

Leila clutched her legs into her chest, stretching her arms in the space between us. "How long have you been playing, Dante?"

"Ever since I can really remember," I answered, laughing a bit as I leaned against the wall. "Tito Clayton coached me nearly all my childhood until we fell out of touch for a bit. But I don't think it matters now that we're back in it." I knew the gravity of the subject matter did not have much founding in the people gathered, so I looked at Damien and said, "You must be Irish, no?"

"Born and raised," Damien answered with a smile. "I figured a change of scenery was needed after finishing my grueling Senior Cycle. I've always wanted to come to the United States. Never did I think it'd be for hockey, but here we are."

"You like it over here so far?"

"I do, yes. Your portions are actually massive. I thought my friend Ajay was being dramatic when he told me about it when he did a holiday here a long time ago."

Leila but in to say, "Is there any kind of girl you like here, Damien?"

Breanna looked at him. Damien met her gaze when he sheepishly tried to avoid the subject saying, "No, not particularly."

"What a terrible liar," Breanna said, smiling. "You can be honest, Damien. Even I know we're just fucking. There's no meaning behind it."

"You're right, and I know that, but still. Didn't want to hurt your feelings."

"If only you were my type then maybe Celena would stop getting on my ass about dating men who are terrible for me."

Breanna sighed. I wonder if such had been said because of Breanna's history with Celena's brother. Even I was unsure what had happened between either of the former lovers, but if someone like Elliot kept Xavier in his company, I didn't have much hope for it to be anything of moral propriety.

"Oh, well. In the meantime, do tell who on the Lions you fancy. Last I heard, there's a bet ruminating on who you'll court."

Leila and Breanna looked at each other, only smirking.

Damien flushed. "Really, it's no one, Breanna."

I then interjected, "If it really was no one, Damien, why the hell are you so red?"

"Well, I don't want you to get mad, Dante."

"Why in the fuck would I get mad at you?"

"Because the girl I like is Davi."

Everyone turned to look at me. Their gazes were eager, as if waiting for my confirmation on some preconceived notion that I lay ignorant to until presented seconds prior by the still handsome Damien Prince. Least to say, I was nonplussed by the very statement. Sure, Davi was pretty. And sure, she was nice. I thought she deserved a good, just, and equally honorable man in her life. Even if I did not hold any of those traits, it did not change nothing could ever happen between us considering where I swung in terms of my own sexuality. I realized with Leila, Breanna, and Damien staring at me as if waiting for me to recite previously untold scriptures, that they did not know I was gay. I don't know what was more shocking, being accused of liking a girl I loved like a sister, or the very notion of the people gathered before me thinking I could ever dare and be straight.

A laugh came up the confines of my throat despite my best efforts to see it repressed. The smoke from the drag I had taken had escaped from the slit of my now open mouth as I then said, "You guys are a fucking hoot. I'm gay. If there's anyone on the team I would like, it would be you Damien."

Damien burned an even deeper shade of scarlet. Breanna and Leila were now chorusing a hearty, out of place laughter I did not think I disliked outright. I smiled, blocking the expression with my cigarette.

Breanna then said, "Oh my fucking God! No way! I'm crying, Dante! I guess that answers our question, huh?"

"You can accuse me of liking any of the men on the team, but not the women," I answered, flicking my cigarette onto the concrete beneath our feet. The thought of comparing Breanna's taste in men to my own lingered, but I did not think such was warranted when this was our first time congregating outside the confines of Celena and Tito Clayton's shared time.

"So, you and Rue?" Leila asked.

"Yeah, what about you and Rue?" Breanna added.

"You like Rue?" Damien also added.

"What the hell are you guys talking about me liking Rue?" I asked, equally nonplussed as when asked the previous question. "Even if I did, there's no way in hell I could make that work."

"You deserve to have love in your life, Dante," Breanna said.

"What you think and what I know are not the same thing."

"Maybe not, but I think someone like you deserves a happy ending. Whether it be with Rue, or it be with your foot on your brother's neck."

"I could argue the same thing about you and Conner."

A silence lingered as I watched Breanna. I blew the smoke from my cigarette out from my mouth when Leila and Damien looked between us.

Breanna kept my gaze before giving a laugh and looking away, then turning back to me to say, "Your hopes at deflection are noted. But I suppose we both have growing to do in terms of the men in our lives, don't we, Dante Hidalgo?"

I smirked a bit. "It seems we do, Breanna Kim."

2 2

ROBYN

THE FRONT DOOR TO Tito Clayton's house held a knock for a few seconds before I rose from my seat at the couch to answer it.

Lisanna then called, "Who is that at this hour?"

"Conner, Alexei, and Rue." I met Lisanna's gaze. "Or, is the new company unwelcome?"

"They're not unwelcome. Well, as long as they are not at direct harm to you, I could really care less who we interact with within the Lions's sphere of influence."

"You seem to have some discontent for Celena, though."

"When her body can support the weight of her head, and she stops sniping at you, then I will like her."

I laughed a bit. I opened the wood to find Alexei leading the pack of his brothers with two bottles of wine in hand. "Thanks for having us, Robyn. I brought spirits."

I took the bottle housing the pink wine from his hand to examine the bottle. "Ah, I actually like this kind. Props to you for doing your research."

"I'm a man of many talents."

"Like pissing off Celena for one."

"And you must be Lisanna Wilson."

Lisanna smirked a bit. "The one and only. Nice to meet you, Alexei Oba."

"Well, now that we're all acquainted, shall we?"

"We shall," I answered, moving from the door so the three of them could enter.

Alexei and Rue moved past me to sit on the couch, leaving a cushion for Conner on the left of Alexei. I then stopped Conner from entering to then say, "Thanks for coming, Conner. I really do appreciate it."

"Of course," Conner answered, smiling faintly. "I hope we can learn to get along, for the sake of our parents."

"You and me both," I answered. "C'mon, let's get some wine in us since Dante won't be here for a good while."

"Tito Clayton know about this?" Conner asked.

"As long as we clean up after ourselves, I see no reason why he needs to."

Conner smiled, warm, hearty, and equally genuine. He tilted his head over for me to follow him, and I did as he asked, moving over to the living room. Lisanna was sitting in the chair across from the men gathered, sticking out a wine cup for me to take. I moved over to collect it from her hands, pecking her on the lips to then say, "Where the hell did you find this?"

"In Tito Clayton's cupboard," Lisanna answered, smiling as she stared into my brown eyes. "I know drinking wine out of a plastic cup is a fate entirely beneath you, so I figured I would find one for you."

"Thank you, love," I answered. I then turned to Alexei, Rue, and Conner to say, "Pour me some of the White Zinfandel will you, Alexei?"

"'Course," Alexei answered, standing to pour me a portion of our shared poison. "Lisanna, you want any?"

"No, no, I'm fine," she answered. "Thank you, though, Alexei."

Alexei smiled, and I sat on the edge of Lisanna's chair, her arm curling around my waist as I leaned into her body. Alexei, Conner, and Rue were staring at us when Rue then asked, "How long have you been dating?"

"Almost a year," Lisanna answered. "We started dating towards the end of our junior year at Wesley last year."

I found it odd she was answering their questions when she was never quite fond of strangers.

"We're childhood friends," I added. "We were best friends in middle school before we fell out of contact. Never did I think we would meet again in the same college. Truth be told, I had given up all hope in seeing her again when she moved away."

"Well, it's good you two are in contact now," Alexei said.

"Any girlfriend for you, Alexei?" Lisanna asked. "Or, you, Conner?"

Alexei answered for them both to say, "No girlfriend for either of us. But there is a girl on the Lions who I do like."

Lisanna and I glanced at each other for me to then say behind the lip of my wine glass, "And who might that be, Alexei?"

Least to say, Alexei had stars in his eyes. "Leila. We made out a Kappa Sigma party, and I've been wooed by her ever since."

Rue then said, "Keep in mind he has made no other progress with her than drunkenly making out with her."

Lisanna and I laughed.

Alexei pouted to then say, "C'mon, Rue. Give me credit. I'm shy with girls."

"Not in high school you weren't," Rue said, leaning back on the peeling, leather couch. I noticed he, like Lisanna, was not drinking. "Bringing home a girl every other week. I was getting sick of them leaving their stuff behind."

"A hoe era?" Lisanna said.

I smiled. "Alexei, you dog."

"I have to agree with my sister," Conner said.

A dull flutter began to beat between the confines of my chest.

"How did Takeshi react to that?" I asked.

"The thing is about not getting caught," Alexei admitted, beaming with pride. "He never found out."

"Shit fucking liar," Rue answered. "Remember how he took your phone away for a month because he told you that you were ruining the sanctity of marriage?"

Lisanna, Conner, and I burst into a hearty chorus of laughter. Alexei moved his hands to cover his face that was now an even shade of crimson as he sank into his chair. I then rose from the edge I was sitting atop of to say, "Well, while you let that marinate, I will make us dinner with the ingredients I have gathered."

"What's on the menu, chef?" Rue asked.

"My father's lechon kawali. I boiled it last night and all I have to do is fry it now," I answered.

"I'll help you," Conner said, rising from his seat.

I smiled. "Sure, Conner. C'mon, I'll show you how it's done, true Filipino style."

Conner laughed, and the two of us walked over to the kitchen. I moved to the fridge, taking out my slivers of prepared pork belly to then move over to the stove. Conner had seemingly read my mind when he conjured the bottle of vegetable oil I would need to prepare the dish. I smiled, finishing off the last bit of my wine before placing the glass in the sink nearby to then commandeer the large, plastic bottle. I held it into my chest, grabbing a skillet before placing it atop the burner and turning on the stove. The click of the gas burner filled the space between my brother and I as I then poured enough oil to cover the strips of meat. Then, I handed the bottle back to my brother who placed it where he had first found it. I leaned against the stove before crossing my arms, and Conner did the same on the counter across from me as we watched each other.

I stared at Conner. He was easily very handsome. I mean, if he were related to me, he should be. But the matter of my pride aside, I could not help but see a part of myself in his own face. The way our wide noses crinkled when giving a toothy grin. The way freckles dotted every conceivable inch of the brown the same shade of the parents who had left us behind. Even the curly hair we had shared, down to the same pattern of ringlets kept atop our heads. Looking at Conner was like looking in the mirror. Looking at him was like looking at the ghost of the person I had once promised Lisanna and my parents I always had been. A woman I could not really remember since three months of a once unmanaged addiction had desecrated her memory. And I, too, wondered if she had been this perfect, elaborate ruse, or if I could ever dare to become her again.

But I don't think such needed to be answered for now.

And maybe one day, I could dare and try without the context of failure beneath a bottle of those same, white pills.

"What dish is this again?" Conner asked, crossing his cloth covered arms. Come to think about it, I had never seen him without long sleeves on.

"Lechon kawali," I answered. "Fried pork belly. With the Mang Tomas sauce is my favorite. But some people are biased to vinegar."

"I see," Conner answered, glancing back at Lisanna, Rue, and Alexei who were in the middle of chatter. He turned back to me. "Lisanna's a hoot. I can see why you like her."

"She's been there for me through thick and thin, and I have done the same for her."

I turned back to the pot filled with oil to hover my hand above it. Once I deemed it hot enough, I placed each sliver of pre-prepared pork belly into it as the crackling of the contrasting temperatures filled the kitchen. Footsteps came toward me until Conner stood at my right, looking into the oil before I turned to him.

He smiled, then saying, "You know, I'm glad we're in contact. I think it's what our parents would have wanted of us."

"Do you know anything about them?" I asked. "My own never told me much, if anything."

"Well, our parents had a history with addiction," Conner said, quiet. "They both died of an overdose."

There was this pang of fear that had taken hold of my mortal frame; seizing my throat and refusing to let me go despite my desperate and unanswered pleas. It would then be with the crushing weight of my failure atop my chest that I could only ever tell the same lie that I would finally see through a redemption. An effort I had long ago scorned in following in the same footsteps as the pair who had helped given me life.

I knew there was only one end awaiting me should I not give up the vice that was rotting me from the inside out. That much was understood both by me and the people I loved. But could I dare and give up the same pills I had become all but reliant on? I did not know. They were still this perfect, sickly crutch that allowed myself to process my most intimate and haunting of emotions, despite knowing what it would cost me should I refuse to let them go. I didn't want to think about it knowing I had a new fix to see through a makeshift baptism, but I knew the circumstance demanded courage in order to see myself withstanding. And in order to be worthy enough to see Conner call me his sister, I had to dare and be capable of such.

"I see."

"This is why I think you should get clean."

"Conner, I am not having this argument with *you* of all people."

Conner looked offended. "And why the fuck not me, Robyn?"

"Because you deserve me at my best."

Conner was quiet.

"Not this hopeless woman who can't give up the one thing that will quite literally solve all her fucking problems."

"I don't think it's entirely that simple," Conner replied. "Holding yourself up to this degree of utter perfectionism is just going to make you hate yourself. I should know. I've tried so many times before only to see myself hurt thinking it was at others's expense."

I looked at Conner, afraid.

"But the thing you need to realize, Robyn, is that the sins of others are never something that's reflective of you. They've never been something that you have to atone for. It will always be their cross to bear. And it will never be yours." Conner was quiet. "And I would never forgive myself should I not tell you this than being forced to learn it through a makeshift baptism see beneath a lighter atop your bathroom floor."

I opened my mouth to respond when Alexei came into the kitchen with Rue and Lisanna, buzzed and equally wine drunk to say, "Smells so good, Robyn. Divvy me up extra portions!"

Conner and I stared at each other before I turned to the frying meat and turning it over with a nearby pair of tongs. I then turned to Lisanna.

She met the expression in my gaze to say, "C'mon, let's not impede on Robyn's cooking efforts, guys. It's clear you all have no conceivable idea what you're doing, and she's the only one who does."

Conner stared at me before turning to Alexei and saying, "C'mon, Alexei, let's get you sitting down. You're too drunk to be standing up."

Alexei gave a drunken laugh when Lisanna and Conner collected him from Rue. The three of them left the kitchen, when

Rue remained. I glanced at him, looking him up and down to then say, "I'm not in the mood to talk, Rue."

"I can tell you're trying," Rue said after a bit. "Really. I can. I can't pretend to understand what you're going through, but I feel bad for you."

I laughed, annoyed. "The last thing I need is pity, from you of all people."

"Don't want pity? Then, see through sobriety."

"You act like it's that simple."

"It may not be, but I know we both know there can be only one answer in who gets the last word on the question that is your life. And do you want it to be you? Or, your addiction?"

I knew Rue was right. Before I could be arrogant enough to question him, Rue looked me up and down before joining Lisanna, Conner, and Alexei in the living room. The only thing then left speaking was the sound of frying pork belly; crackling like the fire of my own undoing I had been seemingly caught in since coming to Schaffer University a traitor.

23

DANTE

I **TOOK A DRAG** of my cigarette while sitting in the window of my bedroom; the acrid taste of nicotine washing a sense of calm over my body I was unsure was founded or not. I blew the smoke out from the open window, the thin slits of gray trailing off into the chill, winter air now taking hold of the Schaffer campus.

The season opener in which I would be facing my brother again for the first time since my branding was drawing closer, and even I was unsure how to deal with the imminent threat of facing him again. I suppose there was an irony knowing the vice he had gifted me would help me stand before him without spurning a complete and total mental breakdown. But the matter of keeping it a secret was infinitely more complicated than it was before knowing the truth of my addiction was shared between my uncle and me. It was no longer something I had given blood to keep from him, aware of the sobriety he would force me to see through should he lay privy to its truth. But the matter of being clean aside, I knew I had an inevitable choice to make. And that was either see through the cause of self-righteousness in terms of myself or in the terms of Celena Božović.

It was no secret what her declaration to make me something great in front of a national stage would come with. It would see me rule this kingdom she had built from the ground up, and I knew being trusted with such was not so much a matter of luck as it was a matter of respect. For some unknown reason, I had done something to earn an attribution of worthiness from, arguably, the greatest hockey players to ever live. I had done something to see Celena wish to take me with her on the world stage, helping her secure her place in the history books where an endless generation of girls would come to look up to her as what they, too, could one day accomplish. And even if I knew asking myself why I had been deemed deserving of such was pointless, it did not change that I had been. And I don't think answering such a question would really, truly change its truth. After all, it was still something I had already been deemed deserving of, no matter how unworthy I would always think of myself as.

There was a knock on the door to my bedroom, and I did not answer it. Instead, it opened despite my lack of permission, and I turned to the wood to find Davi standing in the archway, leaning against the left edge to cross her arms. She stared at me, and I welcomed her inside. Davi then gave a nod before closing the door behind her to lean against it, a silence taking root between us.

I ultimately said, "Davi, to what do I owe the pleasure?"

"I talked with Robyn," Davi said after a bit, almost afraid. "Turns out she's just as much of a victim of Xavier as the two of us might be."

"You don't have to coddle her," I replied, dislodging a clump of ash from my cigarette, equally unsympathetic as the words I had just spoken. "She still excused all Xavier had done to you knowing it was wrong. What good is there to say about her, Davi?"

"I know that," Davi replied. "But, I would not be alive without her."

I stared at her. "You don't have to tell me if you don't want to. I would never be so heinous to ask."

Davi smiled, a sense of comfort laced between the part. "Do you really think I can do it?"

"Do what?"

"Be a person free of Xavier's influence. Live a life without being bound to him."

I stared at her to say, "Why are you asking me that, Davi?"

"Because you're the only person I'll believe no matter what answer you give me."

I was quiet, bringing my cigarette back to my lips to take another drag. I couldn't bring myself to gaze upon the tense, timid eyes Davi was looking at me with, so I moved to look out of the window I was sitting in to give her question proper thought. Truth be told, I had not begun to answer it in terms of self since I had been given away to Tito Clayton eight years ago with nothing to show for the family I had been forced to leave behind but a branding, silence, and a lighter. I had given everything to see myself absolved of this very question and the answer it came with, but knowing this did not change that Davi was entitled to an answer. So, it only begged the question, could I, too, rebuild my life without the weight of my brother's foot atop my neck?

Davi and I contrasted Robyn in this regard because neither of us held equal standing in terms of Xavier. Despite what anyone else might say, it was obvious Robyn had known what she had dared to excuse during her time as my brother's best friend. I think saying she was every bit a victim as Davi and I was both giving us too little credit and giving her too much.

She had made the choice to both enable and coddle my brother every time he sought to do wrong. Even when he picked off Davi from her college tour while she was a junior in high school. Then 'courting' her in an attempt to shape her into a woman that fulfilled his own desires in regard to her image and likeness. Xavier held power over me being my older brother. He was a party I idolized and looked up to, and knowing this, contorted the trust I had in him to see me pay for something I didn't think I would ever be deemed worthy to know. But Robyn on the other hand, had met Xavier during college and probably knew both these truths as intimately as Davi and I did. She had atoning to do. And whether she would see it through was entirely up to her. But I sure as hell would not be waiting around for it knowing what kind of person she had to be in order to call Xavier Alonso Hidalgo her best friend.

Truth be told, my entire life now had been spurned onto me by my brother. The vices I used to cope with my depression and my depression itself were manifestations of his actions well past their immediate consequence. This misery I had found a comfort drowning in was all thanks to the branding he had carved into my face, and knowing such, I did not think this could be some kind of accident.

I knew Xavier was cruel and equally vindictive as I could be, so it dawned on me then that the matter of my addiction, mental illness, and sense of self were a calculated strategy to see me do the dirty work for paying the price of what he deemed betrayal in blood. Celena was right; killing myself was playing right into Xavier's hand and giving him exactly what it was he wanted. It meant letting him answer the question of my life and what it was worth. It meant letting him have the final say.

And even if I could not confidently say I owed it to myself to see the effort of recovery through, I owed it to Celena. I owed it to Chase, and I owed it to Tito Clayton. I think most importantly of all, I owed recovery to the person I used to be. A boy I knew the parents who gave me up eight years ago would no longer recognize. Who was now the man I had been forced to become in the wake of Xavier's signature trait of violence.

I blew the smoke out from my mouth to look at Davi and say, "Do you think Xavier dating you was a happy accident?"

"What does this have to do with the question I asked, Dante?"

"We'll get there. But you have to answer me first."

"I mean, he said I was different. He said I was special."

"But you weren't," I answered, taking another drag of my cigarette.

Davi flinched, but I knew skirting around the truth would do nothing but see her house sympathy for a man who deserved none.

"Xavier knew what he was doing in giving you his number when you toured Wesley your junior year of high school, Davi. You were valedictorian of your fucking class. You were accepted into fucking Harvard. And Xavier first courted you expecting you to be this easily moldable art project to see you become the woman he wanted."

Davi was quiet still.

I continued, "It's obvious why Xavier tried to kill you that night. And it's because you were better than him. You were smarter than him, and you have a future of greatness like he'll never get to have because he peaked in college."

I paused, moving my ashtray within my range of motion to flick a clump of ash from the ember at the other end of my filter.

"And this gets into the question you asked. Because you always had been your own person without him, even if you can't remember. Because I was too. And even if we can't remember and even if we may not like the person we were before he tainted us, it does not mean we shouldn't let the fear that comes with meeting them override the entitlement we owe ourselves in daring to try."

Davi laughed a bit, then saying, "Wise words for a man who never wanted to say them."

I smiled. "I know now what Xavier's intention was in robbing us of stability, Davi. And it was to see us do his dirty work for him. It was so that he won, and we lost. And we all know the competitive fucker I am, I refuse to lose in a game as serious as this."

Davi crossed her arms to say, "So, you're going to let yourself get better?"

"Baby steps, Davi. Baby steps," I answered. "I know the game now. I know what is needed to do to win it. I suppose my next step is figuring out the play to make it happen."

"It's going to be hard," Davi replied, quiet.

"It's either let Xavier win or take away the one trophy he expects to get out of me." I took another drag of my cigarette. "And when you look at it like that, Davi, it really is not much of a choice at all."

"Then, can you help me do it too?"

"You would be an idiot to think I wouldn't."

Davi smiled. She moved to sit atop my bed, offering her hand. I tossed her my package of cigarettes and gifted lighter to watch her siphon one out from the cardboard, then placing the cylinder to her lips. She struck the fork of my lighter until she'd rendered a flame, protecting the ember from a stray gust of wind with her other hand before flicking the metal closed. She took a drag before tossing me back my things, the newfound weight of our shared effort of recovery and the earthy stench of tobacco staining the inside of our noses.

24

ROBYN

I **WALKED INTO THE** Elizabeth Gurley Flynn Library to find two people sitting together I did not think had much business to keep the other in their company.

Rue Oba and Chase Zhu turned to look at me, exchanging whispers before ultimately welcoming me over with smiles and a beckoning wave. I hesitated before accepting their offer of refuge, cutting through the tables and chairs surrounding them on all sides to sit next to Chase. I placed my textbooks and laptop across the table before crossing my legs and scanning their faces to ultimately say, "Chase Zhu and Rue Oba. How lovely to finally meet you both."

"Pleasure is all mine," Chase replied, smiling wide and charming as ever.

Truth be told, I did not know what someone as suave as Chase saw in someone vindictive like Dante, even going so far to call him his best friend.

"I realized no one officially welcomed you to the Lions, so on behalf of all of us, welcome, Robyn."

"I appreciate that even if I'm unsure if such is truly warranted," I answered. I moved to rest my clasped hands above my knees to add, "After all, you lot are friends with Dante, who is not very keen on my presence among his court."

"I mean, can you really blame him?" Chase asked.

And truth be told, I knew I really could not.

"After all, you are the best friend of the man who branded him."

I glanced at Rue. He examined me with piercing, black eyes and tight lips. I smiled, turning back to Chase to say, "Former. I am very fortunate to no longer call a man so heinous my best friend, Chase."

Chase smiled like he did not believe my declaration as to where my loyalty lied. I thought that much was warranted, but knew it would never begin to be fair. Instead of answering the accusation laced between his words, I adjusted the weight they came with evenly atop my shoulders before turning to Rue.

Rue Oba was easily very handsome. While I would never be compelled to appreciate such, I could understand the overall appeal that came with Dante's interest in him. His appearance was almost a kind of pinnacle of masculinity and the pleasing things that came with it. Sharp, defined, and equally rigid. He smelled of fresh mint mixed with clean linens, and I watched him look at me with an expression that gave no illusion to what he was thinking or feeling. I didn't think he would willingly come to my defense nor like me considering the matter of the current object of his affection, but I watched him part thin, pink lips to say, "Chase, I think your judgment of Robyn is unfair."

Least to say, Chase and I were equally perplexed at his statement.

Chase narrowed his eyes to say, "Well, what's your take on Robyn being here, then, Rue?"

"Really," I answered, curious. "I'd like to see what you have to say."

"Well, if we look at this logically, you would only be here at Schaffer if you betrayed Xavier, or Xavier betrayed you."

I smiled, low and equally sweet.

"After all, what business does a woman who helped Xavier scorn us Lions have here unless she, too, was scorned?"

"My, my, my, a brain in there and not just a pretty face? A certified triple threat."

"I mean, me coming to this conclusion didn't require any brain power. I may be loyal to Dante, but I see no reason to let that cloud the facts."

I tapped my fingernails atop the table to then reply, "Speaking of. You need help putting in a good word for your courting? I have no problem with a man who admires a challenge, but you should know Dante is not easy prey to sink your teeth into. Xavier made sure of it."

I glanced at Chase. He met my gaze with a nod, now aware we were now on the same page in regard to where Rue's affection lied. We then moved to gaze upon Rue.

He thought for a moment before saying, "I'm well aware Xavier had a hand in stunting Dante's romantic side. After all he's been through, it would take a man of Teflon to not succumb to the same fate he has now."

"So, I'm right. You do like him. Do you not?"

"I do, yes. It's stupid to lie on things as important as this, no?"

I glanced at Chase, smirking. Obviously, he was not expecting a confession to be spoken of a truth we both knew equally well when it was left unsaid.

I watched him run a hand through his cotton candy pink mullet to then say, "You like Dante, Rue?"

"He's hot, is there something wrong with that?"

"No, no." Chase smiled slightly. A twinge of fondness was laced between the part knowing a man his best friend harbored an obvious affection toward liked him too. "I just don't think anyone's ever told me they've liked Dante before. I won't tell him. But, I can put in a good word for you too. It wouldn't hurt. I think you'd be good for each other."

Rue waved his hand to say, "I appreciate both of your offers in terms of the courting, but I'm more than capable of doing such myself. After all, the challenge is where the fun is to be had."

I smirked a bit, saying, "My, my, my. Rue Oba the chaser. I call dibs on reciting the vows at your wedding."

Rue nodded. "But, getting back to Dante, how do we plan on avenging him?"

Chase and I looked at each other. We then turned back to Rue for Chase to answer, "What the hell are you talking about avenging him? Like beating Xavier in a game or something?"

"Well, you see, Xavier took Dante's life in giving him the scar on his face. Maybe not in a conventional way that a murderer kills another person, but he killed the boy Dante once was for the man he is now to take his place. And there's only one way to make something like that right, is there not?"

I then said, "Are you suggesting what I think you are?"

"Being?"

"Murder."

"Yes, that is exactly what I am suggesting."

Chase glanced at me, his expression not the least bit fazed in regard to the more than grave subject matter. I stared at him for a moment. I then realized both men before me had the same answer in regard to the question of Xavier Hidalgo's life, and what it was worth. And they expected me to come to the same conclusion of what price the man I once called a best friend should pay for the crimes he had willingly committed.

Rue was right. I was only here because of the same scorn Xavier saw through at the expense of most of the Lions, but that did not mean I could willingly absolve myself of the past like

Elliot and Xavier before me. It's not that I still harbored some kind of fondness for Xavier and wished to see him take back his post as my most esteemed confidant in the wake of my assassination attempt. It was just that I had given blood to help Xavier see through his own healing, and I saw him attempt to culminate the effort in small, seemingly insignificant glimpses.

I was one of two people who knew the pain he had been forced to endure, and I was one of two people who had tried to help him accept it. What Davi lacked for in standing, I made up for in equal footing, and Xavier listened to me in a way he never could his ex-girlfriend knowing his entire point in courting her was to mold her into the woman *he* wanted. I had seen Xavier attempt to see through change. And knowing this, I could not condone the taking of his life. There was still a chance he could look his past in the eye and dare to heal from it. Knowing the relationship we had, I would not forgive myself if I uprooted my effort of building a foundation just because of the wrong he had committed against me. And I didn't expect Chase or Rue to understand, but it did not change the fact I would never be the party to sign off on Xavier's death warrant. Not when I had been trusted to meet the man behind the hurt and love him in spite of it.

I answered coolly, "Celena won't be too keen on you murdering her only rival before she gets the chance to beat him in a championship game."

"Then, we just beat him, and then, get to it."

"Why do you seem so keen on revenge in regard to a man you are not even dating?"

Rue looked annoyed both the low blow and an obvious fondness of Xavier I had yet to really absolve myself of.

Chase then said, "Are you saying you still care about Xavier, Robyn?"

"The man was still my best friend, my brother," I answered, not expecting either party to see my side when they had long ago sworn allegiance to Xavier's foil. "You all are free to see through what it is you like. But if you want me on board, I need to know there is nothing left redeeming him, something I know will never be true."

Chase was quiet, then saying, "You really think you're different."

"I was different, Chase. Xavier loved me at one point in his life."

"Key word, at one point."

I was quiet.

"Don't you think you could learn from Davi's same mistake?" Chase continued. "I'm not asking you to agree with us, but I'm asking you to treat yourself with proper tact and respect. If you were ever truly an equal in Xavier's mind, would you be here with us, among the court of his scorned?"

It's not that I did not think Breanna, Chase, and Davi were wrong. Xavier was easily a terrible person, and he easily sought out people he could control in order to behold all the power in his relationships with them. I knew there was no longer any point in defending a man who long ago decided I was no longer worth the same. Xavier had tried to murder me after I told him I was transferring to Schaffer to be among the company of the brother I never knew, and Xavier had taken this as me choosing Dante over him, like his own family had done to him his entire life. These truths were not lost on me, and I knew arguing with such facts was pointless in every regard. I did not want to give Xavier more credit than where credit was due, but I saw Xavier for what he was in a way the Lions never could because Xavier would never allow them such.

And that was every bit human as I was.

And as they were too.

Not that any of the Lions would understand my viewpoint. I knew the time for understanding between Xavier's and Dante's lot was long past. There was no hope for forgiveness between either faction, only rage. And maybe my nostalgia in regard to Xavier Hidalgo would see me keep the same post of unwanted among the Lions, but I could not begin to absolve myself of morality like they could so easily. After all, I had tried to do such in rehab. And I didn't like the person I was becoming in agreeing to fester these dark, unholy thoughts in regard to a man who I had once loved like a brother.

I rose from my seat, collecting my things to clutch them into my chest. "Well, I think my time has long past expired. But, it was nice chatting with you both."

Chase and Rue gave a nod. I walked away without giving a goodbye. I wondered what would become of Xavier Hidalgo by the end of the coming school year knowing there was only so much I could do to stop it.

25

DANTE

"**D**O YOU REALLY WANT to interact with these people?" Davi asked.

"If I didn't want to, why would I be hanging out with them, Davi?" I replied, pressing the buzzer to Breanna's apartment.

There was a dull hum beneath the door, and I opened it before ascending up the stairs of the unit with Davi in tow.

"Fair point. I just didn't take you to be a social butterfly," Davi said, smirking a bit.

"Neither did I, but circumstance sure has a way of bringing people together."

Once we arrived at the floor where Breanna's apartment would be housed, I scanned the doors until I found the corresponding number ten she had told me was belonging to her unit. I knocked atop the wood for the door to open beneath my fist to reveal Leila. She looked between Davi and me with a pleased expression knowing I had only invited Davi in an attempt to see Damien win her over.

Leila gave a sly, all-knowing look before turning inward to announce to everyone gathered, "Guys, Dante and Davi are here!"

Breanna came over to the door, giving me a hug I was unsure how to reciprocate. Awkwardly, I patted her back while tilting downward to meet her reach halfway. She retreated to do the same thing to Davi. I watched her and Leila part to give access to the kitchen before us to find Conner, Damien, and Chase helping set a wooden table that was set lower to the ground than the ones I had grown up with. Cushions rather than chairs surrounded the slate, with Chase then moving to set the table. He, Damien, and Conner were in deep conversation and within the realm of laser focus that they did not notice me, nor the commotion made at the door.

"Welcome to my humble home," Breanna said, smiling. "You're in for a real treat, a genuine Korean feast all prepared by me and my little helpers."

"What are you, Santa?" I asked.

"Something like that," Breanna answered, sly. She leaned in close to then say, "I've told Conner to behave himself. So, I'm hoping you'll meet me halfway, ok?"

I glanced at her to see her expression conveyed ignorance to the reason why I did not like him. Truth be told, it was because of the run around he had been giving Breanna in terms of his feelings. That, and his stringing along of Davi in his pitiful display of selfishness in choosing to hook up with her despite knowing how he felt about Breanna. But I remembered she had confided in me that she and Damien were in the same predicament, and I could not help but notice the parallel between the two. I did not think I was close enough to Breanna's to meddle, but that did not mean I would not call out the impasse she and Conner were caught between because of it. Sure, it may not be listened to nor warranted, but I didn't think I'd like the person it would make me if I did not point out the obvious truth both Conner and Breanna were refusing to admit to.

I then said, "Have you done any reflection in terms of your stance with Conner?"

"Why, should I?" Breanna asked, feigning ignorance.

"I think you two need to have an honest conversation with each other, that's all."

Breanna smiled as if she were trying to scold an unruly child running amuck in the store they had walked into. "I don't want to have this conversation with you to start off the night, Dante. We're here to eat and have fun, ok?"

"Yeah," I answered, half-heartedly. "Then, I suppose I should ask, why isn't Celena here?"

"She has extra practices with Coach Clayton. You know how she hopes to go pro. It makes sense he would train her one on one, no?"

"I suppose so, but c'mon. Enough stalling. Let's eat."

Breanna smiled and welcomed me inside. I examined the décor to see it contrasted the home which Tito Clayton and I inhabited. It was covered in every crevice with pieces of carefully curated furniture and had this sense of feminine touch in the way they were arranged. Plants littered every conceivable surface near windowed, French doors leading to a balcony that looked too small for anyone bothering inhabiting its space. Fairy lights were hung up against the walls where pictures of Celena, Breanna, and their friends were taped against the off-white smeared across the walls. Past the dining room area in which the other men were gathered was a couch across from a flat screen television with a coffee table kept between the items. Smeared across the wood were various Vogue magazines. Before I could wander over to examine the other titles kept atop the surface, Breanna dragged me over to the table. I sat atop the cushion keeping the space between her and Chase, crossing my arms before Breanna looked across the food and then at Conner. Conner gave a nod before she then said, "C'mon, everyone! Let's eat!"

Gathered atop the table were various side dishes with big enough portions everyone gathered would be able to partake. Surrounding the small bowls filled with various foods I could not say I had tried before was a plate of carefully prepared short ribs. I looked at the food a bit overwhelmed considering I had no idea what to possibly pile onto my plate. Breanna took her utensils made up of chopsticks and an elongated spoon before doing the portioning for me. She then said, "Never had Korean food before? That's ok, Dante. I'll walk you through it."

"Appreciate that," I answered. "Did you cook all this food yourself, Breanna?"

"I had the recipes but put the men to work and had them help me."

"That's equality," Leila called sagely. "It's only fair men get up and work. It's all they're good for anyway."

Davi and Breanna laughed. The other men gathered and I looked at each other, unsure if commenting on it would see us be equated under the same metric Leila had imposed on us. I shrugged, more than aware of the fact I did not want to consciously be that asshole. Damien, Conner, and Chase then agreed with a nod.

"This is classic. Can't have a banchan without it. Kimchi. Fermented cabbage. You like spicy food, Dante?" Breanna asked, holding a wilted piece of the leaf smeared in a bright red up to my mouth.

"I do, yeah," I answered.

"Here! Try it."

Breanna cupped her hand underneath the food to place her chopsticks at my mouth. I met her halfway, eating the portion before turning to look between Damien and Conner. Damien gave a thumbs up, while Conner looked annoyed at what I could only assume he deemed to be flirtatious. I laughed a bit before moving my hand to cradle the bottom of my mouth and chew the food given. It was much spicier than I would have thought it to be. The flavor was a deep tang accessorized with an obvious sourness. Despite the obvious fire dancing across the length of my tongue, I did not dislike the taste of it outright, instead, giving Breanna a thumbs up as she began to pile some more of the kimchi onto my plate along with a hearty portion of white rice.

I then said after gulping down some water, "So, I suppose I should ask, is it true you guys bet on everything we do when it comes to inter-team-fucking?"

Chase wiped his mouth with a napkin, smiling wisely to say, "Of course, Dante. It's how we make the Lions economy go 'round. And how I make a pretty penny at the expense of those around me."

"Even me?" I asked.

The table fell silent.

"Now, what the fuck could you all possibly bet against me?" I asked, annoyed. "About my sobriety?"

"Never that," Conner said.

I turned to look at him.

Then, Damien answered, "Just about your dating life."

"And? There's nothing to report on that front."

The people gathered looked at me as if they were calling me out on my obscene, grandiose bluff. Their expressions were a mix of collective unbelieving with a twinge of annoyance at my stubbornness.

Leila then said, "You *are not* slick. You and Rue are so into each other, Dante. It's about time you simply admit to this truth instead of forcing us to do it for you."

"Even if I did like him, what would make me deserving of someone like him, hm?" I barked.

"Let's change the subject, please?" Davi called, an annoyed tone smeared across the words spoken.

Breanna, Leila, and Chase glanced at Damien. Damien then said, "Then do you like anyone, Davi?"

Davi glanced at him, looking him up and down. She settled on his blue eyes, then saying with a smile, "Why, are you interested, Damien?"

"Depends if you're on the market or not, love."

Considering Damien's less than suave reaction when we had first discussed the matter of his interest in her, the total opposite manifesting before me was, least to say, disorienting. I glanced at Conner, who looked between Breanna and Damien wounded, as if they had purposely kept him in the dark in regard to the nature of their relationship. While true, I wondered if I would have to see myself relegated to the fate of meddler. I knew Breanna would be forcing my hand in choosing to keep the man she liked in the dark in regard to the truth of her feelings.

Even if I hated Conner because of his same inability to be honest, that did not mean I was above the fate of being the ultimate harbinger of justice in regard to his and Breanna's tepid and equally undiscussed relationship. Mostly because I was sick of witnessing the impasse they had been caught between when it would be far past them should they simply just sit down and talk to each other. And if solving the issue at hand meant getting involved even if it annoyed me to no end, well, then so fucking be it.

Davi laughed a bit, a light blush dusting her brown cheeks. Then, she placed her utensils down on the table to clasp her hands together and say, "I do like someone, Damien. But I think if someone handsome like you is interested, I should throw away all responsibilities and run away with you, no?"

Conner then interrupted, "Am I missing something here?"

I glanced at Breanna. Leila and Chase did the same. Breanna did not meet any of our gazes, but she turned to look at Conner. Conner then narrowed his eyes, moving his food around in his plate to raise an accusatory eyebrow at Damien and then say, "Last I checked, you liked Breanna, no?"

A silence lingered.

Damien awkwardly called, "No, I don't like Breanna."

Another silence lingered, and I gazed up on Breanna to ask her with my expression what the truth would be. She did not meet my gaze, only smiling at Conner before gripping Damien's arm with her left hand. Damien opened his mouth to say something, but the words died between the confines of his throat. And it was then I knew getting involved was the only way to save the last shred of dignity the wannabe lovers were hanging by, before their inability to be forthright severed their shared, red string of fate.

"Oh, for the love of Christ," I said, annoyed. "You and Davi are just fucking. Breanna and Damien are just fucking. Sorry no one wants to say it, but it's obvious you two like each other and I'm sick of you two using other people as fodder because you don't want to have an honest conversation with each other."

Another silence lingered. Conner then swallowed down the lump in his throat as he looked upon Breanna, who met his gaze. They stared at each other when Breanna put down her utensils atop a wooden shelf with corresponding nooks for her special silverware. She then said, "Well, it seems I've lost my appetite."

"Me too," Conner called.

They watch each other.

"Then, I suppose we should... Talk?"

"I think we should."

Conner and Breanna rose from the cushions they were sitting at around the table, ignoring the rest of us to head down a hallway and into—what I assumed was—Breanna's room. When the door clicked, Leila and Chase burst into a round of a hearty applause. Davi rose from her seat to claim the cushion once belonging to Breanna between Damien and Leila. I ate some of the food Breanna had portioned on my plate to give an annunciated, fake bow with the curl of my wrist.

Chase then said, "Jesus, I didn't think you'd actually say that."

"I was tired of the tepidness in regard to their relationship," I answered.

Leila then said, holding up her head in her hand, "Rich coming from you, though."

Chase glanced at me.

I turned to Leila and then said, "And rich coming from me how?"

"Because you won't accept you like Rue," she answered, taking a bite of her rice. "Tell me, when are you going to put two and two together, Dante?"

I watched Leila's deep, rumbling eyes seemingly dissect my body language and posture. I ran my hands through my hair, rolling my eyes before turning away from her to eat my food.

I was brought back to the topic at hand when Chase then said, "You know Leila is right."

While having Leila claim she knew this part of my own innermost workings was unfounded, seeing Chase claim the same thing was enough to make me reassess the truth of Leila's declaration. I knew Chase knew me infinitely more intimate than I could claim to know myself. Mostly because quite frankly, I knew nothing to attribute to my sense of self other than this depression that had caught me between its piercing, three-inch canines. The blood spilled had long dried over the brown smeared across my skin. Its stain was a truth I could not simply wash away. Especially in something equally sacrilegious as the baptism seen through beneath an even stream of the alcohol I had been stripped of in even agreeing to be a Lion in the first place. Despite these reservations, and not knowing the person I was beneath the years of mental anguish, it did not change the fact Chase knew him, whoever he may be. And I knew I could not ignore such a truth when presented to me by the man I called a best friend, who saw me for all my broken and equally mismatched parts and yet, despite it, dared to stay.

I wondered, what would it mean if I liked Rue Oba? What could ever dare and come from this attraction if it were to ever be reciprocated? The question felt like a sickly, out of body experience. Like vertigo washed over my body when first abusing the liquid tether to sanity, and my tolerance was all but nonexistent. The spinning now encasing my body on all sides began to gnaw a sense of anxiety I knew meant I could not dare and answer the accusation presented to me either by Chase or by Leila. I did not want to smoke in a place that was not my own, but I did not think I could come out of this conversation withstanding if I did not have some kind of vice needed to process its truth and the weight it came with.

But I did not want to come across as a coward who ran from the harder questions when they were presented to him. Instead of getting up and seeing myself regain sanity by seeing the nicotine absolve me of the weight of my mortal sins, I simply began to eat my food instead. The silence that lingered was thick and equally palatable. But I knew better than to lift its weight off my shoulders when the truth of the question asked of me would be infinitely more sickening of a poison to swallow than refusing to answer it ever could. So, I turned to glance at Damien and Davi's flirtatious banter. Davi was leaning into Damien's range of motion, and Damien keeping his gaze locked on her own. And it made me wonder, would I ever want the same of myself and Rue?

Truth be told, I had never given it much, if any thought. Mostly because when you cannot even bring yourself to like the person you had become in the wake of your mental illness and subsequent addiction, it's not really fair to love another despite it. Knowing this and the matter of simply being undeserving of such a thing were two clashing ideals I did not think would come to see eye to eye anytime soon. I was more than aware of the reality that should I dare and be intimate with another person, they would never fix me, and I would never fix them. Such a metric was both unrealistic and unfair. But it did not change how there was this subsequent ache in my chest seeing Damien cradle his arm around Davi's waist and Davi lean into his chest with that told me, *I wanted the same thing despite all I had done in seeing myself absolved of this very truth.*

I shook my head, eating more of my food. I knew Leila and Chase were expecting me to answer their accusation, but I could not be so heinous to try when it meant admitting to what it was I now wanted. I hoped the coming deflection would lift the guilt now holding me beneath the piercing weight of its molars gnawing against my scarred, brown flesh.

"Then, what about you, Leila?" I asked, still nauseous.

She then said, "Your deflection is noted. And what good is a man for me, Dante? All they do is weigh you down when you're trying to rise above. Fucking headache waiting to happen, if you ask me."

Damien and Davi looked at her. Leila waved them off to then add, "Yeah, yeah, you two are gonna fuck after this. We get it. No need to rub it into my face."

Davi and Damien turned back to each other when I glanced at Chase. He looked me up and down, eventually turning back to his food. It was then the truth of what I now wanted had sunk to the pit of my stomach, joining the sinking feeling encasing my body below.

2 6

ROBYN

THERE WAS KNOCK ON Tito Clayton's front door, and I rose from the couch I was sprawled across to find my father beneath the wood.

I watched Max Zaragoza for an endless minute. It was no secret we shared some of the same traits, as seen in our inability to walk away from situations and people no longer serving us. Like in his marriage to my mother which had been drawn out long past its conclusion. In the wake of their finalized divorce, I was torn between two worlds where both co-inhabitants scorned their burnt bridge. The remaining truth of their union was the lingering ashes of what could have been, with me left as their only remaining tether who then had to pick up the pieces. It was something I had yet to really accept or forgive them for. After all, it was what had seen me driven into the thralls of my own addiction. But I knew better than to blame either party outright when I was still the woman who had dared to see through my coming to terms with its consequence in a blurry haze of tiny, white pills. And maybe it was some kind of sick, self-imposed revenge that would see the damage my parents had wrought upon me paid back in the damage I would come to wrought upon them in an even exchange for justice I believed to be righteous.

"Dad," I said. "What brings you here?"

"Your mother doesn't have the best way of wording things," Max said, frowning. "I think you've gone long enough without the truth. And you deserve that much since you're still picking up the pieces, Robyn."

Least to say, it was the absolute last thing I would have ever expected my father to say. Reluctant, I then said, "Alright. We can chat."

Max gave a smile, his wide, flat nose crinkling between the creases etched across his face. Maybe in some distant, alternate universe he and Tito Clayton would have been brothers rather than the friends they were today. And such a thought made me wonder if in that same timeline, would Max come to forgive the man keeping me alive like he had in this one?

My father sat in the recliner on the other side of the coffee table of Tito Clayton's brown, leather couch. I closed the front door behind him, locking it in good measure before sitting atop the middle cushion. I ironed out the creases in my dress with my palms. I flipped my hair to the right side of my face, adjusting my posture to straighten my back and shoulders. I imagined that my father would be divulging the truth on national television where the two of us would be forced to react to it in real time. Thinking of it like that made it infinitely easier to digest the fact it had taken him nearly twenty-two years for us to reach this impasse anyway.

"I suppose I should start," I said. I tilted my head up. "Did you ever love Mom?"

Max smiled. "No. But I wanted to."

I stared at him, tilting my head back to his eye level. "Then, why did you marry her if you didn't love her?"

"Your grandparents wanted me straight. Your mother's visa ran out after we graduated college. It seemed like a perfect scenario to both of us at the time."

Least to say, I could not have imagined those words coming from my father's lips. Staring at his shy, sheepish expression taut between the lines etched on his face told me he could not be anything else but genuine in this regard. I wanted to ask him the arrogant question as to why he did not think he could safely confide this in me in my youth. Of why he sacrificed his own happiness in order to make people he would never owe it to content with his life and what he had made of it. But I knew I could not say such thoughts aloud when I had never lived my father's truth. That, and should he not have seen the union through with my mother, I would become another statistic like my brother, forever lost in the foster system with no family to call my own. And I realized sitting before him with his eyes sage and equally unyielding, that even if our family was no longer what it used to be, that did not mean it was broken. I still had my mother, and I still had my father. And how many people can be lucky enough to say the same?

While this did not excuse the truth of what their relationship cost me, I knew having the childlike expectation of my parents being perfect was no longer fair. Because I had now aged out of its initiation rite. I was a woman now. That meant treating my parents through an adult lens because the three of us were all beholding to this same status. I knew I had an infinite amount of growing up to do in light of what I had done to see myself cope with their hatred of each other. But I did not think blaming them outright for being the party who drove me into the thralls of my addiction was fair. Because, still, I was the woman who had made the choice to see it through. I was responsible for the pain I had imposed at both their—and my own—expense. Just as they were for the matter of their own and its same truth.

I tried to speak for what seemed like an endless few minutes. I then said, "Dad, why didn't you tell me this earlier? I would never have judged you. After all, I'm a lesbian. I would have gotten it. And I think you know that."

Max looked reluctant, but ultimately said, "And live with the shame knowing my inability to be honest has caused you and Bruna all this pain? Knowing I could not live this honest and authentic version of myself until after your lolo and lola passed?

You're so much braver than me, Robyn. I have lived this lie for so long I tried to convince myself it was the truth. That's why when you came out, I could not help but remember the version of myself I tried to see repressed. And it's why I could no longer be with your mother when I realized I had to be honest with myself before it was too late."

I watched him. "I get it, Dad."

Max looked as if the weight of his original sin had finally been lifted from his shoulders.

"I understand why you did what you did. But it does not change the past as much as we wish it did."

"I know, Robyn. And that is why I am going to say it now." Max was quiet. "I'm sorry. I am so unbelievably sorry for everything, Robyn."

I could not help but pity the man I called a father. Even knowing the damage his shame had caused both me and my mother, it did not change how I understood the *exact* situation he had been seemingly trapped in. Every child who deviates from the expected norm present in society has to weigh the scales on whether or not coming out is something worth sacrificing their family in exchange. Because such was something I, too, had been forced to bear the brunt of when I told my mother and father the truth in regard to my lesbian identity. I realized now my father had tilted the scales to the realm beholding to family rather than self. Some could argue it was selfish. Maybe even the other truth of selfless. I stared at my father's tense, afraid, and equally vulnerable expression. And whatever anyone may call his choice, the single truth remained.

And that it had never been fair.

"Thank you for telling me this, Dad." I said, almost quiet. "Thank you for sharing this with me. But I have to ask, why did you and Mom have me if you knew your marriage was for convenience?"

Max smiled a bit. He reclined back in the chair, thumbing his fingers atop the scratchy, white cloth beneath him. He then said, "Your lola and lolo wanted grandchildren. Bruna knew I would never sleep with her, and so we decided adopting was our best bet to see the lie I had been living remain withstanding. But I don't regret it."

"Why don't you regret it, Dad? You've nearly lost your entire sense of self in the process. I don't get it. Really, I want to. But I don't."

"Isn't it simple, Robyn? It's because I have you to show for it. I would do it all over again just to be able to call you my daughter. I would sacrifice every part of myself solely to call you my own. Because when I held you for the first time and gazed upon your face, I knew, this was it. This was what my entire life had been waiting for."

I bit the inside of my cheek so hard I could taste the metallic finish of blood. In an attempt to keep the tears welling in my eyes at bay, I sunk my nails into my arms.

"And knowing I still chose to hurt you by refusing to be honest is something I have been forced to bear the brunt of since I have realized it. I know I'm the cause of your addiction. I know it's because of my shame that drove you into coping with it in a means that saw you hurt yourself. And I'm sorry, Robyn. I am so unbelievably sorry I have done this to you. That I *have done this to us.*"

I smiled, digging my nails deeper into my flesh to not let my emotions show through. I then said, "Dad, it's not nearly that simple, and you and I both know that."

Max looked up at me with tears, too, welling in his eyes. All resolve was lost the moment I saw the salt cascade down the curve of his cheek. I released my inhibitions and then watched a stream of my own break through the cracks of my eyelids, and I tried to wipe them away in a brisk pace to not show such weakness to the man I called a father. I don't know how I managed to say this, but the words came from between the creases of my lips when I heard the sound rumble between my ears in a foreign, out of place rhythm.

"You can't blame yourself for giving me what you thought was your best, Dad. I know now you tried. And truth be told, that's better than never trying at all. And, I'm sorry too. For being the only party who can say they *did this to us.*"

Max rose from his seat, moving to stand before me. He smiled, crouching down to place his hands atop my cheeks and wipe away the tears welling in my eyes. Like when I was a child, he gave that warm, all-encompassing smile. A warmth I had not felt since he and Bruna were together flowed throughout my body. My father pulled me close, kissing my forehead before moving to face me. He was smiling that same smile he had on his face whenever I had made him proud, like when I had gotten into Wesley on a full-ride scholarship, or had graduated valedictorian of my high school class.

He then said, as gently as he could manage, "You should start following your own advice, langga. And I'm ready to atone for the wrongs I had committed with both you and your mother."

I swallowed down the lump in my throat to then ask, "What about Conner, Dad?"

"With Conner too," Max answered, smiling. "If you'll have him, and he'll have me."

I smiled, moving to stand upright. My father and I embraced for the first time since I had been shipped off to college, this time with a shared love linking our beating hearts I thought could have never dared to be felt again.

27

DANTE

"**FUCK, MARRY, KILL: ME**, Davi, and Rue," Chase said, looking up from his phone to gaze up at me and my seat across from him.

"What is it with you and your weird hypotheticals?" I asked, taking a sip of my cold brew. "This question is like asking me if I would go back in time and kill one of two evil, historical figures while being forced to let the other one live."

"I want to know if you'd sleep with me if I were gay," Chase admitted casually.

"Hard no."

"What? Am I not pleasing to look at?"

"You're infinitely too complicated for me to fuck. You would harass me until I took you out on a date. Then, you would force me to pay."

"So, you think I'm cheap."

"No, high maintenance is the more appropriate title."

"Wow, fuck you, Dante."

"Good to know you still have a personality and the bleach didn't fry your brain."

"Girls like men in touch with their feminine side, Dante. Why do you think Celena has looked at me more recently?"

"You are hopeless in every sense."

"When I ask you to be the best man at our wedding, don't think I'm above an I told you so."

I laughed a bit, taking a cigarette out from the cardboard box resting atop the coffee table keeping the space between us. I scanned the room for Tito Clayton, as if he would be there despite already knowing the answer to such. Ultimately, I decided to not see through the only ritual keeping me sane knowing the stench would linger well past. It would only earn the ire from my uncle knowing I had disregarded one of his many rules in regard to my allowance here at Schaffer. And thinking of such made me think of my newfound effort of recovery; a truth I was going to see through for the sake of spiting my brother. Truth be told, I really had no conceivable idea where to start in terms of allowing myself to heal when this mental illness and the symptoms that came with it had defined my life for a long, eight years, and I did not know who I was without its constant, self-degrading truth.

It was more than obvious I owed the people in my life who made the choice to stay such an effort, but it was still something so gargantuan I was unsure how to properly slay the beast without two new heads emerging from the severed stump. And I didn't want to admit to Chase that he was right; that the night where he found me in a blurry haze of blood, pills, and sloshed liquor was something I'd come to regret, and it was unfair to put him through such. But it didn't change that in order to be the person he always thought of me as, it meant admitting to the crimes committed despite all the pain they had once dared to wrought. It meant no longer being a coward. And if that much was ever going to be true, it meant trying. Really, actually trying to be better this time around, and not giving up when I had reached a wave that demanded me to rise above the curl of my circumstance instead of drowning beneath it.

I lost all nerve and siphoned a cigarette from the confines of the white and red package resting atop the coffee table. I then grabbed my lighter resting next to it, placing the filter between my lips before flicking the fork and rendering myself a flame. There was no need to protect it from an outside gust of wind when the air between Chase and I was calm and equally palatable. It sent a sickly shudder down the length of my spine knowing the truth was about to be spoken. I dragged the ember to the other end of my vice, making sure it was burning before clasping it shut and inhaling the tobacco in a long, much needed drag.

Chase gazed upon me, seeming to dissect my entire stance and posture to then say, "Something has obviously been on your mind."

I blew the smoke from beneath my vice to then say, "I'm going to get better, Chase. And I'm sorry it took me this long to realize I needed to see this through. And I'm sorry I did not realize such when you found me on the bathroom floor and lay witness to a sight you should have never been subject to."

Chase moved to sit upright, placing his phone—camera side up—atop the coffee table we were gathered around. He moved to lean over; his gangly limbs looking more like twigs than corresponding arms and legs. I watched him place his elbows atop his knees. He clasped both his hands together, moving to study my face with careful thought before settling to say, "What changed your mind, Dante?"

I maneuvered the ashtray resting between us to dislodge a stray clump of ash. I then took another drag to say between the exhale, "I've come to realize the reason as to why Xavier gave me the scar on my face."

"Being?"

"It was so I would kill myself, and he wouldn't have to do the fucking work himself."

"So, you're getting better for the sake of pissing off Xavier?"

"What, is there something wrong with that?"

Chase laughed, then running a hand through his hair to say, "No. There's nothing wrong with it. Truth be told, it's so you I almost want to take a picture of what you just said and frame it to warn any other fucker who scorns you what would become of them."

I couldn't help but meet the laugh with a smile that poked out from beneath my hand. I then asked, "And what fate is that?"

"Bettering yourself solely for the sake of saying I told you so." Chase placed his head in his hand. He smiled at me, then saying, "I want you to know, Dante, the matter of your life and what it was worth? I could give a fuck on what was the catalyst to have you see it through. I simply just want you to see it through, Xavier be fucking damned."

"So, it's just like that?"

"Just like what?"

"A simple 'I'll support you no matter what' despite all the harm I willingly chose to imprint upon you?"

Chase laughed again. "For a smart man, you really are dumb."

Quizzical, I replied, "I don't follow."

Chase pointed at me, then saying between the part of thin, heart-shaped lips kept across an even shade of taupe, "I've made my choice to stay a long time ago, Dante. I promised you in middle school I would stick around as long as you needed me to. I promised you forever. And I meant every word."

I felt this pang of wounding inside the pit of my stomach knowing I did not remember this instance as intimately as Chase had. Come to think of it, I did not remember much, if any of the childhood I had been forced to leave behind in being branded eight years ago.

"It's ok if you don't remember," Chase called. He crossed his arms, resting thin hands atop equally thin biceps. "You've always been dealing with so much. I never expected to fix you, but I liked to think I helped bear some of the weight you were carrying."

"You did," I answered, almost quiet. "But why me, Chase? Why did you make the choice to stay?"

Chase didn't need time to think about it. "In middle school I had no friends because I had two moms. It's ok if you don't remember this, but I'll never forget it. It wasn't even an hour after you transferred after moving in with Tito Clayton that you got suspended for breaking the nose of one of the kids who was bullying me because you thought it was 'fucking stupid'. You gave me your lighter, and it was the covenant that bound us as we are now. You told me as long as I had it, no one would fuck with me. And no one ever did again. Because you were the only boy in the entirety of that fucking school who saw something wrong and *fucking did something about it*. My moms had tried every diplomatic route to see me defended, but they were never taken seriously. And it wasn't until you broke that fucker's nose that the bullying finally stopped."

"I was just doing what anyone else would do," I answered.

"But they didn't, Dante."

I was quiet.

"And you were the only one who did."

I knew the point Chase was making was one he was not going to relent on so easily. And I knew now that in seeing through the effort of my own recovery, it did not mean I had to believe him just yet when its founding was still in its infancy. Maybe I never would, and maybe the ego death overseen by my brother a long, eight years ago meant I was incapable of such niceties. But thinking this did not change what Chase thought I was deserving of. I would never forgive myself should I let this sickness win; only for its consequence to then pass this misery onto him when there could be nothing I could atone for such knowing I had left this earthly tether and he remained.

It was if I had realized in this perfect, seemingly insignificant moment standing before the best friend who had saved my life once before that I realized I did not need some grand, overarching purpose in order for my life to hold value. That merely the act of living at all—whether for self or for others—was the bravest thing you could do in defiance of darkness. And I don't know what made me more nauseous, accepting I was now going to see through this life until its natural end because of the people who refused to leave, or thinking on the long, eight years my tito had said the same thing and I had refused to listen.

I took another drag from my allowed vice, wondering if this newfound effort in terms of stability and sobriety would be one I could even manage, let alone be deserving of. The matter of inherent worthiness aside, the effort of slaying the beast of my addiction, trauma, and mental illness was an effort too gargantuan that I knew I could never begin to do such alone. But I never had been. I had Chase. Davi. Tito Clayton. Celena, and for some reason, I thought of Rue too. The labor that would come with bettering myself was one these same people who always saw an inherent worth in me would help me bear the brunt of. And even if I had done nothing to deserve such graces, it did not change they had offered me their kindness to begin with. And if these same people who had refused to leave me despite all I had done to drive them away, how could I be so heinous to push them away a final time when they, still, had chosen to stay?

I glanced at Chase, his jet-black eyes shining like an endless stream of oil spurting from the ground in a desolate countryside. He smiled, moving to trace his fingers against the skin of his palm, and I watched him trace the lines creased at the folds holding up his fingers until I met his gaze again. Chase watched me for an endless minute, as if there was something he had been meaning to tell me since our first meeting in an equally inhospitable middle school classroom where my first impression was made with blood.

Neither mine nor his, of course, but still, the red had seemingly tied our fates together into this incomprehensible knot, with no hope to loosen it unless one hacked a pair of scissors across the layered, interwoven edges. And it was then I realized that doing such would leave the other incomplete in every sense; with nothing left holding the other half left behind together but a bleeding, gaping hole taking the place of where the man we once called a best friend had stood. And even if I would never begin to deserve it, I promised myself I would allow myself four more years of this same life I had never wanted because Chase needed me in this way I could never begin to need of myself.

2 8

ROBYN

T **ITO CLAYTON HAD REQUIRED** his Lions to dress up to make a good impression in the coming humbling of Andrei Božović. Most of my male teammates opted for school provided suit coats kept atop an unbuttoned dress shirt, slacks, and neatly polished, leather shoes. I watched Dante join the rest of us Lions gathered outside our coach bus, and I placed my hand atop my eyes to block the stray rays of the sun to say, "It isn't a fucking funeral, Dante."

Dante laughed, annoyed and equally amused at the dig considering his outfit was entirely of black, including his platform leather shoes. I really thought the incredulous loyalty to the color was seriously inebriating an attractiveness I thought would only be more overbearing should he wear tones that complimented the deep and equally lovely brown kept beneath. Again, while I would not be compelled to appreciate such a thing considering where I swung on the human pendulum of sexuality, that did not mean I did not want Dante to reclaim a life that had been all but actively stripped from him in the wake of his brother's violence. Truth be told, while I did not think there was much on my end to be entitled to such, it did not change I harbored some sympathy for him. I knew the damage he inflicted upon self was because of the damage once seen through at Xavier's expense by parents I did not think he even remembered. And how could he when they made a conscious effort to be forgotten knowing raising Xavier meant they could not safely say the same of Dante?

"That's where you're wrong, Robyn," Chase called, his attire entirely identical to Dante's.

"Is someone dying like you've discussed prior?"

Dante did not seem fazed over the moral ambiguity of such a statement. He bore the weight of the life about to be taken evenly atop his shoulders when he glanced at Chase.

Chase smiled, equal parts toothy and crooked to say, "Maybe death is not imminent, but the high horse Andrei has been fond of riding will be all but butchered come the end of today."

"As he should be," Dante added. "Why the hell do you think I'm even dressed up if it were not some grand occasion?"

I didn't answer, only looking between the two of them. I wondered if there was a newfound sense of kinship shared between Dante and I knowing our same truth. I knew better than to think such now, but the coolness of his demeanor was almost enough to convince me there was an inkling of it housed between his piercing, black eyes and thin, brown lips.

The door to the bus opened to reveal Tito Clayton. He moved his gaze between Dante and me as if to accuse us both of harming the other.

I rose above the curl of such an accusation to say, "If I would have killed your nephew, Tito Clayton, I would have made sure I got away with it."

"You can only hide so many things from me when I am the man keeping you from death, Robyn," Tito Clayton replied.

He was right, and there was no point to argue with him knowing such.

"But we have to beat the traffic getting there, and I've waited long enough for Dante and Chase to show up. For the love of Christ, Dante, you really need a phone."

"And what, let people have a one-way mirror into my life, Tito?" Dante called, rising to meet his uncle on the steps of the bus. "The last thing I need is a phone. I'm sure the superficiality of social media I would see on a daily basis would drive me further into insanity at the sheer stupidity of it anyway."

I passed off my laugh as a cough. Dante didn't notice, but the last thing I would attribute to someone like him was a sense of humor.

"We'll have this fight when I'm not going on three hours of sleep pulling this all together for the past three days," Tito

Clayton called, guiding Dante onto the bus with a hand on his back.

Chase spared a glance at me, and I watched the pair descend to the back where Davi, Alexei, and Rue were waiting for them. Celena, Damien, and Breanna claimed the no man's land linking the back to the front. I turned to find Lisanna and Leila watching me with interest with the two of them each having an empty seat next to each other. I looked between them before turning to my left to find my brother sitting alone, staring out of the large, tinted window with his head against the glass. I pointed at Conner and both women nodded at me. Leila then moved to claim my once held seat next to Lisanna.

"Hello, manong," I called.

"Manong?"

"Older brother. In my father's dialect."

"I suppose it's a travesty I don't know anything about the place our parents called home, no?"

I sat down next to him, crossing my legs before turning to face him. "Nothing you can't learn."

"You can only teach an old dog so many new tricks."

"And what does that make me if you're this so-called old dog?"

A smile. I met the gesture with one of my own, aware he did not want to show me such affection laced between the part.

Conner then stretched his arms up in the air to say, "Well, you're my twin, so you must be equally as old."

"Am not."

"Am too. Have you tried speaking with Alexei? He makes me feel ancient."

"Touché."

Conner laughed, moving to fiddle with his tie. Now that I noticed the length, I realized he was the only man besides Tito Clayton donning one. I wondered if this stemmed from a respect for Celena I was unsure was warranted or not. Since the niceties were out of the way and a common ground between us had been established, I then said, "Breanna told me about your situationship."

Conner groaned, noticeably irritated. "Now what business does she have telling you?"

"I am your sister."

"Who I didn't know existed until a month ago."

"You're right," I called, crossing my arms. "Just because we are strangers does not mean I want for us to be. I want to be the family you never had. I want to show you that, Conner. And that means I care for you. Is that so hard to believe?"

"With my history, yes," Conner answered, snappy and almost afraid.

I thought the contrast in our first meeting was more so a defense mechanism in case I bolted rather than anything beholding to an actual hope I would stay. A part of me grew angry over such, but not in terms of self. Mostly in terms of Conner, who never knew what a family was, or what it meant to have one when he had grown up in a place devoid of such comforts. I knew better than to let his venom pierce beneath the skin. He was a wounded child trying to play a man's role, and I knew this same thread well as seen in Xavier Hidalgo. But I liked to think Conner contrasted the man I once called a best friend in a capacity to change Xavier would only be able to be seen with someone's blood paying its price.

"You've had a family all your life, Robyn. What the hell can you know about a situation like mine?"

Now, the ignorance needed to be killed at its root. I didn't know what ideas Alexei was putting in Conner's head, nor could I do anything to improve my standing above the only person in Conner's life who stayed. But their feelings did not change my truth as I had lived it. And it would be doing a disservice to the girl who had survived it to not defend her in the wake of my brother's ignorance.

"Correction, *had*," I answered.

Conner shrunk into his chair, looking at me as if I would lay craters into his face like figures of authority had before.

"You don't know me any bit as I don't know you. You can hate me after I've shown you my effort in terms of family, but until then, all you are doing is letting your past dictate your future." I turned to my brother, leaning my head atop my clenched hand. "Look around you. You are all alone. You have no one. And you don't have to believe anything it is that I'm saying. But you would be fucking idiot to cast me out headfirst because I am equally as much of a sinner as I know you are too."

Conner was quiet, then saying, "So, now you know what you need to do to be clean."

I was quiet too, eventually curling my lips into a smile as I then replied, "Sneaky fucker."

Conner laughed a bit. "Hey, it's the truth. And you're right. I've been unfair, and I really do want for us to be a family, Robyn. It's just that it's hard considering my history. You have to understand."

"Of course, manong, but it's nothing I cannot attempt to teach you too."

"Then, a promise?"

"Of what?"

"That we'll try. I mean, really, truly try to be a family."

"I promise."

Conner didn't answer. Instead, moving to stick out his pinky. I interlocked my finger with his own. I knew this was a covenant I could never bring myself to keep when my pills were weighing down my shoulder, housed in the chasms of my Chanel purse.

29

DANTE

I **LEANED MY HEAD** against the window I was sitting next to, propping up my chin with my hand now resting upright from the armrest belonging to my side of the bus. Chase was eagerly talking among the shared company of Davi and Alexei, and I didn't bother to include myself in their idle chatter despite lending an ear to stay up to date with the subject matter. When they began to divulge in the dating lives of celebrities I had made a conscious choice to remain ignorant to, I let my mind wander elsewhere, the sensation of smooth, highway asphalt propelling us forward washing this sense of calm over me I was unsure was founded or not.

Truth be told considering the context of why we were even going to Boston to begin with was enough to spurn a complete and total mental breakdown. However, Celena needed me more than I needed to succumb to the same pitiful, unassuming stereotype Xavier would expect me to be in making my debut as

Celena Božović's personal pet project. The circumstance commanded courage, and even if I knew I was incapable of exactly that in terms of self, it did not change Celena needed the same of me, and I would be the last person to purposely let her down. And it only made me ask myself, would I ever come to stomach the future I had seemingly given to her knowing it was every bit fluid as the spectrum of addiction I had been seemingly trapped in? And like it, would have to be worked toward despite the shared end goal never being guaranteed despite the blood I had given to see such come to pass?

The future was unknown. That much was beyond obvious to me that I knew better than to try to predict it with cards that gave vague guidance when you demanded clarity, or a system putting you into a box solely due to the month you were born. I knew the truth in regard to my own future was that in order for it to possibly get better, I had to live long enough to risk the opposite manifesting. And to be entirely fucking honest, I could not begin to stomach the truth that things could possibly *get worse.*

Truth be told, I had been at a consistent place of rock bottom for the past eight years, and I had liked the comfort that came with it being known. I did not remember what the surface looked like, and I thought it was too late to try. And even worse, what if I did not like the person I would soon become without the influence of this depression I had come to rely on to have a tangible trait to attribute to my sense of self? The boy I once was long dead. He was never coming back. And I wondered, would the person seeing through recovery come to be his equal, or something infinitely more heinous than I was now?

And even if I knew better than to ask myself such a question, it did not change I now owed Celena the same future I had promised beneath a noose that I would never see. In even agreeing to come to Dylan Rivera's show, I had given her a part of myself I had refused to give anyone else, and it was now too late to rescind such a thing knowing I had already told both Davi and Chase I would be so arrogant to *let myself heal*. What had I ever done to deserve that? What good left me entitled to redemption when I had done everything in my power to see myself absolved of just that? Recovery may mean stability—and in turn—sobriety. But it also meant meeting the same person I had given everything to see as collateral damage to the question of my life and what it was worth. And how could I face him knowing the crimes I had seen through at his expense? Like during sleepless nights where my blood washed away the original sin of my very creation. And I begged a god I could not bring myself to believe in that he would bestow upon me some kind of incurable, terminal illness in place of a child who would never deserve such a thing?

I would wear the badge of death with pride knowing I no longer had to see through self-destruction to finally get what it was I wanted, being the finite freedom of an end. There would be no mourners at my funeral. There would be no people to carry my casket. There would be no tears shed because the death that would soon befall me was expected, and there was nothing anyone could possibly do to change it. And that's all I wanted. But I was no longer allowed to see it through because I had been stupid enough to believe the pipe dream Celena had fed me since childhood. I was going to be announced as her heir apparent to every corner of the collegiate sports world, who would soon become the pallbearers carrying the casket of the man I once was. Every bit a coward as the man I could no longer afford to be as long as the world and Celena Božović were watching.

Rue's head poked up from the seat in front of me, and he turned to face me, arms curling around the headrest. We stared at each other, and I peeled off the wired earbud Chase and I were sharing to say, "You have something to say, obviously."

"You seem to be thinking something over," Rue answered, in a hushed enough tone it would not alert Davi, Alexei, or Chase that we were now in conversation. "You make that same face whenever something is on your mind."

"I didn't think I was so easy to read."

"I just know what to look for."

I laughed, amused. I then said, "Then, what is it that you think I'm thinking about?"

"How you're going to give Celena your future."

I felt annoyed I could be read so easily by a man I could never begin to say the same about. "Then, what's your take on it?"

"I think you're entitled to recovery. Especially someone like you, Dante."

"What makes me special, then?"

"Your brother wants you dead. He has given everything to see that you kill yourself so he doesn't have to get his hands bloody doing the work for you. I know you don't like to think of yourself as deserving of such an effort, but don't you think it'd piss him off if you were to get stable despite that?"

I smiled, slow and equally pleased. "Maybe you are right, Rue Oba."

Rue watched me, his endless pools of black lighting this unfounded fire beneath my chest.

"Maybe you do know me."

Rue smiled, and it was every bit otherworldly as the flecks of red lighting his gaze ablaze. The sun poked through the window next to us, setting into the color to give the same warm, out of place glow akin to this unfounded flutter seeping between the gaps of my ribcage. He moved to rest his chin atop crossed arms, staring at me with this affection laced between his expression I could not begin to comprehend. I mean, what the fuck had I ever done for someone to look at me *like that* anyway?

I knew better than to answer. Instead, I crossed my arms and gazed upon Rue Oba to find his appearance was even more alluring than I had once believed it to be. I noticed the faintest trace of freckles dotting the bridge of his nose that seeped into his cheeks. Dimples creased between his pair of thin, pink lips. I then met his gaze to find the same endless shade of brown staring back at me, daring me to be the party who looked away first. But for some reason, I could not bring myself to meet his challenge as I watched his gaze move up and down the length of body. There was this air of tension taking root between us. Thick and equally palatable. I knew it was felt between the other half before me as it was now entrenched in my entire being. There was this feeling that reverberated across the walls of my heart, smeared across in even coats of a clear, transparent lacquer. It was now flowing through the skin kept beneath even lengths of black cloth. I tried to conjure up a word to possibly describe it but knew any hope to name it was every bit futile as making it go away. I knew staring at Rue Oba that there was something I wanted of him, and I knew then with his calm, unyielding expression it was something he was more than willing to give me. But I could never begin to ask him of such. Not while I remained Dante Alonso Hidalgo; still a man who could never be worthy of such a thing, whatever the fuck it may be.

I turned away, but Rue's gaze remained. I glanced back at it to find he was about to speak, with the words coming next from his lips to say, "You're capable of change, Dante. Even if it's scary. And even if it's hard."

"Thanks, Rue," I answered, unsure if I meant it or not. "I'll keep that in mind."

The bus came to a final stop, and I gazed out of the window to find we were before a foreboding, Boston skyscraper with the letters 'ESPN' superimposed in an alternating red and white font. The letters were guarding comically large satellite dishes and their corresponding antennas; tethers linking us to the magic that would soon broadcast Celena's response to Andrei's declaration of war to the same collegiate world that needed her dead, squashed, and gone. The coming taping was something I was all but dreading, and not because I did not think kicking my brother off his post was a task the lot of us Lions could not handle if we really, truly worked at it. It's just that the announcement of our hope to upstage Xavier Alonso and his Wesley Cardinals would in turn give me the same future I never wanted to have. And worst of all, the glory, riches, and infinite respect Celena had promised me was equally fluid as the hope of seeing through my own stability and sobriety.

But I did not have the capacity to think of such now when the circumstance called for courage. Celena needed me, and I refused to see myself among the same company of the men who had failed her before. The mental breakdown could wait. In the meantime, I had a battle to win. The war was another story. Cowards came home without fanfare, and I refused to be one before the same man I was seeing through recovery in hopes of spiting. The answer to if I could meet such a challenge did not need to be dwelled on now. And that needed to be good enough—if not for the long term—then for now.

"We're here," Tito Clayton called. "Everyone rank and file. Hector will meet us here after the taping."

With that, the thirteen of us rose from our seats, with all the Lions following Tito Clayton out except for Davi and me. Her eyes were watching me with interest, as if to ask me a question the both of us knew the answer to but could not bring ourselves to be spoken. I stared at her before moving to follow our teammates out of the bus when she grabbed my arm and said, "You and Rue seem close."

"He's tolerable. How many people can say the same?"

Davi squinted her eyes. "Am I tolerable?"

"Of course, you are, Davi. What kind of question is that?"

"I just want to know where I stand in your mental hierarchy."

"You're my friend."

"Nothing more?"

"Why would there be anything more?"

Davi frowned, retracting her hand. "Forget I said anything. Let's just get this over with."

She walked past me, descending down the stairs to join our teammates on the concrete they were gathered. I followed her out, more than confused as to what she was asking of me to begin with. I glanced at her as I joined my teammates outside, and she met my gaze before moving to stand between Conner and Robyn and looking away.

"Alright, we're sticking together as I am your chaperone. No wandering off, and no violence. Get me?"

No one answered, and Tito Clayton sighed before recouping his losses and leading us into the studio. The twelve of us moved to the front desk where Tito Clayton answered the receptionist as to who we were here to see. She smiled, using her desk phone to announce to who would come and greet us that we had arrived, and I glanced at Chase while we waited. He was watching Celena as if he had never seen her before, dumb and equally awestruck.

Celena donned a black dress that seemed to be perfectly tailored to her figure, accenting feminine features I had never really paid attention to before. Her roots were now dyed to match the streaks of white cascading over her shoulders, with even length of a glossy black painted over fingernails usually kept the same porcelain shade beholding to her skin. She wore a bold, red lip kept atop a neutral foundation and accessorized with a dark, smoky eye leaning heavily on foreboding black eyeliner that contrasted her light, blue eyes. She was talking intently with Breanna and Damien, not noticing Chase gawking at her appearance less than nuanced in the almost sheer desperation laced between his expression.

I leaned into his ear, saying, "You could tell her she looks nice."

"I will," Chase answered, still staring at her. "When I work up the courage to bask in light as welcoming as her."

I didn't think that much was even true. A rhythm of contrasting flecks of marble against stiletto heels came towards us as a woman with straight, black hair and strong, round features greeted us with a smile. She cut through the Lions to hug Alexei and ignore the rest of us. A mixture of shock and confusion was splashed across our faces when she retreated from Alexei's embrace to cup his face in her hands and say, "My little brother, all grown up! And a college star no less!"

We greeted that with a collective nod and understanding of the nature of the woman and Alexei's relationship. Alexei blushed an even crimson, then saying, "Manang, I told you not to get all sentimental in front of my friends."

"You have plenty of time to be embarrassed after the fact." She turned to us and then added, "Dylan Rivera. I'm Alexei's older sister."

Dylan retreated from Alexei's range of motion to stand before Celena and Tito Clayton, giving a warm smile between the both of them before offering her hand. The pair each shook it, and Dylan then said, "My, my, my, hasn't it been a while. Three years to be exact?"

"About so," Celena called with a smirk. "Good to see you still have that good head on your shoulders."

"The feeling is mutual, Celena." Dylan smiled. "And Clayton, how are the Lions treating you?"

"As well as they can be," he answered, smooth, and equally charming in a way I had never really seen him annunciate before. I was sure the influence of his past in the spotlight certainly helped him come across as infinitely more charismatic than I would ever know Tito Clayton to be. Especially considering the nature of our relationship and the circumstances that prevented such.

"Good, good. Shall we, Lions? My studio is just this way down. Follow me, and we'll get you settled in."

The trailing of stiletto heels preceded our unit, guiding us down the hallway and over to the elevator that would lead us elsewhere. I could see with the now opened doors it would accommodate all fourteen of us, when a familiar face caught my attention I could only ever recognize as Andrei Božović.

I was unsure how Andrei could have learned of the taping when its rumination had been all but a secret as haunting as death kept among us Lions. It had to be this way in order for us to gain the upper hand in this coming war of attrition, but now I knew we lay weak, defenseless, and exposed by the way Andrei looked as if he were going to unhinge his jaw and swallow us whole. I watched Tito Clayton rush forward, but Chase was faster, speeding past my uncle to stand before Andrei Božović. No words were spoken except under the context of a fist that had landed directly into Andrei's nose, earning a fierce curse in his native language. The blow recoiled him by a few inches considering the matter of its abruptness, and I watched as Tito Clayton teleported to grab Chase from Andrei's range of motion and yank him backwards. A wall of people had been erected between our opposing factions, with Chase then yelling loud enough to cut through the bodies gathered between him and

Andrei to say, "See what the fuck else happens when you talk about Celena like that, cocksucker!"

Andrei glanced at his daughter, who did not react to his presence other than housing an expression washed over in a kind of indignant pity. There was no affection housed between either of them, only hurt. It was a truth I felt too when thinking of the parents I had been forced to leave behind, and it made me wonder how I would react should I meet them again. I banished the thought to my stomach as a shudder ran down the length of my spine, reminding me of the task at hand. And it was to face the vitriol at Celena's side rather than having to do with me and my myriad of issues both external and internal.

"You should learn to control your players, Clay," Andrei called, the use of his nickname in an attempt to mock him.

"You could say the same of your own," Tito Clayton replied without missing a beat, digging his fingers into Chase's bicep. "Or, is your knack for degradation genetic?"

Andrei huffed. He did not reply, only moving past us to exit with his own entourage who did not meet our gazes on their way out. Before he was out of my immediate vision, I glanced at Andrei's face to see Chase had warped his nose in a dramatic, left angle, with blood dripping down the length of his top lip. I smirked a bit. Mostly because I was the man who taught him how to throw a decent punch.

Something told me to look at Celena, so I glanced at her to find she was now staring at Chase with this sense of wonder tucked between her eyes I had never really seen her express before. I could have sworn I saw the faintest trace of a blush dusting her cheeks, but before I could ask her about such, Tito Clayton said to Chase, "Now, why *in the fuck* did you do that, Chase?"

Chase glanced at Celena. Celena, too, was waiting for his answer. Chase smiled at her before turning back to Tito Clayton to say, "He said it best, no? Play stupid games and win stupid fucking prizes. He shouldn't have been so surprised when I broke his fucking nose. After all, Dante taught me how to throw a decent punch."

Now, I was the party smirking. I glanced at Celena to see she was already watching me, and we gave the other a nod. Perhaps the cause once deemed hopeless by me and everyone else making up the Lions to see Chase and Celena together, maybe, was not as impossible as we had once thought.

3 0

ROBYN

THE BACKSTAGE AREA OF Dylan Rivera's show was plush and equally elegant. There were two black couches across from each other and split in the middle by a glass coffee table with all kinds of magazines smeared across transparent slate, held up by metal legs. The walls surrounding us on all sides were a pristine white and accessorized with black flat screen televisions. They gave us a view of the studio set where we could see Dante and Celena sitting next to each other in corresponding, plush chairs. There was an empty seat across from the two of them where Dylan would soon be seated, and I watched as various staff members began attending to the needs required of their guests, touching up their makeup and wiring up their microphones. I crossed my legs. I was eager to see what Celena's response would be in the face of unjust, sexist vitriol at the hands of both her family and Xavier Hidalgo; a man I was still every bit dependent on as I ached with my entire being not to be.

I knew the easy answer in terms of where Xavier should rank in my mental hierarchy was near—if not totally at—the bottom. It was not lost on me that the fact I was even here as unwanted moral support for the woman who probably needed him equally dead as Chase and Rue did was because of the matter of his betrayal. I was not the kind of woman to think of herself as a kind of pillar of moral authority, and I knew I could never be in the wake of my addiction. I knew the choices I had made and what would be needed to atone for them, and yet, time after time, I still had refused to see it through. Sobriety would give me and Lisanna a stable foundation to rebuild our relationship knowing I had uprooted the previous one with a jackhammer of my own deceit. But being here among the same people I had once helped to scorn, I asked myself, was Xavier Alonso Hidalgo a man better off dead as Rue, Chase, and I knew Celena, too, would come to suggest?

The matter of revenge gave an obvious answer. In order to be avenged, it meant taking the life of the man who had once dared to try and take my own. Blood for blood was an equal exchange for justice that is righteous. And such would extend to Xavier Hidalgo and what payment would be wrought for actions he, too, had willingly chosen to see through. I knew killing Xavier was the only way to see myself avenged when leaning on bureaucracy to see justice wrought was simply pointless in every regard. Xavier was good about covering his paper trail, and even if he were to slip up, it did not change the company we once shared would side with him in every possible instance knowing I was now a traitor among their court. And even if justice meant Xavier paying the price for his crimes with his life, I could not begin to stomach the execution of a man I had yet to so easily absolve myself of like the Lions around me had knowing they had never been loved by him a long and equally insignificant sliver of time ago.

I knew the other Lions did not know the truth of Xavier's own circumstance, but it did not change that I did. After all, if it were really true I had never been an equal in regard to his mental hierarchy, why would he have trusted me enough to dare and tell me such? We both knew I had made an attempt to oversee the atonement of Xavier Hidalgo, only to be scorned in the process. Such was not so much of a reflection of myself as it was of him, but it did not change how it sure as hell did not feel that way. I had made him my personal pet project akin to what Celena was now seeing through with Dante; to be the woman who finally fixed a man once deemed unfixable. And therefore be able to gloat in being the party who had spurned change upon a man who had once refused to be it through.

But the thing about this predicament that contrasted Celena and I, despite its founding being under the same truth, was that Dante was virtuous in his need for change. Celena was giving him the future he always ached he would never see. It was a truth I knew Xavier would come to find out after Dylan's show was broadcast across a national stage. Dante would then rescind Xavier's ownership of his fragile state of mind and would burn the last bridge linking them together. The only wood left had been near the edge of total calamity for a long, eight years since Xavier branded his younger brother for payback for crimes he thought he committed. But the thing about this lapse in morality that Xavier held above mine, Davi, and Dante's heads was that it had never been our intent to hurt Xavier in the process. But the thing about Xavier was that he was never fair. He was a child trying to play a man's role in regard to the answer on who would be the party to atone for his past. And maybe knowing this meant I had been a fool in trying to oversee his atonement, but it did not change how I had seen it in small, seemingly insignificant glimpses. And knowing that in his scorning, we had become dependent on the same vice despite all the damage wrought upon the other. And this truth, in turn, meant I still could not condone the execution of Xavier Alonso Hidalgo.

The backstage of Dylan's show reminded me of the kind of hangout only celebrities would be able to attend considering their monetary privilege and status. It felt strange to be welcomed into it solely on the basis of a sport I did not care nearly enough about. Truth be told, it was no secret Dante and Celena were the only Lions who had any conceivable hope to one day join the NHL on the merit of talent. Knowing this, it made sense to me that they would be the combined force facing the vitriol as a duo making up both halves of states of play in hockey, being offense and defense. Truth be told, I was unsure how either of them would compose themselves in front of heavy, overbearing studio cameras, but I didn't think they'd be as vindictive to Dylan as they were to me. After all, I didn't think Tito Clayton would have allowed them to inhabit the same space in front of a national stage before his colleagues and peers should they be.

I sat next to Conner with Lisanna on the other side of me. Leila sat on the other end of my brother and Davi sat next to her on the end with the five of us squeezing onto a couch that probably shouldn't fit more than three atop its cushions. Breanna and Damien sat next to each other but kept an empty seat between the two of them. I glanced at Conner. Conner met my gaze before applause rang through the speakers, and the camera panned to Dylan Rivera sitting atop a plush, white recliner. The view of Dante and Celena had been purposely cut out to give an added layer of surprise to their appearance.

Dylan smiled into the camera with a ready, news anchor smile to say, "Welcome back to Dylan River Prime Time. You all heard what Andrei Božović had to say in terms of his daughter and Clayton Alonso last week on my show. And here, we have Celena Božović for her first televised interview since joining the Lions three years ago."

The camera panned to Celena without including Dante in the shot. Celena, much to my surprise, gave a press worthy smile of her own to then say between a bold, red lip, "Thank you, Dylan. The honor is mine to have you give me space to speak my mind."

"Of course, it's the least I could do for someone of your same status, Celena." Dylan leaned forward, crossing her legs. "Let's roll right with the punches. Your father, your brother, and even Xavier Hidalgo have run your name through the mud at every camera they could find. Hell, even most of the press has partaken in the effort to take you down. But you haven't given light to these accusations and misogyny until now. Why is that?"

"You see, I am in a position where my presence is a lose lose. I speak out, I'm a firebrand. I'm a woman who doesn't know her place. I'll be deemed a woman trying to play a man's role who is compensating for a lack of talent with rebukes that have no founding. While nowhere near true, the other face of the coin is not much better either. Silence can be interpreted any which way you want it to be. Maybe some people thought I was afraid. Maybe they thought I bought into the vitriol and knew I could not face the cruelty because of it."

"Do you think it's true, then, Celena?"

Celena smiled, fierce and equally cold. "No. It never has been. I am coming on the record on your show to assert I will prove every one of my critics wrong in the coming season. I know better than to predict a miracle, but the true merit of my talent will be shown to you all soon enough. And quite frankly, I have Dante Alonso Hidalgo here with me to put that much to bed. Because we will both do what is needed to be done to cut the Wesley Cardinals down at their knees. We are two halves of a perfect offense and perfect defense. And quite frankly, I pity any man who has been stupid enough to dare and challenge us in the coming NESCAC Championships."

The camera panned to Dante, who adjusted his posture in the chair that was infinitely too small for his stature. He gave a smile, the camera panning down his face to give perfect light to the scar reflecting the white, overhead lights. The raised skin almost gave this kind of glint to the line, illuminating a shadow cast by his high cheekbones that I knew made the audience gathered begin to whisper.

Dante then smiled, malice-ridden and every bit indignant as Celena before him to say, "Celena intends for me to take over the Schaffer Lions when she graduates. And I have come here to say on the record that I have every bit of an intention as her to see that my brother is humbled in every possible regard."

All of us Lions began to look at each other. It was no secret Dante was every bit a coward as I was, and we had no idea what had brought on this bout of courage displayed by a man who we all knew had none. I glanced at Tito Clayton, who adjusted his crossed arms and was staring at the screen before him with the same pair of dark, rumbling eyes as his nephew before him. There was a slight attribution of fondness creased between the lines etched into his face to show for his age, but other than this thinly veiled sense of pride tucked between his eyes, I could not tell either what he was thinking or feeling. Instead of dwelling on such, I turned back to the television.

"Dante, do you think Celena is a capable leader of the Schaffer Lions?"

"Of course, Dylan. Truth be told, I trust her with my life."

I didn't think that was much of a metric to gloat on like the audience might.

"And Xavier is a small, pitiful boy trying to play a man's role. We all know if he were to take on Celena one on one, he would be eviscerated off the face of the ice without a single remnant remaining to show for his obscenely grandiose ego without any kind of talent to back it up. He can talk a big game all he wants, sure, but he cannot outrun the truth. I should know. Because I'm done hiding behind my uncle, and Xavier is finally going to get what's fucking coming to him, Dylan."

I glanced at Tito Clayton. He was smiling slightly, fierce and every bit spiteful as his nephew before him. I watched him laugh, taking a sip of his water bottle to block his expression.

"And with that, we'll be right back after a short break."

The camera panned away from the stage. A silence lingered between us Lions gathered, who were all watching Tito Clayton, waiting for his next move in regard to his nephew's promise to see through his own stability. Tito Clayton swallowed down the rest of his water, looking among his Lions to then ask, "And what are all of you staring at?"

None of us spoke.

Tito Clayton then said, "You heard Dante, did you not? We have an enemy to vanquish. And I'm content with the blood that will soon be smeared across my hands knowing I will be the force that will help you see it through."

Tito Clayton placed his water bottle atop a nearby table and crossed his arms. I then turned back to the commercials selling cheap, useless products flashing on the flatscreen television. And I knew if a man every bit beyond saving as Dante Alonso Hidalgo would be seeing through his own recovery for the sake of spiting a man better off dead, there was no longer any excuse for me in that same regard.

31

DANTE

"**AND THAT CONCLUDES DYLAN** Rivera Prime Time. Thank you all for tuning in, and we'll see you again next week."

The camera fixated on Celena and me panned away from the two of us. I exhaled knowing the courage I had mustered from the deepest depths of my subconscious had done enough to see me withstanding in the face of the brother I had been forced to leave behind. I knew the mental breakdown that would follow would be detrimental to the already minuscule progress I had made in terms of my own recovery, but I still had enough time not to think about such when we were not yet back at Schaffer, and my newfound fix of my favored vice was beyond my immediate range of motion. I felt like I was about to collapse into a pitiful pile of once working parts when wooden heels atop the hollow, studio floor caught my attention. I turned to find

Tito Clayton coming up to the set, first addressing Dylan with a handshake.

"Wonderful as ever, Dylan. You always do know how to ask questions that aren't stupid. And I really can't say the same of your peers."

Dylan smiled. "Why don't you come and do your own interview, Clayton? Andrei attacked you as well. It would make sense you come and address his vitriol yourself, no?"

"The days of press cameras are long past me," Tito Clayton answered, laughing a bit. "But I'll keep that in mind should I feel the need to come clean."

Dylan smiled again, and they withdrew from each other. Tito Clayton then glossed his gaze over me before walking over to Celena who watched him before saying, "I'll give you two some time alone."

Celena rose from her seat and followed Dylan off the set. The only people inhabiting the space were me and my uncle, and I adjusted my shoulders to bear the newfound weight of my recovery evenly atop my shoulders. We watched each other, seemingly daring the other to speak first when Tito Clayton then said, "You had yet to tell you were going to have a future."

I frowned, replying, "I couldn't tell you the truth. Not after I had done so much to hurt you before, Tito. I couldn't face you knowing what I had done. I didn't think I would come to survive it anyway."

Tito Clayton crossed his arms. "And yet you could face the world?"

"Don't ask me to explain," I said, quiet. "I don't think it'd make much sense anyway."

"Don't worry, anak," Tito Clayton called. "It makes perfect sense to me."

A silence lingered between the two of us, when Tito Clayton crouched down until the two of us were eye level considering I was still sitting atop one of the chairs. He flashed his arms, rolling down the even lengths of dark, opaque cloth covering the skin to reveal scars of his own he had made a conscious effort to hide from me. Littering his inner forearms were a myriad of puncture wounds, with the veins trailing down them darker than skin kept atop. I winced at the sight of them before moving my gaze to meet my uncle's, hesitant and equally afraid. Tito Clayton met the solemness in my expression before rolling his sleeves back down. We watched each other, our shared expression daring the other to speak first.

Even if I don't think it was every bit warranted on my part, it did not change I had gone out of my way to see that I knew of Tito Clayton's past, before he was now finding the courage to tell me. I knew a year after his first and only Stanley Cup win, he had been stripped of his NHL contract and kicked off his team. He then had been forced to rebuild his life without a means to support himself and exiled from the same world he had built his entire sense of self around. While I could not find the reason as to what had spiraled in him into the same myriad of self-destructive behaviors as I, too, had seen through in the wake of my own battle with addiction and self-worth, I knew it had something to do with the woman our hockey arena was named after. And I hoped he found some comfort that in this facet of my uncle's life, I did not choose to ease my own curiosity in regard to the nature of their relationship. After all my uncle had given for me to even still say that I was here, I thought he was entitled to this instance of privacy. Even if I knew repeating his same behaviors of past it probably put him in a position that was less than righteous. Truth be told, I was unsure how to live with myself knowing the damage I, too, had wrought upon him in the wake of his own push and pull with sobriety.

Tito Clayton then said, "I know you know about my truth."

"I'm sorry, Tito, I shouldn't have pried."

"It's only natural you were curious. After all, you were so young when you were given to me. I think you're entitled to know if the man who would act as your step-in father would be capable of doing the job."

"You've been more than capable," I answered, quiet. "I wouldn't still be alive if it weren't for you, Tito."

"You know, you gave me a sense of purpose in the wake of Nora's death," Tito Clayton said after a bit. "After she was murdered, I didn't know what to do with my life. I blamed myself for leaving her behind, for choosing hockey over her and could not bring myself to let myself go unpunished knowing such."

I leaned back in my chair to say, "Did you love her, Tito?"

"I did. A part of me still does."

"Then I don't think she would blame you for a death you had no way of knowing was going to happen while you were chasing your own dreams."

Tito Clayton smiled as if I was too naive to ever possibly understand his past as he had just told it to me. He stood upright, offering his hand to then say, "C'mon, anak. We have the other Lions waiting."

I realized his attempt at deflection. Instead of being so heinous to answer it, I gave a nod before leading my uncle off the set. His hand was atop my shoulder along with the newfound weight of seeing through my recovery for him and self balancing the other out.

3 2

ROBYN

TITO CLAYTON BEGAN TO lead the lot of us Lions back onto our coach bus, and I noticed Davi was nowhere to be seen.

Come to think of it, I had not seen her since we had begun to depart from the ESPN studio in which Dylan Rivera Primetime had been taped, and I glanced at the growing distance between me and the line of Lions to grab my phone from my purse and text Davi.

where r u?

She did not text back a reply but shared her location with me. So, I began to trace her steps until my phone said I was a couple feet from her. When I saw who she was with, my heart began to gnaw on itself, leaving this sore, gaping hole where my stomach and corresponding entrails once stood.

Because standing before me was Xavier Hidalgo and Elliot Božović.

The circumstance did not call for cowardice. Truth be told, I was going to be the last person who would willingly show it when I could not afford to come out of this confrontation on the losing side. I placed my phone back in my purse before sharing my location with Lisanna, then flipping my hair and clicking my heels before striding forward. Xavier curled his thin, pink lips to accommodate my presence and retreated his weight framing Davi in place to meet me halfway. Elliot remained behind him, and I looked down at Xavier Hidalgo to see he was the same pitiful height of five feet even. Short, black hair was styled with the same middle part and framed either side of a face smeared in a light, unassuming peach and accessorized with light, hazel eyes.

I crossed my arms before jerking my hand forward. The shape struck down to move across the skin of his left cheek with the sound filling the space between us as I watched him recoil a few inches backward. Staggering back upright in an attempt to see himself withstanding in the face of my violence, Xavier moved back to face me. And I think there was the one remaining emotion I held for Xavier Hidalgo, being pity. Truth be told, it was the only thing keeping me from agreeing with Chase and Rue that the man I once called a brother should pay for his own mortal sins with his life. Because my rage did not change that Xavier was every bit dependent on the same set of tiny, white pills as we both knew I was too.

"You certainly look shorter than I remember," I answered.

Xavier peeled his palm from his cheek to find my hand had left a red imprint against his skin. "And you are every bit as much of a bitch as I remember."

"Takes one to know one, sweetheart. Are we done with the idle chatter, or can I take Davi and leave?"

"I surely hope you have more to say to me than that," Xavier called, smiling with the slightest writhe of fondness tucked between the part.

I couldn't help but find the same emotion peak through my own expression despite my best effort to see it repressed. Instead of either of us answering to the accusation placed upon us by the other, I glanced at Davi to see she was already watching me, her expression taut and equally tight. She was gripping something in her chest. I knew better than to think I could get past Xavier to get a good look at the vice clenched in Davi's palm, so I flicked my gaze back to the task at hand, which was reducing Xavier Hidalgo into a pitiful pile of ash, soon to be swept away by a stray gust of wind that would in turn leave him finally out of my life for fucking good.

"Davi," Xavier called, opening his palm in the back of his head. "Since there's no need to plant my gift in Robyn's purse when she is not looking like last time, we can simply give it to her instead."

It all clicked in that instance.

Davi was a traitor among our court, and she was working with Xavier.

Emotions began to boil inside of me; like hot, furious bubbles of a teapot kept atop a burner far past its cry for removal. The first thought I had was to tell each and every one of the Lions what it was Davi and done. That she had been the party who had been supplying me and Dante fixes in terms of our shared trait of dependency. That she had been the party who told Andrei we would be here in an attempt to intimidate and belittle the woman he called a daughter but whom we at Schaffer had called our leader. I wanted nothing more than to slap Davi across the face and hurl whatever obscenities stuck for failing to keep her head above the curl of Xavier's rip current. My most primal of instincts felt every ripple of her betrayal and the calamity that would soon befall the Lions because of it. But the moment I caught the bottle of pills Xavier had then tossed at me, it was as if the foundation of morality I had placed myself upon had been uprooted only for fear to take my rage's place.

Because reading the letters printed across the white label contrasting the orange bottle beneath, I knew this vice was not the same Oxycontin I had become dependent on in agreeing to abuse it with Xavier in the first place.

No, this was the Fentanyl that saw me overdose under the guise of one, last goodbye high with the men I had once called my best friends.

The obvious matter of morality meant giving Xavier back the very same gift that would oversee my butchery at the hands of self rather than his own. Xavier was a smart, sly, and equally conniving man I knew I could not underestimate when it came to the question of how he should pay for all the wrong he had done to me. The thing is, though, I knew I was much smarter, and that his self-imposed status as this reclusive, misunderstood genius was not any bit accurate when we both knew he was currently maintaining the baseline GPA needed to still be on the Cardinals's roster.

I knew what the pills meant, and I knew what they represented. It was a means to see me dead without Xavier having to lift a finger; it was a way to see him come out on top despite the only effort seen through to say such was supplying me with the means to oversee my own execution. And I knew a rational line of thought meant saying no to this sinister covenant and telling Xavier Hidalgo to go fuck himself. But, matters of the heart are not so simple when you are bound to a vice. And I'll give Xavier credit, he made good sure that the matter of my own cleverness had long ago been outweighed by the trait of addiction we now shared; despite no longer having the friendship that had once been the catalyst to first see it through.

I also knew that the matter of telling the Lions of Davi's betrayal would then mean Davi would out me and my lying to the very same people I owed honesty to. I glanced at Xavier, who smirked as we met each other's gaze, and I knew this truth was not lost on him either. I bit the inside of my cheek before placing the bottle next to the other inside my purse, then flicking my gaze back up to Xavier to say before he could give a snide remark in response, "You fucking did this to me, Xavier. And don't act like you didn't turn me into this monster."

Xavier smiled. "You've had plenty of times to atone for your past mistakes, now have you, Robyn?"

I was quiet.

Xavier inched closer.

"You know what it takes to be the person you promised your parents and Lisanna you always thought you were." Xavier was now standing before me, and I watched him place a hand on my shoulder, then leaning into my ear to whisper, "But I know the real you. The liar. The cheat. The addict. Because you and I are one and the same, Robyn Zaragoza. And you would be nothing more than the very same liar you are so arrogant to think you're not if you were to think otherwise, no?"

Xavier retreated back to his original post. I stared at him like he was sickly, out of body hallucination as I swallowed down the lump in my throat. My confidence had now been replaced with this full body, all-encompassing fear. And I knew staring at Xavier Hidalgo that the man I had once loved like a brother was no longer there, and the man who had taken his place could only feel one emotion, being hate. He smiled, every bit evil and every bit wicked as I once thought he never could be until he had made the choice to hurt me. I knew staring at him there was no longer any hope for the healing I had given blood to oversee. And truth be told, I was a fool to think there ever could be.

"You should have known what choosing Dante over me would have cost you."

Xavier turned around and began to walk away.

"But I didn't."

Xavier stopped walking.

"But I didn't."

Xavier turned around to look at me. And for the first time in the four years I had known him, I saw sorrow tucked between his eyes and grief etched between his frown.

But I did not have long to admire the emotion I had once deemed him beneath. I watched him turn back around and exit the hallway with Elliot following behind him. His gaze lingered on my own for a moment as if to apologize on Xavier's behalf. But I knew better than to attribute such to Xavier unless I were to hear the words come from his behalf instead of the man who had taken my place. And when the two of them had all but disappeared from eyesight, I turned to Davi.

Neither of us spoke when I heard Lisanna call, "There you are, Robyn."

We turned to face her to find Tito Clayton was with her. I smiled at the pair as if they are the oldest of friends, who I would only come to betray later in a death only a liar, a cheat, and an addict like me could be deserving of. I turned to Davi who was already staring at me, and I smiled and said, "C'mon, Davi. It's good I found you before you wandered off too far and God knows what would have happened to you, right?"

Davi only managed a nod, a little awestruck at how perfect the lie had sounded coming from the tip of my tongue. I turned back to Tito Clayton and Lisanna who were already watching me, only to say, "Sorry for getting lost. I didn't want Davi to get left behind."

"It's not a problem, Robyn," Tito Clayton answered. "As long as you're safe and your head is still on your shoulders, I could give a fuck how long it took us."

"Good to know, Tito," I replied. "I'm sorry for the inconvenience."

"It's all water under the bridge now," Tito Clayton answered again. "C'mon, the other Lions are waiting."

I glanced at Lisanna who was watching me with interest. I gave a tight smile and a nod as Davi and I walked over to join her and Tito Clayton. And as we walked out of the building, it was then I realized the person I had always promised her I would be had never really, truly existed, if ever at all.

ACT THREE

RUE OBA

CENTER #3

JULY 4, 1997

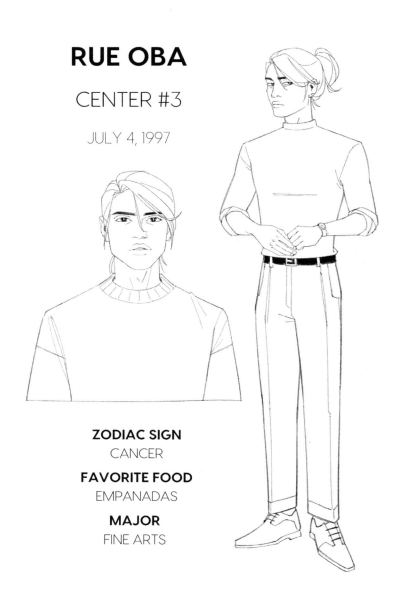

ZODIAC SIGN
CANCER

FAVORITE FOOD
EMPANADAS

MAJOR
FINE ARTS

3 3

DANTE

I **KNOCKED ON THE** door to Max Zaragoza's office when a call to open it greeted me beneath the wood. I opened the brown slate with a forceful push to find Max sitting at his desk, glasses atop his flat nose and buried in stacks of ungraded essays. I glanced between him and the door for him to motion for me to close it. I obliged, peeling off my duffel bag as he offered me the seat across from him. I watched him part the stacks of paper keeping the space between us until I was in his immediate range of sight.

He smiled to then say, "Dante, to what do I owe the pleasure?"

"I wanted to talk about my uncle, if that's alright with you," I answered.

"Well, we have plenty of material to work with, I'm sure," Max answered somewhat dryly. "I suppose our lives are infinitely more interesting than a compare and contrast essay, no?"

"Yeah," I answered. "I have to ask, what made Tito Clayton so successful in seeing through sobriety and his own recovery?"

"His faith," Max answered, leaning back in his chair. "Ciara helped him along the way too. I think that's why he was so lost for so long. He had no one to help guide him back onto the right path. Or, he thought he didn't. But truth be told, even I'm unsure if I had the capacity to help him knowing all he had done because of it."

I swallowed down the lump in my throat. "He hurt you. I take it."

"I'm sure you know how such goes hand in hand with loving an addict," Max answered somewhat rigidly. "They hurt you and you know it's because they're sick. But the heart doesn't forgive betrayal like the mind does."

"Then, what did Tito Clayton do to you, Professor Zaragoza?"

Max smiled innocently, like I was a curious child asking questions I had no tangible intelligence to possibly understand. Max leaned back in his chair, placing his palms on the back of his head before saying, "You and your uncle are a lot alike."

"How so?"

"You think you have to bear the brunt of your misery alone. Because who could possibly understand it like the two of you? But the thing is, Dante, what your uncle and you have yet to understand is that leaning on someone else when you need to is not a weakness. Truth be told, it's essential to our own survival. And to be honest, do you really think you would still be alive if you had not dared to try such before?"

I was quiet, almost afraid when I then said, "Have you forgiven Tito Clayton for all the hurt he's given you?"

"I've made my peace with it," Max answered after a bit. "But forgiveness is something I have yet to be capable of knowing what has already happened."

A silence lingered.

Max watched me with interest before moving to sit back upright in his chair. I knew his relationship with my uncle was the byproduct of what he called an illness, and I knew any hope for its survival would only come to fruition if either half dared to acknowledge its truth. I watched Max smile a bit, as if he could read my mind in this perfect instance. I watched him recline again in his chair and prop his feet atop the wood as if he were waiting for my response.

The room we were gathered in was small and barely had room for the two of us to inhabit its space. A solitary bookshelf was filled in every possible crevice with protruding spines that locked their gaze with my own before my eyes trailed off. They wandered over to the framed degrees depicting the time spent at Schaffer back when Max and Tito Clayton had their shared stint here as students. Thinking of such made me wonder what kind of man my uncle was in his youth; if we were any bit alike as I ached for us not to be, or if he, too, was a boy long ago murdered because of our shared traits of mental illness and addiction that had killed any semblance of innocence left at its very root. I wondered what my uncle, too, thought of the child he once was; a boy I could no longer remember except in perfect, seemingly insignificant glimpses. After all, forgetting the person you once were was a hell of a lot easier when the means that allowed you to remember and mourn him had cast you out headfirst for being this imperfect and equally irredeemable sinner. And I wondered how you could possibly dare and avenge this person when the party you were seeing through righteousness for was someone you had made a conscious effort to see killed. No matter who or what had then become collateral damage in the process.

The words I spoke next felt like spikes sinking into my tongue, "What was my uncle like? You know, before *this*."

Max thought for a moment to then say, "He was the perfect boy to bring home to your parents, truth be told." Max laughed a bit as if memories of fondness had then clouded memories of hurt. "I remember how popular he was among the girls here at Schaffer. He loved the chase, and he loved flirting. But we all knew he loved a woman he left behind in even coming here to Schaffer to begin with."

"Nora?"

"Yes. Lisanna's mother."

A chill ran up and down the length of my spine. The door to Max's office then opened without any kind of warning. Davi came into view, giving the two of us a smile before she looked between us to say, "Sorry, am I interrupting something?"

"No," I answered half-heartedly.

Max looked at me, equally unconvinced that was the truth. Davi did not seem to pick up on such. Or, she did and did not dare to address its truth. Either way, I was content with washing my hands of this conversation and the weight it came with.

"Tito Clayton sent Chase and I to grab you since we have practice soon. He didn't know where you were, so I said I'd find you. Seriously, you need to get a phone, Dante."

I laughed a bit before rising from the chair to collect my duffel bag.

Max then called after me to say, "You need an ear, Dante, I'm always here. We both know your uncle is not the emotional type anyway, and therapists can only do so much when we know where you stand in regard to them. So, feel free to drop by whenever you need."

I looked him up and down. I wondered if this had been some elaborate ploy by Tito Clayton to see me be honest about emotions I could not comprehend inebriated let alone sober. Instead of asking, I gave a nod as I joined Davi in the hallway to find Rue and Chase waiting for the two of us, practice attire and gear in tow. Rue took his foot from the wall to seemingly collect me from Davi, who in turn moved to stand next to Chase. The pair began to lead us back to the Nora Wilson Hockey Center, chatting idly about celebrity gossip I could give a fuck about. Rue and I stared at each other, and once a noticeable distance had formed between us and Davi and Chase, Rue began to follow them. I caught up with him, my arm brushing against his shoulder that sent this sickly shudder down the length of my spine. It was then I lost all mental resolve to come out of the conversation withstanding. But before I could think on such a thing, let alone give proper thought to name and digest this feeling, Rue grabbed my arm.

He then said, "I don't trust someone here."

It was as if he had asked me the explain the entirety of my past despite knowing I never would. Although, thinking on such now, I did not think my prejudice laid my credence when it came to Rue Oba.

"Why don't you trust someone here, Rue?"

"Andrei shows up to our interview with Celena despite him having no way of knowing we would be there. I don't trust Robyn as far as I can throw her, so she could very well be some kind of mole."

I glanced at Rue's hand and then back at his perfect, black eyes. The overhead light hit them at just the right angle, lighting them ablaze in the same way on the bus a day prior. And while he was right in the sense that trusting Robyn Zaragoza was a death sentence, I knew Xavier better than anyone else would give me proper credit. On the surface, inducting Robyn onto the Lions seemed like a perfect ploy to see him acquire an in who would then report everything it was that we were doing to the same man we were actively trying to keep in the dark. All the clues placed Robyn at the scene of the crime, but I knew Xavier was the kind of man to never let a punishment leave the person being punished unscathed.

If Xavier were going to see himself have a mole among the Lions, he was going to do it in a way that kept his cards close and did not draw attention to himself since men like him operated in the dark. And doing the mental math of how all these pieces fit together, it's not that Robyn wasn't the answer. It's that she was *too easy* of an answer. There was no fucking way someone like Xavier, who found a joy in harming and traumatizing other human beings, would want the consequence of his actions to be so blatantly obvious it left no room for any kind of pain to manifest. And I'll give Robyn credit where credit was due, her head was entirely too big to stoop so low to help Xavier a second time when he had already dared to cross her before.

"What do you think, then, Rue?"

"You know what I think. The real question is, what do you think, Dante?"

"The matter of trust is something I can only extend to one person who I know for a fact is not in cahoots with Xavier. But that doesn't mean I like her any more or any less."

We stared at each other.

Rue retracted his arm. "Then, shall we discuss our findings with the wielder of immunity?"

"We will," I answered. "But I will do so alone. After all, we're the only people in the world who can begin to understand how the consequences of Xavier's actions manifested in terms of our addiction."

Rue gave a nod. "I'll be close by if you need me."

"Noted, but I can handle myself."

"The more you say that the less I believe you."

I smirked a bit. "If I say it over and over again it should become true one of these days, no?"

Rue met the gesture with one of his own. "One thing about you, Dante, is that you're a shit fucking liar."

I laughed, moving to place my hand to Rue's back to then guide him out of the building. I blocked my smile with my other hand as we started our trek to the Nora Wilson Hockey Center in a comfortable, homey silence.

3 4

ROBYN

I LACED MY SKATES while sitting atop the wooden bench dividing the women's locker room in two. Davi was the only other person present, looking at me with tense eyes and a worried frown smeared across an already unpleasant expression. I did not meet her gaze but kept my eyes keen on the task at hand when I then said, "So, was it all a lie, or was any of it based in any kind of truth?"

Davi replied, "Not all of it. I think maybe hoping for it to be the truth was enough to convince me it was."

"The thing is, Davi, is that I want to hate you. I want to slap you across the face and give you a piece of my mind. But we both know leaving Xavier is not so easy, now, is it?"

"No, I suppose not."

"What leverage does he have against you?"

Davi did not answer. She looked as if the life had finally been drained from her, and that serving a man who we both knew could never be satisfied had finally run her well dry.

I then said, "I know the reality of leaving Xavier behind is not as easy as others who do not know him like the two of us would come to suggest. I know it's hard, and I know how much blood is required to see yourself reborn outside the confines of his influence. It's not so much that I think there is any hope to convince you of the issue of morality when you have already made up your mind. But tell me, what would Dante come to think of your betrayal? What would Chase? Hell, even my fucking brother whom I came here to be with knowing what it would fucking cost me in the process; my head on a fucking pike and Xavier needing me dead to sooth an inflamed ego because coming here meant following in the same footsteps as the parents who had scorned him before. And I know you know this truth too, Davi. And don't act like you don't."

I tied the last loop making up the laces of my skates, then brandishing my stick and walking out of the locker room to be greeted by Dante. The overhead light illuminating the hallway began to flicker in an annoying, offbeat manner that cast a mood of misfortune between him and I that did not aid the gnawing in the pit of my stomach. Dante was smoking a cigarette, leaning against the wall before me with a malice-ridden expression kept beneath the filter contrasting the ash cascading from the ember making up the opposite end. A thin, faint trail of smoke linked his world and mine. The earthy stench of tobacco washed this strange, out of place comfort over my body, despite knowing better than to think I could ever feel such with Dante Alonso Hidalgo and come out with any semblance of dignity to show for it. I looked to my right. To my left. When I realized I was the party in which he wanted to talk to, I attempted to puff up my posture as if to tell him I would not take any of his forthcoming abuse without seeing him lose a couple teeth for it.

"Is this some sort of sick, deranged surprise party or what?"

Dante laughed, crossing his arms. He flicked the ash from his cigarette onto the ground beneath our feet. "You're the only person on the Lions who I know will listen to me. So, you can either do just that, or I'll tell Tito Clayton that you have the means to relapse."

"This goes two ways, Hidalgo. I'll tell him you have enough vodka to kill a small army. You wouldn't want the only thing seeing you remain functioning be taken from you, no?"

Dante smirked a bit. "You and Xavier sure are a lot alike."

"I like to think not," I answered dryly. "Get to it and get to it fast, Dante. I do not have all day to sit around and entertain idle chatter with you of all people."

Dante blew his cigarette smoke out from his nostrils, straightening his shoulders and back as if he were going to bear some kind of weight atop of them. He then said, "You know Xavier didn't show his face here when he gave us our vices, right?"

"You have a brain in there. Color me surprised."

"So, that can only mean we have a traitor in our midst."

I gazed upon Dante to see if there was any attribution to her identity, or if this confrontation was a shoddy attempt at forming an alliance to sniff her out. Even if I did not like Dante, I knew I could not let the prejudice of past cloud the obvious matter of his intelligence. Granted, he did not put any of it to use in an academic sense, but I knew Dante was a good judge of character except in the instance of my brother. Men like Dante are not so much born as they are made because of the matter of circumstance. And I knew, too, that there is no reward given to the valor shown during lonesome, sleepless nights where all you could hope to do was survive. While the obvious matter of my own relationship with morality meant confessing the truth of Davi's alliance with the very man who had scorned the three of us, I could not bring myself to hurt him in such a way.

Maybe this was the same conscience I had given nearly everything to absolve myself of poking out from beneath the shallow dusting of dirt I had caked it under. Maybe there was still hope for me to become this good, just person I ached to finally become. I realized then that such could never be true considering my circumstance; how this knot I had seemingly been tangled in was not so much a matter of morality as it was a complete and total manifestation of my addiction. If I had simply come clean and confessed to adults and peers of moral standing I had been given a new fix of those same tiny, white pills, I would not be caught between the matter of righteousness and still being bound to the man I was trying to rebuild my sense of self without.

And Dante was right. He could tell his uncle, or even Lisanna this truth at any time, but I knew the matter of doing so was every but an empty threat as the matter of my own. We were brothers and sisters in arms; united in a shared struggle of hurting everyone we loved because the vices we were bound to commanded such of us. And maybe Dante was better in that regard knowing he was going to make an effort to see through recovery and sobriety, but I knew the reality was infinitely more gargantuan than he could ever begin to comprehend. While I did not think he was incapable of meeting the challenge, it did not change that at its core, it was just that.

While neither Dante nor I were alone in the effort to see through sobriety, I did not think unlearning eight years of self-conditioned hate in the wake of your brother's violence would be something he could manage overnight. It's not that I didn't believe Dante could slay the beast of his trauma, mental illness, and addiction. Truth be told, I held onto the hope he could rise to the challenge so it would teach me how to do such in regard to the matter of my own. But as long as he and I are equals, forever bound to the chains of our addiction, I did not think he could make it out alive. After all, I already knew the same fate was one I had deemed beneath me, and I was still so heinous to choose my vice over the woman who I would never deserve knowing such.

"Any idea on who it may be?"

Dante watched me, taking another drag from his cigarette. A noticeable tension lingered between the two of us, daring the other to call them out on their bluff. While I knew better than to trust him, I also knew Dante would not confess the matter of my inevitable relapse just as I would not in terms of his own. Maybe in the afterlife he would come to scorn me for such, but for now, it did not change this tepid alliance in terms of our own hubris was giving us enough of a foundation to build some kind of relationship atop of. I knew Dante would never come to like me because of the matter of my past. However, I did not think that meant I was going to perpetuate the same cycle of abuse as his brother before when I had learned it had not been warranted. I had enabled and coddled Xavier's vitriol in regard to the Lions. This truth and its weight was not lost on me. To me at least, daring to atone for it now was better than being so arrogant to never try. However, that did not mean I could be honest in regard to the matter of our traitor. My careful balancing act beholding to the spheres of sobriety and being clean would soon come tumbling down knowing the sun had long ago melted my feathers of wax. And the only truth withstanding was the inevitable fate of drowning beneath the cruel, unforgiving curl of the ocean below.

"No," Dante answered.

I knew he, too, was keeping his cards close.

"But I need your help in putting the pieces together."

"Last I checked, you hated me. You think I'm a mole working for your brother, and now you want my help in showcasing the head of the traitor for all the Lions to see?"

"I may not be smart enough to earn a full ride to Wesley, but I know Xavier better than you'd like to think. You being the traitor is too simple of an answer, Robyn. And if we both know the man I call a brother, if you were to be a traitor, why would you have your own means of a fix? When it's more than obvious the truth of your addiction is dependent on Xavier and the pills he was given after Celena broke his collarbone their junior year?"

I smirked a bit. Obviously, Dante was a lot smarter than Xavier would ever come to agree with me on. "You know, I think you're seeing yourself short. You are smart, Dante. After all, how many other Lions could have figured out that even with their prejudice tied to my past with Xavier?"

Dante was quiet, then settling to say, "Then, do you blame Celena for the matter of your addiction since it was her violence that saw Xavier even acquire the opioids for you two to abuse?"

"You know the answer to that," I called, flipping my hair. "After all, the circumstances that saw us rely on these same crutches to keep us functioning may be out of our control, but we are still the party who made that choice. Even if it stings. Even if I know it makes you and me both bad people. After all, how many other people can understand the hurt that comes with loving an addict like the two of us knowing we are the party dishing out its consequence?"

"You and I are not the same," Dante said. "I'm going to get better. I'm going to prove Xavier wrong no matter what it fucking takes. And while I know we share the truth, we are not the same vein of liar. And don't fucking act like we are."

I laughed, amused and equally awestruck by the sheer, grandiose naiveté of Dante's declaration. I placed both my gloved hands above my stick, then resting my chin atop the length to give a smile. Leaning my weight into my stick, I then said, "You are not a dumb man. And truth be told, it would be in your best interest for you to listen to me in regard to the matter of your sobriety."

Dante blocked his expression by taking another drag of his cigarette.

I then used this as a cue to continue, "Anyone is capable of change. Hell, even I am. But the matter of your recovery and your sobriety is not something I think can be shed so easily when it has been so entrenched in your sense of self for these formative, eight years. I of all people know shedding the person you once were for sobriety to finally poke through the surface is not as simple as I think you really have a grasp on. I'm all for proving Xavier wrong, but you have to be realistic, Dante. I don't want you to become someone like me. Someone who has sold this pipe dream of being a good, just, and equally honorable woman to the people she loves. And now, has to live with the consequence of never being able to be her again. Not when that version of self has long been butchered by my inability to dare and be clean even if means quite literally solving all my fucking problems."

Dante crossed his dominant, left hand over his right that was clutching his bicep. He tapped a finger atop his cigarette, and I watched the ash cascade down to the concrete beneath our feet. Dante looked me up and down with a firm, unyielding expression. I watched Dante seemingly recoup his losses, then replying, "If that woman you've claimed never existed actually didn't, why do Tito Clayton and Lisanna continue to see her in you?"

Dante took a last drag of his cigarette to exhale the smoke from his nostrils. Then, he ground the butt out on the painted over, white brick holding up his more than gargantuan stature. The ember left a small, circular mark as I watched Dante hold its remnant in his hand to then say, "We may never be friends. We may never reach an understanding considering who you once were. But I would never let you be so heinous to lie about the person you once were and who you can dare to be. I'm not saying this has any merit coming from me. It could very well make me a hypocrite in saying it. But Lisanna chose you. She didn't have to, Robyn. We both know she has given everything to also shed the skin of the person she used to be to be a woman who could dare to give and receive love in return. You're right it won't be easy. But I've come to realize now, I don't need to do anything to be entitled to recovery or sobriety. I am inherently worthy of such an effort because after all I've been through, I deserve maybe not happiness, but a baseline. And so do you, Robyn."

I laughed a bit. "When did you become a wannabe shrink?"

"I have my moments, but don't count on them to be frequent. I've reached my quota of useful shit to say, and I'm ready to show the rest of you Lions how utterly incompetent you really are."

I smiled a bit, moving to close the space between myself and Dante. He looked down at me, and I then said, offering my hand, "A truce?"

Dante shook it. "A truce."

"Then, let's show Xavier Alonso Hidalgo what the fuck we're made of."

Now, it was Dante who laughed. He moved to stand upright and lead me to the ice of the Nora Wilson Hockey Center. I spared a glance at the locker room door. I imagined the same bottle of pills waiting for me when I got back and wondered if Dante was right. Could we dare and meet the challenge of being the person the people we loved always believed us to be?

3 5

DANTE

I **WALKED ONTO THE** ice of the Nora Wilson Hockey
Center to see the rest of my teammates—with the exception
of Davi—waiting for me.

Upon seeing Robyn and I enter together, our teammates
began to whisper among each other with the exception of Rue
and Chase. Robyn and I glanced at each other before I skated
off to join my sphere of influence as she claimed her own. Tito
Clayton gazed between the two of us before looking back at
Celena who was at his right. They stared at each other before
Tito Clayton then said, "Where is Davi?"

Almost on instinct, skates against freshly paved ice came in
from behind the lot of us gathered. We all turned around to face
Davi, who gave a sheepish expression to then say, "Sorry. Got
my period and had to scrounge the locker room for a tampon."

Something told me to look at Robyn. She raised an eyebrow
in a sharp, defined arch. She met my gaze, looking me up and

down before turning around to face the task at hand. I glanced back at Davi a last time before turning back to Celena and my uncle, who waved her off and said, "Of course. But now that we're all here, Celena would like to say a few words. That ok with everyone?"

I knew better than to think that was really a question on Tito Clayton's part. It was understood by his tone that it would be in our best interest to listen, or we would be at risk of doing an unneeded set of suicides. I moved my gaze to meet Celena's, and I watched her give a nod before clearing her throat to then say, "So, we all know what I hope to accomplish by the end of my tenure here at Schaffer. I need to see Xavier cut down at his knees, and you lot are my only shot of making that happen."

I glanced at Alexei, who seemingly adjusted his posture to bear the brunt of his newfound responsibility evenly atop his thick, square-shaped shoulders. I then met Celena's gaze to watch her head tilt the slightest bit downward; a motion I knew meant the coming remark was not directed at me considering our shared basis of talent. I met the motion with one of my own.

Celena then added, "I won't lie and say I have been the easiest to work with during my tenure as captain of the Lions. But with everyone in the world you have given blood to break into wanting you dead, squashed, or gone, it is hard to not take out such pressures on the people working under me. I apologize for this, and I know it has not been fair. But, as long as we are a team, I will make up for the lost time and make you all into champions. All I need from you is a determination to get better; a desire to let me and Coach make you into the best versions of yourselves you can be. We are capable of it if you give me your all, and I promise I will not abuse it. So, are we clear, Lions? Because I cannot afford failure. And I have come to ask you this as an equal before your captain. Please, meet me halfway."

Chase was the first to answer, "Of course, Celena. I am in your hands."

Celena's worry withered by the slightest of margins. I then added, "You've always been capable of making us all into something great, Celena. As long as you're our captain, I will trust you to lead us into battle. I've already given you my future. What kind of man would I be if I were not to give you my all too?"

Celena smiled, warm, vibrant, and equally out of place. I glanced back at Alexei to see his gaze was locked upon her every bit unflinching and indignant as his presence among the Lions as a whole, at least by my standards. Whether warranted or not, I was unsure. I readied my posture to come between the two parties in the face of any kind of violence.

Alexei seemingly croaked, "Then give me the same as you've given Dante."

"I'm sorry?" Celena asked, nonplussed.

"We're all well aware of the fact that you and Dante are going to go pro. We all know most of us here do not have what it takes to meet you and him among players of your same caliber, and we know in terms of beating Xavier, it's the rest of us that will have to carry the brunt of the work in becoming better." Alexei placed his right hand to his chest, holding his stick straight atop the ice in the other. "The thing is, though, Celena, is that I want that too. I want to help you and Dante be this great, hallowed duo of attack and defense because I owe the child I once was a future we were once convinced we would never have. And I don't care what I have to give to make it happen, or how much blood will need to be spilled in seeing me bear the weight of becoming something great. I will do everything in my power to help us become champions, but I need your help in seeing myself, too, become something like you."

Celena had a kind of glint in her eyes I had never really seen before. She then replied, "And what is it that I am, Oba?"

"Something great."

A silence lingered between us Lions. I felt Celena's gaze upon my own and turned to face her. We watched each other, and I noticed how she did not reject Alexei outright. No, her expression was almost asking me for permission on whether or not sharing the dream I had built my entire future around was something worth entertaining for my own best interest. I did appreciate her asking in regard to the future we would share together. However, I did not think it should fall entirely on me whether or not Alexei could come join us in our shared vision of hoisting up the Stanley Cup with both our names engraved on the silver, forever immortalizing Celena and I as champions.

While on the basis of my like and dislike, it was rather obvious what I thought of Alexei Oba, and that he was a fucking idiot. Anyone who was stupid enough to call Conner a brother was probably equally deplorable in regard to character as the man who I, truthfully, did not have much reason to hate. But my like of the foster brothers aside, it did not change that Alexei knew his reality among the Lions. That he needed to see through a total reformation in regard to his own talent to see himself be compared to someone like Celena. A woman who had and redefined a sport that had once been entirely dictated by men on the basis of talent nearly entirely on her own. And the part that I knew showed his true character—my own bias and prejudice aside—was his willingness to swallow his pride. That, and work with both me and Celena, two people I did not think he had done much to prove that he even liked.

I thought of my uncle, glancing over at him as he met my gaze. On the matter of stature, nationality, and ethnicity, Tito Clayton should have kissed his dreams of one day going pro goodbye. The odds were already stacked against him from the moment he picked up a stick and decided this sport—violent, bloody, and equally grotesque—was the one he wanted to play. Truth be told, when it came to the mere reality of his hopes and dreams, Tito Clayton was fucked. But gazing upon his deep, brown eyes, I knew my uncle knew this truth too. And I knew that he looked the abysmal odds of him one day carving out a legacy in a sport that was the least bit kind, and dared to dictate the terms of his own future to the Fates who would one day, too, pluck strings making up the lyre of his own demise.

Tito Clayton tilted his gaze to face my own, telling me with his stern expression that with hard work and a determination to see yourself rise above, quite literally anything was possible. Seeing the faintest glint accessorizing his eyes of sleet, I knew this truth could be told in regard to my own life and the places I hoped to see it reborn. And it was then I realized the truth I had deemed myself beneath had been true all along. I was not seeing through the effort of recovery or sobriety alone. And truth be told, how many other people of my same truth could begin to say the same?

I moved to look at Alexei to find he was already watching me, expression and eyes tight and equally unsure what my coming answer would be.

I smirked a bit, then saying, "It won't be fucking easy. That much I can guarantee. But if you're willing to put in the work, Celena, Tito Clayton, and I will not see it go to waste. But you are to respect Celena, are we clear?"

"Crystal, Dante."

"Good. Then, I suppose we have a practice to be getting to, no?"

I swept my gaze around the Lions gathered. They looked among each other before Celena joined us on the ice.

She then skated away only to turn around and say, "Well, you heard Dante, didn't you? Let's get fucking to it. We have a man to humble, and you all should know better than to keep me and Dante waiting."

Chase was the first to skate over, when Rue led the other Lions over to the goalie crease at my left. Alexei remained, and I glanced at Tito Clayton. He looked between us but did not give the snide remark I was expecting. Instead, he retreated back to the locker room to leave the two of us alone, and I moved to look at Alexei Oba.

As I noticed in our first meeting, he did not look any bit alike to either of his brothers. Alexei was not much of an attractive that I would be compelled to appreciate, but that did not change that in a sense I could acknowledge it for what it was worth. Granted, he did look like an over-glorified frat bro like his foster brother, so I suppose in that sense the resemblance was uncanny. But I watched Alexei frown, sheepishly gazing upon me as if he were going to spew venom from his tongue when he then said, "You really made me beg."

"Now, I did not make you beg. You're shit at making a fucking case for yourself, and yet what did I do for you regardless? You're acting like I owe you something. Last time I fucking checked, I don't."

Alexei frowned again, then saying, "I'm sorry."

"For what exactly?"

"For my bad impression. I'm not very good at those."

"Stop being an asshat, and we'll get along fine."

Alexei smirked a bit, then saying, "You're really all bark and no bite, are you?"

"Why, you like the feeling of losing a couple teeth finding out?"

Alexei stared at me, settling to say, "We should learn to get along. For Rue's sake."

Least to say, I had no idea what that had to do with the task at hand. "And why for Rue's sake?"

"Rue was right," Alexei laughed, leaning against his stick propped upright in front of him. "You really are a shit fucking liar."

I watched Alexei to find his expression beneath the plastic of his helmet was, of all things, playful. It was then I realized his past remarks did not house an intent at indignation, but rather an effort to establish banter between the two of us that had gone completely over my head. I stared at Alexei, horrified and equally unsure what my next move should be when he erupted into a chorus of laughter, akin to a balm soothing over my past remarks in a perfect instance. Alexei then glanced at Rue who was talking to Celena. I, too, looked over. I caught Rue's gaze, who stopped mid conversation to wave to both me and his brother, to which I sheepishly did the same. I then met Alexei's gaze to see he was smirking, beyond satisfied that the gears in my head were finally turning in regard to his true nature and where exactly it was I stood in regard to Rue Oba.

Because if you did the simple math and looked it over, I liked him.

And I knew it was still every bit a death sentence now as it was in first meeting him.

Or, maybe the once self-limiting belief that I could never deserve something virtuous as love was outdated. Like the notion Alexei was an asshole and not someone who was awfully good at playing the part of one like I had once thought.

I didn't answer. Instead, I moved to look at Alexei to see he was still smiling when he then said, "So, you've finally put two and two together, no?"

"I suppose I have."

"Took you fucking long enough."

A silence lingered.

And using it as a cue, I asked myself, could this attraction prove to be fruitful? And even more unforgivably, could it be reciprocated?

The knee jerk reaction was that having Rue like me back was something I could never begin to deserve no matter how much an even concoction of pills, liquor, and blood would try to convince me I did. The bashful voice in my mind, who weaved tall tales of nonexistent ineptitudes, told me such a thing could never be real despite the clear and present reality as seen by Alexei and quite literally everyone else on the Lions. But thinking I was worthy of such a thing and actually being deserving of it were two, very different things.

I will give Robyn Zaragoza credit. She may be vain, conceited, and infinitely too complicated for me to even begin to understand, but she was right in the sense that unlearning eight years of vitriol at the hands of self would take a lot more work than I had once given credit for. Truth be told, I did not like the innate reaction that was ruminating in the pit of my stomach. I did not like the voice that told me the only way to purge it was a razorblade nicking the flesh that would wash away this inherent, original sin of my very creation in blood. The conscience I had tried so hard to absolve myself of was now telling me how I had wrought so much damage to these same people I loved, and what could make a relationship with Rue Oba any different? Robyn could be right, and I may not even be capable of change. But the one thing I knew I could manage was damaging my relationship with Rue beyond repair and having us go back to strangers who flinched at the sound of each other's names. And even if the unknown and constant fate of failure in my life told me it was a terrible fucking idea, it did not change how, regardless, I wanted to try. And really, I wanted to get better.

Because Tito Clayton was right.

Staying this way could only have one end.

It's truth would see myself pay the price for crimes Xavier had committed, and why the fuck should I let that fucker have the last laugh on my life?

The matter of justice could be dealt with later. I still had a whole season ahead of me in which I could dictate the terms of my own revenge. But until then, I had to focus on the matter of sobriety and recovery, taking the effort a day at a time to not overwhelm me into a relapse in any of my favored vices. And that mindset had yet to see me dead, and as far as I was concerned, that had to be good enough for now.

I turned to Alexei and said, "Then, what do you think will come of it, Alexei?"

"Only you and my brother can figure that out. But to be entirely honest, Dante, you and my brother deserve a happy ending. Both of you have been through a lot. And I think it takes a real man to look the sorrow of your past in the eye and dare to give love in spite of it."

I swallowed down the lump in my throat to then say, "This sorrow. Has something to do with Rue's mother, right?"

Alexei smiled a bit. "That's his story to tell you. I'll tell you my part in it, but I never knew her. I was adopted after she passed. Rue doesn't talk about it, but something tells me you can weasel the truth out of him. After all, he has the uncanny ability to do the same to you, no?"

I didn't answer. Alexei smiled, tapping my shoulder before skating over to join our teammates. I glanced back at the home bench to see Tito Clayton had come back from the locker room to take his previous post, giving a nod. I met the gesture with one of my own, moving to join my teammates on the ice. Celena began to instruct us on our drills in the hopes the lessons learned would one day make us champions.

3 6

ROBYN

I **SLUNG MY DUFFEL** bag over my shoulder and walked back into the rink making up the rest of the Nora Wilson Hockey Center. I climbed up the bleachers until I found the one in which Lisanna was sitting atop of. I stood at the bleacher below her, hands in my coat pockets that were thumbing over the pills I had been given that she still lay ignorant to.

Lisanna smiled, warm, gentle, and equally heartfelt. And as much as I did not want to confess the matter of where my allegiances lied, it did not change I had to in order to reclaim the life in which Xavier had dared to try and take from me before. Tito Clayton had been right in the sense that it was the actions after your fuck up that would come to define you. He was also right in saying the only thing that could save you from your own undoing was changed behavior instead of repeating the same vicious and equally unforgiving cycle that saw you hurt the people you loved in the first place. Not to say I was ready to say

I was deserving of such a thing, but in talking to Dante, I had come to realize being an active work in progress was better than the alternative.

Being forced to atone for your sins in death rather than with the people and grief you would come to leave behind is a fate I don't think I would wish upon anyone, not even Xavier. I still did not know if sobriety was something I was entirely capable of, but I knew I had to show Lisanna an active effort in trying in order to have the capacity to truly be deserving of forgiveness. I of all people knew an apology without changed behavior was manipulation. And I knew I could not afford to lose the one woman who saw me for all my broken and equally mismatched parts and despite it, *dared to stay.*

"Robyn, we're still getting coffee?"

I tried not to give the next motion much thought in an effort to not bend beneath the weight of my own cowardice, so I flicked my hand holding the two bottles of pills in my coat pocket to toss them onto Lisanna's lap. A thick, palatable silence lingered between us. She stared at my stashed vices as if she were hallucinating both my and their presence, when I interrupted the tension to say, "Before you ask, no, I did not relapse. And, Liz, that is the God's honest fucking truth."

Lisanna did not meet my gaze but moved to inspect the bottles and the labels taped to them. Her expression was firm, still, and equally unreadable. I felt my rib cage holding up the strings of my heart begin to concave in on itself; piercing the flesh until the blood once shed—in a shoddy attempt at seeing myself clean—filled my lungs until I drowned beneath the thick, metallic finish. There was now this insatiable gnawing taking hold in the pit of my stomach. I waited for Lisanna to say something, anything to make this silence that was now festering between the two of us cease and free me from the same guilt that had come with my own creation. I watched her cool, piercing blue eyes turn to meet my own, looking me up and down in a curious manner rather than accusatory. I knew I could not bring myself to speak when I was not the party who deserved to have the first word, so I remained silent. Then, I sank my molars into the flesh of my cheek, the taste of blood now saturating a bitter sting across the length of my tongue.

"I believe you," Lisanna said.

It was as if a weight had been lifted from my shoulders.

"And I am working on trusting you again. So, I will believe you this time." Before I could say something else, Lisanna then spoke, "Why did Xavier give you two bottles if you only needed one to relapse?"

"When we would get high together, he'd already built up a tolerance. So, he let me use that Fentanyl the night when I overdosed knowing I could not say the same which was his attempt at being my judge, jury, and executioner."

Lisanna was quiet, when she then said, "And this is how I know you did not relapse."

"I'm glad you trust me, but, Liz, I don't follow."

Lisanna shook one pill from each bottle to find they looked exactly the same. White, circular, and infinitely grandiose in terms of absolving myself of my dependence. Lisanna must have seen the confusion etched across my face, and I watched her take out her phone. She turned on the flashlight, moving to inspect each of the contrasting pills beneath the glint. She then retreated back to her starting post once satisfied. The expression now etched into her beautiful, perfect face was an unshakeable grief I could not begin to understand.

Did she not believe me in my attempt to see through righteousness? Was it too late to redeem myself before the eyes of the woman I loved? Or, even before this same God who claimed to save all those who wished to be from eternal damnation? It was a forgiveness I could never begin to stomach. It was the truth that my life—despite all the wrong I had seen through at the expense of those I loved—had this inherent value I had tried so hard to absolve myself of. The pitiful ritual of my own undoing would then be seen through beneath the weight of those same pills I had given nearly everything to keep close in the place of the only woman I wanted to one day grow old with. So, I only asked myself, was it really too late to be honest with Lisanna because of the damage wrought, or could I continue to outrun the inevitable truth of her abandonment for just a little longer while I could say I still had her?

The thoughts now swirling around in my head were a dark, cohesive force. I knew if I did not absolve myself of their stain, it would be the catalyst to see me relapse to come to terms with their truth.

But I didn't want to be that person anymore.

And I knew I could not let my assumption cloud the truth waiting behind it. I owed her honesty. Truth be told, I always did. And I hated that it had taken this long in shedding the person I once was to finally realize such.

"Liz, I didn't relapse, that's the truth. I know I don't have the track record for you to believe me, but I mean it this time. I promise."

Lisanna was a deathly quiet when she then said, "I do believe you, Robyn. Really, I do."

I exhaled. "You do?"

"Of course, I do," Lisanna answered, still quiet. "Because if you had relapsed, you wouldn't have gotten high."

"I'm sorry?"

"These pills are placebos."

"Liz, what the hell are you talking about, Xavier took the stronger stuff so I wouldn't—"

Then, it all clicked in a perfect instance.

When Xavier and I would get high under the guise of doing it together, he never saw it through. Instead, he would take placebos and pretend to be high while supplying me the real thing.

Time had come to a complete and total stop. The world around me was now spinning in this endless, unforgiving circle as I tried to see myself regain my balance despite the vertigo washing this confusion over my body. The truth did not sink until I forced it down the chasm of my throat only to choke on the bitter aftertaste of the twinge of betrayal laced with the sting of deceit. The same rage boiling inside me when I found out Davi was working for the man who wanted her dead began to pop through the skin again, leaving insidious, grotesque burns atop the brown smeared across my body.

I felt this sickly chill run up and down the length of my spine. Because the friendship I had once thought Xavier and I shared had been nothing but a perfect, elaborate farce. It only made me ask myself, had the entire thing been a lie? And arguably most heinous of all, how could I have been so blind? How could I have been so arrogant to think this man who hurt others without care for the consequence would never extend the same brunt for me solely because I had convinced myself I was his best friend? And I don't think that was even the most unconscionable of questions to be asked. Because how could Xavier love and care for me like a sister, but still, attempt to dictate the terms of my own demise; ruining my life by forever binding me to a bottle of pills I had given up nearly everything to keep close?

But still, I had to confirm the truth before acting or judging hastily. Maybe that would be my fatal flaw, always holding out the hope I meant more to Xavier than I actually did. But for now, the truth needed to be explained to me in a way I would understand. I needed to know its coming weight before I made any judgment to a man I still loved, even if he had never thought the same of me.

"How do you know they are placebos?" I asked, quiet.

"Come here and I'll show you," Lisanna said.

I climbed the bleacher to stand next to her, leaning into her space until the pills were in my immediate range of sight. Lisanna then held them up for me to examine, pointing at the letters etched into the white contrasted the usual ones found in the opioids I had abused with Xavier. It only confirmed the truth I had been trying to outrun since meeting him my freshman year of college and choosing to love him despite all the wrong he had done to others.

I did not mean anything to Xavier Alonso Hidalgo.

I probably never did.

And truth be told, I never fucking would.

I smiled at Lisanna, then saying, "Sorry, Liz, I'm going to have to take a rain check."

"Robyn, I'm so sorry you had to find out this way. I'm here for you, pro—"

"I know that, Liz. In the meantime, I need some time alone."

Lisanna watched me. She gave a nod as she placed the pills back in their corresponding bottles. I then watched her pocket the last remaining tether linking my most intimate of emotions as she rose from her bleacher to then say, "I'll walk you back to

Tito Clayton's house. And I'll wait for you until you're ready to talk again, ok?"

I smiled, wounded and equally betrayed. "Of course, Liz. I just need to sleep and forget this day ever happened, ok? We'll get coffee another time. I promise."

"I could give a fuck about the coffee," Lisanna said, her eyes sparkling beneath the overhead light of the stadium before us. "I just need you safe. I just need you alive. Can you promise me that, Robyn?"

"Today I can," I answered in a rare bout of truth.

"Today is good enough for me."

Lisanna strapped her bag atop her shoulder, offering her hand. I intertwined our fingers, trying to ignore the pang of fear taking root in the bottom of my stomach. I then wondered the truth in regard to Chase and Rue's question. Because the one thing still keeping me from killing Xavier Alonso Hidalgo had gone up in smoke before me and the woman he had helped me to scorn. But even I was unsure if I could stomach the reality of becoming like him, a man who hurt without care for its inevitable consequence.

3 7

DANTE

I TOOK A DRAG of my cigarette to find the front door of Tito Clayton's house open with a turn of the keys. Lisanna and Robyn then walked inside; an obvious tension shared between the two lovers I wondered the meaning behind.

Robyn did not acknowledge my presence, not that I felt a need she had to when we were never going to come out of this season friends. She retreated back to her room to slam the door behind her, and the noise shook the rest of the house with its thud. I turned back to Lisanna who closed the door behind her, now leaning against it before bringing her hands to her face and exhaling a long, drawn-out sigh. She fell to the floor; her back still pressed against the door as I watched her place her elbows atop her knees.

Lisanna leaned back when she then turned to me and said, "Give me a cig."

I tossed her my package and gifted lighter. Lisanna caught both objects before siphoning a sliver of the tobacco from the cardboard before placing it between her thin, pink lips. She hit her head against the white wood of the door behind her, tossing the package to her side before using her right hand to strike the fork to render herself a flame. She inhaled, then exhaled rigidly. Obviously, something heavy was on her mind, and I wondered if it had to do with anything in terms of Robyn's sobriety. I knew better than to ask such outright when Lisanna was probably the party most beholding to its consequence, so I watched her spew the trail of smoke from her nostrils as she then turned to me, smiling to say, "Pity I got you into this habit."

"It does the job," I answered. "When every other means to do it for me has been taken from me."

Lisanna tossed me back my lighter. I caught it with one hand, moving the metal back to my pocket. She took another drag of her cigarette before saying, "Xavier fucking Hidalgo." She turned to me. "Tell me, Dante. What price should your brother pay for all the wrong he's done?"

"Last I checked I'm not among the Fates," I answered.

"Are you content with knowing there will be no justice for you if you do not commandeer its means for the greater good?"

"I didn't realize you had a socialist viewpoint on revenge," I answered.

"It's what landed me in Ciara's lap," Lisanna answered, blowing a stray strand of her strawberry blonde hair from her face. "I did what I had to do for my mother. For me. For seeing that all I went through was not for naught."

"And you're right," I answered.

Lisanna seemingly loosened her rigid posture.

"But you cannot say the same for Xavier."

"And why the fuck not, Dante?" Lisanna rose to her feet, jumping upright as if all her energy had been summoned to see through the motion before moving to lean her back against the couch. She tilted her head to look at me over her shoulder, and I met her gaze to see this crimson-laced passion tucked between her iris I had never really seen before. "Your brother will keep hurting people if we do not get to him first. Your brother wants you to take your own life so it saves him the dirty work of doing it for him. You know you cannot exist as long as Xavier remains standing. You two will destroy each other. And why let him be the party to see it through first?"

"Are you suggesting I put a bullet in his fucking head, or what, Lisanna?"

'That's exactly what I'm fucking suggesting, Dante."

I froze almost on instinct to digest the gravity in her declaration. We stared at each other for an endless few seconds before I broke rank and looked away at the ash tray atop the coffee table before me. While I knew Lisanna had merit to say this in terms of her own past, I did not think she had much of a right to say it in terms of my own. To be entirely honest, I had thought of murdering Xavier what had to be a million times before being prompted the question of his life and what it was worth. I thought maybe shooting him in the head, using a glove to cover my fingerprints before placing it in his limp, waiting hand. Another fantasy I had was seeing through justice beneath both of my fists, caving in the flesh until there was nothing left to identify the man I called a brother but an even coat of blood smeared across my arms. But what did not change was that this was fantasy. I could not kill Xavier even if it meant my own life now hung in the balance. Because I would never be successful in absolving myself of the original sin that was my own morality.

But I don't think that's what Lisanna was asking me with the stern expression taut across her face.

No, she was asking me if I, personally, wanted to kill Xavier Alonso Hidalgo knowing there would be no consequence wrought after taking his life.

And truth be told, the answer was not as much of a gray area as I was comfortable with admitting outright, let alone out aloud.

I took another drag of my cigarette, exhaling the smoke with my hand and blocking the stray ash from getting into Lisanna's face. She smiled as if she could read my mind in this perfect instance.

I then replied, "What are you getting at, Lisanna? I don't like being run around in circles. If there's something you want to say, just say it."

"I want to murder Xavier Alonso Hidalgo. But I will only do it with you and Robyn's permission."

"You can't be fucking serious about that, Lisanna. This is a murder we are talking about. You know, like the ones they show on Dateline to warn you of what will happen to you should you see it through."

Lisanna shrugged casually. "You act like I haven't done it before."

"But it was self-defense. This is different. This is premeditated."

"And what makes you think the fate of my father was any different?"

A shudder ran up and down the length of my spine. Lisanna smiled beneath her filter at my nonsensical expression, taking another drag of her cigarette before blowing out the smoke from between her lips as the smell of tobacco lingered to say, "Xavier and my father are two men of the same cloth. They hurt without care of the consequence that will be left for the person they are choosing to hurt."

Lisanna moved to place her crossed arms around the couch's back edge, leaning over it with her cigarette resting between her thin, dainty fingers now propped upright by her left arm. "These men take until there is nothing left. These men hurt until there is nothing left to hurt. They will not stop until the person beholding to its consequence is equally broken as they are. Robyn has given blood to see your brother redeemed before the eyes of this same God that saved Tito Clayton from the brink of death. And all that effort has been for fucking what, Dante? There is no saving your brother. There is no redeeming him. He's made his choice to abuse the women who had tried to guide him back on a straight path where he could finally learn to, if not like himself, tolerate himself without seeing it be paid back to others. You know this too. You know Xavier better than anyone here would like to think. And tell me, Dante, do you think someone like him is capable of even being saved?"

I didn't want to think on the matter of morality when this newfound lens recovery would not give an answer Lisanna would like. "What I want and what is realistic are two, very different things. We cannot simply get away with murder when I am not any bit God as my brother is. That means, I cannot dictate the terms of his own demise, Lisanna."

"But you'll let him dictate yours?"

I was quiet.

"I may not be some stuffy, clinical psychologist. But I know why Xavier gave you that scar on your face." Lisanna smiled, slow, wicked, and equally out of place as I had never seen her before. "With trauma comes a means to cope with it. He knew the memory would cloud this vision of the boy you once were for this man tainted by trauma to take his place. And he was right, wasn't he? He knew you would cope with its memory at the expense of self. And you played your role just like I'm asking you to play mine."

I felt myself start to get annoyed. "What the fuck do you want from me, Liz? To sign off my brother's fucking death warrant? To find glee in the thought of taking his fucking life and become the same person he is by hurting him because he hurt me?"

Lisanna's eyes glistened like the sun setting atop once untouched arctic glaciers. She took a drag from her cigarette, now standing upright to sit on the back edge of the couch. She blew the smoke out from her mouth to then say, "No, Dante. I'm asking you to stick up for your fucking self. I'm asking you to face the damage wrought upon you by a brother who found a joy in hurting others and will continue to do so unless you put *a bullet in his fucking brain* and stop more of the fallout to come."

"Then do it yourself if you're so keen on seeing my brother dead."

"Even if I may not be a good person, I have my rules. I no longer seek out revenge for the sake of self. I will only kill your brother if you, Davi, and Robyn condone it. Because you all are the parties who have been wronged directly, not me."

Lisanna stood upright, moving to ground out her cigarette atop the ashtray before me. I watched her move back to her original post atop the back of the couch, and I met her gaze to see she was already watching me.

I took a last drag of my cigarette before blowing out the smoke from my nostrils to then say, "I will not condone the execution of Xavier Alonso Hidalgo."

Lisanna accepted that with a nod. "Talk to Robyn about what we discussed when she's ready. In the meantime, I'll cook us some dinner before our last practice in the wake of facing your brother again at our season opener."

Lisanna moved to the kitchen, when I turned around to face her and then say, "Killing your father. What was it like? If you can remember anything about it."

Lisanna considered my question for a second before moving to take some of her required ingredients out of the fridge. She then turned to me to say, "Blood doesn't come out easy. It stains your clothes, your skin. It's like the lasting reminder of the crime you saw through that never leaves. Truth be told, sometimes I still feel it sticking to my hands and arms. Of it dripping down into the puddle of blood pooling beneath my feet."

I placed my head atop the back of the couch to then say, "Do you think God will forgive you?"

Lisanna thought for a moment, as if no one had asked the question before. She then met my gaze to say, "If He can forgive my father, He can forgive me. Even men like my father are entitled to redemption if they really are sorry for what they've done. Hell, even Xavier is. But we both know they're never going to see it through while living. And I'm long past the point in trying when they prove time and time again they are incapable of change no matter how many fucking chances you give them, Dante."

I thought about the words spoken, then moving to gaze upon Robyn's door. While I knew any hope for an answer from Lisanna was long past, I knew the matter of our reality as Lions was about to shift in terms of its truth. And I wondered if Lisanna was right, and Xavier Alonso Hidalgo would come to cower beneath its weight.

3 8

ROBYN

T HERE WAS A KNOCK on my bedroom door, which I knew would come since I had skipped our coming practice to wallow in my own self-pity. In my current state of degradation, I knew I had to come to an answer in terms of the question of what my friendship with Xavier once meant and what his same life was worth. And after crying for a good hour, it was safe to say I was at a moral impasse of what balm should soothe my current dangerous line of thought in regard to what justice should eventually be wrought.

"Dante left," Lisanna called from beneath the wood. "We don't have to talk, but I would like to just be with you while you come to terms with all of this, if that is ok."

"Ok," I said weakly.

Truth be told, I was unsure if Lisanna had heard me. But, nonetheless, the door opened and Lisanna came striding in, sitting at the foot of my bed. I peeled off the cocoon of covers I had buried myself in to find her offering me my favored coffee order, smiling as she stuck out the plastic cup for me to take, "Delivery. Don't think I'd be stupid to leave you by yourself in the wake of what it was we learned today."

"Thanks, Liz," I again said weakly. I took the cup from her hand to sit upright, moving to face her again. "Tito Clayton ok with me missing practice?"

"He will be once we explain everything," Lisanna answered, tucking a stray strand of hair behind my ear that made the goosebumps rise atop my skin. "But in the meantime, we need to talk about what you've been through. It's the only way we'll both come to survive it, Robyn."

I knew Lisanna was right and being honest about my feelings was the only way to see myself come out from beneath their brunt withstanding. But the behavior I had conditioned myself to see through when processing emotions among the current mix of betrayal, deceit, and anger now boiling inside of me was between the tiny, white pills that had once driven us apart before. And truth be told, I wanted to get high. I had convinced myself I needed to in order to come out of the constant push and pull of my own feelings with my life—and arguably not my dignity—intact. But as I watched Lisanna intertwine her hand in mind, smiling at me warm, hearty, and equally otherworldly, I realized the answer as to how I could come to terms with the person I was trying to shed had been in front of me this entire time.

After all, Lisanna was the only remnant of my past I had dared to hold onto as I was hers. Life had conditioned us to hate the very thing we had given each other because of the precedents who saw the definition of such warp beneath their own. But despite all the pain that came with my parents's divorce and the horrors Lisanna had been forced to withstand, it did not change how we dared to seek out love in each other. Granted, it was not perfect. I was more than aware of the hurt I had wrought upon her and would continue to if I did not see through sobriety. But as Dante had taught me before, being an active work in progress was better than walking down the path of the alternative and its uneven, cobblestone steps. And I had to show Lisanna I was capable of change if I were going to compel her to stay.

I placed my hand atop Lisanna's to then smile at her and say, "Liz, I am so fucking sorry it has taken me this long to finally choose you over the pills that were driving us apart. First and foremost, before we get into Xavier, I owe you an immense debt for daring to stay in the wake of all I've kept from you. I'm sorry, Lisanna. I am so fucking sorry."

"You're forgiven, Robyn." Lisanna smiled slightly. "Do you know why I even agreed to be your girlfriend?"

"Why?"

"Because you will always be the only person I can love this way with. There will never be anyone else. Quite frankly, I don't think there can be. Because there's only ever been you, Robyn."

I sucked my breath inward, expunging it from my nostrils. "Do you really mean that?"

"Robyn, I have scrubbed every instance of my past from my record and mind in every possible sense. I have tried to love others as I have loved you in the time we spent apart but no one has ever come close. I could not bring myself to forget how you were my first kiss. I could not bring myself to move on when you acknowledged the horror of my past and gave me the answer I needed to hear to make the suffering cease. And that was to kill the fucker who hurt me and the mother whose only crime was staying for my own sake."

"I didn't think you'd actually listen," I admittedly sheepishly.

"But you weren't wrong either," Lisanna answered, a certain fire in her eyes I had only seen once before. "It stopped when I shot him in the stomach and he bled out all over my kitchen floor, no?"

"I suppose you're right too," I answered. "And this is why you have to write back to Aspen."

Lisanna retracted her hand, frowning and turning away from me. She clenched her bicep with her right hand, gazing at me with horror in her eyes.

I placed my hand atop her own, settling to say, "He will love you no matter what it is you tell him, Liz. He was the father you never had. And I don't think some fucking abusive piece of shit getting what was coming to him will change that."

"Yes, but he's paying the price for a crime *I committed.*"

"He could have sold you out at any time. He could have told the police and the courts the truth. But he never did. He knew what would befall you if he did. And so, he was content with playing his role and doing what needed to be done for your sake."

Lisanna was quiet, until she then looked at me and said, "So, this means you know we have to kill Xavier Hidalgo, right?"

It's not that I was surprised by this line of questioning when Rue and Chase prompted me on it prior. It was no secret where Xavier stood in regard to the mental hierarchy of most of the Lions considering the matter of scorning the glue that kept most of them a unit, being Dante. I was not lost on the fact that Dante was really the only man who could freely travel throughout each faction—including my own—and have them all reach a collective understanding or at the very least, a compromise. I knew Celena knew this too. When the time would come for her to pass the torch, Dante was the obvious candidate in terms of tangible skills and leadership capabilities in terms of his unit. But the matter of inherent worthiness aside, I knew I had to answer Lisanna, Chase, and Rue in terms of the question I had been asking myself since learning of Xavier's deceit, being what did I value his life for and could taking his own see a divine equilibrium rebalanced? Or, would it make me among the men of his same like?

The way Lisanna gazed upon me told me I knew the answer to this question already. I knew she did in terms of what justice should be wrought, but her opinion would not matter in terms of my own since she would only see through righteousness if the parties who had been scorned condoned it. I knew she was more than capable of getting away with it too. Even if she was no longer a child and had the veil of innocence to hide behind anymore, I did not think betraying Lisanna Wilson was an effort anyone with an ounce of mental reasoning would dare and see through if they knew what was good for them. But the matter of Lisanna's fondness for retribution aside, I knew her asking of this tied into the matter of what I had told her to see through for her own justice, being kill the man who robbed her of it prior. Granted, I did not think she would actually listen to me, but it did not change she had. And that this truth was the only reason we were sitting before each other, discussing the coming murder of the man I had dared to choose over her.

Blood for blood remained an equal exchange for justice that was righteous. If you wanted to see a debt you had accrued atoned for, it meant paying it back, sometimes with added interest. And knowing Xavier, he had tried to take my life before. He had seen through my addiction and overdose knowing these traits would leave me forever despondent and bound to him. The only way to have my fix soothed over would be through the balm of his supply of those same tiny, white pills he had given me under the guise of taking them together. It would be in the same dorm room that he shared with Elliot where he would offer them with an icy, calloused smile. It was a gesture I used to find this unfounded comfort in knowing I had loved Xavier and, yet, he had never dared to hurt me. I laughed a bit, almost amused by my seemingly obscene hubris daring to love Xavier in the face of his violence. After all, who else was there to blame for the fallout? The only conceivable answer was the party who had once been so arrogant to think the same scorn would never wash over to her shores because the matter of loyalty proved through choice overshadowed that of blood.

While I did blame myself for the bridge burnt because of my supposed choosing of Dante over Xavier, it did not change Xavier knew I loved him like I would a brother. It did not change he knew I would be loyal to him in every possible instance, even when my own dignity would come into question because of his wounded ego and the sins of his parents past. I knew Dante no longer remembered this truth because the codependent factors of his addiction, trauma, mental illness, and scorn of parents long forgotten in their wake.

But Xavier did, word for word, beat for beat. My digressions on Dante aside, Xavier knew I would remain loyal to him in spite of all the wrongs he would see through at others expense because of the matter of a self-worth that had become dependent on his friendship. It was this lack of self-worth that was his in to see me become dependent on the opioids he had supplied me with, and it was this lack of self-worth that would see him remain living knowing my emotions would cloud my rational line of thinking. Truth be told, I had to call a spade for a spade knowing there was only one punishment worthy of men like Xavier Alonso Hidalgo. It was the same crime seen through at the expense of Lisanna's father, and it in turn would be the same crime that would now be seen through at Xavier's own.

And that was cold blooded murder.

Lisanna smiled upon seeing my satisfied expression. She placed her forehead against my own, cradling my neck with her right hand as I gripped her wrist with my own. We watched each other for an endless minute before I spoke first, cementing our newfound covenant made in blood.

"There are two conditions you need to agree with before I condone the execution of the man I once called my best friend."

"Being?"

"All the Lions are on board. And you will write or visit Aspen."

"You have a deal, Robyn Hera Zaragoza."

Lisanna stuck out her pinky.

"And you should know I am not the kind of woman to break something as solemn as a pinky promise."

I smiled, locking my pinky against her own. "I know, Liz. Because you said you would find me again when you left. And look at us here now, together every bit as much as your fuckhead of a father never wanted for us to be."

Lisanna smiled before pressing her lips against my own. It was then I promised myself I would see through sobriety no matter the cost. Of course, I wanted to be clean for the sake of the woman I loved. It was also true I wanted to stop hurting the other people I loved among the same vein of Tito Clayton. But the actual motivation behind the matter of sobriety was that I had to remain clean in order to see that Xavier Alonso Hidalgo failed. It was his effort to have me and Dante have us do his dirty work for him in which I needed to see him be the party scorned for a change. Taking his life would simply be a reclamation of my own, forever free of his insidious, outside influence.

And as long as I was not murdering him alone, it did not matter how Xavier's coming execution would come to pass.

Just simply that I was the party who saw it through.

39

DANTE

I **CONTINUED TO GAZE** out of the window of the coach bus carting us to Wesley. While it was guaranteed we would get there in one piece, I was unsure if we would leave under the same truth.

I had been thinking over the matter of what Lisanna had said to me; how my brother was a man so far beyond saving we had to cut him down at his knees and kill any semblance of his very autonomy at the root. While on the mere basis of emotion, it was obvious what fate I wanted Xavier to pay in terms of coming to terms with my own. Even if the same morality I had tried so desperately to absolve myself of in order to see that its consequence was paid back at the expense of self, in this rare instance, I could not say I had its same truth entrenched in my being. Truth be fucking told, I wanted to put a bullet in Xavier's brain for all he had done to me. He deserved that fucking much, and knowing it was wrong did not change how I had seemingly fantasized about this same vision of truth since he had branded me eight years ago. I always held out the hope he would cross someone who valued themself more than I could ever possibly could. It would between Xavier's spilled blood and their fists that they would see through desires solely kept in the realm of my own subconscious in seeing Xavier finally getting what was fucking coming to him.

What did I want of my brother? Healing, to be honest. But I knew such could never be the case in terms of Xavier, and I knew that meant he in turn would continue to hurt people to cope with his own misery. After all, Davi, Robyn, and I were proof of this very consequence. And when I thought of killing my brother, it was not so much anymore for the sake of self. To be entirely honest, killing him was akin to the same butchery overseen by Lisanna to her father prior. It was the only way to make the suffering at the hands of these same cold and equally calloused men cease. The time for negotiating had long past when Xavier had tried to take Robyn's life after she had attempted to reason with a man I knew now had none. I also knew if I did not kill Xavier first, he would kill me. After all, when giving me the scar on my face I could not remember much of the sickly, sacrilegious ritual other than how Xavier had screeched in a foreign English how he would come to finish the job one day. And even if it was wrong and even if I knew it could very well make me among his same like, it did not change this one, simple truth:

Xavier Alonso Hidalgo held no use to me other than dead.

And that only made me ask myself, how could we possibly oversee his butchery without losing our own freedom in exchange?

The issues of how we would come to cut him down at his knees did not need to be answered for now. No, right now, the only accusation that needed an audience was the inkling of self-worth I had scrounged from beneath layers of bedrock to see my brother now pay for all he had done to me. Truth be told, I could condone seeing through vengeance for the sake of others, but what about the sake of self? After all, the fantasy of murdering my brother had been just that, but I knew it was now a tangible truth considering what Lisanna had suggested. But did I deserve such a thing? Did this person I was now becoming deserve to be avenged? Or, was wallowing in his own self-righteousness the high road of moral propriety? And I realized as soon as I had asked that, it was not me who deserved revenge. After all the damage I had imposed upon others at my own expense, such could never be true. No, the party who deserved to see through the butchery of Xavier Alonso Hidalgo was the boy I once was. A boy I could no longer remember because of years of self-imposed destruction that had tainted the memory of who he once was.

A child long dead.

A child I could no longer remember.

I adjusted my shoulders to beat the weight of my newfound reality evenly atop my shoulders. I brushed up against Chase's arm, and he turned to look at me. We watched each other for an endless moment before he leaned in close to bring his voice to an octave that could only be heard between us to say, "You have something on your mind, obviously."

"What do you think of the matter of my brother?"

"Are you wearing a wire?"

I smiled a bit. "No, are you?"

Chase met the gesture with one of his own. "No. But, do tell. I'm keen on seeing your brother lose his unneeded head."

"Would you kill him if you knew you could get away with it?"

"Without hesitation," Chase answered, his eyes glinting in this endless circle. "Without fucking question."

"Why, Chase?"

"You act like I did not find you on the bathroom floor bleeding out from your arms and a bottle of pills opened at your unconscious body."

I was quiet.

"You act like I have not seen the consequences of his actions first-hand, how they've conditioned you to hate yourself and see that *you* pay the price for a sin *he* had committed. You deserve to get even. He has been so calloused to try and take your life before, Dante. It would only be fair if you are to do the same to him too."

I turned to the seat in front of me to see Rue had been eavesdropping on our entire conversation. Alexei and Davi were too busy chatting among themselves to notice the obvious tension that was now shared between Chase, Rue, and I. Honestly, I thought it was better they lay ignorant to its truth knowing what it would come to ask of them. Chase and I looked at each other a last time before I met Rue's gaze for him to part his lips and say, "I agree with Chase."

"Do you now?"

"We've already discussed this in graphic detail. We were waiting for you to put two and two together."

"We met a good month ago. And yet you're content with seeing through a murder on my behalf?"

"I know what is right, and I know what is wrong."

Rue and I watched each other.

"You getting even will never be wrong."

I watched Rue before looking back at Chase. Chase watched me, saying, "He's right, Dante. Men like Xavier cannot be redeemed no matter how thick the rose-colored lenses you look at them are. Don't you think Robyn has tried such? Davi too? And what do they have to show for it? The same exact shit fucking deal you got for it without even wanting your hand in it in the first fucking place."

I turned back to Rue to say, "And I take it you agree, Rue?"

"You would be an idiot not to with the logic Chase is making."

I knew where I stood in terms of the question of what my brother's life was worth. But truth be told, having other people agree with me was a disorienting experience in and of itself.

"Talk to Robyn about it," Chase suggested. "After all, I think she's the only person who can understand your same viewpoint on it too."

The bus came to a stop before I could answer for such, all of the Lions then rising to their feet. I glanced between Rue and Chase a last time before following them and my teammates out of the bus, moving over to the hatch where all our gear had been stored for the ride over. I commandeered my own, looking among my teammates to find Robyn. When she stood at my right in an attempt to grab her own gear, I turned to face her to then say, "After the game, there's something I want to talk to you about."

"Of course, Dante," Robyn answered. "I'll make sure there is no company when we discuss the coming matter."

I gave a nod. Robyn met that with her own before moving to Lisanna's right. The women and I stared at each other before I mimed a salute and moved over to my own faction. Tito Clayton began to do a head count, and once he had counted all twelve of his Lions, he then said, "Alright, Rue, you're in charge of Dante. Lisanna, you're in charge of Robyn. And Chase, you're in charge of Davi."

Chase beamed at the notion of being trusted to be a chaperone among the more vulnerable of Lions. I'm sure the violence wrought at Andrei's expense saw him as a man of new priority thanks to Celena's influence.

"We know what we've come here to do, so let's do it, ok? I'll give a more inspiring speech once I've pissed. In the meantime, everyone who is not Davi, Dante, or Robyn find a buddy and stick to them like glue. I don't trust my other nephew as far as I can fucking throw him. So, let's move out and get changed, Lions. We have a man in need of an obscene humbling. Got me?"

All of us gathered gave a collective, *Yes, Coach*. Tito Clayton accepted that with a nod as Celena took post in front of us to lead us off to war.

I headed to the locker room but did not change with my teammates since the matter of my other scars did not need to be displayed by anyone but self. I sat in an assigned cubby while mindlessly staring up at the ceiling waiting for my teammates to finish, when footsteps came towards me. A shirtless Rue Oba was in my immediate line of sight, wearing nothing but the hockey mandated base layer leggings that, least to say, put everything I needed to see on full, grandiose display. Keeping my gaze upon his own was all but impossible, and I watched Rue smirk to then say, "I know you change by yourself, so I'll let you know when we're all done. Then, I'll wait outside, ok?"

"Sounds good to me," I answered. "And for the record, clothes would do you some good."

"Don't lie and say you don't like what you see," Rue answered, cheeky. "Besides, my eyes are up here, and not on my crotch, last time I checked."

I flushed an even shade of unwanted crimson. "Get out. You are so fucking annoying, Jesus Christ."

Rue laughed. "Like I said, a shit fucking liar."

I flipped him off, and Rue conceded with a smile and a wave. I rolled my eyes before moving my duffel bag to rest on the bench next to me. After a few endless minutes, Rue then came back with his gear and stick in tow to say, "We're all done. I'll be outside. Give a shout if you need me, ok?"

"Will do."

Rue accepted that with a nod before moving to exit. I watched the door close behind him to then begin the matter of changing into my gear. The meticulous process was probably the most annoying part of the sport. I peeled off my turtleneck to find the same white, healed over scars etched across my inner forearms greeting me from beneath the now shed cloth. I moved my finger across the raised skin, tracing the lines with my fingers as this sickly shudder ran down the length of my spine. Ignoring the gnawing taking hold in the pit of my stomach, I began the process of donning my armor. Once ready, I brandished my stick and helmet, and I turned to the exit to find that a woman who had been watching me the entire time I had been changing. How she had even managed to enter without making a noise, I was unsure.

Another shudder ran up and down my spine when I then said, "Lady, this is the men's locker room. The rink is all the way on the other side of the hallway."

"Do you remember me?" she answered in a thick, Filipino accent. I had heard the same notes of her tone and the drawl that hung onto every word somewhere before. But as to where, I was unsure.

She gazed at me, turning as white as a ghost. She did not move, and neither did I. She looked like she was holding back an infinite stream of tears waiting to burst at the seams. I could not understand such knowing I had never met this woman before in my entire life despite this pang in my gut telling me I had.

I raised an eyebrow, saying, "No. Should I?"

"Your manong told me I would find you here. I did not want to show my face like this, but I did not know when I would be able to next."

It all clicked in a perfect instance.

The sadness etched across her face. The grief seeping into every line. The sheer, otherworldly amount of hurt poking out from between her lips.

I knew exactly who this woman was.

Because it was my mother.

I did not speak. After all, what the fuck could I say to her knowing she was standing before me every bit a stranger as I had once ached for us not to be? I don't think it was her presence that alarmed me. Seeing her again was something I had been preparing myself for. Despite knowing any hope for such had long ago been buried beneath the brush of the same forest that saw my hope for recovery butchered. But what I could not begin to understand nor digest was the *pain* smeared across her face; the anguish greeting me behind the same eyes I saw whenever I looked into the mirror to show me a man I did not think she would even come to recognize. But now, here we were. Standing before the other despite her wish to see me given up, and despite my own to never fucking see her again knowing such.

But if that were the truth, how did it explain her anguish?

Marisol smiled, clutching her chest. She wiped away tears welling in her eyes to then say meekly and every bit afraid as I was, "My, you are so big now. How long has it been since I've seen you, anak?"

Instead of answering, I stared at Marisol like she was a hallucination. Some kind of elaborate, out of body experience that was now dictating the terms of my own demise and inevitable relapse. Because I was more than capable to see through sobriety for the sake of spiting the brother who had spurned it onto me. But what I was not capable of was to cope with seeing my mother again after eight years of an agreed upon silence. I could not begin to withstand it without the aid of something externally illicit no matter how much I ached to be capable to rise above the curl of imposing, black waves of my own misery. The sadness I had once believed myself above had come flooding back in this perfect and equally unholy instance.

The truth of the matter was that I was not strong enough to see through the murder of my brother. To be entirely fucking honest, I was not even strong enough to see through the matter of my own impossible hope for recovery.

I never had been.

And I never would be.

I could never begin to like—let alone stomach—this man I had become who would soon bring ruin upon everyone he loved in order to cope with this same, all-encompassing anguish. And there sure as fuck was no longer any hope in trying to be better knowing I could not wash my hands of this same misery since it had now stained the folds of my mind; smeared across the shape in even coats of an insidious, black stain that could only be atoned for by being so heinous to not feel it at all. Maybe that was my fatal flaw. That no matter how much I ached for such to be true, it did not change that a man like me could never be entitled to redemption. Even despite the blood I shed in an attempt to see that the debt that came with my very creation was paid back no matter the cost.

I didn't answer still. Marisol then smiled again, sheepish and equally unsure of what to make of the man before her as I was of her. I was counting down the seconds until she left, and I could finally see myself gorge on the alcohol stashed in my duffel bag that would see me forget this entire interaction had happened. And hopefully, it could help me forget what kind of man I would soon become. How could I begin to live with myself knowing I would soon relapse despite promising my uncle that I would remain clean as long as I was one of his Lions?

"Ah, the time to talk will be later. After your game. I'll watch you play. I miss you. Be sure to tell your Tito Clayton I will call. Ok?"

I don't know how, but I managed a nod.

Marisol smiled before retreating out of the locker room. I watched her move out of my gaze but did not watch what exit she walked out of. Once sure I was alone, I then began looking around for a means to see me isolated in my coming relapse. I moved all the nearby furniture to barricade the door, quiet and equally still like the dawn before birds woke to recant their morning hymns. Once sure there would be no conceivable hope for anyone to break through my makeshift barricade, I then sat in my lent cubby. I moved the contents inside my duffel bag until I had found the repurposed water bottle housing my only remaining tether to sanity to examine the black in the overhead locker room light.

I knew if I thought on the matter of morality for too long, it would see me reduced to cinders with nothing to show for the coming crime but that of equal portions of blood, pills, and the vodka sloshed in the pit of my stomach. Thinking of the disappointment that would soon befall the people I loved was equal parts motivation to see through this self-imposed degradation as it was motivation to remain clean. But the truth of the matter remained. I would never be strong enough to see myself sober. The fate of redemption was long beneath me knowing I would choose the same vices over being the person my mother once knew me as; every bit her son as I could no longer remember myself as except in hallowed and equally perfect glimpses.

I then began to discard the hockey armor I had once donned to see through the coming humbling of my brother culminate. Once the pads and corresponding armor had been all but discarded, I held the weight of my lifeline in my hand before asking myself if this relapse was something I would really be so heinous to let myself see.

And I realized then the only other answer in terms of how to cope with the memory of my mother now brought back to life was a self-imposed, untimely death.

Once enough of the vodka was in my system for me to feel floaty, I let out a drunken laugh knowing the good, just person everyone had once thought of me as had never existed, if ever at all.

40

ROBYN

"D ANTE, *FOR FUCK'S SAKE*, let me in!"

Lisanna and I used the shout as a cue to exit the women's locker room in a brisk pace to find Rue banging on the door to the men's one next over. Lisanna seemingly teleported over to him, understanding the grief laced in his tone. I remained in place, watching the two struggle to break inside. Once Lisanna realized all hope for to get past the barricades pressed up against the other side was lost, she then turned to Rue and said, "Rue, *what the fuck happened?*"

"I don't know, but Dante's barricaded himself inside and I can't get in," Rue answered, every bit distraught as I would expect him to be. "Lisanna, *please. Please, help me.* I can't let Dante stay there alone."

I interrupted them to say, "You come with me, Rue. I know a way into the locker room that's outside the front door."

Rue and Lisanna turned to me. Rue's expression was an even mixture of grief and an otherworldly kind of anguish that was taut across every line showcasing the horror of what we all knew was soon to come. I knew the full body, all-encompassing fear now shared between the three of us meant the matter of Dante's sobriety—and most crucially his life—was now in the balance. I adjusted my shoulders to bear the weight of Dante's now butchered hope for stability evenly atop my shoulders. I straightened my back and crossed my arms. It was an attempt to display a composure I did not think would be needed any bit by Dante. Unlike how it was needed for self to come out of seeing him withstanding.

After all, I knew the truth of his relapse would make me want to see through the same at the same expense of everyone around me. However, with the differing motive to see the sins I had once condoned atoned for. But I knew I no longer had to pay its price because Xavier was now going to such for me. How we would come to murder him and get away with it, I was unsure. But it did not change how the answer of who had to oversee atonement because of the cardinal sins Xavier Hidalgo, too, saw through at the expense of everyone around him was no longer my responsibility to bear. Truth be told, it never had been. Because Xavier should have known better than to think the pain he had imprinted upon those he loved would not come to stain himself in the process. To be entirely honest, I was done being his perfect victim. I was done hiding behind Tito Clayton. I was now going to do everything in my power to oversee justice at my own hands knowing no one was going to do it for me. And if Xavier had to die to see such come to pass, well, *then so fucking be it.*

Lisanna then said, "And I'll get the Lions."

Lisanna began to run in the other direction to the hockey rink, when I led Rue inside the women's locker room. Neither of us paid much attention to the decor or layout considering the matter of life and death, instead making a brisk run over to the back door. I found it odd it was not blocked off by stray pieces of furniture like it usually was, but I did not have time to think of such now. I tested the handle to see it was already unlocked, the door bucking open beneath the weight of my palm.

I moved my gaze back to Rue who I watched writhe with this full body, all-encompassing anguish. He then bolted to the men's locker room on the other side of the staircase linking the two rooms together. I remained in place, turning around to find Xavier sitting atop the bench dividing the women's locker room in two. I stood a deathly kind of still akin to the quiet in an empty forest; the only two people beneath its cover of overhead branches you and the man you lay ignorant to who was watching from behind the brush.

"Miss me, Robyn?"

"If you have something to say, get the fuck to it." I answered, turning back around. "I mean, look what you've fucking done. To your goddamn brother no less."

"And what about you?"

"What the fuck about me, Xavier?"

I turned back around. In the first time I had known Xavier, I saw regret etched across his face. This sort of understanding I had once deemed him beneath in terms of the damage he had wrought upon others without care for its consequence. This almost kind of penance overseen in his expression by a man who I had once thought was incapable of just that.

I walked over to stand before him, kneeling down until the two of us were eye level. Xavier leaned forward, resting his elbows atop his knees as I held up my head with my palm. We watched each other, daring the other to speak first. When no words came, I flicked my gaze up and down the length of his body to then settle on his face. I knew the factors of my scowl and pressed together eyebrows told him there was nothing left for me to say to him that I had not already. Xavier, realizing such, gazed upon my expression like a wounded animal about to become prey to a corresponding predator, my three-inch canines piercing into the flesh of his neck.

"I've hurt you. And I've come to regret it, Robyn."

I smiled, warm, unassuming, and equally sweet. I did not care that Xavier had grown a conscience in the span of our last meeting. Quite frankly, I did not care whether he was being genuine or not. That much did not matter. Because regardless of his intention, the only use he held for me still was seeing the mortal sins he had willingly committed atoned for with my eventual punishment. I had spent the past few months agonizing over Xavier Hidalgo; yearning for a moment where we could reach a common, mutual understanding. And now that Xavier was offering me the olive branch in which we could use to rebuild our once shared friendship, I realized I did not give *a single, solitary fuck* that Xavier was sorry.

Where was this apology when I woke up from my overdose? Where was the effort to see through atonement when I landed at Schaffer a so-called traitor and deemed a two-faced bitch by everyone on its roster? Now that Dante could be dead and now that I had finally severed my last tie linking me to the man who attempted to oversee my own execution, *the fucker was sorry?* And to make such infinitely more ironic, for a man who claimed to be remorseful, sorry seemed to be a word still entirely beneath him. Now that he was making an attempt at an apology without saying the keywords, *I'm sorry*, he expected me to be so unbelievably stupid to actually fucking believe him?

I suppressed the laugh itching to come out from the confines of my throat. I offered another smile instead, every bit forced as it was fake. I moved to stand before Xavier Hidalgo. His coming butchery had been every bit warranted when I had once refused to condone its truth as it was now that I had made the choice to see it through. Because I knew Xavier. And I knew he was only 'sorry' now because he knew he could not outrun the truth of his past forever. We both knew now that I had cast him out and burnt the last bridge linking us together, I was now the only tether still keeping him alive. After all, my uncanny powers of persuasion had yet to be shrouded over the Lions, and I knew they would all come to agree in seeing our rival captain dead after they saw what Xavier had done to his brother.

But I did not need to tell him such outright. No, I would do as he had done to me. Befriend and gain his trust only to warp it beneath the inevitable weight of my betrayal knowing when the life faded from his eyes his last thoughts would be akin to my own being, *Why would you do this to me if you had loved me?* And maybe at some point I had loved Xavier like a brother. And maybe at some point it had been mutual. But I knew now the man I once loved was no longer real as I once ached for him to be. That our friendship had been some kind of drawn out, elaborate ruse. It was an obscene trickery to see me dependent on a man who could never give love in return. No matter how much blood was spilled in an attempt to see me one day claim I had been the party to teach him such.

"I'm sorry for choosing Dante over you." A lie, but Xavier did not need to know that. "I've come to regret it too, Xavier."

"So, we both miss each other?"

"Of course. Life has been empty without my best friend in it."

Xavier laughed a bit. He rose from the bench to look up at me and then say, "Feel free to call or text. I think we should both learn to forgive rather than let our past cloud our present."

"Of course, Xavier. I am in your hands."

Xavier gave a smile, walking past me to ascend up the stairs when Lisanna came rushing back inside with the Lions in tow. I did not address any of them and they did not address me. Not that I felt the need for such when Dante needed them now a hell of a lot more than I did. I kept to the back of the group when they parted, and all I could see from Dante was that of blood.

The lacquer was dripping down his arms, onto the tile beneath our feet. Pills I had no idea how he had even managed scrounge were scattered all around his immediate range of motion. After all, I, too, had made an effort to study and curtail Tito Clayton's strict search and seizure policies. I suppose that's what made Dante and I equals; every bit dependent on our favored vices as we ached not to be. Truth be told, I did not think such should be held against Dante when I of all people knew how cruel and equally unforgiving the effort of sobriety could be. And I, too, had an endless stretch of road waiting for me in terms of unlearning the emotions, behaviors, and circumstance that saw me abuse opioids to begin with.

But now, I had replaced the guilt that had once been entrenched in every facet of my being with rage. By no means did I think such was at all a healthy mindset, yes, but it was enough to see me remain clean. And truth be told, I give a fuck if seeing through Xavier's execution was righteousness or not. I did not care if it made me among his same like. Because the damage had been done, and the curse had long been set. I had nothing to show for his friendship but the eternal binding to a vice that had been complicit in Xavier's attempt to dictate the terms of my own demise. And despite such, I knew now I was the only maker of my density. Not Xavier. And sure as fuck not the same tiny, white pills I had come to realize now would never love me as I had once loved them back.

Tito Clayton and my mother began to clean up the scene of the crime, when Dante, so off his ass drunk I knew meant there would be no hope for him to remember this coming conversation said, "You know what we have to do now Robyn." His speech was so sloshed I could barely understand him. "And should I live, I am in your care."

"Stop talking," Tito Clayton said, his voice curt and equally strained. Dante did not notice, instead laughing as Tito Clayton tossed his disinfectant and bloodied gauze to the side. "Chase, you're in for Dante. Takeshi will be in charge. I am staying here with Dante with Bruna and Ciara, so if any of you break a hip, ice it until we handle this."

"Yes, Coach," we all chorused weakly.

"Celena, Rue is staying here. You good with playing a whole game?"

"I'll be fine, Coach. Just take care of Dante."

"Good to know we're all on the same page. Now, get out of here and give your best. I'm not worried about winning. I'm worried about survival. If you can give me that today, then that's good-e-fucking-nough for me."

"Yes, Coach," we all answered again meekly.

We all looked around each other when Celena glanced at me. Her endless, blue eyes looked me up and down before she motioned with her hand for everyone to follow her out, leading us out of the locker room. Celena then stood at the doorway leading us back to the women's locker room. Our other teammates filed out, but she had seemingly been waiting for my presence. Once the other Lions—now lead by Takehsi—had exited the women's locker room and the door shut behind them, she then stared at me to say, "What is it that you and Dante are talking about?"

"Dante and I want to kill Xavier."

Celena did not flinch at the thought of taking another life.

For some reason, that much didn't surprise me.

"I'll only see it happen if we're all on board," I answered in a rare bout of truth. Then, I smiled knowing the next remark would get her to see my side. "But, should you help me get the other Lions to see through our cause, I can see that we kill Elliot too. A two for one is good in shopping as it is in murder, don't you think?"

Celena considered my proposal with careful thought. She gazed back at where her Lions had exited prior, whom we had now had no hope in catching up to by the time she would give me her answer. Celena brought her sharp, electric blue eyes back at me, looking me up and down as if to find the answer if my cause was morally virtuous or not. And we both knew it was not. But on the other hand, we also knew there would be no tangible justice for either of us wrought should we not be so heinous to dare and see the coming execution of Xavier Hidalgo and Elliot Božović through.

I knew Celena, too, knew the truth of how men like the two of them operated. How they took from the women they loved until there was nothing left to possibly give, and then in a last act of sheer, grandiose self-righteousness, they would then discard us like used garbage; leaving us to clean off the black of their betrayal now smeared across the walls and strings holding up the seemingly endless chasms of our shared heart. Its stain had driven me to murder. Its weight had forced my hand in seeing what was done to me done to the same man who had been the first to dare and see it through. Maybe in a world where I could rise above the curl of Xavier's betrayal, we could come to forgive each other and rekindle the friendship once shared. But I had given up hope for such knowing how intimately I had once loved Xavier. How much I had given in an attempt to see him heal from his past, only to be cut down at my knees like I had meant *fucking nothing* to him and was not the woman whom he had once called a sister in every sense except blood.

"Do you think murdering Xavier and Elliot is righteous?" Celena asked as if she already knew the answer to the question, but regardless, wanted to hear mine.

"You know it isn't."

"It isn't, yes. But how else will justice be wrought for your and Dante's cause?"

I smirked a bit knowing my attempt to get her to see my side had worked. I then said, "You have yourself a deal, Celena Božović."

"Good," Celena called, monotone. "And I, too, am in your care, Robyn Zaragoza."

Celena stood upright, jogging down the hallway to join the Lions that had already left us alone in the doorway linking the men and women's locker room. I then glanced back at the men's locker room door, hoping Dante would come out of his relapse withstanding.

But I did find some comfort knowing Xavier Alonso Hidalgo would soon get his wish in seeing through an act of penance. That is, with the caveat of us Lions dictating the terms—and its dependent clause of his own undoing—as a singular, cohesive unit he once never thought we could be in the wake of my transfer. But any kind of pity or hesitation in his coming murder was long past me knowing Xavier should not have dared to cross me before.

Because the truth of the matter remained.

Hell hath no fury like that of Robyn Hera Zaragoza scorned.

THE END.

BONUS CONTENT

PROLOGUE
CELENA
SECOND DRAFT

Today was the day I would have my name written among the stars like an ancient mythos. Think Achilles but a million times more important. Think Zeus but a million times more powerful. A kind of queen who was both divinely appointed and had earned her crown through calculated and careful elimination of her enemies. Because today was the day I would face the press after officially becoming the first woman in all of NCAA history scouted onto a men's team. By no means an easy feat breaking a glass ceiling, but I'm not here to make friends. I'm here to win, and I'm here to fucking dominate. I was ready to put my names in the record books along with Wayne Gretzky or Bobby Orr. Because I was going to prove through sheer skill and determination that I was and always would be the greatest hockey player who ever picked up a stick.

Taking a chance like this may seem daunting for anyone. Being the first is not for anyone of a weak will or mind. But when your hockey idol comes to Romania solely to ask you to play in his college team, an offer like that really is a no brainer. After all, Clayton Alonso was good enough for me to respect him and was the man I would come to idolize as my inspiration for getting me into this sport to begin with. And even if he only played professionally for one season, I could care less he may not be a household name like the other greats I'd mentioned. Because on sheer skill alone, Clayton was easily the second-best hockey player to ever grace the ice. After myself, of course.

I looked at myself in the mirror. I usually could care less on what my appearance would look like on a normal day, but today was the day I was being shown off the world as Clayton Alonso's pet project. An experiment that would come to define the question of female athletes and where and what role they would come to play in the future whether it be separate or with the boys. And that meant makeup. Obnoxious heels and perfect everything. And for the sake of Clayton, I'd tolerate it. And I knew the press was going to hate me from the start. That much was obvious. But despite wanting to hurl looking dolled up to an excess like some kind of model on the marble catwalks of Paris, I had to make a good impression since this was my first public appearance. Even if it was beyond stupid how I had to already maintain this dainty, frail feminine image because the media refused to believe I could be anything else.

I heard something crash in the room next over and turned away from the mirror to go investigate. I walked inside a different room in the female locker room to see a high school aged boy who was easily five times my size and more than drunk. Considering my history with men thinking they're bigger than they are and violence, you might think I would turn the other way and wash my hands of the rage to come. But something told me this more pitiful teenage boy in front of me wouldn't be a threat. And even if he was, I knew I could handle it.

I saw that his skin was this kind of sappy, amber color. His head was shaved which let me get a good look at high cheekbones and almost glassy, twilight eyes. Although, the one thing about his appearance that I noticed right off the bat was this thick and glaring scar that started from the bottom of his left eye and dragged all the way down to the edge of a sharp jawline. When he noticed me in the doorway, he laughed as he tried to get up from the pile of hockey equipment that had caved under his weight after carelessly crashing into it only to watch as he failed before giving up entirely to take a knock back from a glass bottle of vodka he seemingly pulled out of thin air.

"You're a little young to be drinking that," I said. He looked at me. "And a little too drunk to be walking around so carelessly."

"What are you gonna do, tell my mommy?" he laughed again. "She doesn't want me anyway. Maybe you'll tell my tito instead, hm?"

"Ah," I said. "You're Dante. Clayton's nephew."

Dante raised his bottle in an exaggerated toast. I didn't meet it, but he drank regardless. "Aw, my pretend daddy gave you the spiel on how Schaffer is my sober jail?" I nodded.

"Good. Saves me the trouble of doing it myself. You must be Celena Božović, no?"

"I am." I answered. "Does Clayton know you're here? And that you're fucking drunk when I need him more than you right now?"

"Now, Celena," Dante said. He finally managed to get up as he walked over to stand in front of me with the alcohol on his breath staining the inside of my nose. "If Tito Clayton won't let me die, the least I can do is make him regret letting me live."

I looked him up and down as a hand came from behind to grab Dante's alcohol. I watched as Clayton Alonso tucked the bottle into his chest and picked his nephew up like he was weightless and slung him on his shoulder. Dante let out a hearty and drunken laugh as I turned to Clayton. "I take it you have priorities. I can handle myself out there. If you need me to, I'll do it."

Clayton looked at me. "I know you can handle it, Celena. But the question I have is how is that fair to you?"

"Life isn't fair. You of all people should know that, Coach." Clayton smirked a bit. "I'll handle it. Come join me once you take care of this."

"Knock 'em dead, Celena. If anyone can handle their collective stupidity, it's you."

Clayton turned away and walked out of the locker room as Dante tilted his head up to give me a salute and a smile before the door closed behind him. I caught a glimpse of my reflection in the mirror before heading out to face the press and tied my hair up in a ponytail. Once I was satisfied with the woman staring back, I kicked my heels and headed off to war.

As I walked into the room where Clayton had staged this press conference, I was almost blinded by the cameras greeting me as I tried to focus on making it to my microphone without tripping over myself in these annoying shoes. Once I was sure I was sitting in my designated chair, I scooted closer and leaned into the microphone. "Welcome. Coach Clayton had business to take care of, but he will be joining us soon. I'll be taking all your questions." All the reporters started yelling as I scanned the room for a face I knew wouldn't say something beyond stupid. And I knew I had found one when I spotted the only female reporter in the room and pointed at her.

"You. You can ask me anything you want. Since I don't think you'll say anything stupid."

Her lips curled into a smile as she tucked a stray strand of hair behind her ear. "Why did you pick Schaffer, Celena? As far as I'm aware, other schools had offers for you to play but on the women's team. So, my question is, what made Schaffer different?"

"Two reasons. The first being Clayton Alonso was too good a player for me not to accept his offer. The second being I want to prove women are just as good as men in sports if not better. And I know if anyone can handle being a first, it's me."

A male reporter but in unwelcomed. "But aren't you scared of falling victim to men's locker room talk?"

I was getting annoyed. "A dumb question, but I'll bite. I can assure you, I'm not damsel in distress who needs someone to save her. If anyone tries to lay a hand on me, I'll handle it both on and off the ice. I didn't come here to entertain your weird fantasy of me being weak and subservient. I'm here to win, and I'm here to make history. Nothing more. Nothing less."

The room fell quiet as the male reporter shut right up and sat back in his seat. I heard the door open, and the room turned to see Clayton join us as the cameras took what had to be a million different pictures. He took his seat at my right. He looked at me, and I gave him a nod as we turned back to face the lion's den.

"Apologies I'm late. Family matters came up. Now, who has questions for me?"

"She can ask you questions," I said, pointing at the female reporter. "What's your name?"

"Dylan Rivera. And my question for Clayton is, why choose to make history? This is a big deal. And I don't think you would have made this choice without giving its weight some thought."

Clayton didn't need time to think about it. "Celena was too good a player for me not to scout her. I've never seen a talent like hers man or woman alike. And naturally when you coach a team, you want the best. And the best is what I got."

And hearing that, I knew this deal to become a first was going to be worth it. And knowing Clayton shared this respect I had for him since the moment I watched him sweep the Boston Bruins in four games in the Stanley Cup Playoffs on my boxy TV told me what I had always known. That I was destined for greatness and would achieve all my wildest dreams with both my skill and the help of Clayton Alonso. One of the greatest hockey players that the world would ever know.

1

DANTE

SECOND DRAFT

Nothing cared for me quite like this bottle of Burnett in my hands. And I was beyond happy to be drunk enough that I was completely numb to anything and everything. And to make this shit-show that was my life even better, I couldn't feel any kind of emotion except this sense of fatigue that gave me the same illusion of safety as a security blanket. And gripping the bottle of vodka and holding it in my chest like I was a sinner in a confessional, it almost convinced me the weight of the glass could magically absolve me of all my mortal sins.

I read the letters on the foggy, matte surface to find the answer on this lifelong question if I could ever really become the good person Tito Clayton thought I was. And the letters told me that the answer was neither yes nor no. That if it weren't for a brother who wanted to wear the weight of my life on top of his head like a crown, maybe I would be worthy of the infinite number of second chances Tito Clayton had given me.

And maybe my tito was right and I really was drinking myself to death. But I could give a fuck that this one-way road of being a 'drunkard' would only end with me burning every last one of my bridges and cost a life I had decided long ago would never be worth living. And I knew the only way to see the misery who was holding beneath three-inch teeth let me go was for me to tie a noose around my neck or slit my wrists and finally wash my hands of this forced and unwanted existence. And don't get me wrong, I really don't expect you to understand my logic or even agree with it. But ask yourself this, if me getting blackout drunk every day and every night would speed up the process of seeing myself buried in an early grave, who am I deny myself that kind of freedom?

"You promised me the moment you signed that contract that you would quit, Dante." Clayton was staring at me, but I couldn't bring myself to look at him. "And I'm going to hold you to that until you meet your end of the bargain."

I laughed. Not because anything Clayton was saying was funny, but because this had to be the millionth time Clayton told me I had to quit, and this would be the millionth time I would tell him to go fuck himself. And I knew I was an asshole for going back on my promise that I would wash my hands of what everyone called an 'addiction', but what no one seemed to understand is that in order to keep the miserable existence that was Dante Alonso Hidalgo alive, I needed to feel that comforting burn running down my throat. I needed to feel this warmth in my stomach that would channel throughout my entire body until I was lulled into a comforting sleep. I just needed to drink and drink and drink until I had escaped the memories I wanted nothing more than to forget but could never cleanse myself of like they were some kind of original sin.

"Tito Clayton." My pronunciation was more than slurred and more than sloshed. "I'm already a dead man. Kuya Xavier is going to kill me whether you like it or not, and I think I should just move things along. Please, just fucking let me go. It's what I want. It's what I need. And nothing you say is going to change that."

Clayton looked annoyed. Although, I knew his expression was directed more at my self-destructive streak than it was to me as a whole. "Do you want Xavier to win or lose?"

I thought it over. Obviously, I wanted Xavier to lose on his vendetta to see me with a bullet between my eyes. You may be thinking, but, Dante, what about this whole suicide pity party thing? And you would be right on the fact that I wanted to see myself dead. However, the absolute last way I wanted to go was for my brother to execute me.

I could see it now. Xavier parading around the Wesleyan ice rink with my lifeless head in hand like the fact he'd finally butchered me was the culminating moment his entire life was leading up to. And if you knew me, you knew that when I was going to kill myself, I wanted it to be quick. Painless. Efficient. I wanted to go out with the least possible fuss and the least possible mess. However, no matter how badly I wanted to tie a noose around my neck or drown myself in a river, I could never bring myself to finish the job. Probably because there wouldn't be a time where I'd be sober enough to see that I actually died this time around.

"Just give up," I said. "Just give up and let me waste away like I want to. Please, just give me what I want, Tito Clayton."

Clayton narrowed his eyes, but his expression didn't change. "If you want to beat Xavier, you're going to have to live in order to accomplish that. And you're on punishment as of now. I don't want to hear any complaints. You made your bed and now you have to lie in it."

Clayton sat me upright against the wall and looked me up and down before he let out a long, tired sigh. And I thought my tito was entitled to that much considering he cared for me even when we both knew I didn't deserve it. I watched as Clayton grabbed the bottle from my hand, but I was too drunk to even think about putting up a fight. I was starting to slip out of consciousness, and the last thing I saw before I closed my eyes were the memories of Xavier's smile.

2

ROBYN

SECOND DRAFT

I was proud to say that I had just walked out of rehab an unchanged woman. And you would think overdosing on Fentanyl would be this rousing and awe-inspiring call to arms, but for me, not so much.

All that I could say rehab did for me was help me look nothing short of a total mess considering this place was a jail and the staff would never let me wear any kind of makeup or heels. I think banning me from those two things was a million times worse than even having this whole opioid habit to begin with. Ok, maybe that's a gross, gross exaggeration but it didn't change the fact this whole recovery thing was all bullshit when I didn't even want to get fucking clean to begin with.

And while I didn't want to get clean and never would, I knew I was going to have to face Lisanna—the woman I would love until the end of time—after overdosing under the guise I would get sober so we could be together. Very much an asshole move on my part knowing I couldn't keep my word and still choosing to make the promise anyway. But being an addict and being honest are two things that go together as well as kitten heels and any outfit. And I was pretty much public enemy number one on the Lions right now, but in all honesty, I think I had done enough to earn that. I mean, I was the asshole who made the team a promise that I would be sober enough to help us actually beat Xavier this year knowing I couldn't keep that one either.

The focus right now wasn't to stay sober. I may be fresh out of rehab, but I didn't really hold any kind of value to this whole getting clean thing. Getting high was my absolute favorite thing to do, and I don't think I could really bring myself to wash my hands of it like everyone wanted me to. And even if I knew this addiction meant sacrificing everyone I loved in order to feel a last, perfect high, it almost didn't matter to me. You might ask yourself, would you rather be loved or be high? And even if I'd hate to admit such, the answer to that question was more blurred than you'd like to think. Because the thing is, while Lisanna, Conner, and Clayton all loved me even when I knew I didn't deserve it, they were still human. Like me, they were imperfect. And most importantly, they judged. And what did a bottle of Oxycontin offer me in exchange? A way to escape all my problems with open and loving arms. A way to forget and cleanse myself of my mistakes that would forever haunt me like the ghost of the man who I once called my best friend.

And to be honest, all that really mattered to me post rehab was somehow managing to pull off the heist of the century and convince Lisanna that my silver-tongued promises weren't empty, and I was never this terrible person who kept breaking her heart. And I knew the only way to do that was to be honest and tell her the truth behind my overdose and my addiction as a whole. And while we both knew I had a problem, I of all people should know that knowing you have a problem and wanting to fix it are two very different things.

Clayton's ancient and shitty Toyota pulled in front. He rolled down the window and looked at me with that same scowl he always had on his face no matter what kind of mood he was in. And I will admit, seeing it after a month of being locked up against my will was almost comforting.

"Get in. We got a long drive ahead of us." I got inside of the car before tossing my duffel bag next to me in the backseat. I knew Clayton didn't like me sitting here, but considering I used to go everywhere with a hired driver, it was pretty much a force of habit. "Rue Oba transferred to Schaffer in your absence. That a problem with you?"

"Not at all, Tito Clayton," I said.

Clayton checked his mirrors before pulling back onto the road. A looming silence filled the car, and I knew the exact words that were coming next. "Robyn, I know you don't want to hear this, but being honest with Lisanna and the rest of the team is the only way for them to stop hating you."

And there they were. I gave Clayton an empty smile. "Maybe one day, Tito Clayton, but sure as hell not today."

After an hour of a tense silence, I was more than happy to forget about everything Clayton had said as I got out of his car and walked into the makeshift prison cell he'd confined me to being the spare room in his apartment. Clayton was somewhat entitled to keep me on an improvised probation considering my history, but it didn't make really help the case that this sobriety thing was something worth keeping my word on. I tried to use my keys to unlock the front door, but I found that Clayton had changed the locks. He came up from behind me to unlock the door for me, and I looked at him before entering. "You take my word for once, Tito?"

"You were Xavier's best friend, Robyn. You knew him a hell of a lot better than I ever did."

Hearing Xavier's name made me want to slit the throat of the man I once called my best friend, but I ignored the homicidal urge to see the man who ruined my life to meet his demise beneath a kitchen knife. My gaze lingered a few seconds on Clayton before turning around to walk into the apartment to find Lisanna and Conner waiting for me. And knowing Lisanna was going to be beyond pissed at me, I looked at my twin brother in hopes his expression would make me feel better, which, it didn't by the way. Not that I could really say I knew what exactly to expect from him considering I didn't know he existed until about a month ago.

"Why, hello, you two." Clayton walked past me and over to his bedroom. He looked at me before closing the door behind him and leaving me with the two people who were entitled to my honesty. "How are things?"

Lisanna walked to stand in front of me and gave me a pained smile. And I knew this meant I was teetering off the edge that would make the damage I had brought upon her heart beyond repair. And you don't know how badly I wanted to stop being this terrible person who kept breaking Lisanna like she meant nothing to me and wasn't the woman I loved. But I couldn't bring myself to wash my hands of this addiction even if I knew it meant I would get a happy ending with the woman I loved. And I knew that made this bad person even if I didn't want to be one. But the thing is, I didn't know how to be good or to be honest. Because I'd been lying for so fucking long I didn't think I could bring myself to stop.

"Welcome back, Robyn." This raw and indisputable pain had seeped into each of Lisanna's words. And it did nothing but make me feel like shit. "I'm glad I could welcome you back."

"Lisanna, I'm so fucking sorry. Really. I mean it."

We both knew better than to believe anything that came out of my mouth as Lisanna held my hands. "I want you to know that I love you. But I also want you to know that while I'm more than willing to fight for us, if you don't extend the same courtesy to me, you have to understand what that looks like to me." Lisanna smiled again. "We'll talk about this later. Once I get all my bearings."

Lisanna smiled again before walking out of the apartment and slamming the door behind her. I pursed my lips before turning to my twin brother, Conner, and getting a good look at him before saying something.

The last time we were in the same vicinity of each other, I was attending Wesleyan University and Xavier Alonso was my best friend. And while the two of us may not have grown up together, that didn't change the fact that we were twins. And that we were identical from our brown skin to our flat nose with the same a set of freckles dotting its bridge. And while I may not know just yet what to make of a brother I didn't know existed until a month ago, I knew I wouldn't be able to live with myself if I didn't sacrifice everything I had in order to give him a chance.

"Conner, how are things?" We stared at each other. He looked hesitant to even be in the same room as me. "What? You've never seen an addict before, my dear? You look like you've seen a ghost."

"You didn't have to follow me here. I would have been more than fine if you just washed your hands of me like everyone else."

While Conner was annoying me saying this, I knew with his history that a response like that was warranted. And that trying to drill the message into his head that I wasn't going to be like the other people of our family. Even if that meant being a little bit of a bitch to get the point across.

"Conner, I made a choice to give you a chance. And I'm not going to be like them. I refuse to be like them."

Conner didn't look convinced. "Being the family I never had means believing me, Robyn. Being the family I never had means accepting what *your parents* did to me was fucked up."

"We are not getting into this fight again. Not right now."

"Don't act like you're some kind of saint just because you made the choice to come here and give me a chance I never asked you to give me."

Conner walked out of the apartment, and I heard a door creak behind me to find Clayton leaning in the doorframe, watching me with a gaze I never quite knew the meaning behind. "Well, tito, what's your take on me being a bad person?"

"You have a choice to make, Robyn." Clayton kept his gaze on me as he crossed his arms. "You either choose the people you love, or you choose the drugs. And the drugs will never need you back."

PROLOGUE
CELENA
THIRD DRAFT

While Dante and Robyn are the ones who want to tell the story of how us Lions got away with murder, they asked me to recant the day news of my initial recruitment onto a men's NCAA team broke to provide much needed context. I'm not sure it will help, but out of respect for Dante, I'm complying. Even if I think it's beyond stupid to be telling the story that could very well incriminate the lot of us should it get out.

But, I regress. Dante needs me for this moment, and I will be the last person to ever willingly let him down. And as mentioned before, my part of this ever-complicated story starts with news of me being the first woman scouted onto a men's team in all of NCAA history. Obviously, not an easy feat for any woman especially one of a weak will or weak mind, but I knew I could handle the obscene stupidity coming at me from all sides whether it be from other women projecting their own insecurities onto me or vengeful men who wanted nothing more than my failure to prove women would never be able to achieve a mythological success like I knew I would see once my time here at Schaffer was over.

But being first shown off to the world, I knew this was under the context of me being some kind social experiment. I was a kind of lab rat; Clayton Alonso's personal pet project that would later come to define the question if women should continue to play separate or with the boys. And what did that mean for me? Makeup. Obnoxious heels and perfect everything. And for the sake of Clayton, I would tolerate it knowing making a good impression at my press conference would help soften the blow of my recruitment before its weight really had time to be digested. And Clayton and I knew playing into the dainty, frail feminine stereotype was the easiest way to accomplish that since the press—at this point—refused I could be anyone else.

I looked at myself in the mirror, unsure who this woman was staring back. I had never—and honestly still don't—cared much about my looks since all that mattered to me when defining my own self-worth was what I brought to ice. I had built my entire being around hockey because it gave me a sense of purpose in a life that was the last thing from kind. To be fucking honest, I only got into the sport to begin with to prove to my idiot tata that just because I was a girl didn't mean I couldn't hold my own whether it be against him or any other beyond idiotic boys who thought I would take their crude, sexist comments by bowing my head and keeping quiet. Hockey was—and still is— a way for me to prove to myself what I am capable of. That no matter how uncomfortable or hard, I will not cower beneath the weight of a man's arrogance just to help him sleep at night.

Because growing up in a house where the men were born to be in charge no matter how unworthy or crude and the women destined to be good, faithful servants who doted on their every need, I promised myself I would *never* fill that beyond backward role expected of me even if it took more than backbreaking and laborious work.

I walked into the lobby area of the female locker room built to accommodate my tenure here at Schaffer when I saw a face on the television I remember looked familiar even if I then didn't know where I'd seen the resemblance before. His skin was a light, almost pasty peach and his hair was the same black as mine naturally without the presence of the new, bleach blonde color I had begun to sport in an effort to distance myself from my fucked-up little family. His eyes were an even mix of green and brown, blending together to give off a striking kind of hazel I had only seen a handful of times before. I watched his lips curl into a smile as a male reporter stuck a microphone in his face and spoke, "News just broke of a woman being scouted onto a men's team, the Schaffer Lions. The team your uncle coaches for. What are your thoughts, Xavier?"

"I hope she doesn't expect special treatment on the ice solely because of the vagina between her legs," Xavier said. "I look forward to crushing her and humbling that obscenely big head of hers thinking she can play with the boys. Let's hope we don't witness a mighty and towering fall from grace, no?"

I knew better than to let this sexist pig's comments get under my skin. But when I recognized the figure at his right, I knew this pitiful misogynist kept my brother in his company. And that, was enough to make me promise myself to slaughter this fucking roach and hang his corpse at the entrance of The Nora Wilson Hockey Center as a warning to any other pitiful man of what would become of him should they try and disqualify my skill solely because of the gender I had chosen as my own since the moment I could think my own thoughts or even form my own words.

I remember hearing a loud crash behind me and turned around to look at it to find Dante Hidalgo with a bottle of vodka pressed up against his lips and a caved in pile of hockey sticks beneath him as he met my gaze, offering an exaggerated toast. The only thing different about him here was that his head was shaved while everything else from his high cheekbones, scar, brown skin, and all-black wardrobe that reminded me of my own high school days were the same as it is today. I remember thinking I was inclined to worry considering my history of men who liked to think they were better than me and violence, but something told me this beyond pitiful display in front of me would be no threat to my safety. And even if Dante was, I knew then I could handle it.

"You look a little young to be drinking that," I said.

Dante smiled behind the mouth of his bottle. "What's life without a little bit of risqué, Celena?" Dante took another swig from the cloudy, white glass as the stench to show for his drunken state had seeped into the inside of my nose. "How rude of me to not introduce myself to the living legend making Schaffer her home. I'm Dante."

I knew exactly who he was based on the name. Mostly because Clayton had told me he hoped Dante would come join me here at Schaffer for the two of us to become a cohesive and formidable team of a corresponding expert defense and an expert offense. "Clayton's nephew."

"Ding, dong, someone give her a fucking prize," Dante said with a hearty laugh. "What's your take on my brother wanting to kill you? It makes two of us, no?"

I didn't know what he meant by that then but would come to find out later once we had gotten to know one another better. I didn't answer his question since I thought then it was beyond idiotic to ask what my thoughts were on a sexist being a sexist. "Does Clayton know you're drunk? When I need him more than you do right now?"

Dante smiled like my accusation was the most fascinating thing he had ever heard. "Now, now, Celena. If Tito Clayton will not let me die, the least I can do is make him regret letting me live."

Wood heels tapping against the solid floor commanded our attention as Clayton Alonso came into view, wearing a gray suit with a white blouse and royal blue tie with a matching accessory of black, leather shoes. Dante laughed like some kind of maniacal, rabid hyena upon the sight of his uncle all dolled up, and I remember raising an eyebrow as Clayton took the vodka from his nephew's hand, tucking it beneath his armpit as he slung a well over two-hundred-pound Dante over his shoulder like he were weightless before bringing his gaze to my own. I of all people knew family matters like this were beyond complicated, so I spoke, "I see you have business to take care of. I can handle myself. You and I both know it. So, come and join me when you're ready."

Clayton sighed. "And how is that at all fair to you, Celena? I'm not saying you need me, but I know this press stuff a hell of a lot better than you do right now. And while I trust you, the cameras and reports don't."

"Dante needs you right now," I said. "Let me handle this. I already owe you for even giving me this chance, Clayton. And this is one way how I will pay it back. That, and by helping you shape what's left of this team into champions. You and I both know I have the talent. So, let me show them that by putting their collective stupidity in their fucking place."

Clayton gave a slight smile. "Alright, Celena. They're all yours. And I will join you when I take care of this."

Clayton turned around and walked into a separate room in the locker room as Dante looked up at me and gave an exaggerated, drunken salute knowing I would be heading off to war. I laughed at that as I walked back over to the mirror and put my long, white hair into a ponytail as I clicked my obnoxious, black heels and walked into the room Clayton had set up for my press conference.

It was hard to keep my balance and remain graceful enough with the combination of the flashing press cameras and five-inch stilettos I was being forced to wear for the sake of upholding the patriarchal stereotype that a woman is only deserving of respect if she caters to the male gaze and be as feminine—and therefore as digestible—as fucking possible. Clayton thought that by playing into this beyond idiotic notion would make this whole woman breaking a glass ceiling thing easier to for—you guessed it—men all across the world to digest.

But to be fucking honest, after hearing Xavier's fucked up remarks made me realize that if I served the role as a dutiful, obeying woman who only spoke when spoken to, that would be doing myself this disservice. It would be putting on an act that was not who I was at all; it would be serving into the fantasy of these men—who already fucking hated me—since I was upending the role of a woman they had all assigned to me. And I remember thinking, if they already hate me, why not actually give them a fucking reason for it?

"Welcome," I said, leaning into the microphone resting atop the table. "Coach Clayton will be joining us shortly. Now, before I take questions, I have something to say to Xavier Hidalgo, who was ever so kind to give his thoughts on my recruitment to his uncle's roster."

The reporters all looked at each other, more than confused as to why I felt the need to address the obscenely sexist comments which only reminded me how idiotic the male half of the population was as a whole. I gave a cold smile as I continued like they weren't already ignoring me and still asking me questions. And, of course, I made sure to raise my voice to practically shout my referendum to be this kind of shot heard around the world. "I want every man who will face me on the ice to know that I will not cower because of the sexism you have all grown too fucking comfortable in because it has been so unbelievably normalized in your fucked up, insecure little minds. I am not weak. I am not subservient. I am a fucking hurricane. I will chew you up and spit you out. I will become the first woman gracing the NHL and you will forget the name of all past greats because I will be the next standard all future hockey players will look up to. You will remember the name Celena Božović. And you will all fucking choke on the insults and names you have assigned to me because I am the first of many women who will be joining me here at Schaffer. Don't project the insecurities of your skill onto me when I never fucking asked for it. Do not expect me to take these remarks and not show you my fucking teeth. After all, even I can only tolerate so much idiocy in my life." The shouts coming from the reporters had all but subsided. A man raised his hand when another moved it back down for him. I smiled. "Now, why don't you all prove to me you're better on the ice instead of talking a big game without any proof or skill to show for it? I have the track record to back up my claims. You can all do the math and figure out my stats. So, save the sexist, petty fucking bullshit for someone who wants it. Because no matter what you fucking men say, I will *never*—and I mean *fucking never*—be the one."

Stunned was a good word to use. Male reporters looked among each other, mouths agape at a total and complete loss at my words, which I will admit, did fucking amuse me. Slowly, they sat down, cowering with their tails between their legs as I realized I had just gained control of this entire press conference. I scanned the room for any female reporters and found the only one standing up against the back wall. I pointed at her. "You. I know you will not ask me something fucking stupid, so you can ask me any and all questions you have for me. What's your name?"

"Dylan," she said, stepping forward and holding a tiny notebook in her hands. "Dylan Rivera. And thank you, Celena. Those were some powerful words you just spoke. We both know this kind of feat is not any easy task of anyone to meet. So, my question is, what makes you capable to meet the expectations placed upon you?"

"Simple. Watch me play without a lens of sexism and you'll come to learn I have the potential and skill set to win against anyone. Talent is not so much given to someone as it is earned. Sure, you can be naturally gifted at a sport, but if you don't have the drive, the work ethic, or that fire in you to become something great, it doesn't mean shit." I crossed my arms. "I came here to prove women are just as capable as the male half of the population. Sometimes we're even fucking better but never get credit where credit is due because of society's patriarchal notion that women are and always will be inferior."

Dylan began to write on her notepad before bringing her gaze back to my own. "What do you expect from this rookie season here at Schaffer?"

"Work. Adjusting," I answered. "Sure, I'm great. But does that mean everyone else here is at my skill? No fucking way. I'll give you a prediction, though. If I don't get voted as captain here at the Lions before my tenure is up? You can write me off as some has-been. Some girl talking a big game who can't deliver. I would promise a championship, but as I said, my skill can only carry so much of a team that is nowhere near it."

The door to the room opened as Clayton walked inside, adjusting his suit coat before taking the seat next to me and adjusting his microphone. "Apologies for the delay. Family matter came up. Now, who has questions for me?"

The male reporters looked around, and I smiled as I pointed at Dylan. "Dylan Rivera will be asking all the questions today, Coach. So, Dylan, have at it. Clayton is now all yours."

Clayton turned to face Dylan, motioning with his hand for her to ask him any question she had either prepared or come up with then and there after I had dropped my atom bomb of a rebuttal to his other nephew. Dylan gave a nod before speaking,

"This is a big deal, Clayton. My question is, why pick Celena to break the gender barrier in college sports? What made her special enough to qualify her to join your roster?"

"Isn't it obvious?" Clayton asked. "When you have a team, you naturally want the best. And in scouting Celena, the best is what I got. Who she was before or even her gender doesn't matter to me. All I could care about is what my players bring to the ice and how I can nurture and grow a skill—that in Celena— is something you only ever see once in a lifetime."

I remember smirking because I knew then that taking this deal to be a first would be worth all the controversy since I had Clayton Alonso guiding me every step of the way. And it was then I made a promise to lead the Lions to the NESCAC Champions before I graduated or fucking die trying.

1

DANTE

THIRD DRAFT

I think everyone every bit as complicit as me in the slaying of my older brother would agree the best place to start would be my sophomore year of college at Schaffer College. An institution housed in a typical, small New England college town that had this never-ending sense of eternal quaintness and virtually no people who looked anything like me. Well, everyone except the roster of wannabe greats making up the hockey team my tito had been ruling unchallenged as head coach ever since I could really remember. I'd grown up in the Schaffer locker room and was almost some kind of honorary mascot for the Division III athletes who called the school home and ever so bravely and ever so proudly wore our team colors of an alluring, royal blue and a saintly white. I was groomed to inherit this kingdom my tito had worked so hard to perfect, but there were a few glaring problems to this peaceful transfer of power.

The first being, at this point in my life I was by all means an alcoholic. But don't fret, this story does have a happy ending for nearly everyone involved. But back when I was living through this period of my life, I was depressed. Suicidal. I was convinced my life was unlivable because of the weight of an unmanaged mental illness I once thought I would be forced to bear between my shoulders until the day I finally jumped off the tallest building gracing the Schaffer campus or put my illegally purchased pearl-handled revolver to some good use. The thing is, though, killing yourself is all but an impossible task when people actually want you here and refuse to let you go quietly. And despite my wishes back then, I had people in my life who refused to give up on me no matter how hopeless and perilous the odds on the Dante Alonso Hidalgo investment were looking at that given time. And maybe I didn't have as many people as I would like who would choose to love me at my worst, but I had enough. And when you're clinging onto the very notion of life as you know it because of those handful of people, enough is better than nothing.

But getting back to the matter of the story, this tall tale starts at my first practice with the Lions. I remember walking into the Lion's locker room with Chase Guo at my right. And inside—almost waiting for us—were all the new male Lions.

I still remember how the three of them almost stood locked in my gaze like a deer caught in oncoming headlights. I figured then that a swift and efficient sizing up of each of them would do me good in preparing for an offhand chance that any of them would prove to be a pain in my ass. Sure, Tito Clayton and Celena were the undisputed rulers of this kingdom they'd spent so much time into shaping from the ground up, but I was also part of the perfect court who helped make a team once ranked dead last become second best only to the Xavier's Ainsworth Bears. I mean, who else picked up the slack to save a hundred goals per game when they slipped through our once shit defense? And to be honest, I think it helped me sleep at night back then knowing Celena Božović wanted my brother just as much dead as I might even if our reasoning behind it was drastically different. Mine being revenge and hers to get the proper credit to her skill she'd been robbed of since she started here at Schaffer three years ago.

The first Lion that had caught my attention was new. Strikingly handsome and extremely so might I add. But totally not my type since there wasn't an ounce of anything ethnic between his pasty skin, blue eyes, and perfectly styled black hair. He gave a warm smile that made me think he wouldn't prove to be as much trouble as Conner was to me back then. The mystery man was in the middle of putting on the shirt of his base-layer that would then go under his pads, and I'll admit, my eyes wandered a bit. He didn't seem to mind as he finished putting on the form fitting spandex that outlined his physique nicely. And hey, even if dating another person—let along some rookie I barely knew—was something beneath me at this point in my life, Chase was right as he always was. It really is never a crime to ogle.

"You are?"

"Damien Prince," he answered with a thick Russian accent soaking up the words coming from thin, pink lips. "You must be Dante Hidalgo. Coach's nephew?"

"That's right," I answered. I could feel all eyes in the locker room turn to me. "I'm sure he told you how this place is my sober jail, no?"

Damien smiled. "He might have mentioned it."

Damien and I were never really the closest of friends in this story. Truth be told, we had mixed feelings for each other. One was a mutual respect since we shared a common like for Davi even if our feelings towards her were always at two different places on the spectrum, which I'll get into later. Although, despite that respect, we also kept our distance since he'd claimed my then mortal nemesis as his best friend during his time here at Schaffer. And because of that, I never found a need to induct him into my hand-picked entourage. And who is this mysterious best friend who still holds that title to this day you ask? Why, none other than the one and only, Conner Zaragoza. And we'll get more into my dislike for Conner—like the matters of Davi and Damien—later in the story. They're all key players in my brother's murder, sure, but I think it would be a crime to not take a moment to mention the deuteragonist in my retelling of events. And that, is none other than Rue Oba.

Rue Oba. Rue fucking Oba. Man, where on Earth do I even begin to describe this man? I still remember when I felt his gaze on mine, I turned to face him and, fuck. Fucking every little thing that made up Rue Oba just blew me the fuck away. He looked perfect with skin that was a warm, olive shade and just dark enough you could tell it wasn't a tan. His hair upon our first meeting was like mine, being long enough to be draped over shoulders. His eyes were round and titled, giving the slightest bit of a curve at the fold. The color was an alluring brown that was so dark the pupils had blended into an equally brown iris to give the illusion of an all-encompassing black. His face was a neutral that told me neither what he was thinking or feeling, but man, will I never forget how seeing him for the first time almost made me believe in love at first sight.

Rue didn't speak but his eyes looked me up and down in a way to almost assess me rather than anything flirtatious. Once his gaze was brought back to my own, he stared at me. Considering the giant scar on my face that dropped from the bottom of my left eye and dragged all the way down to my jawline, I was used to getting wandering eyes, points, and even double takes every single day of my life. I had learned to turn a blind eye to the nosy chatter since all of humankind had an unconscious bias to be a raging asshole to people they may not know or even like. But the way Rue stared at me back at our first meeting wasn't the same kind of pitying, tense quiet I was used to. It was almost like between this steely, unrelenting gaze he knew there was this unspoken worth about myself that I had once refused to accept. And back then, having anyone view me with any notion of value was enough to send me into a full-body shock with this itch to get shit fucking plastered hanging in the back of my throat following behind it.

We stared at each other for what had to be an hour. I refused to give an inch on this one-sided game of chicken I was playing with him since I thought then this was a vain attempt at the hands of Rue to try and assert an unspoken dominance over me—that he wouldn't know then—I would always refuse to back down from. A hand came between Rue's gaze and my own as Rue caught it with a ruthless precision to keep it in place in order to continue our stare down that was starting to kind of freak me out. I felt a hand on my shoulder and turned to it to find Chase with a smile between his lips. "That's Rue Oba," Chase said. "New right wing scouted on behalf of the woman of my dreams. He's gonna do great things, don't you think?"

"If Celena thinks he's good, he has to be," I said, turning to glance at Chase before moving my gaze back to Rue's, who was still staring at me. "Right, Oba?"

"Right." Rue's voice sounded like a hypnotizing symphony of rumbling, unruly waves before a storm. "You must be Dante. As Damien mentioned before."

"I am, yes," I said, looking him up and down.

Rue opened his mouth to speak when a figure blocked my view of him. I remember feeling a bit annoyed because of reasons I was incapable of understanding then, but I looked up at the man to break the mutual death-grip of a stare down between me and Rue Oba to find he was Filipino. Maybe not on both sides like me, but enough of a mix I could tell at least one of his parents hailed from the same island Tito Clayton and my mother had once called home.

"Alexei Oba," he said, offering his hand. I raised an eyebrow as I took his invitation to shake it. And my first impression of Rue's adopted brother? I remember thinking this kid was going to prove to be nothing but a pain in my ass. And in a part, I was right. Although, the brunt end of his stupidity would not fall so much on me like it would Celena Božović. "I'm Rue's younger brother."

Now, this was enough to make me do a double take between raised eyebrows and pursed lips considering the Oba brothers did not look one bit alike. They didn't even pass as distant cousins let alone brothers. Since I was trying to make a good impression on people I would be seeing pretty much every single day for the rest of the season, I kept my mouth shut but glanced at Chase who was already staring at me. We gave each other this look in a language only two of us would know before I turned back to Alexei and let go of his hand. "Pleasure, I'm sure."

"You're looking at the next captain of the Lions, Dante." I sent another look at Chase. He was grinning ear to ear since we both knew in that moment Alexei was going to pay the price for thinking he could ever replace Celena. "I'm going to become the next Wayne Gretzky. Hope you all don't get blinded by the light of my talent."

I laughed. "Humble yourself, Oba the Second. Celena will not let you make a claim like that without any proof to back it up."

Don't mistake warning Alexei as something to come out of the goodness of my heart. Quite frankly, I knew he was going to be devoured by Celena in the coming practice and almost felt bad he was going to bruise his ass after Celena had knocked him down a peg—or two—for having an unjust arrogance. And I was just trying to soften the blow since an angry Celena was by all means a wildcard you could never really control.

I looked at Rue who didn't answer his brother's accusation to tie his hair in a ponytail and come up to Alexei's left before looking me up and down. I'll admit, I did the same but tried to mask any expression on my face to not give any inch of a clue that Rue was easily going to become a new, shiny eye candy. "Let's go, Alexei. They're waiting for us outside."

"Yeah, yeah," Alexei said, still arrogant as ever. "They're gonna go back crying to their mommies once I'm done with them."

Alexei walked past me and to exit when Rue followed him out, brushing up against my arm ever so slightly that I turned to look at him. He met my gaze before checking me out again with an expression that still had no emotion to show for it as the door closed behind him. I looked around to see Damien had already exited, and I turned to Chase who was grinning ear to ear.

"Do not even dare mention it," I said. Chase put his hands up with the same smile. I flipped him off as we claimed the empty locker room to change into our practice gear. "What did I say, Chase? Don't fucking mention it."

"I didn't say anything, beloved."

"Your face is doing plenty talking, asshole."

"But is that the same as saying something?" I rolled my eyes. "Man, winning against you is one of my absolute favorite things to do, Dante Alonso Hidalgo."

"Yeah, yeah, don't blame me when I finally snap and break your fucking face for it," I said with no meaning.

Once I was in my practice gear consisting of a black turtleneck and leggings, obnoxiously bulky goalie pads and stick, and my helmet, I sent a look to Chase to find he was waiting for me on one of the benches. "Let's get going, shall we?"

"Of course," I said. "After all, you have a date with Celena I'm going to be forced to endure even if it makes me want to gouge my eyes out."

"Romance isn't dead," Chase said. "Even if you've convinced yourself it is."

I didn't answer the accusation even if it annoyed me. We walked out of the locker room to find Celena waiting for us, leaning up against the stadium wall with a glass bottle of vodka in her hand.

I would never consider Celena one of my closest friends like I would Chase, but I always held a well-deserved, infinite amount of respect for her. Being a first of anything is not a title for the faint of heart, and Celena handled the vast amount of sexism and hate she got from all sides with such grace it was hard not to admire her for it. As mentioned before, Schaffer was a kind of second home—and then sober jail—for me ever since Tito Clayton had been offered the position of head coach a very long time ago. And that meant I was there to single handedly watch the rise of Celena Božović ever since she was first recruited and I was in my freshman year of high school.

I still remember when Tito Clayton asked me my thoughts on scouting Celena. He was pretty much having a mental breakdown on whether or not he should make that leap of faith and add her to her roster knowing everyone was going to write her off the moment she first stepped onto the ice. He kept saying over and over how much he wanted her on his team but didn't think she could handle everyone being out for her blood without good reason to be. I was tired of having my tito weave never-ending worse case scenarios, so I asked him if she was good enough to be on his team. He answered with a gruff and an obviously. I said then, well, you have your answer don't you? And Tito Clayton waved me off until I watched the world news that same night to see Celena had been scouted and a glass ceiling had been broken.

And I think because I was the push that got Tito Clayton to commit to giving Celena instant name-recognition, Celena seemed to treat me with this respect I didn't think I had done much to earn. And I don't know what exactly it was she saw in me but knew it was something. Celena may be a simple person to understand since the only thing that she demanded of us Lions was a total devotion to a sport that was the last thing from kind. But back then knowing the greatest hockey player who ever lived saw some kind of talent in me from the moment we met almost made me want to envision a future I had once promised myself with a noose around my neck that I would never see.

Celena stuck out the bottle for me to take. I took it from her hand to find it was filled just enough to be a Tito Clayton approved increment to allow me rhythmic functioning. I gave a fake toast to the captain of the Lions before taking the bottle and downing the entire thing in one swift gulp.

"Celena, you look as gorgeous as ever," Chase said. "I'm so very happy to be playing with you again."

I rolled my eyes behind the bottle as Celena answered, "Thank you, Chase." Celena turned to me before speaking again, "You can be something great, Dante." Celena's eyebrows were pressed together and helped make up the rest of the sour expression across her face. "You have so much potential, and you know I don't say that about anyone. But you won't be able to make something of your life if you don't wake up and realize there's more to it than this poison that is rotting you from the inside out."

I wiped the invisible trail of vodka off my lips as Celena collected the bottle from my hands. "Celena, I mean this in the gentlest way I can, but I will never amount to anything. And nothing not even the greatest hockey player alive can change that."

Celena looked annoyed. "I'm not saying this just because now having another addict on the team made me grow a conscience. Do you really want Tito Clayton to keep lying to everyone in order to keep you on this team? Do you really want to die a failure or do you want to be someone, Dante? You have the talent. All you need is the drive, and you'll have infinite riches, glory, and respect. In the time I've come to know you, I see what Tito Clayton saw in me all those years ago. And I would never forgive you if you just let it all go to waste."

Celena left to join our teammates on the ice. And the words she had said haunted me on her way out like the ghost of my father.

1

DANTE

FOURTH DRAFT

Dante Alonso Hidalgo had promised that he would kill himself before he turned nineteen.

In a sense, the ending of his life was the start of another. It would mean the suffering he had come to welcome would cease. And even if that meant moving his consciousness to a realm beyond knowing to make such happen, it was a debt Dante was all but willing to pay. Because a life filled with sadness really was not much of a life at all. A life without hope held no purpose other than to thrive on misery. He and the depression he had come to know were the oldest of friends. Some could even say they found comfort in the other akin to the feeling of when love first blossoms between two halves of the same soul. Although, the cautious optimism would see itself twist into the most toxic of codependent abuse because now there was nothing left to him but the infinite trails of seen and unseen scars to show for its venomous self-degradation. He had given nearly everything to see that this day would never come. But as he watched the stadium clock strike twelve, it was as if his most haunting of nightmares had just been realized.

Because here he was.

Now nineteen.

And very much not dead.

Not that any of his favorite vices to cope with such a wretched milestone would be in immediate access to him. Clayton had confiscated all his razors in their shared apartment knowing the self-destruction that would befall should Dante have access to them in the countdown leading up to today. Clayton had also made sure to hide away any and all alcohol as he did not trust Dante with any variation of the poison alone. Dante thought his uncle was smart for such. Because both men knew if he were to see himself gorge on either of the habits, Dante would be sure to mix enough pills in his manmade concoction of self-righteousness to see that he actually died this time around.

The only vice Clayton had allowed for Dante to consume was nicotine. Dante thought the new, shiny wares of electronic cigarettes were measures infinitely too mainstream for his liking. Dante was a man of tradition in every sense. After all, his uncle had raised him in hopes of such. Every special occasion would be met with uncle and nephew prepared lumpia; where relatives would gather in Clayton's tiny apartment to ask Dante of a girlfriend who would never exist and of a future he knew he would never have. Suits and ties had always been foregone with transparent, embroidered barong tagalogs. Lyrics sung in Tagalog to a catchy, swing beat were the only chorus that greeted him in the mornings where the pair would prepare to meet Clayton's roster of wannabe greats making up his Lions. And most importantly of all, Clayton had made sure that the nephew he raised would follow in his footsteps of one day playing for his alma mater, Schaffer University.

Dante thought his college experience was not among the likes of his peers. College was where teenagers go in hopes to find an independence free of their parents and form beliefs free of their same influence. But Schaffer was more among the likes of a jail; where Dante was forced to see himself sober of any of his favorite self-destructive tendencies under the careful, watchful eye of Clayton Alonso, who was his father in every sense except blood.

Dante took a packet of cigarettes out from the pocket of his ripped, black jeans. He examined the box to find a warning label showing the horrors that would befall him should he never see himself clean. He gave a half-hearted, amused laugh. After all, who needed to worry about cancer when you were going to kill yourself the moment you were free of the forces who would do everything to keep you here? He moved to grab one from the thin cardboard after flipping open the flap atop. Placing the object between thin, brown lips, he exchanged his cigarettes for the chrome lighter than was the only remnant left of his father. It had the name of the man he would never know engraved atop the metal; the curved in edges catching the light of the overhead, stadium lights above. He flicked the fork to render himself a flame, taking a drag beneath the filter before leaning back to blow the smoke above his head. The smell of nicotine and the chill to show for the ice behind clear plexiglass encasing the hockey rink below had now been mixed evenly together to stain the inside of his nose.

Dante could hear footsteps atop the concrete behind him. He did not turn to face the noise. Instead, he moved to rest his elbow atop the armrest of the stiff, stadium seat he had made himself comfortable in, holding his cigarette between thick, stocky fingers. He moved his hand to dislodge a clump of ash, then grinding it out with the ball of his black, leather boots. The cinder left an insidious, black mark as he parted his lips to say, "Tito, I thought I told you I don't celebrate my birthday."

No answer came. Dante turned around to see who the presence was to find it was not his uncle, but the captain of the Lions, Celena Božović. She looked the same as Dante had remembered in their first meeting, minus the added attire of hockey armor. Here she was dressed in athletic leisurewear; bleach blonde hair tied up in a high ponytail at the center of her head. Her expression was stern, forceful, and every bit sharp as her electric, blue eyes. Thin, pink lips were quirked in a motion as if to assign Dante's cause to see himself dead before this very day was every bit hopeless as he subconsciously knew it was. And Dante thought Celena would find comfort in knowing she was right. Because dying sure is a hell of a lot harder than you'd think it was when there were people—like her—doing everything in their power to keep you here.

"You're not allowed to do that here," Celena said.

"I shouldn't be alive, Celena. I have every right to cope."

Celena didn't argue. "Is a happy birthday beneath you?"

"Every bit as calling Elliot your family."

Celena laughed at that. Maybe Dante should have found comfort knowing he was one of few who could make a joke at Celena's expense. Although even if he were to have noticed, it's not that either would comment on such. After all, the future face of the NHL and her ever reluctant protege respected the other too much to think there was any bit of magic behind such a thing.

"Robyn Zaragoza wants to transfer here."

Dante's shock showed despite his best attempt to hide it. He took another drag of his whittling cigarette; the acrid taste of nicotine the only tether that would see him come out of the conversation with enough of his sanity intact to see him survive it. Dante may have made a conscious effort to forget everything about his older brother since they parted ways an endless summer ago where he left the island nation they hailed from infinitely more broken then when he had first arrived. Dante had done everything in an attempt to see himself purge himself of the memories they shared and the trauma that followed with the same vices he had been stripped of in agreeing to play for his uncle for the rest of his collegiate career. But now, a remnant of the past had come back to haunt him. Because what other explanation was there for Xavier's best friend to wash upon his shores, every bit unwelcome as they all knew she was?

Dante knew there was more in regard to her transfer than Celena was letting on. The easy answer was to say that Robyn was a double agent in disguise; a means for Xavier to keep tabs on the brother he wanted dead without having to face the wrath of the uncle who was the only tether keeping Dante safe from his wrath. But despite his wishes, Dante knew Xavier well. He had spent years in an attempt to come to terms with his cruelty and knew it would be unfair to not judge Robyn Zaragoza in the same light. Xavier was a man who valued loyalty. He wanted those he held dear to be dutiful, obedient servants rather than autonomous human beings with their own free will. The only person worth a semblance of dignity was someone *who obeyed him*. And the only explanation behind Robyn Zaragoza wanting to transfer from the best hockey team in the ECAC to the second best was that she had betrayed the very man she had once dared to call her best friend.

Dante may think of himself as a man every bit beyond saving as he was heinous. But he was never a man who would forgo righteousness. After all, why else would he be actively trying to destroy himself if such were not the case? But seeing himself as collateral damage aside, that did not change that Robyn Zaragoza was on his front doorstep, seemingly coming to the place he had called a second home nearly his entire life a refugee. And even if Dante's emotions told him to cast her out and force the notoriously spoiled brat to fend for herself, he knew firsthand how cruel Xavier Hidalgo could be. And even if Robyn was every bit vain, conceited, and annoying as he and Celena both knew she was, that did not change the matter of right and wrong. And refusing Robyn asylum in the wake of Xavier's unjust violence *would always be wrong.*

Dante turned back around, moving to take a drag from his cigarette. He blew the smoke downward in an attempt to not see it fill the space between himself and the woman who always saw a greatness in him that he would never be worthy of. Footsteps came closer until Celena's presence loomed behind him. She moved a manicured hand to rest atop his shoulder. He glanced down at the even, painted lengths of a perfect, shiny black. A hand came into his range of motion. Dante moved his gaze to meet Celena's; her cobalt eyes shining in an endless circle round her pupil as she said, "I don't want her any bit you do. But Coach insists there is more to her than a looming betrayal. I wanted to know your thoughts. For she is the one who wronged you."

Dante took a last drag of his cigarette; the ritual washing a calm over his body despite the subject matter. He blew the smoke out from his nostrils before placing the object in Celena's waiting hand. She did not give a thanks, but Dante knew it was present in the reassuring tap she gave atop his shoulder. Once Celena had commandeered his last remaining tether to sanity, Dante moved fingers painted over in chipped, black nail polish to the top of his turtleneck he wore no matter the season to rest the cloth above the patch of facial hair coating the base of his cleft chin. Celena then leaned over the back of his seat, and Dante turned to look at her to find she was already watching him.

"I already talked with her. She refused to tell me the circumstance, but I could tell it was urgent she get out of Wesley fast. You say the word, and I tell Coach to refuse. If she'll get in the way of making you something great, I will banish her back to the very place she is daring to escape from."

"No." Dante felt as if he were going to vomit. "She can stay."

Celena raised an eyebrow in a sharp arch, obviously seeing through the hesitation laced in Dante's tone.

Dante glanced at her to say, "My feelings do not change the matter of what is wrong and what is right, Cel. What kind of person would I be if I refused a woman refuge in her most desperate, undeserving hour?"

"A smart one," Celena answered, a jaggedness tucked between her accusation. "We both know where her loyalties lie. And you ask me to take her in when we know of her history with *the man who marked you*?"

"You know it's not that simple."

Celena was quiet.

"We have Davi as proof of such."

Celena returned Dante's cigarette to his waiting hand. Dante gave a faint thanks as Celena stood back upright. She began to walk away, when Dante turned to her gaze as she said, "And you should know, I will not allow you to die as long as I have a say in it. *You can be something great Dante.* And it pains me to know you cannot see it too."

"You're the great one," Dante said in an attempt to deflect. "You're the first woman scouted onto a men's team in all of NCAA history. You're going to be the first woman to play in the NHL. Who am I compared to the future great endless generations of children will come to look up to as the titan of the sport?"

"My greatness does not diminish yours."

Dante was quiet too.

"And as long as I am Celena Božović, I will do everything to see that you one day see it too."

Celena moved to exit. And Dante swallowed the lump in his throat knowing a sense of morality he had tried so desperately to absolve himself of would soon be the downfall of them all.

2

ROBYN

FOURTH DRAFT

Robyn Zaragoza knew she had come to Schaffer University a traitor.

Although even she was unsure what fate was worse; forever being the name atop Xavier's hit list or being forced to keep the company of very people she had been conditioned to hate. Robyn knew now in the wake of her best friend's betrayal that there was so much more to the Schaffer Lions than the tall tales someone as heinous as Xavier had spun in an attempt to give credence to his prejudice. It was more than obvious now how truly vile a man like Xavier was knowing the truth of what he had done to her. But even Robyn was unsure what to make of herself knowing she could only ever realize such when it came at the expense of herself.

Robyn placed her luggage on the floor of Clayton Alonso's apartment. Knowing she would now be roommates with the only person alive whom Xavier detested more than her was something she had not given proper thought until standing in the kitchen where she would come to spend the rest of her college career. Seeing Dante would force her to answer to the crimes she had been all but complicit in committing. And she would have to acknowledge the damage caused because the man who called Xavier a brother had a branding carved beneath his left eye that dragged down to the end of jawline to show for it.

Robyn examined the place in which she too would call a jail. It was every bit plain as is it was unassuming. It was decorated in a way that easily told her the only people who dwelled beneath its white, popcorn ceiling and called it a home were men. The tiled kitchen floor did not aid in seeing her keep her balance considering her six-inch stiletto heels. But she was not the kind of woman to back down from a challenge especially when her pristine, meticulously curated appearance was at stake. She moved to stand before a shelf hiding behind a corner of the doorway she had been standing in. Housed atop its shelves were various mementos. Some were pictures of Clayton and Dante as a child. Others were pictures that documented Clayton's hockey career where he would be kicked off the Ottawa Senators before finishing his contract. Even Robyn was unsure if she should pity the man who had given her refuge or simply never speak of what could have been to a man who probably knew its truth and the weight that came with it a million times more intimately than she ever could.

Robyn's phone rang in the pouch of her designer purse. It had been a gift from her parents to celebrate graduating as valedictorian among her high school class, and there had yet to be a moment where Robyn was seen without it. It reminded her of better times before she had to worry about the tattered string her life was now hanging by scorning a man who would not rest until she paid for what he called a betrayal in blood. Robyn only wished she would have never been so arrogant to think she would not befall his signature trait of vengeance because of the once held belief she was better than others who had been dumb enough to succumb to it.

Robyn glossed over the notification to find it was from Lisanna. She knew she was not doing much to earn the favor of a woman she wanted to make a wife after overdosing on Fentanyl and therefore outing her opioid habit to the woman she had made a conscious effort to hide it from. But the truth was now an open wound; rotting the soul they had dared to share whose coming infection could very well kill them both. It was neither above nor beneath Robyn to know of the betrayal she too had been responsible for seeing through. In a sense, Robyn and Xavier were equals even if the motivation behind their failures were intrinsically different. For Xavier, it was to pay for the crimes he had thought Robyn committed. For Robyn, it was the failure of being the person she had promised Lisanna she always would be.

Hope all is well. I've moved into my dorm.
Thinking of you.

Robyn flipped her long, razor straight hair to one side of her head. She then tapped long, acrylic nails atop her screen to text back. The clack of the lengths atop the glass filled the space along with the dull hum to show for the heater.

would luv 2 chat when u get the chance. i know
i have a lot of explaining 2 do

Robyn moved her phone back into the chasms of her purse. She flicked her gaze back up to the shelf before settling her gaze upon an image of a young Clayton Alonso in the prime of his career. The memento before her depicted his first and only Stanley Cup win, with his teammates propping it up for him to drink out of its basin, all smiles. And knowing the reasons that would see Clayton lose it all was enough to make Robyn's body become covered in this sickly and equally grotesque itch.

Because it too was the future awaiting her if she did not dare to kick the habit that was rotting her from the inside out.

"You certainly are taller in person."

A man came into view. Robyn recognized him as one of two people she would dare to willingly betray Xavier Hidalgo for, being her twin brother, Conner Zaragoza. This would be their first-time meeting in person due to the bureaucracy and more than lacking models to keep families together in the same system that saw their own broken apart. Robyn knew it could very well be arrogant to say she was beneath crying over spilled milk because it did not change the present of the two of them standing before the other despite the odds. But even someone as cunning and shrewd as Robyn Zaragoza was unsure what to make of her other half standing before her. A man she did not know existed until Clayton Alonso had reached out to her in her senior year of college and told her of the brother she would give everything to protect but had never known.

Conner and Robyn were the same towering height of six feet and five inches. Each had the same wide, flat, nose protruding from a shade of pleasant, amber skin. Freckles dotted the bridge, seeping into high cheekbones and ample cheeks. Robyn tried to mask a hesitation she knew was splashed across her face despite her wish to keep it hidden, and Conner frowned upon meeting the gaze kept behind eyes such a dark brown they gave the illusion of a deep, all-encompassing black. Each half of their matching set moved their gazes to examine the other, equally unsure what to make of the person before them considering neither had known the other existed until a month ago.

Robyn jutted her hip to the right. Her purse dangled off her arm, resting in the nook atop her elbow. She gave a smile she was unsure if she wanted there or not, but ultimately said, "Conner. How lovely to meet you."

"And to you too, Robyn."

A silence lingered.

The front door gave a click, indicating that it had been unlocked. Both parties turned to the noise to find Dante and Clayton joint them inside. Dante was dressed in varying, mismatching shades of black kept atop the same brown smeared across the bodies of the siblings before him. His long hair was tied back in a ponytail, with thick, prominent facial hair decorating his top lip and chin in the form of a goatee. And of course, kept beneath a pair of sleet eyes at the left side of his face was the scar to show for the wrath of Xavier Hidalgo. The man Dante called a brother who would do everything in his power to see him dead.

Emotions that Robyn had made the choice to bury poked through the surface of the flimsy film she had kept them under. It was as if she were reliving the memory of waking up in the hospital only to learn of the betrayal the man she called a best friend had been entirely responsible for. An insatiable guilt and an otherworldly divine lament that she would never be strong enough to see through considering the matter of her pride. And maybe if she could make the choice to become the good person she always wished she could be, then her and Dante would not come out of this meeting with scorned feelings and equally cindered truths.

Clayton Alonso on the other hand was an infinitely more stereotypical vision of the Filipino man in terms of stature compared to that of his nephew. Clayton looked quaint compared to Dante, who was easily towered over him, aided by his platform, leather boots the same shade of his all-black attire. Clayton had lines etched into the skin to show for his age. A prominent stubble contracted the light, taupe skin beneath to compliment the centerpiece of the same flat, broad nose belonging to his nephew. Both men wore long sleeves, with Dante's shirt coming up to cover his neck.

Another silence lingered.

"Well, speak of the devil," Dante called, every bit venomous as the glare kept between his eyes. "Robyn Zaragoza. How lovely to meet you."

"Cut the shit, Dante. I did not come here to start shit with you."

Dante moved to answer, but Clayton's hand atop his shoulder made him bite his tongue. Clayton then said, "Robyn, mind if the two of us have a chat? Alone?"

Clayton moved his gaze around to ask their now unwanted company to leave. Conner was the first to acknowledge such, moving before his sister to say, "It was nice to finally meet you, Robyn. I hope we can learn to get along. Not just for our sake, but for our parents' sake."

Conner moved past Robyn with a smile. He then exited the apartment as Clayton accused Dante to see through the same. The ravenette smiled, every bit venomous as the words spoken to turn to Robyn and say, "You're every bit unwelcome here as you know you are. And know, I don't trust you as far as I can throw you."

Dante then looked Robyn up and down a last time before moving to follow Conner out and exiting the apartment. Clayton lingered in the doorway for a few seconds before moving to stand before Robyn, their height difference infinitely more drastic than the space once apart could accurately convey. Robyn swallowed the lump once lodged in her throat. Clayton crossed his arms and said, "Dante is all bark and no bite. Don't take his hatred personally. He doesn't like anyone, let alone those who would have once called his brother her best friend."

"I figured my presence would be met with vitriol." Robyn smiled a bit. "But I do not take your offer of refuge lightly."

"I think you should talk with Davi. I'm sure she will be so much more understanding and hopeful to see your point than someone every bit socially inept as my nephew."

Another silence loomed over the pair.

"You talk with Lisanna?"

Robyn should have known better than to admit to the crimes committed. But their truth did not change that Lisanna was the one to even seek out Clayton Alonso and see that Robyn was protected despite everything Robyn had chosen to do to her. And what had Robyn Zaragoza had ever done to deserve such? To be loved unconditionally and without an overarching want but simply in the purest, most virtuous way despite everything it was she had willingly chosen to do. Lie. Become exactly like the person who had once taken from Lisanna before; who Robyn knew she would do anything to bring back from the dead and kill again solely to say she was the party who had at long last avenged her. But knowing Robyn would see through the execution of the man who had harmed Lisanna first did not change that she had become the second. And what could she possibly do to begin to atone for her cardinal sins knowing the damage it had already wrought?

Robyn didn't answer. Instead, she moved her gaze to meet Clayton. His tired, aged face housed an expression that looked as if he could read her most intimate of thoughts housed only in the realm of her subconscious. He flicked his gaze up to her, then settling to say, "It won't be easy. This road to sobriety is not for the faint of heart or mind. But even I know you do not want to lose what you have left. Quite frankly, Robyn, I do not think you will survive it. After all, I know this too. *Because I barely did.*"

Clayton did not say anything else. Not that he had to when the weight of the words spoken was enough to kill any semblance of unjust self-righteousness Robyn had grown fond of; eradicating the very notion that she was not beholding to the misery they both knew she had caused down to its very the root. It could be the very thing that made her realize her life had an inherent value and was worth living. But she would never know this if the opioids she had given nearly everything to keep close didn't get to her first.

ACKNOWLEDGMENTS

Thank you for picking up a copy of *From the Match* and making it all the way to the end! There is no amount of thanks I can give to properly convey my gratitude in you reading a story conceived entirely from my heart and finish it no less. I hope you enjoyed the journey these characters have taken you on, and I hope you'll pick up the forthcoming sequel, *From the Fire* (release date pending)!

Now, to begin my acknowledgments, I need to first and foremost thank the one person who without her, this book would not have come to exist. To my sister, Tara, thank you for all you've done for me since I was a self-loathing child trying to figure out his place in the world to the man I have grown into since then. Without you, this world would not have begun to exist, and without you, I cannot say with confidence I would have remained withstanding too. Ever since I've been writing, I've wanted the first book I've published to be about our characters since they were the catalyst to see me pick up this hobby a very long time ago. It was a means to give them proper tribute for all they've given me, and I hope you come to find the medium they are displayed does them justice. I still remember the late nights we used to spend in your room, imagining this entire world we could escape to and saw it come alive right before our very eyes. Your creativity, passion, and kindness are all things that made this possible. I may have created some of these characters. But without you creating their perfect, corresponding halves, they would never come to life the way I always imagined them. So, Tara, thank you. For all you do for me. For all you've done for me. And all you will continue to do for me. Mahal kita, langga.

Secondly, a huge thank you to Denny for working with me on my passion projecting and breathing light into characters once only kept in the confines of my mind. Thank you for supporting my vision and giving it life; this entire series could not be what it is today without you. I can't wait to work with you on the forthcoming books, and hopefully many more projects to come!

Next, I want to thank one of my best friends, Niko. To think these characters were the catalyst that brought you into my life is something I am eternally thankful for. You're one of my best friends, and I cannot wait to spend my 2024 birthday with you, Nikita, and Malika (and let's kidnap Sumatra too). You're a constant light in my life who shines light even on my darkest of days with your humor, charm, and all-around warmth. I promise Chase will not die this go around, but either way, you've helped driven this story into the best version it can be. I love you endlessly, beloved. I will see you soon!

Next, I want to thank my friend Phoenix. She has driven my work to become the best version it can be, and she has been a constant, supportive warmth in my life. Hopefully Robyn has lived up to your expectations, and I look forward to the day where our books can keep company on the same shelf. Thank you for sticking by me and coming back into my life, there's not a moment where I am not thankful for it. Truth be told, I would not endure the trials and tribulations of social media with anyone else but you at my side. I can't wait until we can meet one day and gush over our characters together.

Quinn, Sekinat, Sushi, Eureka, and Elora. To think my choice to join Twitter (before my departure) brought you all into my life is something I'm so grateful for. You all have driven my writing into the best version it can be while also encouraging and supporting me along the way. You're all so endlessly talented, and I cannot stress enough how much both you and your support means to me.

I then want to thank my friends Claire, Whit, Kelly, Zach, Selena, Raeshma, Cindy, Carbon, Andrew, Megan, Jaxon, Mark, Jack, and Hunter. Thank you all for teaching me what real friends could be when I had gone most of my life without them. It's a gift to share your life with other people, and I am thankful to do so with all of you. Thank you all for helping me be the best version of myself I can be. You all make this life all the more worthwhile.

A huge thanks to my ARC readers, Sanaya, Rosario, Anastasia, Qezia, CJ, Mia, Luce, Jynastie, Maq, Sanaya, Maia, and Matt. Thank you all for supporting me and even wanting to read this story that is entirely from my heart. I hope you'll enjoy this story as much as my sister and I did in creating it nearly a decade ago. Thank you all for supporting my vision, and I am so thankful to have on this journey with me.

Also, I would like to thank my dad and my mom. My dad for taking me in and providing for me in my most daunting of hours when change was as scary as it was necessary. To my mom for sharing a culture with me I feel now with every beat of my heart. I cannot begin to pay either of you back for all that you've done for me, but know, the love I harbor for each of you is limitless.

Lastly, I wanted to thank the girl I once was and her sacrifice to stay. I hope you know this life we've come to share will pay you back for such a selfless and equally arduous act in ways you could never begin to conceive. And find comfort in knowing one day you *really* will find the peace you had always searched for but could never find.

ABOUT THE AUTHOR

Adrian Tkaczyk grew up in a small, quaint New Hampshire town where he spent his childhood writing stories and daydreaming about the characters in them. Now, he writes about complex, morally gray characters you can't help but root for even if you may disagree with their reprehensible actions. When not writing, you can find him drawing, cooking, or engrossing himself in the lessons to be learned from history of past.

You can find him on social media under the username @thneskos or on his website, www.thneskos.com.

Printed in Great Britain
by Amazon

22053389R00278